BACK
THEN

A NOVEL

BACK THEN

A NOVEL

CLY BOEHS

LIFFEY PRESS

an imprint of
OGHMA CREATIVE MEDIA

OGHMA
CREATIVE MEDIA

Liffey Press
An imprint of Oghma Creative Media, Inc.
2401 Beth Lane, Bentonville, Arkansas 72701

Copyright © 2018 by Cly Boehs

We are a strong supporter of copyright. Copyright represents creativity, diversity, and free speech, and provides the very foundation from which culture is built. We appreciate you buying the authorized edition of this book and for complying with applicable copyright laws by not reproducing, scanning, or distributing any part of it in any form without permission. Thank you for supporting our writers and allowing us to continue publishing their books.

Library of Congress Cataloging-in-Publication Data

Names: Boehs, Cly, author.
Title: Back Then/Cly Boehs.
Description: First Edition. | Bentonville: Liffey, 2018.
Identifiers: LCCN: 2018954220 | ISBN: 978-1-63373-403-6 (hardcover) |
ISBN: 978-1-63373-404-3 (trade paperback) | ISBN: 978-1-63373-405-0 (eBook)
Subjects: | BISAC: FICTION/Literary | FICTION/Family Life
LC record available at: https://lccn.loc.gov/2018954220

Liffey Press trade paperback edition September, 2018

Jacket art by Carol Bloomgarden
Jacket & Interior Design by Casey W. Cowan
Editing by Gordon Bonnet

This book is a work of fiction. Any references to historical events, real people, or real places are used fictitiously. Other names, characters, places, and events are products of the author's imagination, and any resemblance to actual events or places or person, living or dead, is entirely coincidental.

*With love, to my sister, Franki Jean Boehs Dennison,
who knows these stories by heart*

ACKNOWLEDGEMENTS

First and foremost I thank my ancestors and relatives, especially my parents, for the borrowing of details and incidents from their stories, stories I heard from the time I was very young. I have taken parts of these and used them toward fictional ends. In no way is this novel a family history or memoir. I wished to create a time, place, and atmosphere of my upbringing, not an account or specific rendering of people in my past. My characters have taken journeys of their own emanating from their natures and circumstances.

This novel has had a long gestation, but its birth has been painless thanks to the expertise and professional guidance of Casey Cowan and Gordon Bonnet of Oghma Creative Media through the publication process. Special thanks to Carol Bloomgarden and Casey Cowan for the fabulous cover design.

I am grateful beyond measure to my longtime writing partner and editor, Gordon Bonnet. His critical skills and knowledgeable feedback made this book so much better for his advice. He challenges and inspires. I value his friendship beyond measure.

Many friends and family have supported and influenced my writing, especially the creative groups I've belonged to over the years—in artmaking, writing, and theater, most particularly the folks in 3rd Floor Productions, The Georges, The 3pm Club, and T-burg Writer's Group. My work truly began, though, in Irene "Zee" Zahava's writing circles, Ithaca, New York, when I felt vulnerable and alone, moving to an area that has since become home. In an atmosphere of trust and support, those of us in her circles wrote our way to confidence and deep friendships, some of which have lasted for decades.

Shade Gomez has been my go-to friend for anything and everything forever and ever. His abiding encouragement, wisdom, loyalty, and unshakable honesty in my life and writing are treasured.

Warmest and deepest appreciation to my dearest friend, Nancy Osborn, who has seen me through daily ups and downs and has read, edited, listened, and shared in my creative efforts. I trust her with my life—with all of my stories.

Franki Jean Boehs Dennison is my sister, my teacher, my inspiration, and loving friend. I am so grateful for her being in my life.

Special thanks to newfound writing friends of the Oghmaniacs and Quillies. They are a home base for continual information and support.

Also, a special thank you to Shirley Brown, whose support during hard times got me started again.

Heartfelt thanks to Elizabeth Wavle-Brown, George Rhodes, Marcelle Lapow Toor, Emily Rhodes Johnson, Joan and Ed Ormondroyd, Bob and Cara Franchi, Leslie Knight, Marcia, Scott, Jake and Will Sheavly, June Wolfman, Anne Furman, Jae Sullivan, Loretta Louviere and to Elizabeth Lyon, whose consult at the Willamette Writer's Conference was invaluable.

BACK THEN

A NOVEL

PORTRAIT

of

JESSE

The last time I saw my Uncle Jesse, he'd gained a lot of weight, and his hair had thinned way out. When he was younger, it had body and a bit of a part to the side. In the photograph I took of him with the family on that last visit, comb marks had left furrows, and a white hairline formed an odd halo over his red, puffy face. He was a grotesque overstatement of himself, an exaggerated buffoon of a man who was anything but funny, a deadly serious man, with leering eyes and a mouth that stretched across his face like a strained rubber band. During this family gathering, we went in and out of rooms, not looking at each other—or rather, I didn't look at him, at least not when he was looking at me. I caught him once, staring straight through me to the wall.

In the family album is another photograph of him taken in the yard of the Dirks home place, undoubtedly during another family get-together. I must've been about three at the time of this photograph, the sepia curling around the edges of the picture like a memory fog. I can't imagine who might have taken this snapshot, as the ones in it, to my recollection, were the only people there. My father, mother, and Aunt Josephine are standing together looking directly into the camera while Uncle Clifford, and Gramma and Grampa Dirks are standing on the other side of Uncle Jesse and me, looking at us to keep from squinting at the mid-day sun. Tommy Don and Roy are squatting on the ground in front of us all, Leon seated on Roy's leg. Uncle Jesse's holding me in his arms, but out a little from him, like a trophy he's just won, his eyes almost closed from the glare of the light coming straight at him. He's dressed like a prizefighter, in a pin-striped suit, high-collared shirt, wide floral tie. He stands looking at the camera as though he's waiting for a reporter to take his picture. What was he? A wannabe gangster in his twenties? Capone's or Dillinger's favorite in the ring? It was inconceivable he could have known such a thing, raised as he was in a non-inclusive religious community. But there he was, with the look and feel of a Mafioso, or more like a movie gangster's lackey.

What was he to himself?

He told me a story once about when he was nineteen—probably at a family reunion, again, sequestered somewhere from everybody. Times I saw him alone or with Aunt Clarice, without the family, stand out with unusual clarity. The story of him at nineteen has that shimmering translucence. He'd been taken to Hopewell by one of his coaches who had continued to help him with his boxing after he left high school in Shirly, an Oklahoma town with a population under a thousand and the hometown of my mother's family. Jesse'd won the district title, as he thought he would—he had remarkable confidence in anything he set his mind to, although things rarely turned out quite as he believed they would. Now the coach had entered Jesse in an advanced tournament.

But his boxing career started and ended on that trip. After his final match, he got drunk, followed another boxer he thought had stolen some girl he'd been out with the night before, and beat the kid unconscious.

"I kicked him into a creek. He woulda drowned if his friends hadn't found him and bailed him out. I never gave what I'd done a thought. I went back into town and had another drink."

I didn't think he'd been bragging when he told me. After all, he'd been saved by then and had accepted the call to preach. But there wasn't a sign anywhere of remorse in the confession either. As I remember it, he was leaning back in his chair telling me this like he was attempting to convince me to buy some car in the sales lot, in that casual conversational tone that's a calculated contradistinction to the high pressure sell. He didn't tell me nor did I think to ask what happened to the girl who had triggered such violence in him. I've often wondered since if he saw the parallel in what he'd done that night to what his father had done to him only a couple of years earlier. It was a Jesse story Mother had told me in secret, how Whalen had beaten him to a pulp by the pond and then pushed him in the water, leaving him to his fate.

My view now is that Uncle Jesse told us his stories to gain credibility. They proved he was who we thought he was. At the same time, they showed us the extreme absolution he'd been granted by the Almighty for the crimes—which he later called his "sins"—he'd committed "back then," before Jesus and the pulpit. For a while, that pulpit was during his seminary preaching days, in a church with steady foundations. Later, after some extenuating circumstances, it was a pulpit he pulled from the back of his pick-up and set up inside a tent he'd purchased from Sears which was intended for small wedding receptions. The forty folding chairs were purchased from the same cash flow—God only knew the source. The plywood platform folded together like the bottom of a flattened gift box. It rose only two feet above the ground when assembled for pulpiteering, but it was enough to elevate him from the sinning congregation who'd come to be saved, in whatever town he was traveling through in California, Nevada, Arizona, New Mexico, or Colorado. I always knew as a kid where he was from the postcards he sent Grandmother, Mother, and Aunt Josie that they seemed delighted to exchange with each other.

I attended only one of his church services, after he was given the pastorship at Southside Baptist in Hopewell and before I turned my back on the family dramas. But earlier, I'd become familiar with his itinerant *mise en scène* in the photographs he sent Gramma Dirks. She proudly passed the photos around at her monthly Sunday dinners. He wanted us to see how his ministry was flourishing, but also what he was enduring for Christ. He had sent at least a dozen or more five-by-sevens, probably copies of those he'd taken for sponsors as evidence of his show's success, as well as for his revivals' advertisements, when he made his tours. He sent clippings from local newspapers, complete with a black-and-white, three-quarter promo-shot of himself in his pin-striped suit and well-oiled, comb-toothed hair. His entire tent operation was taken at panorama, the shots stretching the story of this evangelical enterprise far beyond what was actually there. My impression at the time was that this was the set-up and strike of a small Sunday Service Mud Show, one transported by a couple of trucks instead of two wagons—although these notions of mine were inspired, no doubt, by my father's acute sense of humor.

"Your brother," I remember him telling Mother on the way home after a day of Jesse-photo-gazing, "and a couple of hired has-beens are making a revival like one of those family circuses where the trapeze artist does the entire act, you know, where she hangs in mid-air by her teeth, plays the clown, rides the ponies and sells the tickets, as well as the popcorn and the cotton candy. Only your brother could think up such a spectacle for Jesus." He slapped the steering wheel, laughing himself silly, then adding, "In his case, the pianist leads the choir of two, sets up the chairs, hands out fliers on Main Street, and passes the collection plate. It's a Christ-inspired joke, is what it is, Darlene."

Mother sat in the passenger seat staring out the window. After Dad's spiel had run its course, she only said, "Poor Jesse."

When I was still living at home, Uncle Jesse would sometimes drift in for a coffee at one of the family's places where I was. I never felt indifferent to what he said or did, even if his attitude seemed as laid-back as one of his folding chairs. My parents weren't indifferent to him, either. Mother felt her brother was pathetically sad, a broken man all of his life, from both the disregard and brutal punishment he got from their father, and the over-protection given him by their mother. Dad felt Jesse was simply a thug, permanently damaged to the point of being unchangeable. I have no idea what my brothers thought, though Teddy probably didn't like very much the teasing he took from Uncle Jesse, who would grab him by his head, swing him around in a grip under his arm like a wrestler, while rubbing his knuckles against my brother's hair calling him "Shimps."

Timothy somehow slid by. A quiet, gracefully thin, reticent boy, he was simply unnoticed or slighted by Jesse, though Timothy never showed any sign of caring in the least. In one of the pictures in my album, Timmy's standing off to the side, staring at this supposedly good-natured abuse, as Teddy is attempting to slip out of Uncle Jesse's hold, clawing hands pushing against Jesse's arm, my brother's face hidden under the grip, while Uncle Jesse smiles up at me and the camera.

How did I see this behavior as a kid? Why would I take such a picture? Did he ask me to? Where were our parents?

I think I pretty much grew up always sensing an interior force in him was ready to spring out to overtake me. When he touched things—even simple, inanimate objects—they seemed to yield to him, for fear they would be stolen or broken. He pushed people aside as he walked through crowds. He touched the heads of us kids, as he passed, turning our faces up while speaking nonsense to us. We allowed this until we were old enough to anticipate his moves and back away from his reach, to which he would snap his fingers, shape them like a gun, pointing it at our faces, pulling the trigger, laughing as though we were a part of his joke. All of the family acquiesced to him, even the men who called him a blow bag behind his back, as my father often did, Uncle Clifford nodding in agreement. We hated him for our lack of guts, our inability to stand up to him, but also because we didn't know how to put the fragments of his life together with ours. He belonged to us, but chose to remain apart, separate, the exception, a hovering maleficent presence wearing a heavy coat of arrogance. Nobody would've dared ask him to tell us anything about himself. We all simply waited for him to tell the stories he wanted to tell. He had gone to places I'd never been and had done things I both did and didn't want to know about. He filled me with fear and wonder. But later, when I was old enough to scrutinize and interpret his stories, he shrank in stature, no longer an object of awe but one of targeted defiance.

Because he was my uncle, when I was young I attempted to do what he asked, but learned to look to Momma or Aunt Josephine before following through. It could mean getting caught in something for which I'd get a skinning from my parents, especially Mother. Or worse, put me in serious danger. When I was around ten, I ended up almost killing my cat when washing it with the insect repellent he recommended. "Says it kills aphids," he read from the bottle's label. "So it's dang sure to kill fleas." Once, I almost set myself on fire while attempting to destroy an ant hill in the backyard with a blow torch he'd offered me from the garage, starting it up with a flint-striker, and leaving me to the task while he went to "grab a smoke." I must have been around eleven, barely able to lift and hold the torch steady for any length of time.

He was full of what Gramma Dirks called "foolhardiness." It had a decidedly sinister edge. He put a devil-chaser on a backyard fence post when we lived on Tenth Street in Hopewell, aimed it toward the house, and set it afire. It tore through our back screen door, zoomed around the house like a smart bomb, exiting the way it had come in, finally dying against the side of the garage in an explosion loud enough to bring the police to our family backyard picnic. It had almost zipped across my mother's face as she turned from the kitchen counter with a tray of hotdogs and buns for this outdoor Fourth of July bash. We all stood in the backyard watching as Jesse talked the cops down. He even closed the door of the cruiser after one of the young policemen slid into the passenger's seat. Laughing, he slapped the window frame, then waved as they drove away.

But Jesse's biggest agreed-upon-in-the-family malfeasance was when he got caught deviating from his ministerial path. I'd always been told he was in a Conscientious Objector camp as a Mennonite pacifist during the war. This didn't really jibe with his later Baptist ordination, but I figured it was similar to my Aunt Josephine's decision to become Baptist after her Mennonite upbringing.

During a visit back home, after I'd moved to New York, as Dad and I enjoyed an early morning coffee before Mother was up and about, he said, "Jesse never saw a C.O. camp. That he went there was a little unrefuted assumption perpetuated by the family to, once again, save Jesse's hide. It's what he told everybody, a-course, to keep his slate clean." I looked over at my dad, his clear blue eyes merry with hidden laughter, hair thinning more than when I'd seen him last. "Caroline, you know how this works by now. You put something down on your application for a job, and most of the time nobody checks it. They just look to see what's there, how good it looks for the job they're wanting you for." He brushed his pant leg as though it had collected lint from the last washing, then he cleared his throat and folded his hands on the table. "But right after the war, some employers hiring people wanted to know what they did during their war years, especially if the employers themselves had served or their kids. Jesse told them he'd been in a C.O. camp doing public works, because he didn't want to put down that he was in prison. Being a C.O. may sound like it could put a fellah to a disadvantage but it actually helped Jesse's cause because—in Mennonite territory, the Midwest especially— this was expected. He applied mostly to churches for sponsorship to seminary, or later for a pastorship. I mean, Jesse was in or going into the ministry so it made sense, and it was a story in circulation, see what I mean?"

Dad drank from his cup, his eyes on me as though I was going to get up and leave. I drank as he did, our cups coming down on the table at the same time. He smiled, looking at his cup and then mine, satisfied that I was still attentive and welcoming his story.

"Well, what really happened—this is between you, me, and the fencepost, a-course—I mean, you let Ava know that you found out something other than what's traveling around, I'll be in trouble and so will you, you understand? But what really happened was when his grades began to fail, after his first year in seminary, Jesse went meandering thorough local bars and whores, not abandoning classes but barely cutting the marks. When his behavior didn't straighten out after some leniency given to him—some good talking to and some probation, I think it was—the authorities at that seminary in Corpus Christi kicked him outta school and turned him in to the draft board."

My father stopped and stared heavenward. "Oh, what was the name of that place?" He nodded as though he'd been heard somewhere up beyond the ceiling. Looking back at me, he stated with certainty, "South Texas Baptist Theological Seminary in Corpus Christi, it was. Well, anyhow, he ended up as a cook at *Leavenworth*. Oh yeah. He was in prison for the remainder of the war. The government's selective service folks don't cotton to being fooled around with. But Jesse never paid any attention much to what anybody in authority had to say. I get why. I mean, Whalen didn't treat him the best, that's for sure. Well, hell, let's be honest. Whalen beat the shit outta him more than not, as I've told you. But Jesse was always pushing the limits with Whalen, school authorities, everybody, really, and this time he got caught by somebody who could tell him 'no' in a way that mattered. Where Jesse got the money to even begin seminary, none of us will ever know. He did have sponsorship through the Baptist church in Shirly—tiny place, couldn't help much money-wise, but you have to be referred by a church to get in. I think they gave him their endorsement because that's where he'd been saved."

"It's hard for me to see Uncle Jesse surrendering to anybody, let alone a minister behind the pulpit during an altar call."

Dad slid his empty cup back and forth between his hands like he was a cat playing with a ball. When he stopped, he looked up at me. "Yeah, you got that right. Who knows what he had in mind. But why the church'd do that for him, it's anybody's guess. Everybody in the community knew him and all his shenanigans.

"Here's the thing, Caroline, what I want you to know about this guy. He got outta the service because he was a member of the Mennonite church, not the Holdeman one that Ava wanted to join, but the one she joined in town—the more liberal one. When he turned twelve, she and Whalen pushed him into membership, because they saw a kid already losing control in life—in school, in just about anything he undertook—and they thought this might help. Never mind, that Whalen didn't join the church himself until he got cancer and was dying. But Jesse got to stay home and farm with his dad while other farmers' kids were getting called up. Then he bypassed the draft again when he went into seminary."

He stood and asked if I'd like more coffee. I shook my head, so he walked with his cup to the stove and poured from the pot. "You sure?" He raised the pot high in the air.

"Oh, all right, but only half a cup."

As he was pouring, he smiled, shook his head slightly and walked the pot back to the stove.

"What?"

Seated at the table again, he answered my question. "Baptists don't accept the kind of baptism Mennonites do, what they call sprinkling, pouring water over your head. When I say he was saved at Shirly Baptist, I mean that he went forward during a revival altar call and then became a member there through immersion, you know, the baptismal dunk, because that's what Baptists require. I think that's when Jesse got it in his head he was going to become a minister. He hated farming, and he saw his ticket away from his father and into another life.

"But about Jesse and these things, who knows for sure? In any case, the guy's had a shadow following him around his whole life. It started with his dad. Whalen had zero tolerance for laziness, and Jesse was the kind of kid who didn't want to work from the day he popped outta the womb. I'm talking about work, work like normal. He wanted to play, but more than that, he had it in him to spend more time trying to find ways of getting outta legitimate work than simply doing it. He thought like a criminal. Still does. He schemes, you understand? That's how he works! It's why I've told Darlene I don't want him over here. She wants to see him, I tell her, we can go visit him over at her mother's place on Elgan Street."

When he hesitated, thinking he had finished his tale about Jesse's hidden life during the war years, I asked him how Jesse could enter seminary when he didn't have a college degree. He hadn't gone eight years to seminary, surely not, I reminded him. It didn't add up.

"Oh, nothing adds up with this guy, but yeah, you're right about the college thing," he conceded.

"After Jesse's fiasco with boxing, Coach Wilmore Stout suggested Jesse get himself a college degree through correspondence courses. Think about this, Caroline. Jesse nearly kills a kid at a boxing tournament, and the coach suggests college to him! This is the thing about Jesse and his whole history. People either feel sorry for him or are charmed by him, regardless what he does, usually both at the same time. He has the goddamnedest luck of anybody I've ever known this way. At any rate, with Stout's influence and recommendation, Jesse enrolled in some small religious college in the Midwest, I forget exactly where. Baptist, I remember that. So for almost four years, he worked on a degree in education, with courses in psychology. He graduated without a word to anybody, though he told me he was working toward it during the time we were all running around together before your mother and me got married. I had to swear on a stack-a-Bibles I wouldn't tell Darlene or anybody. I kept my word, because I keep my word, always, as much as I can. But I also didn't want to start trouble with Whalen in particular. To tell you the truth, I think Jesse got this college degree to get even with Whalen, something he had on his dad behind his back, since Whalen was so big into education and thought Jesse was a prize-one screw-up. At any rate, it was one of the smartest things Jesse ever did."

"But he was living at home, right? How did Grampa and Gramma Dirks not know what was going on? Correspondence, textbooks and such coming through the mail while he was farming at home?"

"He musta done it through a post box, General Delivery in Hopewell, or maybe through Stout. Who knows? Some school chum covering for him. He could drive so anything's possible. I don't know the details, but when he applied for seminary in Corpus Christi, he had an acceptable degree to offer. It's probably another reason why Shirley Baptist sponsored him, come to think of it. He showed promise, some initiative."

"Did Grampa ever find out?"

"If he did, he never let on to anybody. I can't imagine him not finding out in a small place like Shirly. Hell, Whalen knew everybody, I mean everybody and then some. But your mother was as surprised as the rest of the family when she found out. The guy's a complete puzzlement. On the one hand, he acts like he doesn't give a shit about anything. On the other, he always has some plan underneath that devil-may-care attitude."

But in those family pictures that show him as I remember him most, Uncle Jesse's whole appearance was different from the rest of us, an air about him of another society, even after he went into the ministry. His religious bent seemed, to me, to be a veneer hiding desire. He wanted to smoke cigars and drink out of brandy glasses, swirling his alcohol as he paraded around in Italian-designed shoes, maybe not as Mafia-like as I made him out to be, but a stereotype nonetheless. He longed for an audience. He longed for fame. After he was saved, he wanted to wear well-tailored suits and stand before a microphone proclaiming the love and wrath of the Almighty, but perhaps not with the crowds Sister Aimee, Billy Sunday and Billy Graham could draw. He wouldn't want that much scrutiny. In any case, he didn't have to worry about becoming a McPherson or a Graham. Even though he made headlines because of his ministry, he would always have to pay for his own advertisements.

Jesse stories were passed from Gramma Dirks to Josephine to Mother and then to me, and the starting point in that correspondence line could begin with any one of us. There would be later tales by Mother, filling in so many of the details I always wondered about, but those came after I was in college.

In one of the most startling tales to circulate while I was younger, Aunt Josie told us that Jesse'd tried during his early preaching career to connect with evangelist Aimee Semple McPherson's Interdenominational Foursquare Pentecostal Church when he lived in California. That's Foursquare after the four gospels and the four persona Sister Aimee attributed to Jesus—as savior, healer, baptizer of the Holy Spirit and Second-Coming King. This was right after the war when Jesse was released from prison. Sister Aimee had died in 1944, but her church organization had been taken over by her son, and Jesse was drawn to it because she had begun as an itinerant, preaching in huge revival tents to large gatherings, reaching to thirty thousand. The National Guard had to be called out to help control the crowds. Jesse liked the idea of traveling for the Lord, reaching out with the Word to thousands at a time. It had everything in it to carry him out of his prison slump and get him moving forward again.

After his release from Leavenworth in the fall of '45, going back home was anathema to him. From scattered letters he'd received from Josie within the last couple of months, he knew his father had sold the farm that summer. Whalen had been diagnosed with colon cancer that winter, and was weakening rapidly. Josephine had pleaded with Jesse to return home before it was too late, while he could still see his father alive.

But returning must have felt like failure, like going back to the viper's nest.

Of course, going back to Shirly was ridiculous in any case. It was a small place, without any promise for Jesse outside of farming, and with his parents now living in Hopewell, it seemed the more logical place to call home. But Jesse had mapped out other plans while in prison, and going to Hopewell immediately upon his release wasn't one of them, especially with Whalen on his death bed.

While serving time at Leavenworth, Jesse had heard of the Foursquare Church's training program for pastors and missionaries, so he decided to by-pass the usual church ordination process and try for what he thought would be an easier route to his endorsement for preaching. Jesse was guessing that Foursquare's primary prerequisite for ministering out in the field was a demonstration of having been called by the Holy Spirit. There wasn't anything about this that Jesse felt he couldn't validate. After all, he had been called. The expression of that calling, to him, was pre-ordained.

He hitchhiked his way to the Los Angeles area where four of McPherson's churches were located, and while working as a cook at burger joints and diners, he attempted to enter Foursquare's educational program. But for reasons that weren't exactly clear to Aunt Josie in his one note to her, but which she thought probably involved information about his prison record or skirting the service, the International Church of the Foursquare Gospel ignored his two dozen letters of appeal to his application. That's if any of this can be believed, Aunt Josie told us. If not, it was still a good Jesse story, because, years later while on his death bed, he would claim to my mother that he'd even joined a Foursquare healing line and was taken into a sacred side tent in an attempt to get himself an audience with somebody who would listen to him, but without success.

All was not for naught, as he told it, because through his many trials and inquiries with the Foursquare Church, he'd learned a great deal about how to conduct and organize himself for revival evangelism. And he had seen Sister Aimee in film news reels, memorized whole sections of her sermons and studied carefully her intonations and gestures. We were left to our imaginations as to how he could've gotten all he said that he did from a few film clips or even how these clips had been available to him. The problem was, he'd confided to Josie, the style of female evangelists simply wasn't one that men of God could use. It was too simpering and suggestive—in a devotional sense, of course—but it was also heartfelt, obviously coming from Sister Aimee's sincere belief in what she was doing. Her large-audience preaching went beyond aimed performance to genuine attraction. Whatever it was that she had, audiences fell for it like a ton-a-bricks—those being his words, not Aunt Josie's. "The way he talks," my aunt told Mother, "you'd think he's in love with the woman, dead as she is."

When I was older I would realize that the characteristics Sister Aimee McPherson had founded her ministry upon, the ones Jesse was striving for, was charisma. And by the time he had established himself as a preacher in Hopewell, he had it. He just needed a larger place to practice it. Unfortunately for him, by the time he was ready, his time was past.

It was after his rejection by The Foursquare Church that Jesse decided to use the year he'd spent in seminary—and the three in Leavenworth—to his advantage. He was thirty by then and had enough maturity to peddle himself in just about any way he chose. He never lacked nerve. So, via fliers, posters, and brochures, he sold himself as an itinerant preacher fully ordained by the Southern Baptist Convention, and launched his own revival circuit.

It took him the winter of '45 to plan this circuit, and while he cooked in diners for a living, he gathered supplies and assistants. In the spring of '46, he launched the *Dirks Ministries for God* with an itinerary through the western and southwestern states.

The Convention didn't have time to catch up with him, even if it had heard of his forgeries in its name, because his itinerancy lasted seven short months, and he was on the move constantly. The newspapers and radio weren't particularly attracted to him since he didn't draw the crowds that warranted their attention. So Jesse's little mobile revival, for all the talk and excitement it engendered back home, only left a dusty trail through five states during the long, hot summer of '46 and into the fall.

Hard as I try, I can't imagine the ministry netted him any monetary gain outside of paying for its maintenance, which included all the ads and hypersell, the gas to make it through all those states, his room and board—and that of his employees—that's if they even got paid. Did they travel with him all that way? After each family get-together, Jesse's exploits were hashed and rehashed like leftovers from other meals. As a kid, my chief concern, which was more legitimate than I knew, was that he didn't end up back in prison.

And then the family lost track of him for almost a year.

Ava kept her grieving to herself. She'd lost a husband, and now her son. But Josie had her say, at least to Mother. "He missed his father's funeral. Maybe that's forgivable, with his rushing through the western part of the country, all hell-bent for the glory of God, and even missing the sale of the farm in Shirly. *That* I can understand, although just barely. He was never involved in farming, leaving as soon as he could. But not coming home to see his mother after she'd moved to Hopewell, the farm sold, her life utterly destroyed? Not even a week away from his—his what?—*his itinerant preacher show?* As though the postcards and sales clippings from his ministry would cover it all! It's just downright wrong in God's eyes, and in anybody else's who's got any sense in his head. Right now, don't even mention his name around me. I've no use for him. None. Zip. Zero tolerance."

Later, we found out that when Jesse finally threw in the towel, he really threw in the towel. He played poker and gambled on anything anybody would lay stakes on across California and Nevada, coming out five thousand ahead, more money than he'd seen during his entire life. Five thousand in 1947 could buy two cars and still leave enough money for a down payment on a house. Jesse was sitting right where he wanted to be.

But he paid a price for it. He was jailed twice for drunken-and-disorderly conduct and had been booted out of town a couple of times for illegal solicitation and gambling. Aunt Josie said she didn't want to know what those meant, but she guessed the gambling had been for betting on cock fights and the solicitation had been for pimping whores.

But then, just as unexpectedly, Jesse walked into a Baptist revival in Reno, Nevada, and reconsecrated his life to Christ. He believed he had never lost his faith, he'd only been derailed. As a Baptist, he had what he called "believer's security," which meant that once he was saved, he was always saved. As his mother would tell it years later, it was the time in Jesse's life when he truly found his way. He quit smoking cigarettes, drinking whiskey and sweet wine, swore off women—well, off swearing altogether—and other sundry sins and crimes against God and humanity.

Through some miracle of God—Ava's view—or special touch he had —Josie's view—he entered Wichita Theological Seminary "as pure as driven snow"—which was both of their views, one expressed with sincerity, the other with sarcasm. This time his source for the money to enter divinity school was clear, and with that security as leverage, he was able to find a church sponsor in Hopewell faster than anyone from our family could have imagined.

The one telling detail, to my father's mind, was that Jesse continued to wear blue pin-striped, double-breasted suits with careful creases in his trousers despite their lack of fashion, only switching their color to solid navy blue in later years after he'd undergone misfortunes none of us could have dreamed up. Jesse's life was taking on a surreal quality far past even our overblown imaginations.

"Evidently Jesse had decided by then that the association to the tougher element of society wasn't helping him any," Dad said about Jesse's choice in suits. "In fact, pinstripes and those fancy silk ties were inching him closer and closer to the devil's abyss. Especially the two-toned shoes. He had to've seen that his image—after his cockeyed, raving hiatus and his cockeyed, raving commitment to the evangelical life—wasn't going to play well at his second go-around at seminary."

My view was that Uncle Jesse became infatuated with an idea of how he wanted to be, then plummeted fast and hard when he wasn't able to live up to it. But I couldn't see or express this until years later. I was only eleven when Jesse entered Wichita Seminary.

The family had lots of disagreements about what motivated his actions. Most importantly, they didn't agree on why he couldn't give up on religion, and his role in it. Mother and Aunt Josie thought he was a troubled man who sought to right himself as best he could, though Josie saw in his search a hopelessness that Mother didn't want or seem to grasp. The way she saw it, one never stopped trying to find their way to God regardless of where their troubles took them. Ava protected him at all costs and in any way she could. Most of the time, it was a stretch and strain. She would retreat from family gatherings or stand in the kitchen, filling canning jars with spiced and pickled vegetables and fruits from the last pick of the orchard and garden, or bend over the sink, sullen and silent, while the rest of the adults tore Jesse to shreds. Uncle Clifford sat grinning as the discussion went around the table. Dad thought Mother's brother was a good-for-nothing low-life who was bent on covering that up with whatever he could pull out of his hat, easy tricks on crowds wanting to be deceived. "Jesse did his altar calls just like he played his hands at cards, with a poker face," Dad told us.

Before Whalen passed away, he sat in silence when talk and photographs circulated around the table about Jesse's ministerial life down in Corpus Christi and his itinerant preaching afterward. Whalen's jaw tightened with each comment, but he never uttered a word.

Everybody agreed that the one thing Jesse did have going for him, for good or ill, was an appealing preaching style. It seemed that, despite her seduction and simpering, Sister Aimee had mentored him well. His early preaching and speaking voice was never loud. It resonated through a space. Everyone was aware when he was speaking, however soft the utterance. His delivery was attractive, like a hushed baritone at a regional opera. As time went on, it grew into another kind of attraction, the one of a drug abuser or chain smoker—hoarse, like sandpaper to the ear, ground down through hidden friction and abuse. It was the sound of the Del Rio, Texas, strung-out radio evangelists, of the later Johnny Cash and Willie Nelson. It was haggard, with heartbreak in it.

I heard him preach only once, before I graduated and then left Hopewell for college, and I was astonished by his command of Scripture and his tight, constrained enthusiasm. It was held in check by a purposeful modulation of tones. I could envision him in an opera, speaking instead of singing the parts, especially those demanding gravitas and tragedy. And he was a gifted writer, forming ideas in simple, straightforward, emphatic sentences but using that emphasis sparingly. In this his charisma came close to McPherson. He read the sermon I heard him preach but with such seamless oration it appeared to be spontaneously inspired. It gave what he had to say authority and dignity in a profession that too often descended into gut-wrenching bellowing and howling, especially on the radio, a medium that would have suited Jesse well, but one he surprisingly didn't pursue. I wasn't sure why, since his appeal could have reached a large number of people without the constant pressure of the crowds. But I'm guessing he decided to keep his preaching presence immediate, for the intimacy of those crowds, regardless of their size. Jesse was a personal persuader, the salesman standing with the customer in the parking lot, directly in front of the car.

As I left the church the day I'd heard him preach, he shook my hand in the reception line at the door and waited for me to comment on his performance. I withheld, as family members so often do, and simply told him I had enjoyed the service. I didn't look to see what response was in his eyes.

The stories about him whirled around me, but they really began when I was old enough to understand he was more than a simple flesh-and-blood relative. One day—I must have been around ten at the time—in a photo box at my grandmother's house I found a picture of a strange woman with a baby in her lap. I had been through the box many times before and knew most of the photos in it, as well as most of the people pictured in them, but did not recall this one. I took it to my grandmother and asked her who the woman in the picture was.

"Oh, my," she said in a peculiarly perplexing way. "Where did you find this, Caroline?" Gramma Dirks always called me by my birth name instead of the nickname, "Shike," used by the rest of my family.

"In the photo box, Gramma, the one you let me go through when I'm here, remember?"

"This must be where I put it, then. I can't imagine why. Well, never mind. It's just a picture of a friend of your Uncle Jesse's from some time ago. Why don't you give it to me and I'll put it away."

"Away?"

"Well, out of the box." She hesitated just long enough for me to see the embarrassment in her eyes.

"Why?"

"Why?"

"Why out of the box? Why do you want to put it some other place?"

"It belongs to Jesse, Caroline, and I don't feel it belongs with the other photographs. It's his to do with as he chooses."

"She's pretty," I said, still holding the photograph.

"Yes, she was."

"Is she dead?"

"Oh my, I hope not."

"Where is she?"

Gramma's voice was strained. "Caroline, you're asking a lot of questions. I'm not sure I can, or even should, answer them."

"Why not, Gramma?"

"It may not be fair to your Uncle Jesse. He has a right to his privacy."

I handed her the photograph and asked, point-blank, "Is the baby his?"

My grandmother stood as though taken by an intense memory or pain. She stared down at the picture.

"Where would you ever get an idea like that?" She walked toward the bedroom, me following behind.

"Momma told me once that Uncle Jesse was 'fast.' She said he did everything fast—drinking, driving, and women."

Gramma turned around and stared at me without saying anything.

It was an admonishment, I knew, so I quickly added, "He used to."

"Your momma oversteps her bounds sometimes." She turned her back to me again, continuing to walk ahead. "Especially where her brother is concerned and in matters that should never have been mentioned to her children." She said this like I wasn't one of them.

"Is it? Is the baby his?" I insisted.

"Well it is, yes. But Caroline—" she hesitated, as if considering how much truth she could tell without betraying her son's confidence. "This was a woman, a wonderful woman your Uncle Jesse met when he—when they were very young. She loved your Uncle Jesse very much and wanted to marry him, but he denied the baby was his." Gramma opened a dresser drawer and put the picture inside, then closed it again, straightening the scarf on top. "It's ancient history now. So it's best kept out of sight, tucked in here. Away."

"Did she send the picture to you, Gramma?"

"Caroline, stop this. I've answered more than I should. And you mustn't—"

"But I want to know. Did she?"

"Well, yes she did, but why do you want to know?"

"I want to know the truth."

This seemed to stop Gramma for a second, but she gathered herself quickly. "The truth sometimes is hard for others to accept. It's the reason for lying, always, or at the very least, keeping silent." She put her arm around my shoulders and began walking us back to the living room. I didn't think of it then, but grew to understand, that most lies are conceived in silence, in secret, especially Uncle Jesse's lies.

I stopped her in the hall and looked up into her eyes. "Why did she send the picture to you, do you think?"

"Probably to keep in touch—to touch us all by this child's presence. Who knows? I never answer her letters."

"She still writes to you?"

"Oh, not so often anymore. A year here or there... I get a letter, a picture. I never keep them. This one happened to be one of the first when the child was still very small. I didn't remember I even had it."

"How old is he now? It looks like a baby boy."

"Well, it is, was. Maybe he's—" She stopped and thought. "He was born about the same time as you were, Caroline. I'm remembering that now. So he's about as old as you are."

"Ten? This story is a very old Uncle Jesse story."

She hugged me and laughed. "Yes, I guess it is."

"Did Uncle Jesse ever see him again?"

"He never saw him to begin with. He wouldn't listen to reason or let me ever mention her name, let alone the child's." She looked at me, tears around the edges of her eyes. "Elenore. Her name was—*is*—Elenore," she whispered.

"Uncle Jesse has a son he hasn't ever seen?" I asked in amazement.

"That may be true, I'm afraid."

Where this conversation went beyond this, I don't recall. It surely didn't end up in the air like this. I was too inquisitive. The questions that had provoked the exchange wouldn't have stopped in mid-discovery. I would've wondered if my mother and father knew, Aunt Josie and Uncle Clifford. Surely my grandmother warned me to keep this knowledge to myself. Thinking on it now, I'm amazed Gramma told me such an enormous family secret.

I was to learn years later, when I went back home to visit while living in New York, that Elenore Mary Decker was a girl of eighteen—to Jesse's twenty-one—when she became pregnant. She and her parents were members of the Holdeman Mennonite community in Shirly. They had packed up and left for Nebraska before the baby was born. Mother told me from a memory-story Uncle Jesse had shared with her in the last days of his life.

Years later still, by some ironic twist of fate, I was searching in the library for names for girls—for a friend who was pregnant and was ambivalent about a girl's name, but wanted it to be old, traditional, even possibly from the Bible—and ran across the name Elenore, spelled in that precise way, in a small book entitled, *Baby Names From the Scriptures*. The meaning ascribed to it was, "God of my youth." When I searched for reference to it in the Bible, I found none.

After his wayward gambling days, Jesse limped back to Shirly, staying long enough to shake hands with the bartender and look up a couple of chums from high school who worked or owned their fathers' farms. Of course, he avoided altogether the Shirly Baptist Church minister and its congregation. He had no desire to explain his behavior while at the Corpus Christi seminary to which they had sponsored him, thinking the administration at the school probably had sent them notification of his expulsion. He had a speech ready in case he ran into a member of the church on Main Street. It wasn't likely any would be found in the bar, but out on the street in town, it was possible he could cross paths with one or two. He had not done himself proud, or the Lord proud, he would tell them, and then pull out the Nevada revival reconsecration card and lay it on them. It was a play he was sure most would fall for.

He saw his mother, now living alone in Hopewell in the house she and Whalen had bought before he died. Jesse stayed with Ava for some time before sharing a room with a friend in town. He found a job as a cook at a small Italian restaurant, and once again began the search for a sponsor for divinity school. He found it in an unlikely place— Calvary Baptist Church, the second largest church in Hopewell. The new young minister was willing to put real effort into persuading his board that Jesse Daniel Dirks had brought himself up from overwhelming odds to become an instrument of the Lord's work.

Jesse had adjusted his resume to meet his present need—the years spent in prison continued to be touted as work in a C.O. camp—part of which he claimed was as a cook at Leavenworth. It was always his tendency to skate as close to the truth as possible without sliding over the edge. Never mind that these camps usually did not do this kind of social work. What fabrications did he invent to convince the board of his grand side-stepping? And how did he get past his fake Southern Baptist ordination during his revival preaching days and his follies afterwards?

"There's nothing like a prodigal son brought back home to the Father," was my dad's comment about Jesse's sex-laden sins, with a sarcastic addition, "in Jesse's case back home to the *mother* who favors him."

Mother retorted that Mary Magdalene had been as close to Jesus as any of His disciples, and she had been a prostitute, so before Vernon or anybody else went shooting off their mouth about carnal sins and fake contrition, they should take a second look at the Scriptures to see how Jesus responded to such accusations. To her recollection, she argued, Jesus wrote something in the sand when He was presented with the adulteress. 'He who is without sin, should cast the first stone.'" To Mother's mind, that's exactly what happened during Jesse's interview with the board—of course, without the writing in the sand. If Calvary Baptist and the grace of heaven forgave him any waywardness, then so should his family.

Dad told her that the Scripture doesn't specify what Jesus wrote in the sand, that she could look up reference to what the sand had to say in John 8, if she was so inclined. And if she did, she might be surprised to learn that what she'd quoted Jesus as saying was what the Savior had said *after* He wrote whatever He did in the sand. But then, John 8 or not, he was willing to concede to her point as he'd understood her message about forgiveness well enough.

Jesse was granted the sponsorship under the condition that part of his internship would be served as assistant pastor to their minister. But this too was waived, because by the time Jesse was close to finishing his course work at Wichita, he was married to Clarice Abt, a woman from a well-established Baptist family, had two children—a boy of five and girl of four, adopted through a special agency from Germany—had delivered a number of notable guest sermons in churches while attending seminary, and had served as student representative on the college council that advised and helped orient entering divinity candidates to their programs. It would appear that Jesse had a flow-chart that connected all the right people and circumstances to keep him moving forward with his work for the Lord.

—

So when Uncle Jesse called and asked if he could see me, in his church, the little mission past the tracks, in the colored section of town, I hung there at the other end of the phone listening to his soft-spoken, totally unexpected invitation, imagining his full-moon-round, red-bloated face and wondering what in heaven's name could have prompted such a request. It was in the Fifties, so we still thought and talked about "colored town," the dividing line between the folks who had a little and those who didn't have anything. A few white families were scattered on the periphery of the darker south side of Hopewell. At one time, my family was among them. Those who had more than enough lived so far on the other side of Hopewell they couldn't even see the streets leading to where Jesse's church sat.

"Well, I could, I guess, but why?" Clearing my throat, I asked, more directly, "This about Mother?"

"Your *mother?*" He puffed like he was smoking. "No. But it's not anything I care to talk about on the phone. I need to see you in person and as soon as you feel like you can make it over here."

As soon as you feel you can make it over here was one of those long-ago, from childhood, requests he used to make with a well-understood, but underlying threat. He meant that I should leave where I was and come to him immediately. I wondered how he got my telephone number. It was my senior year in high school, a year after I'd been to his church to hear him deliver a special Mother's Day sermon. I had moved away from my mother and home. At the time of this call, I hadn't talked to her for months. I wasn't listed in the phone book. I had no friends but the people I worked with at a short-order restaurant whom I'd urged not to give out my number or whereabouts. It wasn't likely he got it from them. I wanted to ask him, but he probably wouldn't have told me, and anyway, I was slowly forming a possible answer—Aunt Clarice had given it to him.

"It sounds urgent," I said, feeling around.

"Well, it is, in a way, at least to me. But, look, I don't want to be mysterious about this. I'm calling because I need your help, and it's something I think you can give pretty easily. Can you come some night this week?"

At night? A queasiness seeped into my stomach. "I don't know."

"I can't see you during the day. I have a conference and some house calls I have to make this week," he pronounced, like a doctor on his rounds. "How's Tuesday at eight, here at the church?" He was in command. I acquiesced, thinking there was no point in resisting. He wouldn't give up until I fulfilled his request.

Before I could manage an excuse in order to take charge the way I wanted to, I said, "Okay, give me directions," even though I knew very well where his church was located, and he knew I did.

I drove my beat-up Dodge into the parking lot and stared at the sunlit windows without stained glass. A carefully hand-painted sign planted at the head of the drive told me it was the Southside Baptist Church of Hopewell, Rev. Jesse Daniel Dirks, pastor, and in smaller letters, Mrs. Camilla Smithson, pianist and choir director. The building looked barely a mission, a shack of a church in need of paint and repair, the sign being the most cared-for feature of the property.

When I stepped inside, the atmosphere was transformed by that particular odor churches have, regardless of their age, of varnished wood and freshly polished pews. It was a bit like a one-room school house, but with a couple of offices to each side of a two-step, elevated podium and, placed at front center, an intricately hand-carved pulpit.

Sunset had settled on the windows in slanted streams. I felt momentarily as though I were seeing a vision. Once my perceptions realigned, I realized it was déjà vu from a childhood of churchgoing, three times a week on a normal schedule. I stared in the dimming light at the hymnal board with the title of the sermon and the numbers in the songbook for the hymns to be sung. Uncle Jesse had preached on "Standing on the Promises," the name of the first hymn for the service Sunday last.

The flow of my thoughts was interrupted by the sight of him, standing still as a post, a silhouette on a pulp fiction cover, the tungsten glow from behind stretching into shadows in front of him, eliciting drama and fear. He stood in a doorway, which led presumably to his office next to the choir. The bright light gave him an incongruent halo, suggesting a dark specter with powers I didn't want to test.

After I walked through his office door, he closed it behind us. I all but heard the sinister twist of a lock, but it was in my head. I stood there waiting as he walked around his desk to the leather chair.

"Thanks for coming. Did you find your way here okay?" he asked, facing me.

"Sure. Easy enough."

He wore dark navy trousers, his suit jacket hung over the back of his chair, his stiff, white shirt open, without tie, but sleeves buttoned at the cuffs. His belt was new, slick cowhide, the buckle shiny but narrow and slim, to match his Gruen wrist watch with oil-tan leather band. In every other way, his appearance was as it had always been. Except for thin, sagging lines under his eyes, he carried his age and wear well. My guess was that he'd just crossed over into his forties.

When he motioned me to the seat across from his desk, I had the odd sensation that I'd been called to the principal's office, waiting to hear what infraction I'd committed. When we both were seated, he folded his fingers together quickly on his desk and cleared his throat—a good little boy ready for recitations and prayers. "You're wondering no doubt why I called you."

He wore a thin gold wedding band on his thick, left ring finger.

"We could begin there." I tried to keep the distaste out of my voice.

"Okay. Right."

I didn't think I'd ever seen Uncle Jesse nervous before, not once in the long history of him with my family. But now, he attempted to hide trembling hands by squeezing his fingers together tightly. For a second I wondered if he'd been diagnosed with Parkinson's, and some such pronouncement was part of the reason for my being summoned. But, of course, that was ridiculous. He didn't need my solicitations over such a thing, and anyway, I would've heard this sort of news from Mother or Aunt Josephine, but then, our communications had their fault lines lately.

He shuffled some papers around. My father and Uncle Clifford's "self-assured blowhard" wasn't evident at the moment. I allowed the silence to manifest between us, hardening into a wall. I wasn't about to help him.

"Your mother—" he began.

"I thought you told me this wasn't about my mother," I interjected, trying to keep the glee out of my voice. I was enjoying the shift in power.

"It's not. I told you that on the phone, remember?" he declared, his voice gaining some confidence. He moved some papers around again. It occurred to me he might have a list of grievances in front of him. He looked down at one paper as though reminding himself what he was going to say first. But he slipped the paper aside, paused, looked at me straight on, hands no longer fidgeting, his fingers folded together once more, thumbs touching. He leaned forward, the insecurity vanishing, replaced by the posture and glare of a bully on the playground. "Recently your mother visited with my wife, your Aunt Clarice, and said some things to her, and to you as well, which have brought me a great deal of distress."

"I'd say it's Aunt Clarice who's the distressed one," I shot back, anger rising. The visits my uncle was referring to took place over a period of time, was my guess, first to my parents—which I was just now learning about, though I wasn't surprised—and then to me, and not just a couple of visits like he was making it sound. I was guessing Clarice had shown up at my parents' door, battered from a knock-down-drag-out fight she'd just had with Uncle Jesse, one eye nearly swollen shut and darkening bruises fully visible on her face and arms. Pretty much the way she'd looked when she showed up to talk to me at work.

She'd had a conversation with a friendly male newcomer, at a church reception, but Jesse saw it as flirtation. "Jesse's jealousy is going to get me killed," Clarice said. "And if he doesn't do the job properly, I just might reverse what he has in mind!"

Since I wasn't talking to my mother and didn't call my father unless I really felt I needed to, I had no way of knowing exactly what they knew, even though I had the creeping suspicion they had been contacted before me. Clarice didn't mention seeing anyone else in the family, and I was so overcome by her story, I didn't think to ask. I sensed that her letting me in on her dark secret was a demonstration of how desperate she was becoming.

Now Uncle Jesse stared at me, his face reddening. I thought he might reach across the desk and strangle me with one hand. He could. God knows, he was large enough, and furious. But he leaned back, rocking in his chair, regaining composure.

"Caroline, I don't think you truly understand the implications of what you are doing." He lowered his chin and grinned beseechingly at me with a tilt of his head. The emotional switch was mesmerizing. His entire physical projections shifted, perniciousness pooled in his eyes, floated to his hands and swelled his chest even as an extending smile stayed on his face. He seemed to expand toward me, then hover with sinister, near-sexual innuendo without leaving his chair.

"What exactly am I doing that's— "

"You are saying things that could jeopardize my ministry here. This is a small community—well, the whole town's a small community—but on the South Side, it's like a family, with the dynamics of family." He paused for a beat to let the personal allusion hit its mark. "I've served these people faithfully for the short time I've been here, taking the place of a man who'd been pastor to them for over thirty years. I've worked hard to fill his shoes."

"Why am I here? You said you had something to ask of me, a request I could easily fulfill. So now I get a history of your ministry at Southside Baptist and a slap for something I might have said that you find threatening?" I knew I was being snide, outright provocative. I didn't care. Most of all, I was having a problem putting together my aunt's bruised face and limbs and what he thought I'd done to provoke this meeting. Her appearance in the community would be self-explanatory.

"Okay," he leaned in again, and I felt the pending menace rise.

Why had I come? Why hadn't I insisted he tell me on the phone? I wanted to simply not ever see this man again.

"My wife's former life, before she met me, is none of your business. Keep whatever you think you know to yourself. That's my request. I was only attempting to explain why I was asking it of you."

So his abuse wasn't the problem? He was worried about some gossip about her former marriage. Why? "This is about Aunt Clarice having been married before she met you? What does that have to—"

"I said you didn't understand the implications of what you were doing, and I see all too well I was right. Let me draw them out for you. This is a very, very small community. Divorce is not accepted by Southside Baptist. It states very clearly in the bylaws that no pastor may preach or baptize in this church who has been divorced or has had more than one wife. I Timothy 3:2 is cited which extends to the pastor's wife, as they see it. In other words, no pastor can be married to a divorced person and preach in this church. *My* church. Can I make it any clearer for you?"

"I know Baptist preachers who have been divorced," I argued as though I was well-versed in the edicts of the Southern Baptist Convention, as though I was a respected church policymaker and this issue was important in my life.

"I know." He leaned back, apparently softening. "Michael Lukejohn of Cavalry Baptist, on the other side of town, is an openly divorced pastor, but he has never re-married, which to his congregation is the difference, evidently. Michael has assisted me and my ministry from the start, and I don't intend to let him down. I will not drag him through any difficulties that could arise out of what might be perceived as an insubordinate act because of me. Let me be clear on this, Caroline. The Southern Baptist Convention does not dictate what local churches put in their bylaws concerning such matters. Local churches have jurisdiction over their own governance in this." He held up a hand like a traffic cop. "And before you argue with me any further, no, I'm not open to going to another church that may allow divorce. When you become pastor of a church, especially one with conservative views, you go through an in-depth screening. I could never have obtained this pastorship had I been divorced. But the hiring committee did not extend their inquiries into the life of my wife. I have my own idea as to why, but it's not germane to the discussion you and I are having now."

He held up a hand again to stop me from interrupting. "Given my checkered background,"—he rocked in his chair and smiled amiably—"I was most fortunate to get this pulpit, largely due to Michael and his board's approval, and I intend to keep it." He lifted a couple of pieces of papers from his desk, not looking at them, letting them fall to the surface again and running his fingers back and forth over the pages as though he was dusting them off. "I do good here, Caroline. I believe I truly do right by these people. It means everything to me to keep this pastorship and continue in the service of the Lord." He paused for effect.

He was now the salesman I'd known him to be throughout my life, the one who attempted to get the deal made, regardless of what it cost. He was probably right about his service in this little church in the back woods, at least as far as his own needs and those of his parishioners went, though I wasn't so sure about his contribution to the larger community. And he undoubtedly was doing more good here than if he were somewhere else, selling something else—like cars, which would undoubtedly be a front for something more diabolic. And that was it for me with Uncle Jesse. I wasn't sure if I wanted to get even for all of those intentional meannesses he'd done to me and my brothers as kids, or if I had some deep need to set right the general wrongness that followed him like a fatal scent.

I shook inside to think what he could threaten me with should he find out I knew about his illegitimate son somewhere in Nebraska, and what kind of response he'd have when he realized it had been his mother who'd told me many years ago.

Keeping my voice even and my face as inscrutable as I could, I asked, "You have a Bible handy in your office?"

A flicker of a smile spread across his face, like a candle flame about to be extinguished. "Of course, but why would you—"

"Mind handing it to me?" I interrupted, adding, "No, I'm not going to tear the Scriptures asunder before your very eyes."

This seemed to put him at ease. He smiled easily, or smirked, and swirled his chair around to an antique oak bookcase directly behind him. Perhaps, he thought I wanted to check his reference to divorce, to verify his reasons for my silence. Without getting out of his seat, he lifted the front glass, took out a black leather-bound Bible, and handed it to me.

I knew by heart what I was seeking, but I wanted to read it to him directly from The Book—his lauded book. My fingers knew where to go. First Timothy was about two-thirds of the way through the New Testament, so I flipped to it easily, running a finger down the first page to Chapter Three. I stopped and recited, *"Verse two, 'A bishop then must be blameless, the husband of one wife, vigilant, sober, of good behaviour, given to hospitality, apt to teach;' Verse three—"* I continued, knowing exactly what it said, *"Not given to wine, no striker, not greedy of filthy lucre; but patient, not a brawler, not covetous."* Ah, here's the verse that covers them all—*"One that ruleth well his own house, having his children in subjection with all gravity—For if a man know not how to rule his own house, how shall he take care of the church of God?"*

I snapped the Bible closed and slid it back toward him. I didn't say anything, just waited for him to fill the gap between us.

"Well, that's a pretty big order, and one no man can keep one hundred percent of the time, even when trying his best," he said, solemnly, the smirk fading.

"Please don't say, 'But God is merciful.'"

He searched my face.

"When was the last time you hit Aunt Clarice, Uncle Jess? Isn't that what 'striker' means in the passage I just read? Or is that what you think it means by 'keeping your house well, your family in subjection'?"

He was up out of his seat in an instant, his palms flattened on his desk, I was certain, to keep them from flying over and smashing into my face. "You listen to me, you little—" He muttered something foul through gritted teeth, but I couldn't make out exactly what it was. "You just listen to me, you hear?"

"Sit down," I instructed him, as a teacher might a schoolboy, the words out of my mouth before I knew I was uttering them, but he had already fallen into his chair. It almost rolled out from under him, and he grabbed the edge of his desk to keep from sliding back into the bookcase. His face was so red I feared he might have a coronary. He reached across the desk, grabbed the Bible, and threw it across the room. It smashed against the wall, taking down his seminary degree and certificate of ordination with it. I stared at the wall, then at him, my heart beating in my ears.

He glared at me, disregarding the pile of shattered glass on the floor. In a voice far too quiet and calm, one that sent shivers through my body, he said with carefully-delivered enunciation—the devil's messenger now in the pulpit—"I'm not building this ministry, this church, to have it trampled underfoot by a stupid bitch-cunt like you, little girl. You want to take me on, you just go ahead. And don't think you can relay anything I've said or done to your parents or any member of the family. I know tricks you can't even think of in your most perfect mind. And don't even suggest to yourself that we are anything but what we've always been to each other—*nothing*. You think or do anything, anything at all, that might elicit suspicion upon me from anybody, I will hurt you in ways you can't even comprehend. Now, get up very quietly, walk out of my church, and don't ever come through the sanctuary doors again."

It struck me, after I left, that he might find enough inspiration in what had taken place between us to write a good deal of his next sermon. I couldn't have articulated it then, and am still not sure I can hold any definition of him steady to this day, but, it seems, looking back on this time, Uncle Jesse had matured into what he had been all along. He had evolved from a semi-private, egocentric sociopath into a paranoid, socially-manipulative psychopath. He was no longer simply agitated into compulsive volatile behavior. He now exercised calculated cruelty on anything or anybody he perceived as an obstacle to what he wanted. He was controlling his condition by embedding it in a persona of virtue and community service.

What kind of man was this, who could administer goodness and evil in perfect balance and measure?

———

I was so deeply troubled by the encounter with my uncle that for days I thought of little else. During my ruminations, I deliberated long and hard on who I could approach about what had happened to me in his church. There may have been a time when I felt insulated from his omniscience. Not anymore. Since I hadn't spoken to my mother in months, this meant that Aunt Josie and Gramma Dirks were also off limits. Well, Gramma was out of the question, in any case. I decided to call my father at work and ask if I could see him. If a secret needed to be kept, he was the surest bet.

"Your mother know about this?" he inquired. He meant my calling him instead of her.

"I can't come home yet, Dad. I'm sorry. But I need to see you about something that's really bothering me. I wouldn't call if I thought it would put you in a difficult place, well, I know that it is, but—"

"No, I can see you. Want to see you. It would be a good thing. It's just that I don't like so much meeting behind your mother's back, but I will. And I don't know quite when and how to do it. Let me give it some thought," he said and hung up.

Two long days later, when I thought he wasn't going to get back to me at all, he called the restaurant where I worked after school, and we agreed for coffee in Clover, a small town outside Hopewell. I told him that my car wasn't dependable enough for me to make the drive out of town but insisted he not pick me up. I didn't want anybody we knew seeing me with him, compromising his delicate situation between Mother and me. My landlady, Ruth Gifford, had promised to drive me to Clover. Dad found this difficult to agree to, but he finally consented, if I'd allow him to drive me back to a bus line on the edge of town where I could catch a ride home when we were through with our talk.

When I walked into the restaurant, he was already seated, drinking coffee, dressed in clean khakis and a shirt from his locker. He waved like he wasn't the only person in the place. It was late afternoon, not a usual time for him to be away from his mechanics job at Davenport Motors.

"How'd you get off?" I asked, sliding in the seat across from him.

"Oh, I've been known to tell a story now and again. There are too many other sins I've committed for me to go to hell for this one."

It was a line I'd heard from my mother about herself more than once over the years. The thought occurred to me, as it had countless other times, that when people live together long enough, they not only begin to look alike, they think and sound alike as well. However, in my parents' case, their appearance couldn't be more opposite—my father's thin-as-a-bean-pole, angular frame to my mother's round-as-a-beach-ball, cushiony build—but their expressions were beginning to repeat themselves in each other.

"So what's got you so tied in a knot you have to see your old man in secret to get untangled? I take it, it really isn't your car needing repair or you would've told me over the phone, though it sounds like I need to be taking a look at it sometime soon." He was grinning but there was concern in his eyes. He knew he wouldn't have to hide a car repair for me from Mother.

"I wish it were the car, Dad." I paused a moment while the waitress took my order for a Coke with no ice. "It's about Uncle Jesse."

"Jesse? Well, I'll be hanged. What's that bag-a-crap up to now? Don't tell me he's trying to get you to join his church." He snorted, looking at me over his cup.

He and Mother attended the First Baptist in town, having left the Mennonite church into which they both had been born and raised, and in which they had raised me and my brothers. When I moved away from home about a year ago, a good deal of the reason was my strict refusal to attend any church, including one that I might pick for myself. Neither of my brothers was old enough to decide for themselves at the time, but their religious futures would prove to be problematic—one becoming a Mormon, the other totally without church affiliation. Concerning me, at the time, my father was of a completely different mind from Mother, stating outright that I was of an age to make my own choices, including where I wanted to go to church and what I wanted to study, if and when I decided to go to college. He never suggested I didn't need to attend either one, but Mother didn't leave an opinion unsaid.

"How dangerous do you think Uncle Jess really is, Dad?"

He looked up again, this time holding my gaze. "To who? To you? Where's this coming from? Oh." His eyes narrowed. "This is about your Aunt Clarice, I take it."

I gave him a sketchy view of my encounter with Uncle Jesse at his church, and half way through the story I realized that I needed to delete Jess's threats so my father didn't get his hackles raised and make a visit to my uncle himself. I concentrated on Uncle Jesse's distress over my finding out about Aunt Clarice's early marriage and divorce.

"Well, that's an easy enough secret to keep, isn't it? Your mother and me've known since Clarice visited us, well, when was the last time? It was about a year ago, I think, just after you left home. She showed up at the house beaten to a pulp. I wasn't home, but your mother told me about it. And this wasn't the only time either. We've known about her taking his abuse for a long time, but there's no reason to make their life and yours miserable by spreading the word about it, is there?"

He didn't seem to realize he was mixing up the information about Aunt Clarice's divorce with that of her abuse. Dad had his own battles with temper, but he clearly saw a distinction between Jesse and himself. He would never have hit my mother despite years of her taunting and nagging him during her mental illness and his response to this by drinking. I think I saw him slap her once during my entire childhood, and that was mostly to get her attention, bring her out of her trance-like depression. And, despite his heated outrages toward us kids, none of us were ever in need of an emergency visit to the hospital.

Dad rushed on, not waiting for my answer. "But that pair do have their secrets, don't they? Clarice asked that we not tell anybody about his beating her up, because it would make it just twice as rough on her if he found out she'd shown herself to us. Your mother wanted to go to the police, but Clarice wouldn't hear any of that, a-course."

"Then why is she telling us, Dad? Coming to us? I mean, if she doesn't want any help from anybody?"

"Well, she's shown up on our doorstep several times pretty battered," he said, evading my question. "You know your mother. She can get fierce. Hell, she's not afraid of anybody when it comes to this kind of thing. It took everything Clarice had to keep Darlene from confronting Jesse with it and the police, as I've said. Clarice told us that she had her own ways of dealing with it. And I don't doubt that for a minute."

"Like what?" I imagine my aunt threatening to shoot him in his sleep or to tell his parishioners that he was pounding her brains out.

"You mean, like actually bashing him with a baseball bat when he wasn't on guard?"

"Yeah, while he's sleeping. It's crossed my mind after I saw her the way I did."

"So she's come to you as well? That kinda surprises me, Caroline. She's got to be getting desperate, feeling maybe she's used up all her other resources." He meant him and mother. I couldn't see Aunt Clarice seeking assistance from other members of the family. Uncle Clifford would probably kick her out of their house, despite Aunt Josie's sympathies. He'd made it clear enough over the years that he wanted nothing to do with Jesse's ins and outs. And Ava was out of the question, especially since she was living now with Tobias Wiebe, though it was hard to believe she didn't know anything about what was going on, having been in their home when Jesse and Clarice first moved to Hopewell.

"I'll tell you about Clarice's visit, Dad, but I want to know what you think she's capable of. She told me that if Jesse didn't finish her off properly, she might finish the job on him!"

"She vents a lot, Caroline. It's why she comes to us. Well, and tries to get some justification for herself. I'm not sure if she'd actually do him in, but I can imagine her threatening him with that, yeah. Now, if you were Jesse, that'd give you some anxiety, don't you think? But let me tell you something about those two. They go at it more than not. I'm talking about both of them, at each other. When the courts hear that this is the kinda fighting going on, where both of them have smacked each other around, I just don't think very many officials are gonna take her side. Though I gotta tell you, the authorities could take the kids. Remember, these kids of theirs are adopted from another country. And the courts aren't gonna put up with the likes of their parents' physical feuds in the home. Authorities'll get the agency where they got those kids involved, and you don't wanna know that story!"

"Whoa, wait a minute. What story? About how they were adopted?" These Jesse stories seemed to have layers upon layers *ad infinitum*.

"I'm not sure I know the whole truth about all a-that, what strings they pulled to get them the way they did, as fast as they did. But, you better believe, Clarice knows they're walking a thin line. Doesn't want the agency stepping in. She's as good as told us so. It's one of the reasons she's silent most of the time, I'm sure of that."

He drank more coffee before continuing, tapping the air to let me know he had more to say. "But these two, Caroline, they were fighting openly when they first got to Hopewell. Remember the potato salad she dumped all over him while you were sitting with them in the back seat on the way to some picnic or dinner?"

"I don't, Dad."

"Okay, then maybe only the boys were along. Anyhow, your mother was driving. We were on the way to some family get-together, probably in Shirly, and they were going at it like they do, you know. Darlene slammed on the brakes and told them to get outta the car. Clarice did, but your uncle refused. We drove him home. We liked to never got him outta the car. It took a threat of calling the police, and then we went back and tried to find Clarice where we'd left her, but a-course she was long gone by then, even though Darlene'd told her to stay put."

"I thought this was before he went to seminary, Dad. I remember the story. I wonder why I wasn't there? Where did he meet Clarice? In California, during his evangelical days?"

"No, no. He met her when he was in seminary the last time, in Wichita. Jesse did change after he met Clarice, I gotta say that. She helped him through school, though her family had something to do with that, I believe. Her dad had a hand in helping him find his present position by putting a good word in with the minister at Calvary Baptist. The Abts were well-known in their church organizations. Clarice's dad was head of this and that. I'm not sure how all that worked, but right after Jesse graduated seminary, that's when he and Clarice got their two kids and came back to Hopewell. They adopted because they found out she couldn't have kids.

"There was a little time between him taking over the pulpit at Southside and the current pastor retiring. So Jesse went to work on a farm for some months because they'd run outta money and had these two kids to feed. Jesse wasn't old man Abt's idea of a son-in-law, but he did what he did for Clarice, you know?

"Problems seem to start for Jesse every time he comes up with a plan. He can't hold onto whatever he's trying to do. Usually that's because his past shows up to bite him in the ass, and he has to take off, find something else."

We were silent as the waitress set down another Coke in front of me and topped off Dad's cup of coffee. He nodded his thanks and ordered a slice of cherry pie.

I began a silent litany of Jesse's accumulated past—there was Elenore Mary Decker's pregnancy that he ran out on, then his failure at the seminary in Corpus Christi during the war and his term in Leavenworth, then his try with the FourSquare Pentecostal Church education program from which he was rejected, next his failed California itinerant revival ministry, and finally his entrance into the Wichita Seminary where he made it through only with help from Clarice, her father and the minister at Calvary Baptist in Hopewell. Now he was in a permanent position at a church where there was some promise for security and starting anew but with the potential for any of these past lies and secrets to explode at any moment. It was as though he'd constructed this elaborate barrier between himself and success.

And seeping between each of the blocks of failure in this wall were his lies. on his resume, about his Southern Baptist ordination for his touring evangelical ministry, and his total omission about where he got the money for Wichita

Theological Seminary. Added to all this were his wife's divorce—a state-of-affairs that wasn't condoned by his present church and the shaky—or *shady*—means by which he obtained his children, and his abusing his wife over each imagined infraction. His entire adult life had been built on a foundation of secrecy, lying, duplicity and self-indulgence.

I was silent so long my father asked, "Where are you? You look a million miles away, Caroline."

"I'm sorry, Dad. What were you saying?"

"I was saying that I don't think Jesse can hold a line for very long with anything worthwhile. He's got the kind of desires that once he acts on the temptations, he creates situations that can't remain hidden. I think he knows this, even when he's doing half this stuff, but can't help himself. He's self-destructive in the way the criminal mind attempts to manipulate its environment to its own advantage even when it knows that what's being manipulated can, and likely will, call attention to itself to the point of getting caught."

"You talk about 'the criminal mind' as though it's a thing, a force or agency from the outside that takes over a person. Like it's living in them, but not actually that person, what they are."

"I don't know where criminals and their kind of thinking come from, Caroline. But I know Jesse's like many of them. Sometimes I think bad people were just ordinary folks who made wrong decisions for their own gain—whether that's money or power or some personal need or want or whatever. We talk about them like they have sin in them that none of the rest of us have, which we all know is absolutely not true. But with a guy like Jesse, it goes way beyond bad behavior and wrongdoing. He's one of those people with a wicked nature—maybe not downright evil—but who's been shaped by circumstances over which they've had little control. To tell you the truth, I don't know which is to blame, their natures or the circumstances that made them. It's almost like those are the same, you know what I mean? It's like they were conceived by the devil, and his designs for them, and they're living out their fate according to some preconceived blueprint that's in their blood by dark forces outside themselves."

That sounded like the definition of evil, of Biblical proportions, but I let it pass. The waitress set Dad's pie down in front of him and turned the wedge like an arrow to face him. He looked up at her and grinned his thanks. She nodded, holding his gaze with a smile, as she set a fork down on his napkin. Then she walked back to the counter. Was that a flirtation? I decided not, since I couldn't see my father being overtly aware of his charm. He took a bite of pie, chewed and swallowed before going on.

"You give guys like Jesse a helping hand, and they'll take it and turn it around against themselves, even when they think they're making plans to do good in the world. Thing is, before they end up destroying themselves, they destroy a lot of unsuspecting people along the way by ensnaring them in those plans. Maybe World War II, with its horrific consequences has done this to me—how I now think about guys like him. Death camps, the Axis of Evil, the atomic bomb, all created by people thinking they were inventing a better world. But it's how I look at criminals now. I don't know if they were always that way, or if the war made them. Don't know if they need to be understood or forgiven. I just know that it's tremendously dangerous, even fatal, to associate with them. Criminals like this rarely take responsibility for what they've put in motion. They're always looking for somebody else to blame their troubles on, especially when those troubles start exploding in their faces."

I was stunned by my father's ability to articulate this to me. Obviously, all those talks he had with Mother's father, my grandfather, Whalen Dirks, about the war, their endless discussions on what was in the newspapers at the time, had a tremendous influence on him. And just as obviously, I wasn't the only one who was reflecting on Jesse—who he was and how he behaved. I was certain my father and Grampa Dirks didn't discuss Jesse to any degree, at least not in this regard. It wouldn't have been in Whalen to confide in Dad about what he thought of his son. But it didn't take a mind reader to know Whalen acted out his contempt toward Jesse without caring much who saw it.

I nodded, but it took me a moment before I finally said, "I don't know what I think of Jesse, Dad. I've always tried to understand, if not forgive, but I can't go where Mother and Gramma Dirks do. I just don't see him as a victim, a screw-up like they think he is. I am cautious toward him in a way I wouldn't be with other people. He may look genuine or spontaneous at times—especially the rages he can go into and how he conducts himself with his parishioners—

but there's something cunning in all of Jesse's actions. He knows what he's doing, and does it for effect, almost like he's performing, in an odd kind of way. There's self-consciousness in it."

"My point exactly," Dad said.

Our waitress came back and took Dad's empty pie dish and asked us if there was anything else we needed. When we shook our heads, her eyes lingered my father's way, but when he didn't lift his eyes to meet hers, she left after placing our check on the table.

"He's been at Southside Baptist for at least a couple of years now, right?" I asked and Dad nodded. "And it looks like he's going to muck it up with his bad treatment of Clarice and whatever else is coming to surface, which seems to be her divorce. So is he going to see these public revelations as her fault now?"

"Or yours." He sighed heavily, placing his empty cup down carefully on the table. "Probably both."

"Is it because we're women? Does he see women as trying to trip him up?" I thought of his long-ago problem with Elenore Decker. I'd never told the secret my grandmother entrusted to me, and no member of my family ever mentioned Elenore to me. Who, if anybody, knew about Jesse's early indiscretion? But there was also Aimee McPherson, a woman he idolized, whose organization rejected him. And it was anyone's guess how many women he'd prostituted and pleasured himself with who'd spit in his face, and to whom he'd retaliated. Clarice's darkly reddened eyes, swollen cheeks, and bruised lips flitted through my interior vision.

"I don't know about that," Dad replied. "I do think he's met his match with Clarice, and she's tripped him up plenty and intentionally too." He paused. "You wanna know the truth as I see it? They enjoy fighting. But I gotta tell you, the last time Clarice came over, she was beaten up really bad. I was frightened by how she looked. I'm just surprised they haven't killed each other. And I don't think that's something to overlook. In fact, that's why she said she came over. She wanted somebody to know what she was calling the truth, in case she ended up dead. She stayed with us overnight and then flew out the door to Kansas where she hid out for a while."

"He didn't look for her among our family? That surprises me."

"It shouldn't. He's not welcome here, and he knows it. I've made that abundantly clear to Darlene. Since Clarice and Jesse've got back to Hopewell, they've been pretty much to themselves. A few family dinners, but they mostly use the excuse that they're busy with church goings-ons. He probably didn't think she'd come to us, and I'm sure he wouldn't want to alert Ava of any troubles he was in. Well, now, after talking with you, he knows, you understand?" Dad looked away with a worried frown. "Anyway, come to think of it, she actually went to Chicago after she spent the night with us, as I remember now, because she'd gone there before and stayed with an old girlfriend from her schooldays, your mother told me. She was afraid that if she went back home—to Kansas, I mean—he'd find her there right away, or maybe she was worried her father would do something rash to Jesse. There's a lot to protect, her being Abt's only child and him hating Jesse the way he does. The Abts don't believe in divorce, and they've been through this once with her already, remember. So I'm sure that despite their reservations about Jesse, they've gotta feel they're stuck with him as son-in-law. I'm sure Clarice has to be careful how she calls on her family, when and where, in order to keep that for whenever she needs it. Who knows how all-a-that works? But she's learned how to disappear, evaporate for a while. It was how the church members never saw her bruises. She's had more flu and family emergencies than any preacher's wife in history, and a-course, Jesse was probably careful where he landed his blows, though that isn't what I saw this last time."

"Why doesn't she divorce the son-of-a-bitch?"

"I just told you, there are her parents. She's their only child, and she's especially close to her father. And she's also told us that she can't divorce him, because Jesse's threatened to find her and kill her if she ever tries. He probably doesn't look for her real hard, because she always comes back—and there's the kids. She leaves them with him when she takes off like this. Think on that! And if he hurt her bad, he couldn't stay at the place where he's preaching, could he? He's gotta be thinking of that as well."

"But he's hurting her now, and he's not in trouble."

"Not yet. If she leaves for any time at all, I mean, my God, he'd have to answer to why she was gone so long or for good—and that's if he didn't kill her. If he did that, a-course, all of the cats would get outta the bag. That's why I think he'll never really do it. Not intentionally. Unless he decides to give up the life he's trying so hard now to save." Dad drummed on his cup. "She's always gone back home to him and the kids. Would you leave the kids with him? Hell, I don't know, Caroline." He wiped his hands over his hair, what little he still had. "Maybe it's an understood thing between them. He beats her up out of rage, but then shows he's sorry, and they decide she needs to leave to cool things off. She comes running to us when she's still upset and knows where to go to hide until it's time to go back home so they can start it all over again."

"So she leaves to let the bruises heal? Jesus, Dad."

He shrugged. "Then again, maybe she doesn't have a choice." He reflected a few moments, then added, "He doesn't hit the kids, never seen any evidence a-that, and she says not. But, about killing her, I believe her on that. There's a real possibility one of those two people is going to end up dead by the hand of the other. He tied her up with an electric cord one time, she claimed, and beat her unconscious, then left to do a wedding. I have no idea where the kids were in all of this. Who knows if it's true, but it's something she's told us is all. Listen, Caroline. Don't mess around with them. I mean it. He broke your mother's leg with a tree branch when they were kids, when he was mad, and he tried to lie his way out of it with Whalen, telling him she fell off the horse. But Whalen beat the shit outta him anyway 'cause even then you couldn't believe anything he said. Your mother has protected him at times, it's true, but she's given him a wide berth through the years. She claims she's not scared of him, and I don't think she is when she gets mad enough. But she tries to keep out of his way at other times. You'd do well to do the same."

The waitress poured Dad another cup and asked if I wanted a refill on my Coke, which I declined.

After she'd walked away, my father asked, "So she came to see you? Beat up and all?" He was talking to himself, really. He shook his head, stared at his coffee. He didn't seem to be done with this Jesse story yet. It was festering, deep inside, and he was examining it to find the sliver under his skin.

I answered him as though he'd asked again if she'd visited me. "Yes, and she looked awful."

He nodded. "How'd she find you? Ah, she came to your job, didn't she? I can't believe she'd expose herself like that."

"She didn't come inside. She knew where I worked because she'd come into the restaurant with the kids for soft serve cones when I was on duty one evening. When she came to see me, when she was a mess, she waited in her car at the curb not far from the restaurant and honked when I came out the door. It was raining cats and dogs, and I didn't know who she was at first. I started walking away, so she got out, called my name and motioned for me to get in on the passenger's side. I hardly knew her. She had on a scarf and sunglasses—*in the rain*, mind you—but I recognized her voice and, well, I just knew it was her. But I was shocked. Her face had been pummeled. It looked like he'd taken a board to her, Dad. Mom had told me Clarice had been mistreated by him. But Mom hadn't told me about *this*, and I hadn't asked for details, not wanting to hear any more at the time. So I had no idea what Mom really meant. I just thought they fought."

I glanced over at my father, but he didn't look up. He and Mom had their bouts as I was growing up. He knew why I was reluctant to take on more feuding and fighting in the family.

When he remained silent, only drinking coffee and nodding at the table, I added, "I have a hard time understanding why Clarice puts up with him, so I asked her."

He looked up at that, in his eyes was a pleading sadness. "What'd she tell ya? Probably what she told us—that he didn't know what he was doing, that he didn't mean it, not really."

"Basically, yeah, with an exception, that if he didn't kill her first, she was gonna 'kill the fucking bastard.'" I made air quotes. "And she wasn't going to wait until the next time, she said. I asked her why she came to me. She said she needed to tell somebody, and she didn't know where else to go."

I stared out the window. Nothing was in the lot except for Dad's truck. I suddenly felt terribly alone and isolated, even with the scattered sounds from the kitchen, and Dad sitting across from me earnestly listening. When I turned to him, he was shaking his head.

"It's why we took her in the times we did. It's a mess, but you need to be careful, I'm telling you, Caroline."

I went on as though he hadn't admonished me. "I know she wouldn't, couldn't, go to Grandmother. Coming to me was a desperate cry for help. Clarice didn't want me going to the police. She took me home and, after I got out, she drove away with a little wave. I felt awful, but I was afraid to do anything, not just because of him, but her."

"Same with us. She came, let us see her like that, and then wouldn't allow any help."

"But Dad, I was left with this idea that she was feeling around to see if I would do something. Inform the family or the police, or get one of us to take him on. Or *something*. Maybe it's as simple as her wanting us to give her permission to leave. But if we did turn him in, especially after what you've told me, I don't see how she could ever come back. And he had the kids. I can't believe she'd give them up to him.

"I gave her my phone number. That must be how he knew how to reach me. Is she so scared of him that she can't keep secrets from him? Or is she taunting him, using us as leverage?"

My father sighed, and shook his head. "I don't know how they think, and I don't wanna know. Those two are gonna kill each other or one kill the other, and you don't want to get caught in their sights."

I looked down, hating to meet his eyes, because I knew what his reaction was going to be. "What she really said to me was that she wanted to kill him and then kill herself *except*—"

"—for the kids." Dad's jaw flexed, his fingers tightening around the cup.

"No, she 'wanted to live after he was dead.' Her exact words. Not that she could live or would live but *wanted* to live after him."

Dad shook his head vigorously. "Clarice may look and sound like a victim, but you just don't know what's really going on in her head—or his. I told your mother, when she was all poised to go to Jesse or the police, I told her, 'Wounded dogs bite, Darlene. You won't come outta their mess unscathed.' For once in her life, she listened to me."

"I'm not sure I wouldn't be a lot like Aunt Clarice if I got beaten up consistently like she is. I'd think seriously about killing him."

"I don't think for a minute Clarice is like she is because of Jesse. She *enjoys* goading him, spends time thinking up ways to get him. These two found each other the way that hardened criminals do sometimes. Whatever produced either one of them, we may never know. I don't know anything about Clarice's upbringing, but Whalen and Ava both had their hands in how Jesse turned out. And we can be as sorry about that as we want, but the reality is, Jesse and Clarice are who they are, and it isn't anything I want to be near."

He held up his cup for a refill. I was amazed at the amount of coffee he was drinking without a restroom break. We remained silent while his attentive waitress filled his cup. When she had swished her way down the aisle past us, he took a gulp and continued.

"Anybody who takes sides in their battles is going to end up in trouble either way. We're talking Bonnie and Clyde, only Clarice and Jesse've turned their craziness on each other. Promise me right now, you're gonna let this be. I don't wanna get a call about you from the emergency ward."

Or the morgue.

I recalled how Jesse grabbed his Bible and threw it across the room.

As though reading my thoughts, Dad said, "Jesse's the kinda guy, Caroline, who'd kill your pet dog in front of you to keep you from telling anybody on him."

A shiver flew up my back as we stood to leave. Dad threw a five down on the table—a *five?*—and insisted on paying the check. We both were silent on the drive to my bus stop.

When I started to get out, he said, "What I'm afraid of more than anything else, Caroline, is his way of enticing you in. It can have a kind of momentum."

My hand on the door handle, I asked, "What you mean by that, Dad?"

"He's good at getting people in his clutches, and it's hard to extricate yourself. Goes for her too. You asked for my advice on this, and that's it."

I thanked him, and he told me not to be a stranger, to come home soon, that he knew my mother was ready for me to come back, at least to visit, that she'd show me some real respect if I did. I nodded several times before closing the door, and he drove off as I sat down on the bench and waited for my bus ride home.

Two weeks later, I arrived home from work to find a note taped to the door leading upstairs to my room. It was written in Ruth's neat, old-fashioned hand. *Your uncle called to say he'd get in touch with you about your dinner with them next week.*

Of course, there were no such plans. Jesse and I hadn't talked to each other.

He phoned that evening, and I took the call, knowing he'd never give up until he reached me. I didn't want to put Ruth through his barrage of constant messages. I tried wiggling out of his trumped-up dinner date, but he pushed me to give him a time.

There was no mention of his threats. No apology, nothing. His invitation was curt but congenial. However, that strange emotional shift was there again—from irritation and frustration to normalcy—with far too much ease. It left me cautious, but despite Dad's warnings, strangely curious.

With deference to Clarice, I agreed to the dinner, telling myself I might be able to pick up more information. If nothing else to affirm or deny my father's view of them both.

Perhaps if I demonstrated a kind of *savoir faire* in this tense situation, Jesse might see me as harmless and leave me alone. The important question was if this would be the end to an escalating state-of-affairs, or if it would be, as my father suggested, the first step toward a never-ending set of encounters. I wasn't certain how I could possibly pull an easy-going attitude for this dinner out of my built-up, strung-out emotions over my recent encounter with him and my conversation with Dad, but I had three days to sort this out. Perhaps this dinner would be the real information I needed to find out what it would take to keep him satisfied. Yet I couldn't rid myself of the persistent image of the Uncle Jesse of my childhood, calling me to him, lifting my face to meet his, delivering an exhortation he knew I'd not forget.

I began preparations by scripting the evening in every *mise en scène* I could imagine. No matter how much effort I put into this, none of my plausible scenarios morphed into good outcomes for me. Jesse always ended up on top, Clarice in the middle, and me at the bottom. I finally settled on two approaches to every storyline I invented—I'd feign casual surprise, or become overwhelmingly nonplussed. Then Jesse or Clarice, or both, would have to explain themselves further.

Turned out, the evening wasn't about me, unless it was about me watching them and they studying my reactions, especially Jesse observing me as a bug under glass again. I initially did get a brief, oblique third-degree from him about my life and the family, but it was in an off-handed, glib fashion, which struck me later to be a kind of rehearsal for the parade going on before me for the rest of the evening. His little exhibitions had a sinister, partially-veiled feel to them. But a more and more direct message became all too clear as the evening progressed. What I had to do, for the role written for me, was show up, delight in the meal, and appreciate what was unfolding, demonstrating as little disapproval or puzzlement as possible while they told me what they each wanted to say. I already knew *why* they wanted me to know it.

The table settings, the four-course meal by Clarice, and the hostess-and host-generated conversation were all done with that obsequious fluidity they no doubt used with a visiting pastor and his wife. Clarice had set the scene with porcelain china, crystal, silver, and linen in a manner both ostentatious and casual. The table was a gorgeous display, while their attitude toward our eating together was easy-going. They knew my parents couldn't afford the likes of this splendor, nor could anybody else in our family. It contrasted greatly with the church's meagerness and even the parsonage's dining room where we sat, with its vine-patterned wallpaper and grey oil-painted floor partially covered with fake, though well-done, oriental carpets. They were clearly demonstrating that they had the resources to lay out at least upper-middle class elegance in the middle of Hopewell's Harlem, despite their dubious past. Once again, Jesse was managing to live above his means on resources bound to raise my eyebrows, generate questions in my mind, while he seemingly sat before me detached from any of it.

In most of the important ways perhaps he was.

The presentation—the meal, including the flowing banter—was all Clarice. She'd come from some money, though how much she could claim now wasn't known. From the scattershot story Clarice had told Josephine over a couple of coffees, Mother and Josie had pieced together a picture of Clarice and Jesse's near-starvation, panic, and desperation the last weeks before they had made it back to Oklahoma from Wichita. They had survived their last months in Wichita by living off of what Gramma had given them from Whalen's inheritance. Even with Jesse's work on a farm while he waited to fill his present ministry at Southside Baptist, it was difficult to figure how they accumulated such fine table accoutrements.

If they were family heirlooms, somebody with an ironclad will must have named Clarice as beneficiary, and the rift with her parents was greatly exaggerated or mended. Perhaps they were wedding presents. If they were purchased with Jesse's money, I didn't want to know what that might mean. I couldn't tell if any of them were antique or not. Mother would have known instantly.

In the time that Jesse and Clarice had lived in Hopewell, none of the Dirks family had ever been invited to their house. If Gramma Dirks had visited, none of the rest of us had heard about it, but then we probably wouldn't, as Ava was always tight-lipped about her son. I was now the exception.

I was pondering why and how wine could be served in this oh-so-very-conservative Baptist parsonage, when they escorted me into the dining room area and indicated my place to sit across from both of them. Four eyes, the better to see me with? It was a little disconcerting but perhaps it was to all of our advantages since I could see their solicitations and reactions individually and together. No sleight-of-hand gestures or eye-signals without my catching them at it.

"Where are the kids?" I asked, surprised with only three place settings. I had thought their children, my little-known or seen niece and nephew, might be upstairs, out of sight until beckoned.

"Sent them packing." Jesse laughed a little.

"They're doing a sleepover with friends from the church," Clarice added, ignoring my uncle's remark, filling the crystal water glasses that reflected sparkles of candlelight on the white linen tablecloth. "Sleepover's the right term for the boys, Junior informed me. Kitty is the one having the slumber party!" She smiled at me, rolling her eyes in caricature.

"We're lucky," Jesse interjected cheerfully, "to have friends in the church who have a boy and girl about Junior and Kitty's ages."

About the time I was entering high school, Junior was around five and Kitty, four. Now they must be eight and seven.

"And, wonder of all wonders, they actually all like each other." Clarice smiled in his direction. "Would you like wine with dinner, Caroline? We have Sauterne or Chablis." She hesitated a beat, "Or a Riesling if you're like me and prefer German fare."

"I'm not—"

"Oh, faddle. You can drive, you can drink." She waved a hand. "We'll tank you up on coffee before you leave. What's your pleasure?"

"You choose," I said, playing my *savoir faire* card. I didn't know the first thing about wine. I'd had one glass of port during my entire time on earth, the full extent of my alcoholic life.

"Riesling then. Unless you want the Chablis, like Frenchie?" Her voice rose musically, landing on a falsetto, as she glanced at her husband. "Or would you prefer both?" The question hummed in the air. She turned to me and whispered conspiratorially, though fully audible to him, of course. "Jesse drinks anything and everything and when that's done, he drinks cold duck."

"C'mon, honey." Jesse's jaw muscles tightened slightly. He sat, and indicated for me to sit, but I waited to see if I could help Clarice in the kitchen. It seemed they were waiting for me, for each other, for—what? Everything was on the table or on the sideboard ready to be served. No appetizers, straight to the entrées. Straight to the point?

"You enjoy your drink, is all I'm saying," she said to Jesse, not looking at him, sighing toward the ceiling before sliding her hands under her legs and skirt as she sat down with us. "And if my memory serves, you don't get to do this all that often, so— when you do, you drink the dregs." I wondered what would happen if suddenly he had an emergency in his parish or if some lost soul unexpectedly knocked on their door.

She said to me, "That's what cold duck is, did you know that, Shike?"

I bristled at the sound of my family nickname. Nobody called me that anymore—Mother's orders, and then mine—but I didn't correct her. "It's pouring the last of the leftover wines together."

"Actually," Jesse explained to me, not looking at her, "cold duck came from pouring all the dregs together with champagne."

Clarice set the bottle down ceremoniously and gushed her approval in a couple of high notes. "You've always known your wines, Jess, and other drinking necessities. Recipe for success." She raised her glass. "Here's to cold ducks everywhere."

I had pulled my chair in when she did, so I was sitting and raising my glass before taking a small sip, just as she was—puppet, ape, mime. Slightly sweet, mellow heat slid down my throat, but I managed not to cough.

The talk was hurl-and-dodge all through dinner. I was the wall between them, and off which they lobbed their volleys. But as the evening wore on, the image I had was of linens being taken off a line and snapped viciously in the wind before being folded and stacked neatly in piles. Everything bristled, electric with potentiality. I attempted to break up the circuitry with comments or questions, anything I could catch and hold long enough to claim a stake in the conversation. They never took their eyes off of me, unless they were busy with their plates, but their sightlines were on each other, obliquely, in askance, then sizing, aiming and discharging, *pop, pop, pop* and *pow*. Clarice was cloaked in armor thick enough for cannon balls. Jesse lost over and over again, but when he did, she often rushed in and saved him, mewing subtle and not-so-subtle tendernesses, verbally kissing the spots where she had wounded him.

Halfway through dinner, I felt exhausted. I still couldn't reason out why I was there, so when the meal came to an end, I was close to throwing down my napkin and leaving the host and hostess without a word when both sets of eyes focused on me expectantly.

"So." Jesse leaned back in his chair.

The succulent turkey with oyster stuffing, and all the other traditional accompanying dishes, lay scattered and half eaten, including homemade jellied cranberry sauce and pumpkin pie with whipped cream. The dinner, it would seem, was meant as some token of Thanksgiving, the ultimate symbol of the American family celebration.

"Are your visions for your future resting on advancement in the restaurant business? I noticed the manager was a woman of considerable fortitude, who could manage her way in and out of just about any situation, I would think. Wanna take her place some day?" He winked at Clarice and took a slurp from his porcelain coffee cup. I couldn't remember a time when he'd actually been in the restaurant where I worked, but I didn't work constantly. It was possible he took the kids in, as Clarice had, for ice cream.

"I'm saving for college," I replied.

Now their full attentions were riveted on me. I was sure they knew this, despite the feigned surprise.

"Ah, college. High aspirations. I was the first in the family to graduate from college. Did you know that?"

"Guess that's right."

"No women as yet." He glanced at Clarice and then back at me.

"I'll be first to make it, I guess." I waited a beat. "Not that we're counting."

"Perhaps, now that we are counting?" Clarice stared at Jesse.

The silence that followed seemed a cue for my leaving, but as I folded and put down my napkin quickly and showed signs of standing, Jesse said, "So, you've left home and started working on your own while you're still in high school. Not many kids do that nowadays. What makes you different?" His voice was flat, no challenge in it.

But Clarice protested lightly, "That's not very well put, honey. I think it's commendable for a woman to make her own way, have her own mind about her future. I did!"

Evidently she was referring to Jesse as her chosen career. I'd thought she'd graduated from college but evidently not.

I sensed another round of indirect heat-generated bantering. "It's no family secret Mother and I have had difficulties over what I want to do after high school. She says secretarial school, and I say art school and then on to an art profession. Not sure what. Probably teaching, but I aim to find out." I smiled, attempting lightness. "Mother's strong-minded, especially with her religious values."

"Strong-*willed*'s probably more like it, and I understand that—"

"Uncle Jesse, I don't know what you've heard—"

"I haven't heard anything. It's just not so hard to figure out when something's amiss, and it's doubtful it would be your dad and you."

"Mothers and daughters," Clarice interjected in a sing-songy voice. "I'm not looking forward to Kitty's and my growing-up pains, our periods of adjustment." She laughed at her obliquely distasteful joke.

Lips tight, Jesse looked at me. "Your Mother's a bit hard on you, isn't she?"

It was then I knew I had to get out of their adolescent schemes. I placed my napkin down on the table and began scooting back my chair.

"C'mon, Jess," Clarice said, standing as though on my behalf, smiling slightly toward me.

Jesse smiled hugely, a smirk lurking underneath, while Clarice took our empty dessert dishes. I started to help her, but Jesse said, "Sit down." Perhaps it came out more curtly than he intended. "Please," he added in a beseeching, preacherly tone.

I sat down slowly.

He added pleasantly, "No need to rush. It's been a while since we've had a decent tête-à-tête." Coming out of his mouth, the phrase sounded like distant rifle shots.

"I'll get this. You two tête-à-tête." Clarice mimicked his exact pronunciation. Her light laughter had a deep-throated sarcastic edge.

Jesse's face puffed up and turned pink, but he didn't say anything or look at her. He sat with a sideways shrug, head tilted against his shoulder, lips pursed, tapping the fingers of his right hand on the table. He was deciding. The table had been cleared. Nothing left to throw except the fine china cups?

When Clarice was in the kitchen, he sat up straight, cleared his throat, folded his fingers as he'd done when I sat across from him in his office. "We have a choice about how we'll behave from now on, you and me." He was the preacher behind his pulpit, the authority in the room. "I'm opting for civility and seeking to put our mistrust behind us."

"Jesse," I said, standing once again. "Thank you for dinner."

Clarice burst out of the kitchen with the silver coffee pot. She stopped with her shoulder against the open swinging kitchen door, a look of surprise on her face. Was I deviating from their script or had he?

I looked directly at her. "I appreciate all this. I really do. It's been a feast. But I must be going. I have early shift tomorrow."

"Sure?" She held up the pot. I shook my head, and she backed into the kitchen, allowing the door to swing into place. "Then I insist you take some leftovers with you," she called from the kitchen, with the clattering of dishes.

Jesse was waiting, obviously demanding an answer to his proposal. I wanted to ask him how civil he would be if I decided to tell his church board that he was married to a divorced woman and drank sweet Riesling with his dinner. But I didn't, of course.

I pushed my chair back into its place under the table, placing my hands on its back.

"That's fine, Aunt Clarice." I called to her, but she was already walking toward me with filled dishes in her hands—glass dishes, fine glass dishes, returnable dishes. "No, really—"

"You mustn't be rude," she said, instructing me like a child. She put the dishes on the table. "Please, Shike, sit down and have a cordial. Then you can go."

Cordial? Shike?

"Aunt Clarice, I'm no longer Shike. It's not my name anymore. And, thank you, but I really can't drink another drop, eat another bite. I'll accept your leftovers in aluminum foil or something I don't have to worry about returning to you, if you don't mind. I'll enjoy any part of the meal you want to send home with me."

She kept staring at me, immobile, as though I had upended her evening. Was she failing at her mission, failing for him? With an almost imperceptible nod, she said, musically, "Fine, your terms then. I can do that." She picked up the dishes and disappeared into the kitchen. I turned to Uncle Jesse, his face bloated with anticipation, or was it anger?

Perhaps it was the alcohol and the relaxation from the sheer exhaustion of the tug-of-war evening that had now come to an end, but suddenly, he didn't seem as frightening to me. Tension left my body. Resignation or acceptance took its place, either would do.

"You've no worries concerning me, Jess," I said, deliberately choosing to use his first name in its shortened form without the familial address. The less formality right now, the better. I hoped my voice carried the exhaustion I felt. "You're right, totally right. We're exactly what you said we were in your office, and it's how I'll be interacting with you from now on. We are nothing, absolutely nothing to each other. I don't need to prove anything to you or you to me. We're just two people who happen to be related to each other. I enjoyed the dinner. You went to a lot of trouble for me, and I do appreciate it. But I'll be as honest as you have been. All this has made the impression you were hoping for." I let my gaze roam over the table and back to him, looking at him steadily. "So don't contact me again. I'm leaving this town, hopefully for college. I'll leave everything behind. But I'm smart enough to not burn bridges as I go."

I accepted the paper bag Clarice held out to me when she arrived on cue from the kitchen, and I walked to the door, not saying another word when Jesse opened it. I left them standing there together.

Once home, when I opened the bag to put the leftovers in the refrigerator, I found a note attached to one of the wrappers—*Don't think too badly of me. We each make do as best as we can with what we've been given. Clarice.*

I reflected a long time on the evening. Except for a few direct comments from Jesse at the end, the evening had been pure Clarice. From the spread of the table, to the control of the conversation, it was designed and delivered as only Clarice could do it. Jesse could never have made such an evening possible. I realized how hopelessly dependent on her he was, especially in his ministry. And this dependence must fuel at least some of his rage against her, as well as his attachment to her. But for the life of me, I could not figure out what her motives were.

The unfathomable question was why she would subjugate herself to him. What was she getting out of this marriage? Dad may have been right. They were a perfect match, caught in an enormous web they constructed together, watching and waiting to see what each could catch and consume to the other's delight and dismay.

—

One night two weeks after my dinner at the parsonage, I received a call from home. My high school graduation was near, and I was content in my waitressing job, my studies, and my room, away from the family drama. I missed Dad but I kept up by giving him a random call every now and then at his job. If he ever told Mother of this, I had no way of knowing, but it became less and less troublesome to me if he did.

Ruth Gifford took the phone and held it out to me as I made supper at the stove. I shook my head, but she said, gently, "I think you should take this one. There's some urgency in it."

What would prompt Ruth to give me such an instruction, I couldn't imagine unless it was under dire circumstances. It was very unlike her. If anything, she'd been overly protective of me. I turned off the stove, took the phone and fully expected to hear my mother crying on the other end of the line. Instead it was my father's strong, steady voice. He had never called me at the Giffords', so I was instantly on the alert, panic rising.

"Caroline? That you?"

"Yes, Dad. Is there an emergency?"

"I'm 'fraid so...."

A sinking feeling filled my chest and throat. Oh God, it was Mother. I'd put off the reconciliation until now when it was about to swallow me up in unrelenting guilt and despair.

When I asked him, in a halting voice, if it was what I suspected, he replied quickly, "No, no, we're all fine. We're fine. Your immediate family. *Us,* damn it." He made strained guttural sounds and tried again. "Before I start, though, Caroline, I need to tell you that I'm calling not just for myself but for both your mother and me. I'm emphasizing 'both' because we feel like it's time for you to come to see us." He stopped short of telling me I needed to come home to live. "And I'm talking about tonight. Right now. Can you do that?" He didn't give me time to answer. "Something's happened that we as a family need to see through together."

"Dad, for chrissakes, just spit it out, will you? I'm dying of fright."

"It's Jesse, honey. He's been mur—very, very badly hurt. It's ugly. He's been beaten to unconsciousness and stabbed more than once. They're saying it's unlikely he'll make it. He's in the hospital in a special unit and the police have your Aunt Clarice down at the station."

"Oh, dear God." Could I have said or done anything to trigger this?

But just as quickly, I recalled Dad's prediction at the diner. Now it seemed it had found its time.

His explanation about Aunt Clarice at the station came quickly, reassuringly. "No, no, nothing like what you must be thinking. She's as upset as the rest of us, it seems, though I honestly can't tell you this, since we haven't seen or talked to her for ourselves. Your mother's at the hospital with Jesse, well, as much as they'll allow. Clarice's lawyer has talked to her and Ava, on the phone. Darlene said the lawyer suggested I stay put, at home, because there's no need for me, or you either, to come rushing down to either the hospital or the police station. They won't let us near Jesse tonight and after the police finish their interview with Clarice, she'll be released to go to the hospital herself. We'd just have to sit outside in the lounge. Personally, Caroline, I'd like to be there when Clarice shows up, but that's been squashed before I could even suggest it."

"Why do you want to go, Dad?"

"Hell, to see for myself. I'm getting everything second-hand, and you know your mother and Ava. You could send them out to get the alphabet, and they'd come home with thirty-two letters instead of twenty-six. Ava could screw up her own name. And in her best moments, your mother wouldn't be far behind. Be that as it may, I'll just have to settle for what I can get out of them over the line for now. Your mother said somebody from the police department is coming out here shortly anyway."

"At the house? Your house? The police?" I ask inanely, knowing full well what he meant.

"I think you should be here when they arrive, Caroline. They're gonna wanna talk to you eventually, especially since you saw him in his office not that long ago, you know, at the place where he was attacked. I'm sure that'll interest them."

"How would they know that, Dad? I've only told you."

But as soon as I said this we both knew how ridiculous it sounded. Clarice would be the most likely candidate as Jesse was sure to've told her I'd come to see him. The dinner proved that. I was beginning to understand they told each other everything despite how hostile they appeared.

"Does Mother know?"

"Know what?"

I sighed.

He answered, rapidly, but carefully. "Well, I'm not sure how she'd get word of it. I didn't tell her. And I didn't tell her about our meeting at the diner, either, if that's what you're wanting to know. My lips are sealed on both accounts. But the police are another matter. After talking to Clarice, they probably know about this visit of yours to his office. How Clarice is choosing to look on any of this, and what she'll see as important to tell them is anybody's guess. She's going to lay it on Jesse, is my guess. I can't imagine her putting herself in jeopardy, can you?"

"I think you're making some fast assumptions. But I hear you. Why does she need a lawyer if she's not under suspicion, if they're only talking to her?"

"I didn't say the police think she's innocent. She's just not been charged with anything. I think the lawyer was probably her dad's idea. She found Jesse, after all, and made the emergency call."

"I'll be there within the half hour," I told him.

After I hung up, I cleaned up the kitchen, informed Ruth of my circumstances, then ran to my room and threw an array of clothing and needs into a couple of suitcases as though I'd suddenly planned to move back home.

The police showed up close to an hour after my arrival, so Dad had time over his boiled coffee to fill me in before the doorbell rang. The story he told was sparse, but filled with some interesting details. Mother had told him the lawyer didn't indicate Clarice was a suspect. Probably her saving grace—this was my father's conjecture—was that the choir director, Camilla Smithson, had found Clarice in hysterics, talking to the police on the telephone. Smithson, of course, noticed Clarice had blood smears on her hands, face, and slacks, but that her demeanor was one of a woman totally overcome by circumstances. Shaking from head to foot, she was barely able to talk, her voice coming out in gasping sobs. It was obvious to Smithson that it would be natural for the reverend's wife to look for Jesse's vital signs, to touch the wounds to staunch blood flow so the blood smears made sense to her. She told police that when she walked in, Clarice was reporting her husband had been murdered in his own church, stabbed in the back, although she wasn't sure how many times.

Clarice had been asked to check to see if the victim had a pulse, if he was breathing, and to see if he had any signs of consciousness. She told them she hadn't detected signs of life, and thought her husband was gone. But that didn't mean, of course, he didn't have any—which, as it turned out, he did. The ambulance attendants discovered a pulse, however feeble, and despite the large amount of blood loss, Jesse hadn't bled out. He still hadn't regained consciousness. He was hanging onto life by a thread. It was simply too early to give any kind of an accurate prognosis.

The police interview with Dad and me was routine, we were told, and it certainly appeared that way. The officers' questions could have been scripted in any of Bogie's or O'Brien's noirs—where were we during the hours of six to nine on the night of the crime? Had we any idea who might want Reverend Dirks dead? Had we noticed or heard anything suspicious leading up to the night of the incident? Did we belong to his church or know any of the members who might have done such a thing to him? What were our perception of the dynamics in the Dirks' household? What were our relationships to the victim? On and on it went. I hesitated when asked about my relationship to Uncle Jesse. I told them I had seen him two weeks earlier at a dinner in his home, that I had stayed a relatively short time—a couple of hours as I remembered—and it was a purely social evening. I did not mention the meeting in his office, and though Dad looked on a bit wide-eyed, he said nothing.

One of the officers asked if I was close to my aunt and uncle.

"No, I haven't seen them very much at all, except for family gatherings. When Uncle Jesse called to ask me to dinner, he said the evening might be a kind of celebration for my approaching graduation from high school. My uncle appreciated I was the first woman in our family to plan to go to college."

It was a gamble not telling the police about meeting Jesse in his office, but my hopes paid off. Clarice remained silent in all respects having to do with me, except mentioning the dinner and, as though reading my mind, gave the police the same reason as I had for the dinner invitation.

Jesse's misfortune read like a murder scene from every mystery novel on the shelves. The detectives' report stated—large parts of which were given in the newspapers—that it appeared he was preparing Sunday's sermon at his desk when he was bludgeoned on the head from behind, then stabbed three times in his upper back, all falling—within fractions of centimeters—in the same spot. Jesse was hit with great force, and as he was falling forward after receiving the first stabbing, was then stabbed twice in rapid succession. Bruising indicated the attacker must've held very tightly onto Jesse's left shoulder during the strikes. The police investigation centered on the puzzling fact that from his desk, Jesse could have seen anyone entering the room as the layout didn't allow for any hidden access. A window was some eight feet to the left of where he sat, and the door leading into the room was directly in front of his desk. There were no other outside entrances into the room.

I couldn't imagine how an attacker could get behind Jesse without his knowing, especially in order to do the kind of damage he'd had done to him. There wasn't much more than four or five feet between the back of his chair and the antique bookcase from where he'd found me the Bible I'd requested when I'd visited him. Perhaps the perpetrator had been standing behind him, with Jesse perfectly aware, even inviting the visitor to come look over his shoulder at something he wanted him or her to see or read from a paper on his desk. Then, when he least expected it, the assailant hit him. No weapon was left on the scene and nothing was missing from the room. The object could not have been very large—something the attacker would have to have carried, possibly in his pocket, undetected.

Clarice had told the police that, to her knowledge, nothing had been removed from Jesse's office. The police reports stated that nothing in the room seemed to fit the description of the object with which Jesse had been knocked unconscious. It seemed likely that the same object had been used for the bludgeoning and the stabbing, because two objects would have been unwieldy. Even though it was possible to carry two weapons, one in each pocket or in a satchel strapped to the back or waist, why think in terms of two? On the other hand, if only one weapon had been used, what kind of weapon could it have been?

I attempted to picture it, even draw it. A knife with a short, but effective blade, one with enough heft for the blow. It certainly would take something quite heavy to knock out a man of Jesse's size with a single strike, as well as one with a blade no longer than two or two and one-half inches at the most because of the depth of the injuries Jesse had sustained. Such a knife could fit into a pocket or purse, but might have caused the perpetrator concern, being either too large or too heavy and attract notice. A gun could have been the object, but if it were used as the clubbing weapon, why not fire it outright? The noise, perhaps? But there were silencers.

Actually, the gun theory didn't evaporate as readily as I thought it would or the two weapons theory either. *The Hopewell Herald* a day later reported that the police, at that point, believed Jesse was traumatized by a heavy, blunt object much like the handle of a gun, and stabbed with a short-bladed knife. The authorities had no ideas to offer about why there had been such a convoluted attack.

In the days following the evening of the stabbing, I spun facts around and around as they became known to me. Even though no scenario brought me closer to a satisfactory conclusion, I settled on the one weapon theory. The oddity, of course, was the character of the knife. Jesse had been stabbed repeatedly in the same area without having his spine severely injured, a major artery severed or his lungs or heart penetrated. So why not a longer blade? Why take the chance on his survival?

It was one of those times when Jesse, once again, made it by the skin of his teeth. But, perhaps, this time by so much more—by the luck of the wicked. How many times had Hitler escaped assassination?

When Clarice was asked by reporters if she knew if her husband kept a gun or other weapons, such as a knife, in his office desk, she said she was shocked to even have the question put to her. "Absolutely, unequivocally not. My husband is a man of God, not a street thug."

This statement came back to haunt her when the police discovered a week later of Jesse's dealings with Duane Smeets.

I had to admit my suspicions fell immediately on Clarice as the primary suspect. Her comments to me during her visit after Jesse's abuse and those to my parents would undoubtedly get the attention of the police, and certainly a jury, if it ever came to that.

But intending isn't *doing*. If it were, we'd all be in prison or hell. And hard evidence that Clarice was the perpetrator wasn't forthcoming.

The family did its part. There's nothing like family protecting its own, or destroying its own, when it needs to save itself. In this case, neither my parents nor I told the police of Clarice's threat if Jesse beat her again. And our silence seemed to extend to the church family as well. If any of the members breathed a word of suspicion to the authorities, we never heard anything about it. Undoubtedly, there was great concern about fingers pointing or shovels digging around in the church basement for buried skeletons.

But I began to feel very wrong about keeping incriminating information to myself. In my mind's eye, I could see Clarice standing behind him, possibly looking over his shoulder at something he'd written, and then attacking him from behind, fulfilling her long-standing desire for vengeance over his cruelty. On the other hand, I had a hard time believing she could be calculating enough to commit this crime. A crime of passion, yes. Most of her protestations about killing him came directly after he'd beaten her badly, and she was in a state of great agitation, venting her heart out.

But I also reflected on the minister's wife and aunt who'd laid out the immaculate dinner for me only weeks before. Her strange ambivalence about Jesse, her waffling emotionally where he was concerned, seemed only a little like battered women behave. Most seek the approval of their husbands even while they are terrified of them. Clarice was a different creature, seeming to be Jesse's helpmate and religious partner on the one hand but a she-devil seeking her own desires and needs on the other. I had seen her acting out both of these contrary roles of helpmate and provocateur simultaneously, conscious manipulations of the most outrageous sort.

Her alibi relied heavily on Camilla Smithson's statement as a witness stumbling upon the immediate crime scene. Nobody saw Clarice walk to the parsonage after she claimed she could not reach Jesse by phone—this claim was verified by police reports that calls from the parsonage to Jesse's office appeared during those hours on the telephone company's record. Since there were no weapons found near or around the area of the stabbing, and Clarice had called the police within a reasonable timeframe—given her walk to the church from the parsonage six blocks away and the discovery of her husband—the police suspended her as a suspect and waited patiently for Jesse to regain consciousness.

It took three weeks before he did wake up, but as soon as the doctors allowed him to be questioned, he quickly absolved Clarice of any wrongdoing.

He stated in a deposition that he had no idea who attacked him, and that he had not seen his wife from the time he left the parsonage at noon the day of the crime. When asked how he couldn't have seen his attacker who had to have crossed his line of vision in order to stand behind him, he replied that by the time he looked up, after hearing somebody approach, the attacker had knocked him unconscious. It was a small room, after all, and he hadn't seen anything, he declared, except a shadowy figure rushing toward him, dressed completely in black—the only image left swimming in his mind. The perpetrator had swiveled his chair around and smacked him from behind before he could physically respond. When asked how he was so certain it wasn't his wife, and for that matter, any other woman, Jesse stated that the figure was much larger than Clarice, had considerably more bulk and didn't move like his wife or any woman. He was certain, beyond doubt, that his attacker was male. He soon had become uncooperative with further questions that cast suspicion upon his wife.

About their children, Junior and Kitty, Clarice said she had left them with a member of the congregation earlier in the day, as she often did most Saturdays so she could get work done for the church. This Saturday she'd gone to the printer to pick up the bulletin for Sunday's service, called all the women on the charity bazaar committee to remind them of an upcoming meeting, and picked up the baptismal curtains from the cleaners just up the street with the intention of putting them in place before she and Jesse left to get their kids at the end of their work day.

They only had one car, so after picking up the bulletins, she left the car in the church parking lot, in case Jesse needed it. She did not go into the church at that time. On her walk home, she'd circled around to the cleaners on Randolph Street and picked up the curtains.

She and Jesse had agreed she would return around six o'clock, hang the curtains and then together they would pick up their children. But when she didn't get her husband on the phone, she went immediately to his office, finding him as he was. All of her claims had checked out. The police even found the baptismal curtains on a table near the font where she'd stated she'd placed them on her way to Jesse's office.

Making her the culprit meant disregarding Jesse's description of the attacker. Assuming he was not covering for her, she would have to have walked down the street in dark disguise or somehow changed at the church, leaving her other clothing behind, which was not mentioned by the police. I had to admit that my Clarice-centered scenarios left too much unresolved, the most challenging being her calculation in carrying out this crime, her disregard for the violent nature of the stabbing, and her hysterical response on the phone before she even knew that Camilla Smithson had come into the room, which was, of course, Smithson's view. But as guilty as my suspicions made me feel—especially given Uncle Jesse's heinous treatment of Clarice—there *was* something in her that allowed me to see her turning such an emotional act toward her own ends.

I also kept reflecting on her disturbingly manipulative "innocence" the night of the dinner at the parsonage. But as puzzling as it seemed, she was all I could conjure up as a suspect unless I surrendered to not having any lead at all. I'd already run through the other possibilities of the two women planning the stabbing together—why would they?—and of Smithson doing it, and Clarice covering it up. Smithson had no known motive and no blood from the scene on her clothing or person. If they did do it together, or even if Smithson covered for Clarice, why wouldn't they tell the police some made-up story? All of these conjectures grew increasingly ridiculous.

But if it had been done, as the police now suspected, by an outside assailant—the wounds indicated that it had only taken place a short time before the two women's discovery of the crime—how did the assailant miss being seen fleeing from the scene? Investigators stated that blood had not dried upon their arrival, but blood dries at about the same rate as water, so this was only a small factor in determining the time of the crime. Jesse was discovered so soon after the stabbing that most of the blood had not coagulated at all. From this and other evidence gathered at the scene—which investigators were reluctant to reveal initially—they estimated the time of the crime to be within an hour to half-hour of Jesse's having being found by his wife. If this were the case, it wasn't so hard to see how an assailant could disappear without having been noticed. Nobody had seen or heard Clarice walk from the parsonage to the church and only one elderly neighbor thought she'd heard

Camilla's car in Southside's parking lot around six o'clock but couldn't be certain of the time. In the words of my father, whoever had committed this crime "was gonna get off scot-free."

—

Just when I was about to give up on Jesse's whole ghastly ordeal, believing, like Dad, the authorities would never catch who did it, a development appeared out of the blue, to Jesse and Clarice's undoing.

Seems that when they first moved back to Hopewell, before Jesse had been granted the pastorship at Southside Baptist, there had been a period of around five months in which he worked at a local farm as a hired hand. During this time, Jesse made some shady connections with the son of the long-established bootlegger, Harold Smeets, who at one time had farmed in Clearview while also living and farming in Shirly. Duane had gone to school with Jesse, and they accidentally ran into each other when Duane made a delivery of horse-and-cow manure to the farm where Jesse was working.

It was during this time that Michael Lukejohn, minister at Calvary Baptist, acted as a reference so Jesse could become the pastor at Southside.

However, it only took this one-time connection with Duane for Jesse to make a profitable alliance with Smeets to smuggle liquor over the Missouri line into Oklahoma for some fast cash. It was an easy night's drive to Joplin and back—seven hours' round trip—that could net them hundreds of dollars within hours of returning to Shirly, enough for Jesse to pay the rent and buy groceries and gasoline for almost a month. Missouri laws were lax and enforcement shallow. In Shirly, there was only the local deputy on duty, usually coming in from Hopewell two or three times a week, so running liquor was a slick trade without much, if any, surveillance. Tulsa police kept watch on Route 44. A dip down to country roads around Muskogee and Okmulgee added an hour to the trip, but could keep the men pretty much out of harm's way. Smeets had several vehicles, with interchangeable plates, so they could appear to be traveling from Arkansas, Iowa or Colorado on Route 44. His father, then Duane, had worked the fake plates exchange for years. But because Duane made the trip often, he used Missouri and Oklahoma plates more than any of the others, changing just over the border, coming and going. Smeets knew all the back roads and byways and undoubtedly had his bribes working for him. But it wasn't all that difficult to do. It was why some Oklahoma politicians were incensed at the loss of tax revenues to the state of Missouri.

Why more men weren't doing this smuggling, Jesse would tell my father later, he couldn't imagine.

My father had done a little illegal liquor activity himself before he met my mother, making distilled liquor with his brother, Willard, just outside Clearview. Later in his life, though, when he wanted liquor during Jantz family get-togethers on Sundays, he'd catch Harold Smeets at his farm up the road from the Jantz homeplace in Shirly.

Smeets had other farms, his sons manning them as cover and foundational income throughout the counties where he operated his illegal liquor trade. But Jesse told Dad that any runner from around Shirly and Hopewell had to be invited into the smuggling by the Smeetses as they had, over several generations, garnered a reputation for bootlegging in a wide area of Oklahoma. Actually they'd held the exclusive reins on this activity throughout Garfield, Cleveland and Major counties from the Land Run in 1889. And they'd done so with not one day spent in jail despite several questionable beatings and one or two unsolved killings in their territory over the years.

The question came to my mind—and Dad's as well—as to why Duane Smeets would divide his profits with the likes of Jesse. Perhaps it was as simple as Duane wanting a buddy to keep him company on the lonely trips going and coming and having someone to help with the lifting and loading. It could be they took two automobiles and that way doubled the amount of liquor they brought back each trip. Smeets undoubtedly had any number of younger men to do this, but it might simply have been that Duane picked Jesse for old time's sake. After all, Jesse was a charmer, a colorful companion, giving Duane somebody new to tell his stories to and Jesse's to Duane. Who knew?

It was clearer to me why Jesse felt that running with Duane was a pretty sure thing. Jesse had run liquor before he left Hopewell for seminary in Corpus Christi. He'd never done it for money, though, only for the liquor he wanted for himself and his friends, which had included my parents during their dating years. But now it was through just such trips that he was able to keep himself and Clarice surviving until he was granted his ministry at Southside Baptist.

How much Clarice knew back then about Jesse's liquor escapades is still a mystery. He sometimes worked the farm late and would stay over until the end of the next working day. They only had one car, so Clarice would often drive him to the farm and return later to bring him home, or Jesse stayed in the bunk house one or two nights. It's true that Clarice had all she could handle with two children, and Jesse's trips to Joplin could easily have been disguised as overtime, which would account for the extra money coming into their bank account. For that matter, Jesse could have been stashing cash in a jar somewhere in old man Crighton's hay loft without her ever knowing it. The police had been given the liquor-running tip—to which Jesse, of course, remained totally silent—by Christian Crighton, for whom Jesse worked. Since Jesse and Duane's activities couldn't be verified, it remained only Crighton's speculation.

However, with this new angle on the crime, the authorities began to write a different script for the investigation. Over the next few weeks, they concluded that Jesse's assailant could have been some supplier from Joplin who saw an opportunity for blackmail, once the reverend was an established pastor. And when Jesse did not rise to the bait, he fell victim to an overwrought blackmailer, one that he may not have even known.

The whole scenario had to be stretched, but it was possible the assailant came into the room, Jesse didn't react in time, and the attacker, upon reaching the desk, swiveled Jesse's chair around so as not to be recognized—he had worn a dark ski mask if Jesse's deposition was to be believed. The assailant then bashed him over the head with a handle heavy enough to do the job, slashed his back three times and then fled with the weapon. The perp could have been drunk or even drugged. But if he had blackmail demands, wouldn't he have waited to make a money exchange? One of the weakest links in the whole puzzle was Jesse's sluggish response to the attack. And why would the assailant use an instrument that wasn't available at the scene or appropriate for a sure kill? To me, the act had revenge written all over it—a desire to maim but not kill—as a reminder of the attacker's ability to enact more of the same if necessary.

I didn't know of anybody but Clarice who fit that description.

Jesse would tell my father later, at a family reunion, much of the investigative information that I was to find out years after all this was said and done. At the time of his telling, Jesse was still annoyed there had been no evidence to warrant the kind of speculation that took place in print. It had ruined his career, at least in Hopewell. It didn't matter that he had actually done the smuggling, he told Dad. It was that they couldn't prove any of it, and he had been railroaded anyway. To Jesse's mind, running liquor was a victimless crime—if it could even be called a crime—since Prohibition would be rescinded in Oklahoma in 1959 only a few years after his and Duane's smuggling trips. How Jesse saw it, alcohol was something that people wanted and religious nuts were keeping temperance laws in place. For the love of God, he told Dad with a smirk, even Jesus drank wine at His last supper, to say nothing of the wedding at Cana where He turned water into wine.

"That reference in Proverbs that everybody likes to quote so much, about how wine is a mocker and strong drink is raging, well, people forget that that scripture is only giving advice, not laying down a law. It says, 'whoever is deceived thereby is not wise.' Basically, if you're *over*-drinking, you're a jerk!" He laughed, adding he was glad the anti-liquor laws were in place in Oklahoma at the time of his trouble, because they earned him some badly-needed cash during hard times.

But he had to admit he paid a pretty penny to put wine on his table before the liquor stores finally opened for business. Once he'd taken the pulpit at Southside, he had, of course, stopped his association with Duane Smeets.

The police questioned all the principal players again and again, hoping for a slip-up, some vital, new information that could break the silence surrounding every lead in the case. They visited Smeets several times without success. Suppliers in Joplin had been undoubtedly sufficiently paid or were smart enough to know a good supply line when they had one, so they kept their mouths shut. And local clients certainly weren't stepping forward to destroy their personal supply line, some of whom were most assuredly on the police payroll. Detectives reviewed Duane and Jesse's friendship during their school years together, but found nothing truly incriminating. The extent of the boys' crimes had been to slash a teacher's tires for whipping a kid in class who stuttered, and the ordinary mayhem expected of high school teens—a few mailboxes destroyed, a stolen car or two for joy rides, the town nympho yelling rape without evidence and a couple of minor fires from dropped cigarettes—none of which could be attributed to Duane and Jesse singularly or together without a host of other boys being suspected along with them.

About Crighton's accusations, Smeets remained utterly silent. The farmer's accusations finally ran aground, especially since nobody else would verify they had seen the two men together after work. What kind of evidence was there in Crighton's overhearing some oblique talk between the two young men about making some money in a hurry in Joplin? And the man wasn't the most reliable witness after the cops found out that he was disgruntled over Jesse quitting his job with only two days' notice.

However, there were grave consequences for Jesse and Clarice. For a while it looked as though their ministering days were a thing of the past, unless they chose to go back to Jesse's itinerant revival circuit, which wasn't likely as they now were parenting two young children. Jesse had not been immediately dismissed from his position at Southside Baptist, but from the rumblings in the congregation, he and Clarice knew it was a foregone conclusion. For one thing, the reporters showed up at the parsonage and the church at the most inappropriate times. One reporter had even sat through a Sunday service to unnerve Jesse and unsettle members of the congregation into possibly telling something still left unsaid.

And the frenzy was hard on the family as well. A good six weeks passed before the telephones stopped ringing and reporters stopped stepping out to block our paths in an attempt to get interviews or more information, any information, that we might blurt out in frustration, so they could keep the news pot boiling.

Since Jesse was not likely to remain in his pastorship and his and Clarice's news-worthiness began to fade with no solution to the crime, eventually even the police stopped knocking on their door. The victim didn't seem interested in solving the puzzle of what had happened to him, so why should they?

But Hopewell hadn't seen the likes of this kind of violence since the Hopkins murder case when I was in my mid-teens. However, that one hadn't been a mystery. Sordid, to be sure, but nothing coming close to a mysterious stabbing of a local minister living on the wrong side of the tracks. In the Hopkins case, a wife shot and killed her husband when attempting to shoot her daughter, Sara, a close friend of mine from school. Sara's mother was felled by the police. The case had Hopewell buzzing for a good year, especially since the crime had been committed by and to a family from the privileged side of town. It certainly got its press, but nothing like it had happened in a decade, so reporters were all over Jesse's ordeal like flies on manure. To be sure, the Dirks crime had less intrigue than the Hopkins case, but for sheer local entertainment, it couldn't be beat. Hopewell was hardly a small town but it often acted like one, with its ingrown social and political conservatism and its incestuous financial network.

In *The Hopewell Herald* the crime became labeled simply as "The Southside Stabbing," but the popular tabloids took a different tack. "The Baptist Black Widow?" was one headline, and as the investigation progressed and Jesse's smuggling came to light, banners read, "Dirks's Dirty Dealings" and "The Reverend's Private Hell."

If Clarice hadn't known about his illegal arrangement with Duane Smeets before, she knew it then. The rows in their household could have made the potato salad dumping in our family car seem like a silly prank. Then again, Clarice could just have easily gone the other way, and tipped her hat to the guy who put the crystal and china on their linen-covered table.

My graduation was one of the greatest understatements in my life. I didn't go through the ceremonies as reporters were into a feeding frenzy the last of May just before Uncle Jesse came out of unconsciousness to make his deposition statement but immediately following the time of the Duane Smeets revelations. I didn't even return to school after my finals ended. I had my diploma mailed to me.

My feelings toward my uncle were mixed. I was hurt, confused and angry, but after his church voted him out of the pulpit, I felt both sad and vindicated. If Jesse and I had been nothing to each other before, his final months in Hopewell certainly brought that into question. He was beginning to be somebody of considerable importance to me and my family, filling too many of my thoughts and theirs. Dad and I discussed the crime as often as we were together at the house, with Mother throwing in her two cents' worth.

But mainly I obsessed on imagined scenarios of how and why this happened to my uncle. I felt an overwhelming compulsion to understand how this thing had been done, especially if what Jesse had told the police was a cover-up for somebody he knew. If it hadn't been Clarice, the *"why"* remained unchanged for me, at least in general terms. It simply meant she wasn't the one who did it. It had become more and more impossible for me to view Jesse outside the range of other people's hatred and hostility. But he had pastored a successful—or at least, a surviving—community church. That cannot be done when people's opinion of that pastor is one of contempt and fear. Beyond my narrow view of the man, of course, was his Janus-faced personality.

I had visited Jesse only a few weeks before the attack, sitting across from him, a dry run of what was to happen to him later. The whole ordeal felt oddly as though I was simply missing a clue, that I had sat in a chair across from the attempted murder scene, much as one would sit in a darkened theater watching a film, realizing all the facts were being given that would later be arranged and scrutinized into a revealing pattern of the crime and its solution. Frustrating though it was, I couldn't see or remember the one missing piece that I needed to set everything right.

I went over and over the night of the stabbing, slowly transposing what had been described about Jesse's attempted murder with what had actually happened on the night I'd visited him in his office. I saw the shadowy figure entering the office, much as I had done, watched Jesse's invitation for me—and the attacker—to sit down and talk, observed the unfolding of a great emotional outburst from him, then watched as I-and-the perpetrator were verbally thrown out of the room. But instead of leaving as I had done, the attacker rushed around the desk before Jesse could rise, swiveling his chair, battering him from behind as he attempted to stand, and stabbing him as he slumped forward. Jesse was a large man. It would have taken him time to get out of his chair, but his resistance would have been enormous. Even if the attacker had moved fast enough, Jesse could have been upon him before he could have acted, a perfect metaphor of Jesse's own violent behavior, that of a burning match always ready to be thrown in an intentional trajectory toward its target.

Why turn Jesse around? Why not hit him straight on and stab him in the stomach, which is how the greatest number of stabbings take place? Was it because a struggle could have ensued in a way that it could not in an attack from the back? Was the attacker intimidated by Jesse's size, seeing an advantage in an assault from behind? I saw Jesse slumping forward so that the attacker was able to strike him on the upper part of his back but not lower, because the chair would have been in the way. And the knife—Where did it come from? It was conceivable that the perpetrator came carrying the knife as a possible threat, and when Jesse did not respond as the attacker wanted, he reacted quickly and violently. And on and on it went, over and over in my head until I grew exhausted with it and slowly, like a survivor hanging from an edge of a cliff, felt the hold I had on it, slide from my grasp.

―

The perpetrator was never found, which felt to all of us like an enormous let-down. Because of the immense amount of energy we'd given to what had become "Jesse's ordeal," we took it personally. Even though it was a high profile case in Hopewell, the police seemed satisfied with the script they had written for the act, leaving the case unsolved, one of hundreds of other cases in communities as large as Hopewell.

Most of the members of Jesse's church remained silent, except for an occasional interview that netted very little in the news—a phrase or two at most. There were only two letters to the editors about the crime, berating the police for not finding the assailant, and for giving up on solving the attempted murder of a prominent minister of God in an otherwise peaceful community.

After a time, Clarice and Jesse went on with their lives. Well, that wasn't exactly accurate. Southside Baptist dismissed Jesse, but the church board chose to do it in increments, with a delicate veneer only the self-righteous—my mother's word for them—can brush over such ugliness. The teetotalling Southern Baptists evidently felt that accusations of liquor smuggling couldn't be overlooked.

Ultimately, Jesse was forced to resign, but he and his family were allowed to stay in the parsonage until he could move elsewhere. The congregation took a vote by ballot, with Jesse seated on the dais facing the audience and Clarice with the children on the front pew facing him, while the senior deacon counted out the yeas and nays. The vote was fifty-nine to twelve with four abstentions, the audience down twenty members less than normal, but enough for quorum. Oddly, the church promised him a positive reference since Jesse had "suffered a great grievance," as the board stated in his severance letter. The grievance they referred to was Jesse's partial right-side paralysis, causing him difficulties in writing.

Jesse apologized to the congregation for causing the church such tremendous defamation due to the suspicions brought on by his person. He had done this with "great contrition," in tears... though without an admission of any wrongdoing.

There were a couple of follow-up stories in *The Hopewell Herald*, first about Jesse's recovery progress, and then about his decision to seek a pulpit elsewhere. In a statement to reporters he said he'd not been accused of a crime, and he would not bring disrespect to himself or his family by defending himself and them against false and unproven accusations, but he wanted to release Southside Baptist from the burden of what he had set in motion through suspicion and doubt.

What he told reporters was simply not true. Jesse left in bitterness, feeling that he had been betrayed. He had not been charged, had undergone great suffering through uncontrollable circumstances, and had shepherded Southside into a contributing church of goodwill in the Hopewell's community.

"Quite frankly," my father was to say to me when we had time to ourselves, "I think if Jesse had been caught in an affair in his office, it would've boded better for him."

Clarice kept her distance from us after the attack, and since Jesse was resentful of anybody who attempted to console him other than his wife, Mother began to drift away from them. Jesse and Clarice gave chillier and chillier receptions to family visits and phone calls. During Ava and Mother's final time in their home, Clarice simply told them that she, Jesse, and their kids needed time to themselves. There was too much pressure in their marriage, parenting, and, finally, with the parting activities from the church, to take on either of their families. The rejection was hardest on Ava. Jesse was her only son. When he was discussed in the family, she remained silent. Often, she simply got up and left the room. If she was ever invited to visit Clarice and Jesse while they were still in Hopewell, none of us ever heard of it.

Jesse found a ministry in Kansas, which didn't take all that long, probably because of Clarice's father and Southside's recommendation. Clarice and Jesse did come to a final family dinner where everyone was overly polite and nobody made reference to the ordeal and its aftermath. They moved to Dodge City, a place known for Wild West stories similar to the one Jesse and Clarice had actually lived through.

We learned about their Dodge City lives through Ava, the ever-so-silent Ava, who began talking, carefully and selectively about Jesse after being invited to visit them. He took a parish with a small, but swelling membership, and turned it into a hub of the community, doing its share of revivals and charity work, just as he had done at Southside. Clarice was pianist and choir director, service and charity organizer and often sang solos on Sundays to approving applause. But as Jesse aged, the injuries he had sustained began to physically trouble him, so he retired within ten years of their move.

I saw Jesse and Clarice very few times after their flight north, always at family gatherings in Hopewell, once when they celebrated a wedding anniversary, their fifteenth as I remember. I would never have flown back to Oklahoma from New York for such an event, but it happened while I was visiting my parents. I was careful to never be with either Jesse or Clarice alone. Hatred is based on fear.

One evening late, I caught Clarice as she came out of the bathroom and, as indelicate as it might have been, I thanked her for keeping the secret of my visit to Jesse's office only weeks before he was attacked. She did that sideways grin of hers. Tilting her head and touching my arm, she told me it had been a fair exchange, that all was fair in love and war. It was the last thing Clarice said to me. She died of a brain aneurysm shortly afterward, five years before Jesse passed away.

She remained faithful to Jesse to her end. She nursed him through his recovery, helping him to and from bed, the bathroom, and table. She stayed with him during his therapies, his recovery sooner than any of them anticipated, only months instead of years.

Jesse returned to active life a little hunched over and with a slight tremor in his right hand, enough for his Kansas parishioners to believe he had overcome much in order to continue the work of the Lord, seeing in his infirmities a sign of great character. They knew of his brush with death, of course, but how they escaped rumors of his sullied reputation, God alone knew. Perhaps they did know. Perhaps the letter of recommendation from Southside cast the stabbing and liquor smuggling in a light such that the dark reflections in the newspapers could be put aside. Nobody knew for certain about any of it except the family, and the family knew because we knew Jesse.

And he was faithful to Clarice during her couple of weeks of hospitalization, whispering Scriptures as he sat waiting. She lay silent and unmoving, living on morphine—as he had done. Jesse prayed over her bed for her recovery. But God had remained distant and silent, so he gave her a grand funeral which brought hundreds from the area. Several made the trip from Hopewell. Our family was notably absent, except for Mother and Ava who, after the service, stood with Jesse Junior and Kitty by the hearse before it left for the transfer of her coffin to Wichita.

—

Times after Clarice died were difficult for Jesse. At each family reunion—he attended three after her death—he got more toad-like. He continued to thicken until he had no neck, his shoulders sitting almost at his ears. At our last dinner together, with his third plateful of food, Momma admonished him, "You'll choke, one day, Jesse, you keep this up." And he did in a way, dying of throat cancer, coughing up blood and crying like a child for drink and sustenance. He came each reunion, driving without his children, whose pictures he passed around. Kitty attended college in Boulder. Jesse Junior was a cop on a beat in San Jose, California.

"Queer as a two-dollar bill," Jesse said to Dad when they were alone in the backyard, having a smoke. "My only son's a cock-sucking Sodomite! I gave this kid my name, for the love of God. He was born Jens Horst Bueller! When we took him, I looked at this child's perfect face, and told Clarice, 'What kind of silly name is Jens? They'll laugh him off the playground.' So I had it legally changed to Jesse Daniel Dirks, and now look what I got for it." Clarice had told Mother earlier they had adopted German children, because Jesse felt it made right his avoidance of active duty during the war.

Dad simply left Jesse without comment. "What do you do with a guy like this?" he asked me in the kitchen, as though I might actually know.

The next day, Jesse left for Kansas, and we never saw him again.

One visit back home, after Jesse and Clarice were both gone, I asked Mother how in the world these two people found each other, the question I had asked Dad in the Clover diner so many years earlier. My father's version remained steadfastly unchanged through the years. Jesse was a criminal, pure and simple. But when I asked Mother, she invited me to sit with her.

She told me she wanted to answer my question by disclosing a story given by Uncle Jesse on his death bed. "When he had nothing to lose or gain by the telling," she said.

Mother had traveled to Dodge City to visit him one last time, because he asked her to come—"If she only would" is how he made the request. Jesse asked her in a whisper, as though each breath took enormous effort. His exact words were, "You are the only member of my family I want to see before I fall into the eternal light or darkness, heaven or hell, according to God's will."

When I became indignant with his request, she shrugged my protests aside. Mother's view was whatever reasons carried her to his side, she would never regret having gone. He didn't ask for forgiveness or even for her to believe him.

He needed to tell his life to somebody, one story at a time, until he couldn't talk anymore. So she had sat and listened.

He'd been given sedatives and some kind of throat therapy so his talking wouldn't be so obstructed. His speech seemed a caricature of his own preaching voice toward the end of his career—raspy, persuasive, with a terrible longing in it.

"If he could've sung half of what he told me," she said, "he would've left his kids millions."

What Jesse told her answered my question about how these two people found each other.

—

Jesse realized immediately that the board at Calvary Baptist of Hopewell did not view bachelorhood as a virtue in a minister. He not only needed a wife as a model for appropriate familial life for the young congregates, he needed one for the other-gender side of the ministry. He was thirty-three years old. He had never married, but he knew that was about to change.

When he was in his second year at seminary, he met Clarice Lea Abt. She was in her second year of music education at Municipal University of Wichita. She had a head of brown out-of-control curly hair, bobbed down, that bounced when she walked, even talked, and shook vigorously when she laughed. Her laugh was infectious. She often slapped Jesse lightly on the arm as she bent over to catch her breath. Her face seemed at odds with her hair—all of her features were carefully made-up. She penciled her eyebrows—he was to learn she shaved these off, and then drew them back on, in the manner of the early Hollywood stars—and sculptured her lips and lashes. Her dark brown eyes glistened from fire smoldering behind irises with flecks of green, jade sparkles that could cool conflagration in an instant, but could be set ablaze as quickly, finding expression in every detail of her face. Tall—she was half a head taller than he without heels—lean and angular, she could hardly be called beautiful, but notably striking, soliciting much attention, easily triggering Jesse's proclivity to jealousy.

Simply turning her head to smile at a man nearby or wink at a woman who held her gaze too long triggered his instant fury.

But her ebullience was fetching and catching.

He liked the effect she had on him. He smiled and laughed more, hearing jocularity in his talk and manner that shocked him. Around her, he felt beyond himself, someone who could turn what he ordinarily said and did into an art exceeding his knowledge and understanding.

Still, with this easy good feeling came an undercurrent of tension and nervousness he wasn't able to control. Her mood swings were drastic. She could fly from high spirits to flatness in a flash. When he least expected it, her expressive smile and sparkling, brown-green eyes transformed into a far-off, stony stare plastered on an immobile face. Ultimately, her inability to remain constant became her most upsetting and unsettling quality throughout their life together. When he became serious, even angry, he seemed to have little effect, which drove him to increasingly greater and greater attempts to get the reaction from her he expected and wanted.

But it was her smile that initially drew Jesse to her. In time, a short time at that, her mouth taunted, cajoled, baited, teased, seduced, and swallowed him before they had slept together or even had a prolonged conversation. He was initially excited by her control over him.

He melted when she called him names, which she seemingly could pull from the air but most often came from some attachment to what they were doing at the moment. The first time it happened, she'd laugh at the way he held his fork at a restaurant, calling him "pitch" for the rest of the evening. He was delighted. Within weeks, this name calling became a litany of endearments—"speed" for his fast driving, "spoon" for their first kiss. After their early lovemaking, he became a clichéd, "buck," "shaft," and "rod." She didn't try at invention, her monikers were as forthright and bold as a child's. Once, copulating in front of a mirror, he reached orgasm before she did, and she called him "flash" for a week. Each time she did, his penis stiffened, and he had to move in his seat, slide into a distracting conversation so that she wouldn't notice, even as he knew she did.

She was filled with notions about extending the intensity of coitus through role-playing and risk-taking. They fucked in the park, several parks, on the periphery of a family lake front, finger-fucked in a cab, screwed several times in the bathrooms at a restaurant they frequented, a filling station, and the storage room of a small grocery. They did it once under water at the Wichita swimming pool, with children paddling around unaware. During all of these escapades they were never caught, to their knowledge, not even suspected, not one eyebrow raised or glaring glance. It became a challenge to increase the risk and excitement of a near public display while remaining as outwardly detached as possible.

When he wasn't with her, he felt lonelier than he thought possible. It was as though he'd discovered the secret of fire, and he longed to burn.

Her sexual desire and excitement was voracious. She would cuddle and coo and in an instant, pull him to such violence, he feared he couldn't break the momentum of the emotions she stirred in him. She clawed, scratched, bit, whipped and jabbed, while she was very aware of her marks, where she placed them. She was never out of control, a dominatrix in ritual, tottering constantly on the verge of foul play, even felony.

But after six months, he realized she was too much for him, and he took an emotional turn. He felt sluggish, heavy, and inert. His hands became paws, his arms short, squat extensions of a thick trunk, his hair a thinning skein sitting on top of a lumpy ball, his face a mugshot of scarred stupidity. Her nicknames became trials, their sarcastic edge a sharp arrow that pointed toward his mirror. He dreaded, then hated, seeing his reflection there. When he was with her, he felt he couldn't keep up. Never quick enough with the comebacks, his slowness made him feel sick, but he couldn't resist her. He was doing some things right, he knew, because she continued to see him, sleep with him, but he wasn't certain anymore what those things were. He found it hard to stay focused on his studies. His grades began to slump, and he dismayed that once again he was falling into the cycle of not living up to what he had set for himself.

The need to give her up preoccupied his mind—"Break it off," "let her go" became his mantras for every waking hour. But when she was with him, a tingling filled his belly, spread to his genitals and down his inner thighs, grounding him, even as he grew increasingly tense and nervous. He was obsessed, addicted, finding relief in sex, which was reaching greater and greater fervor. She could lead him to blinding pleasure through pain—they were tying each other up, fauxfighting, pushing and pulling on extremities in violent wrestling matches. He was panicked that she might leave because of his raging outbursts, but disturbed that her staying would ruin him, terrified she was carrying him deeper and deeper into dark woods where he would never find his way back to himself without her.

Clarice showed no such signs of ambivalence or doubt. She breezed through her student teaching classes, piano labs, regaling him for hours with hopes of bringing music to children who didn't have chances to aspire.

When not at college, she was always with him, in his room or her apartment. He couldn't fathom who her friends might be. They never invited anyone to join them, so he envisioned her living pretty much as he did.

Because Clarice was an only child, she did visit her parents on weekends, her and Jesse's only days apart. She hadn't offered to take him to her family home, even though it was in Wichita. But she had told him her family's story. Her father was the last in a line of deacons in Baptist churches in Kansas since her family settled there from Bavaria, first in Hutchinson, then Topeka and finally Wichita. The Abts, and her mother's family, the Vogels, had come from Anabaptist ancestry.

To compliment her story, Jesse told her he entered the Baptist faith during a revival meeting as soon as he left a Mennonite C.O. camp, where he had worked in projects during the war, one as a cook to prisoners at Leavenworth and juvenile delinquent facilities near and around Kansas City.

The revival meeting conversion, of course, wasn't exactly true, because he had been saved more than once. The first was forced on him by his parents, with Mennonite membership in Hopewell at age twelve. The second was in his twenties, at Shirly Baptist which sponsored his first attempt at seminary school in Corpus Christi. He felt this one was authentic as it had been a voluntary action. The Baptist revival meeting he mentioned to Clarice took place in Nevada where he reconsecrated his life to Christ following his period of debauchery after his failure at itinerant preaching. He didn't give Clarice all these entangled details, since they only complicated his story.

It would be one of many of his sins of omission to her.

Clarice accepted what he told her without a moment's hesitation. She was delighted with his family heritage and his later choice to become Baptist. Clarice was close to her family, especially her father. Jesse felt that when he was invited to her home, it would indicate that she was committed to him in the same way he was to her. He knew instinctively to press her for this invitation would put their relationship in jeopardy.

It did come, but many months after they had been together, and the initial visit hadn't gone well.

Zachery Wilcott Abt was a man with considerable pride, and, it seemed to Jesse, that he had formed an opinion of him before he entered this man's familial circle. The three Abts had a bond that didn't allow for intrusion. In time, Jesse was to excuse himself from their togetherness, reassuring himself that nobody under the sun would have suited the old man's marriage aims for his daughter unless they had been hand-picked by him. But he was to learn Clarice had disappointed her father in this as well. She had taken her father's choice for her first husband, divorced him in a little over a year, retrieving her family name and keeping it, until she claimed Jesse's as her own. Jesse didn't find out about her former marriage until they applied for their marriage license. It didn't matter to him then, but he hadn't thought it all the way through, not realizing the consequences of her divorce on his career as a Baptist minister.

How could he not have known she had her own little sins of omission? She was, after all, twenty-nine years old when they met and only then working for her Master's in Music Education. Surely he asked about her earlier courting years, but if he did, he couldn't remember doing so. He was dumbfounded by his lack of curiosity. Perhaps he assumed Clarice had hesitated to pursue her own aims and desires, because she was terrified of disappointing her father. After he met the man, this seemed utterly plausible.

When Clarice announced her choice in Jesse, Abt begrudgingly gave her a wedding. Jesse felt after this he recused himself, letting his daughter find her own way out of her second mess with marriage.

"Divorce was abhorrent to him," Jesse had told Mother. "So he was forced to swallow a mouthful of bitter pills. The old man had been disappointed with her first failed marriage, and then he found himself only mildly hopeful for her second."

He had softened when Jesse and Clarice adopted the two children, but he was selective in fulfilling his daughter's requests. Jesse's appointment to Southside had been one of them. Abt knew that without his intervention, his daughter would have lead an utterly humiliating religious life. Clarice never gave Jesse up on the altar of loyalty to her father, but she didn't break ties with him either. She was her own woman, and it grieved The Deacon, as Jesse always called Abt, to his dying day.

"Old Man Abt was so self-centered, he couldn't see his daughter straightforwardly," Jesse told Mother. "But then, if he had, it wouldn't have saved him. He'd have died sooner than he did out of shock and despair."

Jesse and Clarice's courtship continued along the path they'd set for themselves, until the last year of his seminary work when they settling into a more congenial routine. Jesse pulled out of his academic black hole, due largely to Clarice's tutorage, and resumed his goal toward graduation.

And then out of nowhere, the unexpected happened. One night after dinner at a local restaurant—they so rarely ate out— they passed a tent revival on the outskirts of Wichita. It was a Negro gathering, and Clarice, bristling with excitement, decided she wanted to go inside "to sing Negro spirituals with the people who had created them." Jesse pointed out that these coloreds were singing ordinary songs from just about any Protestant hymnal.

She retorted it was *their* singing that made the difference, singing with the abandonment only the coloreds had, turning simple hymns into spirituals. He pointed out they would be the only whites in the audience.

"These salt-of-the-earth people aren't going to care." She pointed to the banner overhead. "The invitation is for all to attend. Why else would they hold it in such a public place, a stone's throw from the busy commercial part of Wichita, not in colored town itself?"

Jesse conceded, but as they approached the tent, two policemen walked up to them and requested they leave the Negros alone to their service. Clarice told them, with all her charm, she and Jesse only wanted to sit in the back quietly, sing songs for a short time and leave. Jesse was from the seminary, training for the ministry. Wouldn't it be all right, this being a public service? She couldn't imagine they wouldn't be welcomed to worship the Savior of the World in a House of God regardless of who had put up the tent.

During this exchange, a colored man from the audience invited them warmly to the service. Clarice was animated during the singing and sermon, a long, rambling message about the wages of sin and the gains of heaven, the suffering of both the poor and the rich without the saving grace of Jesus. The posters and fliers announced the sermon, "What Profit a Man?"

As the altar call began, Jesse took Clarice's hand and, nodding toward the exit only a few steps away, began leading her from their chairs. When she didn't follow him, he turned to see she was crying. And before he knew quite what was happening, she dropped his hand, slid past him, and walked down the aisle to the front where the pastor and his assistants knelt with her in prayer. Jesse watched helplessly from the back of the tent as they escorted her into a prayer room to the side of the stage.

Since he knew from his own experiences this was a private time between the counselors and the newly saved, he would not be allowed with her. He was utterly confused. Clarice was a member of the First Baptist Church of Wichita where her father was right-hand man to the minister. She had become a member of the church from the age of twelve, immersed in the baptismal font in front of an audience of hundreds. Perhaps she was reconsecrating her life as he had done.

He sat back down on his folding chair, wrapping his arm around the back of the seat where Clarice had sat, clinging to the hope she would return and all would resume as before. He watched two men break up and carry chairs one by one to a rack at the front of the tent. Several worshipers leaving the tent stopped and asked if he needed assistance. He thanked them both, shaking his head.

At the moment Jesse had no choice but to take his folding chair up front like the others, Clarice came out of the prayer room, walking alone toward him, her head bowed, a twisted handkerchief in her hand. He pulled her trembling body into his arms.

"I've committed my life in service to the Lord." Her voice had an oddly strained tone, an unusual change in her demeanor, as though she might burst into laughter the minute they walked toward the car. But she didn't.

Once seated next to him, she leaned against his shoulder. "Let's get married, Jesse. I want to be a minister's wife." The next day without saying a word, she dropped out of her classes and, from that moment on, devoted her life to his career.

"He's found his peace," Mother declared, crying over the phone when she called to announce Jesse's passing. "I feel bad because, in a lot of ways, he never lived." She said the same thing about her mother, and would, in time, express this about all the members of her family—her sister Josephine, the exception. What she meant by this, I never quite understood, especially about Jesse, since he was absolutely greedy with life, and Grandpa Dirks was anything but passive in his. Perhaps Mother was attempting to describe, without quite realizing, a destructive quality running through the family, one that invited distortion of reality, especially through religion, such that what happened to each of them was self-abusive in a way that extinguished hope of sustainable aliveness they might have generated through energy and intelligence for their futures.

"You probably don't remember enough about him to feel much of anything," she stated flatly. How was it possible she had forgotten my part in The Jesse Ordeal? Or my listening to all the family gossip and her own final tales of his life?

But I let this slide. I had my own view of my uncle.

It was impossible for me to see him in his coffin. I couldn't picture his lips without the slightly sneering, half-hidden smile that told everybody everything he ever did—and everybody else around him did—had been his great planned joke on God.

After Mother hung up, I sat very still in my chair, waiting as he came pushing his way through the crowd toward me.

I am four or five years old, dressed in a puffy sleeved dress with white tie-up shoes and lacy anklets. I stop and turn to look his way in response to his calling my name. He calls me "Shike," the shortened version of the nickname Uncle Clifford gave me, "Shypoke." We have finished dinner at the Dirks' farm,

Momma's homeplace, and now, we are spilling out into the yard to take a family snapshot. When Uncle Jesse reaches to pick me up, I fall slightly backward as he attempts to lift me. I have the terrible sensation of being jerked toward him at the moment I am attempting to get away. Sensing that something is amiss, Momma rushes to my side just as Uncle Jesse finds enough of me to seize and hoist up to his shoulders, my legs dangling down both sides of his neck onto his chest.

"There," he says, with a note of self-satisfaction, "Here's where you belong, right where I've put you." Momma stands in silence, her eyes shifting from me to her brother's face.

"Well, you're steadier now, I see," she says to me. And I have to admit I do feel more comfortable away from his grappling hands and threatening eyes.

PICTURE

of

DARLENE
& VERNON
with WILLARD

When Vernon Jantz came courting Darlene Dirks, he was thin as a rail, feisty, and grinning behind his brother Willard's red puffed-up face. They were both a little tipsy. Darlene could see that plain enough. But when he first asked her out, he was sober and alone, shy and standing there playing with something in his hands. She saw it was a half dollar. After he asked her to a movie, and she said yes, he threw it hard and silly-like, with a yelp. It landed way past the car shed where he was never going to find it again.

"What's that for?" She shook her head in disbelief. A half dollar could take them both to the movie and then some.

"I feel like a million bucks!" he said, and she liked that.

He took her to the newly-constructed Hopewell motel one night, picking her up from her Shirly farm, forty-three miles to the northeast from where he lived and worked on his own family's farm in Clearview. This was after they'd gone to the movies every Saturday night for three months. He didn't ask. He just drove there, went in the office, and, when he came out, he parked in the back and told her he wanted to marry her. When she said yes, she said it more to God than she did to Vernon—this was so going in with him seemed more like a small transgression and less like an out-and-out sin.

It didn't take Darlene long before she was liking the trips to the Mexican Sunset Motel. The washrags smelled of Clorox and her back could rest against the glaze of slick sheets and pillows while Vernon pumped out his sex against her. But in time she grew to like more than the smell of the soap bars and the squeaky-clean feel of town water without the sulfur in it. She found that she liked sex. It was Vernon she didn't like all that much. But when she didn't get pregnant before they got married, she took it as a sign of God's approval, that Vernon was the man she was supposed to marry. That she had sex with him before her wedding vows was her promise to the Almighty that she would, beyond doubt, have Vernon's children and live her life as his wife. It was how she explained to herself that what she was doing wasn't hell-fire-and-damnation wrong. It was how she could lean back and enjoy the risk without too much worry.

Eight months later, Vernon told her that he had a vision in the middle of a wheat field, while furrowing for spring planting, that told him in a scene complete with a burning blackjack tree and cumulus cloud configurations—close to those one could see through the windows of Leonardo da Vinci's *Last Supper*—that he was going to have two girls and two boys with her as his wife. Darlene knew by now that Hannah, Vernon's oldest sister, had hung a print of da Vinci's famous painting on the dining room wall of the Jantzes' homeplace, despite Mother Jantz's religious disapproval. Darlene had looked at it often while eating Sunday dinner at the Jantzes' table, sitting in silence by Vernon's side. So she had suspicions as to where the articulations, if not the source, of Vernon's vision had come from.

But it was after his epiphany that Darlene felt her life take a predestined turn. She didn't exactly trust the convoluted description of his vision, but the urgency of the message struck her as gospel. She hadn't seen the full metaphor of the harvest after the planting, so she hadn't grasped, at the time, the irony behind the symbols of seeding and conception—well, how could she? What did she know? She was seventeen and on a farm isolated from social contact except for relatives and a few neighbors whom she saw when she took her mother to the Holdeman Mennonite Church on the road to Weather Springs. She no longer even had her classmates as she'd left high school only months before graduation. She just knew that she had to marry this man or reap damning eternal consequences, so she did, within a year of having met him on the farm. And one year and one month after her marriage, she had her first baby, both of them seeing the child's birth as the beginning of his calling and as the fulfillment of her contract with God coming to life. They named the girl Caroline, after Vernon's mother. It would be the first and last name Darlene would give away to the Jantzes, although she would have three more children with Vernon, staying long enough—as such visions go—to make both of their lives prophetic. Darlene left Vernon forty-five years later, almost to the day. But that hadn't been part of what either of them could have seen when it all began.

—

One afternoon not long after Darlene had set herself up in her own apartment those forty-six years later, or was it forty-seven?—she told herself she had ceased counting her lifetime in distance from Vernon anymore—Caroline came visiting, asking questions about her life with her father that Darlene didn't know how to answer for her daughter, let alone herself. She had been thinking about her former life a lot since she started living alone, despite her attempt to put it aside.

Her searches had come in spurts and starts, sometimes with a burst of insight so piercing it actually hurt. She'd sit at the one table she had in the apartment, in the dining area, on an afternoon off from her job as a food preparer at the Red Lobster, and with a cup of coffee, she'd stare across the tiger oak-veneered surface as though there was somebody seated across from her listening to her story. Now that her daughter was actually there, filling that spot, she was overwhelmed, anger seeping around the periphery of her thoughts. Darlene felt suddenly *quizzed* about what she considered a private conversation with herself, but why she felt that this disquieting conversation was sudden, she couldn't say, as Caroline had asked her poignant questions from time to time on the phone since her separation from Vernon, especially as the divorce's final date came closer. She just knew she felt invaded, as though Caroline's questions were intended to scold her or bring her to task for what she'd given her life to. But she was still surprised when she heard the teeth in her own voice.

"Don't think I don't have in mind that he's your father," she said testily, as she began her answering, wanting to tighten her lips, shrug, and throw her hands in the air. "I've deliberately chosen not to talk to you like this." But that was a lie. It was true now, this moment, in her apartment after the life had been lived, but she was all too aware that she'd used her daughter as a journal for years, running things about Vernon past this child long before Caroline could even say a word, let alone understand any of it, and then on and on into Caroline's own courting years. But since her plan to leave Vernon, Darlene'd pretty much kept her resentments and confusions to herself. This was when Kat was in high school, and Caroline had just turned forty, living with some woman in upstate New York Darlene'd never met, the boys scattered to the winds, one in the Southwest with a shrill wife, the other, well, God only knew where. Now her earlier withdrawal was backfiring, creating a vacuum she hadn't seen coming, hadn't wanted. Caroline's questions were becoming insistent, her mood more and more belligerent as Darlene's reticence grew. So now, here was *the visit*, the one she'd finally agreed upon, that was supposed to expose what hadn't been voiced from what she was longing to forget.

"Why did you marry him in the first place?" Caroline asked, point-blank, her eyes searching her face.

"What are you asking? Has it ever dawned on you that if he weren't your father, you would be a totally different person, if you existed at all? What a question this is!"

"I just want to know. You've never said. I have both of you in me. I'm aware of that more than you know, maybe. I lift one arm and I see you doing whatever I'm doing, and I lift the other arm and I see him doing it. You're both in there for better or for—"

"Worse!" Darlene filled in, sighing. "I needed to leave the farm. I have too said. I've told you this before. No surprises for you here at all." She paused hoping to end it there, but Caroline stared, waiting, both of them standing as though drawing battle lines. "Crazy as it sounds now, I thought I'd try to do some good back then," she added before she meant to.

"Some *good?* What the hell does that mean?"

"Well, I don't expect you to understand this, why would you? You were there, a good deal of the time, of course, but you were a *child*. My God." Darlene leaned over and picked up her coffee cup, walking to the couch in hopes that her daughter would follow, which she did. If she was going to talk for any length of time, she needed to be comfortable. She motioned for Caroline to sit down on the sofa and then dropped into the place next to her daughter, after setting her cup on the coffee table. She sat looking down at her hands in her lap, as though they were holding some cue sheet on which was written what she could say next.

Talking felt awful, like an illness brought up from her belly. The silence she had given herself with the divorce, the move away—which had taken a year, an exhausting year—was now pushing breath down her throat. She sat next to Caroline, resisting the pull of memory back to those times she'd wanted to leave for always, well, at least until she could look at them again with more self-assurance. Thin lines of sweat formed around her neck and forehead.

"I've not meant to but I've made a mess of it, haven't I?" She hoped Caroline could fill in the empty spaces on her own, see the sad end of her life with Vernon as his wife, and be satisfied. But it was a question she'd asked herself over and over and it, whatever in the hell *it* was, wouldn't be satisfied until it had drained her dry—her and perhaps now that Caroline was asking, her daughter as well.

"You know I don't think that."

"It's living, you see, by the seat of your pants, is all it is," Darlene said in her own defense.

"Oh, Mom!" Caroline reached across the space between them and attempted to pull her over by a shoulder.

"No, no. I've done a lot of that. Still doing it, too." Darlene sat up stiffly, pulling away. "Instinct!" Getting up, she walked toward the washer which had spun loudly to a stop.

"Survival," Caroline corrected with a light smile that Darlene caught when she glanced back for a moment.

Darlene's slippers made a clapping sound on the linoleum of the utility room. She opened the washer and looked in.

After she and Vernon were married by a judge, in the courthouse, the judge's wife as witness, she had felt the sudden slap of her future staring back at her. She stood close to her new husband, smelling the homemade whiskey on his breath, looking into his face and eyes. She knew that well-worn grin, the flicker in those cool, blue irises, with him holding her loosely, waiting for the kiss the judge had told them to take. What's in there, Vernon? You never say. All I can see in your eyes is me staring back at myself, and if I'da wanted that, I coulda stayed by myself on the farm. This is what she thought back then, and what she would say now, but young and feeling small like she had on that day, she kissed him in silence instead.

That's all there is, Darlene, she heard him reply in her mind, seeing him shrug after the kiss with the grin still on his face, looking away, the way he did, as though studying something else.

She lifted the towels out of the washer, flipping the dryer door open, holding it with her knee while she threw the damp wads in harder than she intended.

"His own brothers and sisters told me not to marry him," she called out to Caroline, gaining some courage with the distance between them. "But they were so set against me, I didn't know whether they just wanted me out of the way or didn't want him to have something he wanted. They hated him that much." She slammed the dryer door closed, twisted the time setter to forty minutes and pushed the start button. She leaned against the oscillation, the weight of her belly and breasts vibrating with the machine. She closed her eyes, resisting the urge to not return to the living room, to burrow down into her own laundry.

"Vernon'll never amount to anything," Willard had told her. "He's a little man wantin' to be big." Willard had been such a liar, though, and worse, much worse. Despite his show at being Vernon's older brother, he was part of the family's hostility toward Vern, so how was she to figure it all out, with her so young, when all she wanted to do was leave her parents? And then later, what was she to do when she had gone and set up house with it again, living Ava and Whalen's meanness over and over with Vernon, even if it wasn't exactly in the same way? She pushed herself from the dryer and forced herself back through the utility room door.

"I don't know," she began, walking back to Caroline like she had walked and talked to her for so many years, in and out of rooms, and while she stood at work, talking in her head like Caroline could hear, like she did hear when she was a child. "I'm never sure that anything I think up—" she said out loud, then stopped. "And that's it, isn't it? It feels like I've made my life up and that I'm still making it up as I tell it. Against him, I mean. It feels like anything I say about it to you is twisted in my favor, because I've done that with you before, you see. When you were little and I needed...." she paused, the catch in her voice warning her. She cleared her throat. "I needed someone to talk to, so I used you for that. You were too young. It was wrong." She stood in front of Caroline, lifting her arms, finally slapping her hands down against the sides of her legs. "It wasn't right," she said sadly, looking away. As an afterthought she added, "Anyway, you probably don't remember, most of it—a lot of it, I wouldn't imagine."

"I guess I don't," Caroline said, her eyes and hands reaching out, pulling Darlene toward her, demanding that she look at her. "Well, of course, I remember some," she corrected herself, looking away too and then quickly back again. "It would be hard not to remember—how you and Dad *were*. I think that's why I'm asking now. I know things, but I'm not sure I've put them together the way they actually were, I mean, the same way you have."

Darlene sat down beside her daughter again. "Okay honey, what is it you really want to know, exactly?" She tried not to sigh.

"I really want to know why you married him. I want to know for *me*—not for you—for me and not to get even or put you on the spot, not any of that. I think I wonder how I got here. I look at you and I look at him and I just don't know how it happened."

Darlene sat silent, her breathing uneven.

"You, I understand." Caroline went on. "It's easier for me to see how I'm part of you, probably because we talk every week, on the phone. I'll just say, it's easier for me to lift that right arm than it is to lift the one on the left." She grinned as her mother held her gaze.

To Darlene, Vernon was in her daughter's face just then.

Caroline went on, as though reading Darlene's thought. "He's part of me, but—not so much a *big* part of me. But the both of you *together* in me seems bizarre sometimes or a little crazy—unreal, actually, like one of those accidental hospital switches people talk about all the time, you know? Or some secret affair you had that I don't know about—"

"You were born at home," Darlene protested loudly, far too loudly and quickly. "You have a picture of the house. I gave it to you. You weren't even born in the hospital and your father was there—"

"Momma!"

Finally she added, "Okay, okay. But all kids feel like this, Caroline. Surely you know this. We all look at our parents like they're people not connected to us and wonder about them together, especially their making love or thinking about how they met and dated together, all that stuff seems strange."

"That's not what I mean, either," Caroline persisted, screwing up her lips in a knot, bringing both hands down on the sofa in disgust. Darlene recognized the anger. She'd known the same frustration, with Vernon and with herself, a lot of it with herself. But she just couldn't talk anymore, not even in her head, definitely not to Caroline. She had to make the thoughts and talk about this man she married so long ago stop or she'd be swallowed up in regret and sin, yes, sin. She'd known better back then, and she'd done it, anyway, and, damn it, there was that "it" again, with its constant pounding at her door for acknowledgement and remembrance.

She looked around dim-wittedly. She'd taken not just his, but all the voices with her, into the silence of her own rooms, hadn't she? Even when she was moving away, without Vernon there, with these two strangers lifting her life out of one place and carrying it over to another, she still heard him following her, not asking exactly what Caroline was asking but asking his own questions about why she'd married him, especially if she was going to leave him like she was.

When had the idea of Vernon-and-her presented itself to her? Had she just fallen into it, like she told herself so often? Had it even been recognizable as an idea at all? Maybe it had actually been determined, like she had imagined it for so many years, given by fate, by visions, by signs from God. But she knew she had come too far for those beliefs to have ground anymore. She'd known at least this much, sitting here, alone, waiting for divorce, searching for something to say to her children. It was her doing and not anybody else's.

Most recently something had been added to the circling ruminations, though. Lurking now in the back of her mind was the idea, the possibility, that she had married Vernon out of sheer stubbornness or possibly something even worse, out of spite, a deep desire to get even. She knew she had reasons for the feeling, but she'd put them down so far that she felt she'd lost them forever. And now they were growing until they felt huge and watchful, vulture-like, inches over her shoulder, always circling back around to her and Vernon's brother.

At first, when she saw that Willard was always there, by Vernon's side, drunk way past the beers in the fields, cooing in the kitchen to her, wooing her for another meal, she wasn't quite sure what was going on. Willard was married so he wasn't openly flirting for himself, she didn't think. It took her a bit to figure out that he was showing Vernon what to do, then when he did it, Willard made it seem like Vern didn't have any sense to consider it. She had seen too late the game in Willard's eyes, the reckless play with their lives as if they were his. And she'd decided then to do something about him. She had known she would see to it but just hadn't been sure how or when. Beyond doubt after she and Vernon were married, she'd known she would never invite Willard into their home, the house that Vernon was building for her in Clearview, in town, miles away from the Jantz's homeplace and miles and miles from her own with her parents in Shirly. Her plan was to leave Willard standing there outside her family, like he had never accepted her in his. And it had turned out that way, but not at all like she'd hoped for it to.

"I know you have questions," she said to Caroline. "I reasoned out what many of them must've been before you even asked me. But the answers are a little harder for me to come by."

"I should've waited. It's too soon. I know it must feel like I'm hounding you. It's just that it's close... not just to you, you know, but... it's close to all of us."

"You can say it, honey. Divorce. There, it's been said, and I do want to answer your questions. But you may have to get what you want in bits and pieces, that's all."

She wanted to say she was still mystified herself, that she hadn't begun to untangle over forty years of hope, confusion, and despair. But instead, she sat still while the dryer spun off, sounding an alarm. The silence grew so long, Caroline stood up, ready to leave. "Look, I'll go back to Dad's place and catch you when you feel up to this. It's only fair, even if it means another visit, a flight back at another time—"

"Sit down. Please sit down, honey. I just have to gather myself. Now that we're actually talking about it, I'm going to try."

Caroline stood there awkwardly in front of her. "Mom, it's not the divorce so much as—well, the divorce just made what I've wondered all along more curious to me. I know why you got married, that you wanted to leave home and Dad was your way out, that you married against both of your parents' wishes, on the sly in Wellington, Kansas, that you eloped all of a sudden."

"I didn't have to get married, if that's what you're wondering.."

Caroline sighed. "I think you know what I'm wanting, Mother. And it may be unfair to ask you now. It's just that I'm here, and I would like to have this conversation sometime soon, if that's possible."

Darlene nodded, waiting a moment before speaking, pulling inspiration out of the air. "I'm going to tell you a story." She smiled, leaning over and nudging Caroline on her leg. "Maybe this'll help you, maybe it won't, but we'll think of it as a start, okay?" She grabbed a pillow and pushed herself into the back of the couch. Caroline sat down, looked at her mother, without moving a hair, not saying a word. Darlene shuddered, then began her story.

"I knew from the beginning your father had a drinking problem. No, no, I'm not going after him about this right now, Caroline. Just listen. I have to tell this my way." She began again, but only after Caroline had nodded her encouragement. "We hadn't been married a month before his first binge, with his brother Willard, on their own homebrew. But I knew it long before then. What I'm going to tell you took place before I was married. So I can't say I didn't know. I knew.

"I told myself it was all Willard's doing. Sometimes even yet, I just can't get past the idea that if we'd moved away, if Vernon hadn't been so close to home and his older brother, things would've been different. I still play with this over and over, but I really know better now. But back then, I kept waiting for an opportunity to show Vernon what his brother really was to him. And occasionally, I'd get my slams in. I'd take some swipes at Willard here and there as if to say, 'Aha, you see there Vernon, see how he drags you down?' But Vernon was never too bright about people, especially his family. He just didn't seem to be able to see how they felt about us both. I realized, no, more than this, I finally admitted that they all overlooked him, maybe even hated him, because he was little and shy, playful really, and had laughter in him, and they just thought he was the runt in their litter, a kid that wasn't ever going to grow up—grow up like *them.*"

Darlene laughed a lazy little laugh as though this thought had suddenly presented itself to her. "How they thought was a stupid, backward way of thinking, you know? So I let myself be carried along, thinking they were all blind about him and me, eventually it would, of course, be toward you kids too, because you were his family. And I tried in my own way as he did in his, I suppose, to win them over, get them to see that we were part of them. Vernon wanted a family. And since then, I've grown to understand that I craved family myself. As you know so well by now, my parents were like oil and vinegar.

"Looking back, I know that I was trying to start over again with Vernon—making a family—only doing it my way which, of course, was going to be better than my parents. This is, no doubt, how most young people think, usually without knowing it, of course. Don't the wedding vows even say something like this, or some damn Scripture that tells us how we're supposed to do about marriage and such?" Darlene waited a moment and then recited, *"'For this reason a man shall leave his father and his mother, and be joined to his wife, and they shall become one flesh.'* I think that's how it goes in Genesis."

"It's actually in the New Testament a number of times, almost exactly as you quoted it from Genesis." Caroline grinned at her mother. "But I think how it goes in the wedding vows is 'forsaking all others,' which would include one's parents, no doubt."

"How in the heck do you remember such things?" Darlene knew her daughter didn't attend church.

"I've had enough religious instruction, don't you think? Some of the verses I memorized when I was a kid have stuck with me, believe that." Caroline laughed. "But I think I get your meaning now, Mom. When you marry and form your own family, it's analogous to forming one as your parents did, you know, raising a family, of which you are a part... at least, this is according to the Scriptures."

"Well, okay, yeah, that's right. Anyway, one of the problems I had that I couldn't see so well then was that his family didn't include me, and I came to understand that was because I was part of him. But I knew he wanted to belong, was bending over backwards to belong to them, so I tried to be a good wife and do everything possible to get them to like me... *us*. So when he first started drinking with Willard, I didn't like it, but I didn't speak out. Vernon always went back home, it seemed to me, for the drinking or maybe the drinking made him feel better about being back home. He didn't do so much of that around me, but then I didn't allow it, except when we were out running around on those rare occasions with Nita Jane and Sherman, Josie and Clifford, sometimes Jesse and a girl of his too when he was around—anyhow, a lot of this was earlier, when Vern and I were still just dating. But, Caroline, drinking or not, I was young and mixed up, how the hell would I know what to do with his family? I hadn't a clue as to how to start one of my own, even though I never would've admitted that then.

"The story I want to tell you happened one Sunday afternoon a coupla months or so before we got married. We didn't marry at Christmas like he told Willard we were going to. We eloped back in August. It was sudden, nothing we planned exactly. I mean, we got the license, but we weren't sure when we were going to do it—that's exactly when. I planned ahead, I remember that. But we did it on the sly, you know. We were actually on this rip-roaring trip through Kansas and the northern part of Oklahoma, like Bonnie and Clyde with the booze but without the guns!" Darlene stopped and waited while Caroline had her laugh. "Well, that's another story, for some other time maybe.

"Anyway, this Sunday I'm telling you about, I went looking for him after one of those dinners at the Jantz place, and when I saw that none of the men, including your father, was in the house, I went out to the yard just in time to see Vernon and Willard, Clifford and Sherman high-tailing it out the drive in Willard's car. So I ran back into the house, got the keys to our Plymouth, yelled at Josephine and Nita Jane to follow, which they did. We all jumped in, me slamming the car down the driveway so fast it brought Vernon's dad to the porch looking out after us and believe me it took a lot to get him out of his rocker on his day off. We caught up with them one mile from the bootlegger's where I knew they were headed, and I decided it was time for a showdown. Drinking was something I just could not take. My father had drunk a lot. But during harvest mainly, on his own homebrew. After that there wasn't much during the year. But I could tell you a few stories about that, too, because Vernon helped my dad with farming. In fact, after the depression, after my father lost everything, he rented equipment from Willard and worked with him on his own place to pay for the use of his machinery. It's how I met your dad. He came sometimes to deliver or get the equipment and work with Willard and my dad during harvest.

"I knew Vernon drank. He drank with Dad, even at the house when Willard wasn't around. And I knew he drank with his family, like I said, that part I knew about, but I hated the way he acted when he had been drinking. He got all cocky and defiant. He was rude to me to make the men laugh. He was a smart aleck a lot, but it got unbearable when he was drunk. So I was determined that alcohol was not going to enter my home. 'When he carries me over the threshold,' I told Josephine, 'he leaves the bottle on the steps.' So there on the country road, right around the bend from Harold Smeets's likker-place, I drove the car past their smirking faces, rammed it around toward their front fender, slammed on the brakes, and jumped into the road, ready for a fight.

"It was Willard who came running out of the front seat first. He looked at me with those squinting eyes of his, god, I grew to hate those little narrow eyes of his. He was opening and closing his hands, rubbing his thumbs over his index fingers like he always did. 'What the hell do you want?' he yelled at me. 'Why're you here? You're driving like a hell cat.' Josephine finally piled out of the front seat then and came over to where I was. I thought maybe I had her on my side, but I found out that wasn't true soon enough. She just stood there, saying nothing, sort of grinning.

"'I'm not wanting to talk to you Willard,' I said. 'I wanna talk to Vern.' I saw Vernon sitting in the back seat, laughing with Sherman, Nita Jane's husband—you know Nita Jane, Vernon's youngest sister. She's closest to his age. Well, each of them was flipping the other back and forth with his hand, laughing like crazy.

"'Doesn't look like he wants to talk to you,' Willard said, 'so why don't you just mosey back home, and we'll be along in a little while.' Then he grinned at the men in the back seat, the car rocking from their laughter. I was so sick of this kinda shit by then from him, from them all, I thought I'd die on the spot from heat and rage. And that gave me a lot of courage.

"'Vernon,' I called out as Josephine started to walk back to the car. But I didn't let her off the hook this time, 'Josephine, don't you think Clifford needs to come home, you pregnant and all, don't you think he has some responsibilities he needs to think about?' I said this to her so the others couldn't hear, but she kept walking over to the car and leaned against the door, still not saying anything. Then I yelled right at Willard so that the others could hear, 'I think you ought be coming outta there and talk with us, Vern, because if you don't, and I leave without talking to you, you can forget about coming out to my place tomorrow.'

"Out of the side of my eye I saw some movement in the back seat, and I knew without really looking that Vernon was getting ready to come out of the car. Before Willard had time to protest, I said, taking my time now so he would see I wasn't afraid of him this time, 'You best be keeping outta this, Willard, if you're smart, because this is between Vern and me, and I mean it.'

"Willard started to say something, but Vernon stepped in front of him, winked and said in a real sugary voice to me, 'Darlene, what do you want? We're just having a little Sunday fun, and it's no cause to be upset. Why don't you go back—' He got that far before I interrupted him, making my voice sugary too and a little more than hostile as well. 'I want you to come back with me now, Vern,' I said, like you'd tell a child not to eat dirt right before he's going to.

"'Oh, now, Darlene, we were just planning—' he started up, but I motioned him to follow me up the road, and I started walking like I expected him to follow. When he didn't move, I turned back around and said, 'I'm asking you polite, Vernon, to talk to me in private.' Josephine had inched her way to the car door and wanted to sit down inside, I could see that, but she was scared to because of what I might think—she felt caught in the middle—so she stood there leaning against the door, nervous and smiling with her fingers around the handle. Nita Jane was paralyzed, I guess, because her thinking was that we shouldn't talk like this to the men. Well, I did to Vernon, but they didn't, I guess, anyway, not when I ever heard them.

"Vern began moving over to me finally, whispering to Willard. 'It won't hurt to talk to her and calm them all down,' I heard him say. 'It'll take just a minute.'

"'She's got you bamboozled, Shorty,' Willard called out as Vernon started walking toward me. His whole family called him Shorty, which I simply detested. 'You're making a big mistake, little brother, I tell ya. You give in now, you'll be giving in a lifetime.'

"'I heard what you said, Vern,' I yelled back, overlooking Willard and his mouth. 'You better plan on the others going ahead if they want to and their wives don't care, but I want you to come home with me now. I know what you all are doing. It's to Harold Smeets's and then whiskey on top of the beer, and I won't have it. I don't want you coming back like that, and then being sick all the way home, and me taking it like always. You've had enough.'

"When Willard heard that, he broke open, yelling at me with his fist tight by his sides. I knew he would hit me if he could. 'Who the hell do you think you're talking to here, Darlene? Vernon, stop right there,' he bellowed turning red and barely able to swallow. He always reminded me of a bulldog or a rooster. He was a barnyard bully, was all. 'We're doing what we set out to do, and no women are gonna stop us,' he yelled and looked at me with sheer vengeance, his fist in the air. 'See?' he screamed, like he was saying, 'You see this?' about his fist in the air.

"Well, for a few seconds everything seemed to stop right there, and we all stood kinda squared off in the middle of the road with dust picking up all around us. It was one of those Oklahoma days when the air was too hot to breathe, and the wind came like dust that could be tasted in your mouth and touched on your face. I remember brushing my hair back outta my eyes, holding it with my hand so it wouldn't blow in my face. I simply wasn't going to be put down. I made up my mind. Josephine had her hands around her swollen stomach, rubbing them around and around like she was turning some huge balloon in front of her. She still was leaning against the car door, her skirt flying up in the wind, and her face scrunched up with that silly little grin on her mouth. I looked at her, like, well, aren't you going to do anything? But she continued standing there, of course. She's standing to this day like this with Clifford, by his side, saying what she does under her breath or with him at home where nobody can hear, if she says anything at all.

Finally I broke the silence. '"Willard, who the hell do you think you are, speaking for everyone the way you do?' I asked. 'Don't you think these men get tired of you talking all the time for them? You blow and go and because you're a little older you think they're gonna do everything you say, but they're not. So stop playing the big man and go get your own whiskey and leave them out of it.'

"It was more than he could take. 'Silly sow,' he yelled and took some fast steps toward me, raising his fist up to hit me when Vernon came stepping into him shouting, 'Stop right there, Willard,' he yelled. 'You're not hitting my woman, you hear that? I think she's right now, you've had enough. You wanna drink by yourself, you do that, but I'm not going with ya anymore.'

"So Vernon walked to the car with me and got in, sitting there with his head against the window he'd rolled up in spite of the heat. I got in beside him, fairly shaking now. I felt a little woozy myself from all the heat and excitement, and I gave him one of those looks that told him he wasn't out of the woods yet. Josephine and Nita Jane pulled out of their stupors, yelled to their husbands, who followed them, believe it or not, and everyone piled into the car, leaving Willard on the road cursing our names as we drove off. Then I really was giddy and strong, god, I can't tell you how strong I felt that day.

"When we took off, I really was driving like a hell cat. I yanked the gears around, but still not saying anything and finally laying down the first rules of the house Vernon hadn't even built for me yet. He had tears in his eyes. When I saw how much he didn't want to cry in front of everybody, how he was twisting toward the window and struggling hard to keep from bursting into sobs, I realized how drunk he really was.

"Once we got home, we sat there while everybody left the car and went into the house. I told him I'd leave him before we were even married if he ever pulled that shit again. He kept his head against the window and cried himself sober. 'Willard's a drunk,' I told him, 'and everybody in Clearview and Shirly knows it. And for you to drink with him means to everybody that you are too. I won't live with a drunk, Vern. Get that in your head straightaway. I want somebody to talk to after the night sets in.'"

Darlene couldn't keep the trembling out of her voice. She was overcome by the tears that were welling up. She felt confused and terribly vulnerable. Here she was crying once again. How could she be touched this way by her own recollections? It was the storytelling of it, she decided. It had to be. But she also felt desperate to reveal the abyss yawning inside, the terrifying longing to tell the silence and let come what may. Caroline saved her by sliding over and folding her tightly into her arms for the second time that morning. Darlene let go and cried harder than she had since her move to her own place. Her daughter sat very still, holding her mother embraced until Darlene was able to sit up and move on with her story.

"He gave me candy with his next paycheck, in a box with real flowers and a note scrawled in cursive, 'Yours after the night sets in,' it said, and then he'd signed his full name in carefully scrawled hand, 'Vernon Leland Jantz.' He had taken his time with it. He never could write worth a damn." Darlene wiped her nose with the back of her hand, then ran her fingers under her eyes. Caroline got up to get a Kleenex but came back carrying a long ribbon of toilet tissue instead.

Darlene blew her nose and dabbed her eyes once more. "Josephine would tell me later about all this when I was married, after you were born, when I didn't even think about it anymore. Who can remember all the stuff? 'We were all scared and skittery as rabbits,' she told me—you know how she talks. 'But you never moved from your spot. You went after what you wanted like a tiger that day,' she said. 'You were aggressive but careful too. You were always like that about what you wanted. You didn't want Vern right then so much as another life, something past our Momma's that got swallowed up in all the poverty and meanness.'

"She's right, of course. I just shouldn't have chosen your father as my way out." Darlene looked down to find the toilet tissue now in twisted lumps in her lap. She started gathering the pieces, picking at them one by one, shaking her head side to side. "I never loved him, Caroline, and that's just such a terrible thing to tell you outright, it seems to me."

"Oh, not so terrible." Caroline pressed her mother up next to her again. "What you've just told me is so much better than my own memories. And anyway, who else but dad could it have been? Sherman and Clifford were already happily married and that only left Willard and a divorce." They both burst out laughing. Darlene laughed more than she thought she could over it all. Caroline's laughter was infectious, approving. She felt vindicated, wonderfully absolved of a burden she'd been carrying for ever so long.

After her daughter had left for the afternoon, she sat on the couch without moving for a long time, shaking her head again and again as though somebody was still watching her, listening to her thoughts as though they were being spoken. Finally, she gathered herself up from where she was sitting, took the laundry out of the dryer, and folded it neatly before she started her day.

"Sunday dinners at the Jantz homeplace were beyond just boring affairs," she announced to Caroline when they were both seated for lunch in her apartment, the afternoon of Caroline's evening flight back to New York. She had decided to tell her daughter more, but wasn't sure what that might be, or much more dangerously, what might rise to the surface. She'd also decided to trust herself. At least the conversation with Caroline had begun.

She'd lain awake far into last night wondering if what she was telling her would get to the boys—well, to Teddy, at least. She didn't know if Caroline was in touch with Timothy or not. The subject was so delicate she hadn't wanted to jeopardize communication with her daughter by asking.

"I don't mind you talking to Ted. But about Vernon, I'd rather you'd let me pick what, when and where, if you feel you can do that."

And Caroline had reassured her of confidentiality with her father, and also with Teddy. These were Darlene's own stories to tell, was how Caroline put it to her. She wasn't going to turn them into family hearsay. It had given Darlene the boost she'd needed to add to what she'd started with Caroline two days earlier.

"Did you go every Sunday to visit Dad's family?" Caroline asked, nudging her forward with her story.

"No, we went every other Sunday, anyway, that's what we did until you kids came along. Then we had a way out when we felt like we needed one, or I should say, when I needed one. They didn't seem to care one way or the other, really. Only Vernon cared. I could see he wanted to go, so I went along, well, until I simply couldn't stand to anymore.

"But these dinners, Caroline, oh god, they were totally lifeless. I had to lift my head from my plate every now and then to check to see if the rest of them were breathing, I kid you not. And Vernon fell right into their rhythm. I can still hear the ticking of the cuckoo clock. It got so I'd watch for the bird to come out, on the hour, to honk at us. You could hear the damn clicking of the knives, forks and spoons. I dreaded, just dreaded, going, days and days before. But once you were born, I had something to pay attention to, other than these crazy dead people of his. You'd think with a house full of women in the kitchen together, cooking up a storm, we'd have enjoyed talking and being together, the way most women are. Forget that with Vernon's people! None of the Jantzes talked, not even Nita Jane who giggled here and there—over what, I couldn't tell you. Maybe Sherman was tickling her under the table.

"Frankly, I think she was nervous around her own family. I can tell you, Vernon was. If Josephine and Clifford didn't show up, it was serious cooking and eating and that was it—*for the whole day*, because we stayed until evening. And there weren't even the men to listen to. Smoking and drinking weren't allowed in the house, so they spent their fun time out by the side of the house or behind the barn. I'd hear a roar of laughter from them every now and then, while working in the kitchen. I wanted to go out there and join them, is how I felt.

"It got so I'd beg Vernon not to go. But of course that was out of the question. He felt left out, as it was, so his connection with them on Sundays was important to him. And until Willard disappeared from these scenes, which happened after we got married, I think it was Willard that Vern went to see. When I complained, he covered for his brother by saying that Willard treated him roughly at times, but they still were able to be civil for old times' sake. He and Willard had worked together while Vern was in his teens and early twenties, harvesting especially, even following the crews up into Kansas and Nebraska for money in the summertime. So, back then, they were close."

"Why did Willard stop coming?"

"Oh, I think the confrontation with me on that road to Smeets's for whiskey that Sunday shortly before we got married had a lot to do with it. It showed him up for what he was to all the men. Willard had an exaggerated sense of self-worth. The others knew this, of course. So they were embarrassed when their women called them on it." Darlene hesitated, then added, "But even after Willard and his family didn't show up for the dinners anymore, I knew Vern went for the drinking. That's how the men were able to connect with each other, is my guess. Once you've got enough booze in you, you start talking until you don't make sense anymore. And then you laugh together like hyenas over anything and everything."

"Did the women drink?"

"Are you kidding? In *that* house? Where hanging a picture, even one of Jesus and his disciples, was questioned by his mother? No, Caroline, I don't remember ever seeing a Jantz woman take a drink, except Nita Jane, when she was out running around with us, after she was first married to Sherman. And she was careful about that, because she was diabetic."

"Was it because they were religious?"

"Heck, no. I mean, some of them were. Most of them went to some church. I don't think Hannah went anywhere, but Elizabeth was Baptist, and Bennie and his wife went to a church that was very conservative, even cultish. But the Jantz women wouldn't've taken a drink, in any case, because it wasn't *proper*. Their idea about all that was somewhere back in the nineteenth century. Women simply didn't do such things, especially things *men* do, for heaven's sakes, smoking and drinking, playing cards, spitting on the sidewalk, whatever. Who would know for sure, but that's the sense I got." While Caroline was laughing, Darlene thought for a moment, then added, "They probably didn't drink because the buzz makes you talk, laugh, pee, *do something* other than next-to-nothing."

Caroline laughed harder. Encouraged, Darlene went on, "You know, I've tried over the years to figure out what these people thought about, cared about, hoped for, might have done, other than work. But I couldn't come up with anything. They *worked*. They were all farmers and farmers' wives, except Elizabeth. And I do get that there's so much to do out on the farm. My god, I was raised on one. We saw really hard times. So I thought that was probably it with them. You work your guts out on a farm. I hated the farming life for this very reason. I was more than glad when I found out Vernon didn't want to, when he'd decided to stay with mechanics full-time.

"Josephine was so different from these women. She got out there and worked right alongside Clifford and the hired hands, especially during harvest but during spring planting as well. I can just imagine what the Jantz women must've thought of her. Well, it showed on some of them, especially Hannah. But Josie didn't care. The Jantz women gardened like crazy. I have to hand them that. But farmer's wives did that back then. Josephine had an orchard which she shared with Momma and me, giving us bushels of peaches, apricots, apples. There was constant canning during summer days.

"But as hardworking as we all were, my family wasn't tight-lipped the way the Jantzes were. Well, except for Mother. My god, if anything we couldn't shut up. We spewed out every thought we had, and, of course, that had its own problems. But we knew what each other was thinking, even about what was going on in the world, especially around Shirly.

"Caroline, the war was brewing during the early part of Vern and my being together. Hitler had become Chancellor of Germany two, three years earlier. My dad was out of his mind. He couldn't stop talking about it, even to Ava, who he rarely talked to, if at all. You know, now that I'm thinking about it, Mother was a lot like Vern's people. But Dad? My god, he'd talk to a fence post. You couldn't shut Dad up about the weather and where we were getting our next dollar. The economy was dead, not going anywhere.

"This was the Dust Bowl. We were in the middle of ungodly heat and drought. In August of 1936, Caroline, when Vern and I got married in Kansas, the temperature hit an all-time high of 113 degrees! And these people, the Jantzes, they were farmers. Maybe the men talked about money and the weather behind the barn but not a word at the table. We sat in heat, water dripping from our chins, the makeshift water-coolers fanning the air. Nothing. Not a word.

"And there were *gangsters*. Bonnie and Clyde had already been in Oklahoma several times. The newspapers had reported their stealing guns in Hopewell, for godssakes, and from someplace in the northern part of the state, some armory, I think it was. They killed a policeman near Commerce, Oklahoma, kidnapped the chief of police and stole a car in Pawhuska. I remember this in particular, because it was right before Vern and I met and started dating. And not too long after we did, they were gunned down in Louisiana. I was, what, sixteen? I was terrified. People in Oklahoma couldn't stop talking about them and Pretty Boy Floyd. They were being pictured in all the newspapers, *The Hopewell Herald*, *The Daily Oklahoman* and detective magazines that my dad read religiously—I kid you not, a lot more than he read his Bible, believe me on this. Plus there were stories in *Life*, *Saturday Evening Post*. Vern talked to my dad about this stuff all the time. Nothing from the Jantzes. Not. A. Word. The whole damn world coulda been on fire, well, what am I saying? It *was*, and they were totally oblivious or seemed to be to me."

Darlene's sigh came from deep inside, from a long time ago. "Caroline, Commerce is just north of Interstate 44 on the way to Joplin. It's half a state from Cleaview, so I guess that's the difference. Anything they can't see from their backyards they don't bother themselves with."

When Caroline only nodded, Darlene went on, hoping to elicit some response. Her criticism of Vernon's family might be putting Caroline in a difficult position, her daughter wanting to be true to both of her parents, but now that she'd started, Darlene couldn't resist the pull of her story. She kept talking while she went to the stove and back for more coffee for them both.

"I mentioned Bonnie and Clyde one Sunday, just to see if I could get a rise outta somebody, anybody—this shortly after they'd been shot to death, slaughtered really—the newspapers saying they each got 50 bullets, which turned out to be an exaggeration, but this was *big news*. That car went on tour for decades at amusement parks and carnivals and such. There was a damn national obsession over what happened.

"Well, at one of the Jantz Sunday dinners—when Josephine and Clifford were there so I didn't feel so shy—I talked a little about Bonnie and Clyde. After I had my say, Willard said, 'just deserts,' about them getting shot to death. And that was that. Everything fell silent. Finally Clifford, who rarely opened his mouth, said a thing or two, followed by Josephine, and finally Vernon squeaked out his two cents worth, looking down at his plate while he did. After that, you could forget it. Everything from then on was dead air. I looked over and caught

Willard staring right at me, as only he could, his arm over the back of his wife's chair, as though he owned her. He had this stupid grin on his face, staring at me like he thought I was dog's puke. I felt like it was a warning, you know?"

"A warning? Of what?"

"For me to keep my mouth shut, stay in my place, where a woman's supposed to be, stay quiet and do what men tell them to do. Men do the talking, didn't you know? That's if there's going to be any. You should've seen his wife. I have to try hard to remember her name. Mary, it was Mary, well, of course it was. She sat there next to him with the 'wife's calling' written on her forehead. Submissive doesn't begin to describe that one. If the meek are going to inherit the earth, she'll be queen at the Second Coming."

Darlene was shocked by her own blasphemy. She felt the old anger tearing at her, trying to get free. "I can't believe I said that," she said, apologetically, but she couldn't help laughing with Caroline who was bent over her coffee until her hair came close to failing into her cup. "I don't know, Caroline, maybe they all felt like I did, downright scared of him—Willard, you know—despite our contempt for him. He was a creepy, creepy guy."

She stopped and watched the cream she poured in her cup swirl around and around with her spoon until it disappeared, leaving a pale, beige brew behind. Her talking had suddenly taken a sinister turn she hadn't intended.

"You're saying they were afraid of him, his own family?"

"They had reason to be, Caroline. He had a raging temper, and maybe they waited to see if he was gonna say anything before they offered their own opinions, is all I'm saying. I've ceased to doubt how they felt anymore. I remember too well when he said something, how it was always and forever followed by silence. I think they probably didn't want to chance setting him off. And he could be, oh could he ever be, set off. I've seen him throw dishes, food and all, against the wall and walk out. It didn't happen often. I only saw it a couple of times, but when it did, one of the Jantz women would get up from the table, oh yeah, just like that, and clean up his mess while all the rest of us continued to eat like nothing had happened. Take my word, Willard could be terrifying. You never knew when he would erupt."

"He did this when his wife and kids were with him?" Caroline was seriously engaged in her story, and it was liberating for Darlene, but also frightening to be so close to the edge of the telling.

Darlene cleared her throat. "That's interesting, because they often didn't come along. Come to think of it, both of the times I saw him throw food, they weren't with him. As to why they didn't show up with him sometimes, the word from the women—one of their rare moments of sharing anything with me—was that Mary was a bit 'hysterical,' which to them meant 'unstable.' I don't know for certain what they meant by this, because 'hysterical' to me means throwing a fit, being out of control. Mary was anything but. She sat with her head glued to her plate. When she did come with him—the two kids always came too, of course—she just blended in, because she worked without talking like the rest of them."

"So they meant she was emotionally sensitive, is that it? Sounds like she was nervous and tried not to show it."

"I think so, yeah, that's right. When all the kids finally grew up enough to start running around, you livened up the place. Hannah had her say about that, attempting to keep everything as soundless as possible. She ruled the roost, from the other side of the hen house. But Willard, I'm living testament to his insanity."

Darlene stopped and let some breaths out of her mouth. Caroline looked at her steadily as she continued, "Well, you heard how he was when he confronted me on the road to Smeets's place that Sunday. He would've hit me if he could've." She flipped a hand in the air dismissively and began again.

"I just didn't understand how his people were, and when I talked to Josephine about it, well, her way of expressing it was to say they could kill a pep rally for Jesus! We laughed like crazy fools over that one. But Josie could laugh about it, couldn't she? She and Clifford came once in a blue moon, when Sherman invited them, so they didn't *have* to be there—Sherman and Clifford helped Willard out with the Jantz homeplace from time to time—so it was an exchange kind of thing. Everybody doubled up that way back then to get things done as quick as possible because of the weather. Harvest time especially.

"A few years after my shy-and-silent spell though, when we'd been attending their dinners a while, after I was married, I found my legs and my tongue, especially after you kids entered the picture. Vernon was sometimes mortified by what I said and did around his family." Darlene sighed and leaned back.

Caroline stood and walked to the kitchen, placing her dishes in the sink. Darlene wondered if her daughter was thinking about leaving, and was oddly surprised by her disappointment. Now that she'd started talking, she wanted to tell her stories to Caroline.

"My dad was social, as I've told you." Darlene added, hoping this would entice her daughter to linger, but evidently Caroline meant to stay, because she came back with coffee and filled both of their cups. "He talked to anybody who'd listen. Including the Holdemans who read the newspapers. They're different from the Amish that way. No radios, mind you, but they read, choosing carefully, of course. In fact, about the time Vern and I married, one of their prohibitions was talking about politics. They argued and changed these rules off and on, you know."

"So they could read about current affairs, but not talk about them? Lord."

"They had lots of crazy notions about right and wrong, to my way of thinking. But Dad was interested in the news and spent quite a bit of time with the men in Shirly discussing it, and it wasn't long before he and Vernon hit it off, because Vern liked to read the newspapers too. Actually my dad became Vernon's salvation. I think you need to know this, Caroline. I'm not sure I ever expressed how important Dad was in your father's life.

"Well, once they connected, Vernon took off like a rocket. He could be opinionated, but he was open to hearing what Dad had to say, and more often than not, changed his mind. But the rest of the Jantzes, you woulda thought everything was just going on without change day after day from the time of the Garden of Eden until their Sunday dinners. You wanna know the truth, I got more outta their mother than any of them. Actually I learned most of what I knew about Vern's family from her."

"I didn't know she allowed such a thing, visiting with her, I mean," Caroline interjected. "But I only remember her from a few photographs that you've shown me from time to time. One of them was a snapshot of Grandma Jantz, you and Kat—three generations of Jantz women, Jantzes by marriage, of course. And it was because of Kat, I think you told me, that the picture was taken, because she was so much younger than the rest of us grandchildren. You gave me a copy of that photo. Grandmother Jantz allowed this photo to be taken not long before she died, right?"

Darlene nodded. "She was ninety-two. Kat was still a baby. It was the beginning and end of a line of births from her to Kat, the youngest granddaughter. That's what Elizabeth used to convince her mother to allow it, although it was strictly forbidden by her Holdeman church. The old woman wore her kerchief for that picture, but I saw her quite often without it, when we were in her room alone. I remember one time in particular, after we had been talking an hour or more, there was a knock on the door. Before she let anybody open the door, she put her kerchief back on. I felt very privileged by this."

Caroline asked, "So how did you manage to talk with her? I thought she didn't allow anybody in her room."

"Well, here again, that's one of those Jantz myths. Nobody in Vern's family explained this or anything else about their mother to me, so I asked Vern about her being by herself so much of the time. He said that she didn't like being social. He left the impression she was a recluse, only coming out of her room very early in the mornings to do cooking and baking, so that she could retreat to her hide-away before most of the house was up and about. After her children were older, she left the child-rearing, cleaning and running of the household to the oldest girls, especially Hannah.

"Given her reclusiveness, I never thought about visiting her when we first started going to the Jantzes for Sunday dinners. Heavens, I might break the code of conduct laid down by God Almighty on the last day of creation. But after I'd been going a while—remember we lived in Clearview because Vernon worked at his Dad's automobile shop when we were first married, and our apartment was only a hop, skip and a jump to the Jantz homeplace." Darlene stopped and stared at the rows of framed pictures along the top of the bookcase on the other side of the room.

"Caroline, when I think about my loneliness, about how this actually could have been, but wasn't, I feel like crying even yet. I mean, Vernon's sisters were all right there in Clearview, all of them, all four of them, until Sarah moved to Hopewell and the others left for Kansas and Nebraska—leaving Hannah behind. But with them right there... we coulda all been friends. They coulda given me advice and helped me with you when you were born and with Teddy, who was born in the house Vernon built for us in Clearview. What was wrong with these people? I couldn't figure out why they were so dead set against him.

"It was like a brood of chickens when they pick one out, one that's small or doesn't smell the same or looks and acts different, so they peck it to death. In a lot of ways, Vernon was like them, but in more ways than not, he wasn't. He was lively and inventive. Industrious is how I'd put it. He worked as much, more, than they did, I'd say, but he put his heart into what he did, worked with enthusiasm. Maybe they resented that. Who knows?

"So, out of sheer boredom, I started going and knocking on Caroline Jantz's door, though I never would've dreamed of calling her by her first name."

"What did you call her?"

"I tried not to call her anything. I had a lot of respect for her, not because I thought she was old or even because she was Vernon's mother. I was in awe of these Holdeman women for their commitment to their beliefs. They had to overcome a lot, especially if their husbands didn't join the church with them. My mother lost some respect over this with me, because she didn't join and wanted to. In Momma's case, she just couldn't do what Caroline Jantz was doing, because she didn't want the constant pressure from the preachers to get Whalen to join when she knew he wouldn't.

"Vern's mother gave quite a lot to the church in Weather Springs, even before she died. It probably got the preachers off her back about her husband, and God knows what else. The money she gave was Carl's, of course, at least far as I know. I don't think she inherited much. But if it was Carl's, he allowed her to pay the tithe and then some. My mother was a proud woman. She never would've wanted her church to know she couldn't pay the tithe. Well, they all knew we were poor, of course, but by her not joining, she didn't have to confront it.

"You know, Caroline, it may have been curiosity that gave me the guts to knock on this woman's door. I wanted to know how she was doing something my mother didn't have the courage to do, even when Momma believed she was probably losing her soul. She did believe the Holdeman church was the one true church. And my mother had put the fear of hell for not believing this in my young mind. I watched her living her days, one after another, feeling she was eternally lost in the eyes of God, or at the very least, wondering if her efforts were enough in the church she did join. This belief in the Holdeman church as the true faith didn't seem to bother Josephine—and certainly not Jesse—in the way it did me. Maybe I wanted to find out for sure myself, to see if Mother Jantz would reveal some divine secret to me. Ah, that's what I called her, when I did call her anything. Mother Jantz."

"What divine revelation did you think she could give you?" Caroline was genuinely interested, so Darlene found it easy to talk, to tell what she hadn't told her children.

"Well, of course, I never would've asked her this directly, but I wanted to know how you could be sure you were on the right path with your life, doing God's will. How could I know, for certain, God's purpose for my life?" Darlene held up her hand as though to stop Caroline's interruption. "Maybe a lot of it was simply fear. I didn't want to be lost any more than my mother did. Perhaps that's what Mother Jantz was afraid of, too. She told me she spent a lot of time reading her Bible and praying. And, as crazy as this sounds, I could feel fear in her."

"This explains a lot to me about both of my Grandmothers, Mom. Do you remember the first time you went to visit Grandmother Jantz? I wish I'd been old enough to go with you."

"I know this. It had to've been after the table was cleared, and the dishes were back in place, or I never could've slipped out to talk to her. Can you imagine what they must've thought, my doing this? But Mother Jantz was delighted. I was pregnant with you. I do remember this, so, I guess, it was the year after I was married.

"Later, I took you kids with me, after you were old enough. So you did go in with me sometimes, Caroline. She'd kiss you and offer you cookies and candies she'd made, that she'd stashed in a small cabinet. She'd bring out tins of candies and small cookies, and let you take what you wanted. But I didn't keep you in the room with us very long. I think she frightened you with her kerchief and foreign language. I'd send you to run around outside, while we watched you from her windows as we talked."

"I must've been very young, because I don't remember any of this."

"I'd say, three, four. The boys were too young to have memories of it at all, I'm sure. And I say boys, but I'm not sure about Timothy, because by the time he came along I wasn't well. I often stayed home with you kids when Vernon went to visit. Those were the first years after the war. I did drive out there sometimes with you and Teddy. But it got so I was afraid to drive, especially with Teddy so little." Darlene suddenly felt very defeated. "I wasn't well. I didn't trust myself."

She glanced at her daughter. When Caroline didn't ask more, she went back to reminiscing about Mother Jantz.

"I spoke just enough Plattdeutsch to stumble through conversations with her. She loved it. I understood, in time, that it was her shyness, together with her religious beliefs, the clannishness of her church, that made her feel more comfortable being by herself. I wasn't of the same mind. With my sickness, the isolation was terrifying. I didn't want people to see me like I was, but the withdrawal from others made me feel something was very wrong with me. Vernon used to tell me that his mother was afraid. And although I admired her religious strength, I was also fearful I'd become like her. Maybe I went to visit her to compare, you know? To see if I had the same feelings she did.

"But I began to realize Vern was more like her than I was. He told me he hid behind the sheds or the barn when people drove onto their property. This was when he was young, before he went to school. But still. I don't think he's ever quite rid himself of this fear of others. It comes partly from being an immigrant, don't you think? Mother Jantz was a baby when she came to this country with her parents. And Vern's father was a young boy. They were with parents from another culture. Backward, is how I see it."

Caroline nodded. "I can't imagine choosing to spend most of your time in a room away from everybody else, though, even from your own family, for heaven's sakes."

"Fear and anxiety can make you a little crazy, I'm here to tell you. I think Vern understood this, and maybe why he loved her so much. And, come to think of it, fear of the world outside our own didn't have just a little bit to do with why I connected with Vernon."

"This religion sounds so typically immigrant, Mom. Its severity escalated with the insecurity stemming from the pressure from the outside to integrate into the established culture, the one around them in America. They felt that if they stayed true to their religion, it would shelter them from these outside differences. So the more insecure they felt, the greater their efforts to stay 'pure,' to meet what they thought would please God, the one comfort and hope they had."

"But it's my understanding that they were like this even back in Russia before they moved to America," Darlene explained. "At Vernon and my family reunions, I've asked our older uncles and aunts about our ancestry, and they all said our families were to themselves, not even interacting much with other Mennonite clans, and especially not with the Jews, who lived close by."

"Maybe the circumstances in the old country, weren't that different from those in the States. From what I've learned from Grampa and Dad, our ancestors moved, during the Reformation, from Lower Saxony, across Friesland into Poland and then on to Russia. Who knows for sure what path they took—there's so many different stories—but we do know they moved from country to country because of their pacifist beliefs. And when your survival depends on sticking together, the way to remain secure—to be certain in the face of grave uncertainty—is to become a singularly identified group by language and religion. It's my understanding that this is exactly what our people did. They stayed clannish because this meant they would survive, and they did, didn't they?"

Darlene nodded, interested in how Caroline was interpreting what she knew.

"They were even granted great exemptions until Catherine the Great died," Caroline added. "When their language and religion were threatened, they immigrated to the States. When you give this kind of historical survival a religious sanction, it's not likely it will easily yield to outside influence. I look upon my family history, even my upbringing by you and Dad, as an extension of this kind of security-seeking. It's what happens to all people who are tied to each other in small groups that eventually start to move out into another world. But that can take many generations. I think of you and Dad as miracles. Not many of your generation have come so far. I'm proud of you."

Darlene stared at her daughter. It was a compliment she rarely heard, coming as it was, right after her divorce and all the guilt it had provoked, especially from her children.

"I'm touched by your telling me, honey. How in the world do you know all of this?"

Caroline shrugged. "How you usually learn about such things. I listened, especially to Grampa. He told me stories when I was a little girl. And Dad too. I became curious, and in college, I did some searching and reading." She reached out and touched Darlene's hand. "So did your friendship with Grandma Jantz continue until she died?"

"No, not really. Most of what we had was when you kids were quite young. After Teddy started to school and Timothy came, I sank into a long depression. We went out to Vernon's home only once, twice a year."

"Did you find out what you were searching for?"

"Well, certainly not in the way I expected. We would spend thirty minutes or so talking together at first, and later sometimes an hour or two. She told me about her life as a girl in Kansas, her parents, how she missed her family. She's the one that told me she'd been baptized by John Holdeman when she was sixteen years old, converted on the spot in some relatives' house, while she was visiting them in Kansas. *Converted* might not be the right word, as she'd been raised Holdeman. It was more like she declared her commitment to live her life according to the Scriptures and God's will—as interpreted by the Holdeman church, of course.

"John Holdeman went to the kitchen, she said, filled a pitcher full of well water, and baptized her in the name of Jesus Christ and the Holy Ghost, pouring water over her head, dripping it on the floor.

"She cried when she told me. She had eighteen pregnancies and gave birth to fifteen children, Caroline. Only eleven of those children lived to adulthood. Shortly before she died, she told me that if she had it to do over again, she'd bar Carl from her bedroom door. We laughed together over that. I liked that old woman." Darlene paused, then said, "You know, I always remember her as old, and I'm not sure why, because she was exactly my age now, in her early sixties, when I talked with her. Maybe I think of her as old because of her plain dress and her isolation, staying in her room more and more as she aged. She's the only Jantz who really liked me, other than Vernon, of course.

"But I remember her now mostly because of something she told me toward the last of my visiting times with her. I'd heard quite a lot of nasty comments over the years about your father by his brothers and sisters, mostly asides, their way of joking, you know. But Mother Jantz told me outright—'Vernon's a crybaby. I thought he was sick when he was a boy,' she said. 'He was so little. He wouldn't grow. His brothers didn't want him around, and you couldn't blame them with all his silliness. So he just hung out with me and his sisters in the kitchen. He's been spoiled. And it's made for bad blood with the others.'

"So there you have it, straight from the mouth of the mother who bore him.

"Says it all, doesn't it? It's how they looked on him, on everything that was different from them and their notions of what people should do and be. I didn't like her for this, of course, but about the other things we shared, I appreciated her frankness and honesty. She was strong underneath all those fears."

Darlene pushed through her weariness. "So the simple answer to why I married your father even though I didn't love him was that we'd had sex before marriage, and I felt sorry for him because his family treated him so awful," she said, with a sigh. "And too, there was this unspoken understanding between us about being afraid of the world, the one apart from how we'd been raised that we both wanted to be a part of but didn't know how. Well, you know how that turned out, not so well, did it? After you were born, we slumped back into the world we knew, felt we belonged to, were at home in.

"Maybe you think people don't really marry for these kinds of reasons, but I did. And I thought that since I *had* to marry him—and I want to say again, it was religion that was under that idea, not because I was pregnant with you—well, I thought that I could help him after we were married. I thought I could help him become the man his family never allowed him to be. I know this must seem strange to you, but you wanted to know the truth, and that's it."

Darlene looked up, adding quickly, "And, this sounds strange to me now, too. I wouldn't do today what I did then. My god, Caroline, I hear myself telling you stories like these, and I'm *ashamed*. It's why a lot of women never tell them to anyone.

"But surely you've found similar things out about yourself. Think back on your twenties and thirties, and the things you did, and why you did them. It isn't just that we each grow up and change. It's because times change as well. Things are acceptable now that weren't back then."

"I suspected most of this," Caroline said, after finishing her coffee slowly. "But I needed you to tell me. You know I had a friend from college I saw not too long ago. She told me when she'd go to a women's gathering, a baby or wedding shower, that sort of thing, she'd walk into the room and say, 'I'm a divorcée. If that bothers any of you, tell me now, and I'll leave. I don't want to find out I'm a leper after I have food on my plate.' This was in the late fifties, right after her divorce. Most women wouldn't have been that direct. Most simply took it on the chin, suffering in silence, while the gossip swirled behind their backs." Caroline made a swirling motion with her hands in the air.

"Well, it's good you mention this, because how it would look to my family and friends was another reason why I waited so long to divorce your father. But even given this, I couldn't have done it earlier, because I couldn't've left while you kids were young. Kat's not long out of high school as it is. Her being on her own made this so much easier. So there's lots and lots of reasons."

Darlene sat shaking her head, hiding behind her cup, before setting it down. "It was a mismatch from the start, Caroline. But it happened, and it became finally one of those situations where I felt I couldn't be myself if I continued to stay with him. So, you see, it's so much more than what it appears to be. It certainly is greater than his drinking."

—

After Caroline had left, Darlene sat alone at the table, exhausted from the telling. She had skipped on the rim of the abyss but pulled herself back before vertigo lured her into its darkness. There was so much more to say, but it could wait, and some of it—she felt beyond doubt after today—would never be told. In some ways, she thought, it takes more courage to not tell than to give in to the longing and tell it all.

Darlene glanced at the clock. She had taken the day off for Caroline's leaving. But now that her daughter was spending time with her father, she had the afternoon to herself. Before the evening's send-off supper and the drive to the airport for Caroline's red-eye to New York, she needed to fill her time, or she would sit and drink far too much coffee, not allowing sleep later when she needed it.

Her talk with Caroline had started the memories churning. She was becoming anxious that her earlier vow of silence was starting to crumble. What might slip out in an unguarded moment was draining her of the needed energy for the relevant telling. Caroline was a far too willing listener, the person she had confided in when she shouldn't have. Her stories were coming too easily and too quickly now that she was past the defense she'd worked so hard to construct on her way out of her marriage.

Cooking needed to be done for the rest of the week, but when she stood to go into the kitchen, she drifted instead toward the bookcase in the dining area where she had placed her photograph albums. She knew exactly the picture she wanted, though *wanted* didn't seem the right word. Perhaps *needed* was the more accurate choice. She had taken quite a number of the photographs out of these albums over the years, mostly those with Vernon and his siblings at the Jantzes, even those with her and the children included in them. When she had left Vernon, she had carefully weeded out any with Willard, leaving these and the rest of Vern's family pictures with him. Short of tearing up the Jantz photos with her and her kids that she had kept, she decided to consign them to boxes. She had gone to the camera store and after talking with the sales clerk, had ordered archival containers.

So what she'd told herself—that she wanted to destroy the images—simply wasn't true. Her rationalization for keeping them had been that sometime in the future Caroline and the boys might appreciate having photographs of their family history, especially snapshots of when they were young. And the albums and other pictures in the boxes were about all she had to leave them after she was gone.

But now that the storytelling had begun, maybe these images had more to reveal than she had thought. Curiosity had aroused feelings resonating behind her stories and set her to wondering if these pictures might not only clarify and intensify those feelings but place them, give them a home. Her feelings had seemed free-floating and willful lately, jerking her this way and that. Now she was beginning to suspect they emanated from specific times and places which she had pushed aside or buried in the hopes of not remembering. At the very least, the stories could explain some of the pictures that Caroline would take, and, of course, the boys as well, should they ever decide to want any.

Photographs were so deceptive, she thought. They weren't evidence of the truth as so many thought they were. What she was to find valuable or significant in any of the pictures in her albums—and the archival boxes—or even what was actually noticed, would likely be at odds with what others would see in them, even the people who were in the pictures. The last time Vernon sat with her and looked at these, he told utterly different stories about them than she did, often about the same picture they were looking at. It wasn't just that memory might have been shaky for either one of them. It had to do with what each picture held for them, individually, the content of it, which seemed to her to be shaped by what they were searching for, expecting, hoping to find.

She pulled the album from the shelf, dusting it off with her fingers. After laying it on the table and sitting down, she opened it, not at the beginning, but at random, wondering, not what she would discover—she knew each snapshot in this book by heart—but where the pages might open. This wasn't that far from the divine revelation the Holdemans used to choose their preachers, at least from what she'd been told. In a stack of Bibles a marker was placed and candidates each picked up a Bible at random. The candidate's Bible that opened to the marker was God's choice for their ordained minister.

To Darlene's amazement, as though through just such divinely-inspired revelation, the album opened to the photograph she had in mind. It was placed next to several others taken a few months before, most of them with members of her family, all of them in front of the house, with the porch running along the entrance way, the cedars to the left and the long driveway to the right. Why did these old photographs all have so much background in them? She wanted to zoom in, scrutinize closely all of the faces. Perhaps clues were there she had missed, the finger of God pointing to the future or more likely some trace of each person's destiny in the look in the eyes or the set of the mouth.

She took the sides of the photograph she wanted, pulling it up and out of its black corner sleeves. It had those curved undulated edges that lots of snapshots from the thirties and forties had, with a black-lined border framing the image. Vernon was in the middle with Willard slightly in front of him, and, in an odd trick of the camera—how it was angled in the light—she appeared closer to him than her husband-to-be. Vernon had somehow slipped back a step or two into Willard's shadow, the light dimmed on his entire figure and face. She hadn't noticed this before, how clearly shown she and Willard were next to him. Willard had his hat sitting back on his head so that his face was completely visible despite the shadow cast by the brim of his fedora. He, like Vernon, wore a suit for Sunday dinner, so this must have been taken after such a meal at the Dirks's farm. Willard's suit gleamed in the sun like polished armor. It appeared overly-large for him as though he had been given a hand-me-down from a much larger man, one that he never would grow into. How old would he have been here? Probably in his early to mid-thirties. His tie seemed an afterthought, bulging out from under a tightly-buttoned jacket. His trousers were limp and lifeless, their cuffs hanging over well-worn shoes.

She had labeled the photograph as though having a viewer other than herself in mind—*Picture of Darlene with Vernon and Willard, soon after I met Vernon, at our Homeplace, Fall of 1935.* How odd to call herself by her first name and then use the personal, "I" and "our" in the description. The label had been written on the page in fountain pen so she couldn't change it now, even if she wanted to.

When had she put these photographs in this album? Why this picture here, with all the others of Vernon with her and her family? Obviously, Willard had been visiting at her homeplace, which he often did during the time she and Vernon were dating. From the beginning, he had assumed a role in her life since he had introduced her to Vern, and since Vern and his brother had worked for Whalen. Maybe she hadn't removed the picture because she had labeled it so permanently, because the entire page on both sides would have needed to be redone, the album disassembled and rearranged. Perhaps it was easier to leave it.

Then it came to her. It was the only picture of Willard and Vernon together without other members of their families. Vern had drawn her attention to this and requested it be put in the album. Was it because his brother was viewed by him as properly placed with her and the Dirkses as he himself was going to be? But once she had left Vernon—taken everything that she viewed as belonging to her from their house to her new apartment, leaving all of his family pictures with him—why had she left this one photograph behind, placed in an album she considered now to be exclusively hers? She stared at it. This picture was the only reference to Willard in her new life.

She did remember well the day that she first saw the photograph. She had taken a day off from Caroline and Teddy, leaving them with Josephine and going to Ava's to help her with blueberry and blackberry jelly making. When the filled jars were on racks to cool, she and Ava had decided to drink some iced tea at the dining room table. Abruptly, her Mother stood, walked to the sideboard, reached in a drawer and came back with photo packets in her hands. Ava had handed Darlene two packages and then realized she had only meant to give her one. Her mother's hand fluttered toward her hair, then landed lightly on her chest.

"It's only the one that has what I want to show you," she told Darlene, reaching out tentatively to take back the package on the bottom of the two she'd handed her.

Darlene started to hand it back, but stopped. "What's in it?" She pulled the packets away from Ava's outstretched hand.

"It's Jesse's. Whalen brought them both back when he had to go in to Hopewell for feed."

Ava had this unbearable habit of not answering directly. When Ava looked away, Darlene opened the one Ava had wanted to retrieve. Two could play this cat-and-mouse game. She never knew if Ava was provoking, perhaps even tantalizing, her with obliqueness and silence, or if she was genuinely guarding her privacy—or someone else's. What kind of secret could this package of photographs hold for her mother? But Ava didn't seem particularly upset when she began looking at the pictures, one by one, putting them face-up on the table as she went through them. They were pictures of Jesse farming with Vernon, Willard and Whalen and several of him with some blond-headed girlfriend who had accompanied him two, three times on dates with her and Vernon, and sometimes with others.

The picture of herself with Vernon and Willard was the last in the package. It hadn't struck her at the time as anything more than a casual picture taken at some family gathering after an evening meal.

She looked up at Ava. "These are several years old."

Her mother nodded slightly, then, as Darlene waited, the silence growing between them.

"Where did you get them? The roll, I mean."

"Jesse left it behind, on the shelf." Ava waved dismissively toward a shelf in the living room.

"So you gave it to Dad to develop with the one with the pictures you want to show me? Did you know anything about any of these?" She flapped Jesse's photos in the air. "The one of me with Vernon and Willard has to've been taken before we were married, not long after Willard introduced us."

"I thought that too," Ava said with unusual directness. "He hung around for suppers, remember that? I never liked that man."

Darlene spread the photographs on the table, tapping the one of her with Vernon and his brother. "Neither did I, but Vernon should see this, Momma. He might want it just like Jesse wants his, maybe."

Surprisingly, Ava smiled and nodded. "I think that's fine. I thought Jesse had forgotten to develop it, so I just threw it in at the last minute with the other one."

"I think I remember the girl. Jesse brought her along when we all went out for the evening, when Vern and I were dating. But Jesse had a number of girls back then. I couldn't keep up with all of them."

"Well, he's in seminary now," Ava said, as though this forgave any wrongdoing her son had committed in the days before the present.

Darlene nodded, but lingering on the pictures of her brother she had just seen. How old was he in them? In his late teens, early twenties, she guessed. The pictures had been taken over considerable time. Why hadn't he ever developed them? Did the roll just get lost on the shelf?

And then a thought surfaced with clarity. Ava knew what was on this roll, and she had waited to process the film until Whalen was likely to see the pictures on it! Ava was wanting to remind Whalen of their son's early days on the farm, when Jesse hadn't spent all of his time horsing around, as Whalen constantly claimed and told everybody in the family he did. But today, her mother hadn't wanted her to see the pictures of the girl, reminding her of Jesse's dalliance.

It was so like Ava, protecting her son, rewriting his history. But Jesse had no intention of ever developing this roll. By the time he got around to it, it was apparent the pictures had been taken over several months, some at harvest out in the fields, some during the fall and winter in the barn, some even later, as with the one of her, Willard and Vernon. Jesse must have thought it was of no use to share them with his father and less use to himself. Why be reminded of his father's constant displeasure with him, regardless of what he did?

He had taken these pictures to belong, Darlene was sure of it, to be a part of the farm work with Whalen, his right-hand man, and Vernon, Willard, and Ava had stood helplessly by, watching what was happening.

She studied the girl with interest. Jesse had cared so little about her that he didn't even get the roll developed for her sake. She was left, literally, on the shelf, forgotten. In that moment, an enormous, swelling sadness for her brother, for his lost youth, came over her. It would be several years later before she would connect this young girl in the picture to the woman and child in the photograph she had discovered in her mother's suitcase of pictures from the nursing home, the photo that now was in some archival box in her own closet. She would never be certain that the woman and the girl were one and the same, but her strong sense of Jesse's character, together with some of the stories he told her shortly before he died, lead her to the conclusion that this was so.

Darlene gathered up the pictures except for the one of her with Vernon and Willard and put them back in the envelopes. When she looked up, her mother was staring at the table with glistening eyes, hands folded in front of her. Darlene handed the packets to her. Ava took them, holding them to her breast and sat in perfect stillness for a long while before she laid them on the table, her hands on them as though they might disappear or Darlene might claim them again. When Ava finally looked up, Darlene could see the mixed emotions on her mother's face—embarrassment and pride, but also guilt.

Darlene knew why.

Ava was pictured in most of the photographs in one of the packages, along with a few of Whalen with Ava's brothers, Fred and Joe. She was lovely in a chintz dress with ruffles down the front. She had chosen to wear this dress to her anniversary dinner. In most of those with Ava, Darlene noticed her mother holding something in one of her hands, her fingers tight around a hidden object. In one snapshot, Ava had even slipped this hand into the folds of her skirt. When Darlene asked her mother about this, Ava shrugged, while walking to the sideboard, opening a drawer and putting the packets inside.

"It was a brooch," Ava had said, stiffly, her back to her daughter. "I didn't want to cause Fred anguish." Ava's small laugh came out with a sarcastic edge. Her mother's brother was a substitute preacher and full-time elder in the Weather Springs Holdeman Mennonite Church that Ava sometimes attended.

"I shouldn't have been wearing it or the dress, for that matter." Darlene wasn't certain if her mother was chiding herself for disregarding Fred's feelings about his conservative beliefs or if she was expressing regret concerning a forbidden belief of her own.

"These were taken at Dad's and your thirtieth wedding anniversary, weren't they? We had the dinner several weeks ago, isn't that right?"

Ava nodded. "Everybody had left for the day, after the dinner, after you and Josephine had gone. It was by chance. Joe saw Jesse's camera from the living room on a shelf in the hallway and talked us into it."

"So why isn't Dad in any of them? With you, I mean?"

"I took them out," Ava said simply.

"The ones of you and Dad? *Why?*"

"Fred's upset about it." Her mother hesitated, then admitted, "Whalen was in a hurry, not wanting to stand there and wait. Joe'd gone to his car to get his comb. What man keeps a comb in the glove box of his car? His vanity knows no bounds. So, while we waited for him to come back, your father handed the camera to Fred who snapped a couple of pictures of us, because Whalen said if somebody didn't take our picture right then, he wasn't going to wait any longer.

"I was surprised Fred allowed his picture to be taken, let alone that he snapped the pictures of us. I think it was because Selena wasn't with him. She was sick. And Fred's always been more easy-going about church rules than she is, though the camera is to him *sintlijch*." Ava slipped into Plattdeutsch for the word 'sinful.' "Joe was by himself, too. Susan was visiting relatives up in Kansas. Maybe Fred did it, without thinking, since there wasn't anybody around to chastise him for it."

When Darlene started to speak, Ava interrupted her quickly, "What I think, when he got home, he told Selena what he'd done. By then he'd become convicted over it. So yesterday he comes, wanting all the photographs, not just the ones he was in, but the ones he'd taken as well. That would've been nearly everything we took that day. When I wouldn't hand them over, he went flying down the drive in a temper, claiming he'd be back to talk to Whalen when he came in from the fields." She waved her hand dismissively. "Well, you know your father. He brought the packet to me from getting them at the store in Hopewell without even looking at them. I don't think he has still. He doesn't care about such things, you know that. He posed with me only because Joe insisted that he do it."

Ava shook her head. "But Fred, well, he won't be satisfied until he gets what he wants. I took the two pictures of your father and me out, because I don't have any of us—*not any*. Fred doesn't have a right to them or the others either. It isn't fair to me, or Whalen and Joe—that's if they care."

"I'm as astonished as you are about Uncle Fred agreeing to any of this. Having his picture taken with his brothers, I can see that in a way, but *taking* some? It's deliberate, willful participation in wrongdoing, what he considers voluntary sin, I would think."

Ava was near tears. "I just know he wanted it changed after he'd done it."

"Go get them," Darlene said, gently.

Ava was puzzled. Then her eyes widened. "You'll keep them for me until this blows over with him?" She walked quickly to the sideboard.

"I can do that, Mom. But I want one."

"What?"

"I want one, Momma. You're beautiful in them."

"Oh." Her mother laughed, hiding her delight, as she walked back with the pictures. Not looking at Darlene, she handed her the packet. "No, surely not beautiful, but if you want one, I wouldn't mind." Then she shook her head. "But there aren't enough for Josephine and Jesse to each have one too, and I don't—well, your father certainly doesn't want them but...." Ava looked pleadingly at her.

"You want to save at least one of you and Dad for yourself. Okay, that's fair. In fact, you should have both originals. But I'm wondering if I could have one copied? I'll have enough made for Josephine and Jesse as well. How's that?"

"Okay," Ava said, walking toward the kitchen. But at the door she turned and added, "I'm asking you to not show around the ones you make. You put them in one of those picture books, that's fine, but not in frames, up so everybody can see. Promise me that."

"Of course. You want me to take them all, then? For safekeeping?" When she saw Ava's face, she added quickly, "Not Jesse's, of course. I'll take only the one of Vernon, Willard and me from that roll."

Obviously, Ava was pleased, but she came back into the dining room, telling Darlene she would feel better if "those other pictures" were out of the house as well, until she felt it was safe to take them back.

—

So she left that day with both packets of photographs.

Darlene chose only one other picture to frame besides the anniversary picture of her parents, a family photograph with Ava standing next to her brothers Joseph and Fred, each in his high-collar shirt, with no ties, buttoned tightly to the top, and dark suits, a look on their faces that Caroline would have called "the immigrant stare." They wore hair-styles and apparel that never changed for them—hair parted down the middle and jackets that were either too big or too small, as though this, as with Willard, was a manner of dress dictated through uncontrollable circumstances. They all stood stiffly, as though the picture had been taken by a professional photographer in a studio. Even Fred was standing ramrod straight, staring directly into the camera.

Darlene walked to the shelf where she'd retrieved the album, took this framed picture down, and looked at it closely. Her uncle Fred had either had his photograph taken some time in his life before he joined the church or had simply aped Joe's posture and stare.

She kept the packet of pictures for her mother for years, and, in the end, never gave them back, because when Fred returned to talk to Whalen about retrieving them, Ava refused to tell either of them where the photographs were. Fred left that evening shunning his sister and her family for the rest of his life. He died unexpectedly of a heart attack shortly after this incident, but Ava's sister-in-law continued the shunning in the name of her husband.

And it had remained so until, in the seventies, at Joe's wake, she and Selena finally spoke to each other. The silence had lasted for almost three decades.

Over the years, Darlene attempted to return the photographs to her mother, mentioning them a number of times, but Ava always shook her head sadly, telling her in Plattdeutsch that what had happened was God's retribution—*ne Strof üt Gott* were the words she used time and time again—God's *punishment*, God's *chastisement*—for what she'd done. It had been her vanity, she declared to Darlene that had created the distance with her brother and sister-in-law. She wasn't going to ease the pain she was meant to carry to pay for it.

After Ava's death, Darlene discovered a suitcase of scattered photographs deep in the closet of her mother's room in the nursing home where Ava had lived for the last three years of her life. This was a day when Josephine's church commitments kept her from helping Darlene with the retrieval of Ava's belongings. Darlene carried the suitcase to the car, not telling her sister or brother of her find. It was a treasure trove of her mother's life, which seemed a symbol of both her mother's defiance—the sinful photographs—and resignation against a world that had framed her life according to its views—the closet-cave where she'd hidden them. After Darlene thoroughly searched through the pictures and taken what she wanted, she gave the suitcase to Josie, who accepted it with raised eyebrows but without significant comments or questions.

One of the two photographs—her mother and father on their wedding anniversary day in 1942—was in a frame on Darlene's dresser in the bedroom of this new home of hers. She placed the other two copies in the suitcase along with the extras from that fated packet her mother had left with her. The packet of photographs of Jesse's early life on the farm she put in an archival box, waiting for Caroline or her sons to decide what to do with them.

After her mother's change of heart, she hadn't offered the copies of Ava in her beautiful anniversary dress to Josephine and Jesse, not wanting to upset her mother further. And once Darlene gave Josephine the suitcase of photographs, she never asked her sister what happened to them. Josephine might have passed some or all to her boys or simply placed the entire collection in her own closet and shut the door on her mother's past, as Ava had done.

Where Jesse was in all of this, Darlene didn't know or care. As she saw it, he forfeited his right to any of it when he left the roll of film on the shelf in Ava and Whalen's living room. As far as she knew, Jesse had never inquired about or asked for any of his parents' possessions. He lived and died in the world he created for himself.

Darlene kept the picture of his young Holdeman lover with her child, having learned that story from Jesse himself as he lay dying. There was no inscription on the back of the photo, but her instincts claimed this photograph as Elenore Decker and son. Jesse didn't tell Darlene the name of his child. Perhaps he never knew.

She thought about all the photographs fated to be saved and then lost in and out of our lives. She wondered how these pictures of hers would be viewed by strangers who might pick them up from boxes in antique stores when nobody in the family was left to keep or care for them. She wondered what her mother was preserving in the suitcase in her closet, or, for that matter, what she herself was trying to save in the archival boxes and in these albums on the shelves in her new home.

Perhaps this photograph contained demonstrative evidence of where she'd been, and how far she'd traveled to be where she presently was. Then again, it could be she was attempting to save the person she was back then, remembering, treasuring and honoring her, even restoring her to her rightful place in her history. Many, many times she'd wondered if she wanted to go back to this or that time and take another path, redirect her future.

Was that what she was doing now?

As she entered what so many called "the senior years" of life, was she attempting to pivot from what had gone before, to begin her life over again, with only herself in it, using just as many references from the past as she needed to remind her of what could happen if she didn't watch where she was going? She didn't have very many chances left, did she? Or was what the sages proclaimed really true—that a new beginning was in every choice that presented itself to us?

She pulled the photograph of her, Vernon and Willard closer and looked at it carefully. Was forensic evidence there?

Photographs were used as evidence in police investigations and reporters verified facts with them for news stories. Cameras were so accessible to everyone. Photographic "evidence" could come from anybody who happened to snap a picture as they came upon a scene. With this sort of immediacy, photographs gave the viewer the notion that they captured the truth of a situation. It was assumed that what had been taken was accurate, because there weren't any manipulations between what was snapped and what was seen-on-sight, at least, no calculated interventions as in the old studio set-ups, with lighting and darkroom development.

But how could this be true when so much in this picture she was now holding didn't seem to give enough clues as to who these three people actually were, what their characters were in reality, how their lives were connected or what their futures might be? Willard looked much the same as any farmer down the road in any small town in America, a faint, scornful smile carrying anger about his hard times and the extremes he had been driven to in order to survive.

But Willard had hardly been that poor dirt farmer, certainly not one of the thousands of hapless ones who'd lost everything during and after the Crash and into the Dust Bowl years. He'd done very well for himself, living off the desperation around him, such as her father's. And later, when Darlene had gained some maturity, she realized how the younger Vernon had carried himself through the troubles on his brother's coat-tails. It bothered her, especially in light of Whalen and Ava's tragedy of losing all their livestock and equipment, but since many in the thirties were struggling to sink or swim, she hadn't made more of it at the time. Pointing it out to Vernon would've been too much like beating a dead horse, especially after she saw his complicity in his brother's schemes. And when Willard left Vern behind—it made sense, after all, that he would, because Vernon didn't want to work for him as a farmhand forever, especially after he married her—there seemed little reason to hold Vernon accountable for the hay he'd made while he was younger, especially since it was just a few short years before their married life together. She continued to study the photograph in her hands. It was Willard who held her attention.

Was this what she'd gone searching to find, after her visit with her daughter?

Years had passed since she'd looked at this picture, really looked at it. She realized that if she'd seen Willard before she'd known him as part of Vern's family, she wouldn't have given him any notice. There was an insignificance about him, a man lacking stature or composure. The only discernible sign of life was in his eyes, which seemed to be hunting with gun-barrel focus for their prey. Here, they were aimed at the camera or the person behind it, which had been Josephine—she remembered now—with Clifford standing lazily off to the side. Willard had turned his right shoulder somewhat into the camera's frame as though he were getting ready to walk past her and Vern or with a few rapid steps, seize the camera box from Josie's hands and throw it to the side. Looking at Vernon more closely, he appeared oddly self-contained next to his brother, an open grin on his face, oblivious to Willard's ability to capture the attention of anybody who would be viewing this photograph later.

Who was she in this picture?

Young, so very young. But she'd been saying that too much lately, especially in her recollections with Caroline. At eighteen, she'd had a lovely complexion, carefully cut and combed hair. Did she do this herself or with Josie's help? She had on a simply-made dress, one she had sewn herself. The only hint of style was in the gathers around the waistband. But she was slim and self-assured, no, it was not confidence so much as pride, an awareness of her own identity.

She liked what she saw, the beginning of a person she felt she'd grown into over the years, tough years, through money worries and sickness, but she had endured, and, well, Vern had too, hadn't he? Surely he didn't see this in her then, her resilience and fortitude. It's unlikely that she even recognized it in herself, back then. This picture had been taken several months before the Smeets incident and before Willard disappeared from their lives for good. She was so keenly aware in this moment of how it all fit.

She would remember Willard in the years ahead exactly as he appeared here, standing with feet apart, hands at his sides, curled into loose fists. And suddenly an unbidden memory seeped in, a forgotten conversation she'd had with Ava sometime after her confrontation with Willard on road with the men. She couldn't rightfully place the conversation with Ava, but she knew it was shortly before she and Vernon were married.

"I don't like this man, Willard, who comes to help your father in the fields. He drinks too much," her mother had said.

"I know, Momma. I've told Vern I won't have it, and Vern must've talked to him, because Willard's keeping his distance. He's stopped coming around."

"He's stopped coming here too, and I'm glad."

If Ava knew about her encounter with Willard on the road to buy whiskey, she didn't acknowledge it. It's doubtful that Josie kept this from her or Whalen. But silence was Ava's way, and Darlene didn't want to get into the Willard incident with her mother right then. She'd have to listen to Ava's vitriolic pronouncements on what she viewed as a litany of sin—the drinking, especially on Sunday, the men behaving like animals, the wrath of God coming to visit their futures.

"Good," her mother had replied. Darlene was surprised by Ava's straightforwardness. Although she had shown strong feelings about Willard from the beginning, Ava had said something so unusual, Darlene had been taken back by it and puzzled by her lapse in recalling it until now.

"Why do men follow rascals like him?" Before Darlene could answer, Ava added, "I don't know why Whalen found him to help. I didn't like how it felt in the kitchen when he was around mooching a meal." Her mother slipped into Plattdeutsch, adding, *"Hee ess Klaum."* Darlene was shocked by the rightness of the description to express Willard's character. He *was* clammy. To her, the word suggested the moist and doughy-ness of rising bread, the flour sticky and clinging to one's hands with the first kneading. But Ava hadn't left it at that. She had turned and looked at Darlene directly, spitting out, *"De Beesa."* The evil one. "This man has a family, you've said to me?"

"He does, Momma. In fact, he's married and has a child with another one on the way."

"His wife's *pregnant?* Ah, and he liked especially when he was over here? What is this with Vernon? Is he sleeping? I don't like it. You watch your step around Vern's brother, my girl. He's up to no good. Never any good."

"I know," she'd told her mother quickly, seeing Ava's impatience with storms gathering in her eyes, lips and cheeks. "But why do you say this?"

"I recognize the devil when I see him. Willard doesn't bother with the sheep's clothing. Maybe that's because he wears them all the time. You tell me you don't see Satan in his eyes? Well, okay, you look at this as you need to, but I'll tell you once, this man likes being around people he can put under his thumb. Whalen's too smart for him but...."

"Vernon's not, is what you're trying to tell me, Momma?" Darlene had bristled and rushed to Vernon's defense.

"Vernon's a little innocent," her mother had said, gently. "He looks away from what he doesn't want to see. *Deist dü festone?*" Of course, she understood. She just didn't want to look at it more directly than she already had for fear of upsetting the equilibrium she had established with Vernon about his brother. And anyway, hadn't she taken care of the problem several Sundays ago, there on that road, showing all the men where she stood. Anything more from her would mean struggling with the man she was going to marry over the closest member of his family to him. She wanted Willard and the incident to remain silent, remote, away from them so that she and Vern could slip into their own life and slowly drift away from the whole Jantz clan.

With this memory, Darlene grasped with stunning clarity just how wise this series of conversations with her mother had been, and she had squandered it on denial and self-protection. But Ava had been modeling out this denial herself in her inability to look directly at Jesse and his self-indulgent irresponsibility with women, drinking, and his lack of dependability with Whalen in the farming.

We see what we will.

―

Though Darlene didn't think, at the time, Vernon knew his brother for what he was, through Vern's stories and descriptions of Willard's actions, she was able to piece together a picture of the man that corresponded with what she'd suspected him to be. She didn't totally agree with her mother's assessment, because Ava had given him that severe religious interpretation she used with so many people and situations in her life. It was true that her mother wasn't often as outspoken as she'd been the day they had talked about Willard, but it was easy for Darlene to disregard what Ava had pointed out because of who she was.

To Darlene, Willard was the sort of guy that liked to be alone, to himself, even though he put on a show of being the gregarious fellow to the people around him. Over the first few months of dating Vernon, she had noted that most of Willard's congeniality was manipulative, used to gain trustworthiness from others for his own wants and needs. It wasn't difficult to see, since he wasn't exactly deft at his moves. In fact, at times, he was so openly shifty and downright conniving, she had a hard time with Vernon's disregard for this. Sometimes she swore she could feel Willard's mean-spirited nature crawling on her skin, while he stood in front of her and Vern, covering up his real intentions with casual attitudes and sarcastic jokes. Some of his jokes could be quite witty. When he was light on his feet, he came close to being fun to be around. But he could also be coarse as sandpaper, and she never knew which of these two sides of him would show up.

But these insightful glimpses of Willard didn't concern her until they developed, during the following months, into an unlanced boil between her and her fiancé. They didn't out and out fight over Willard. They sparred. She would thrust—usually as carefully as she could—and Vern would parry. But after a while she began seething inwardly while Vernon simply ignored or didn't see her distress. At least, he wasn't with Willard as often since he took on more and more work at his father's automobile repair shop, and when he did see his brother, it was usually with others. But Vern let her know that his older brother was still a person of value to him. Willard was his family.

From first sight of him, Darlene knew Willard had a temper, a big one, with a short fuse. And after the food-throwing tantrums at the Jantz homeplace, she thought him capable of just about anything. Looking back, she wondered why it didn't worry her more, probably because he could mask his rage well when he had a mind to—although Darlene always sensed a threat underneath, especially toward her. Willard could wait for weeks, even months, to "get even", but when he did, his revenge came at a time and in a fashion which left no doubt he was settling a score.

Vern told her a story about Willard and a kid he had hired to help with the livestock. One of the kid's many duties every day was to bring a truck load of feed and 10-gallon milk cans to the pond, fill the cans and drive the water and feed out to the far pasture for the dairy cows. One summer morning the kid got caught up with feeding the pigs and forgot to bring the watering cans as Willard had asked him to do. He remembered the feed but forgot the empty cans. When the kid got out to the pond, Willard was waiting for him, and when Willard saw he had forgotten to put the cans on the truck, he tied the boy's wrists to the side of the pick-up—after slapping him around to bring him to compliance—and forced him to walk at driven speed a good deal of the forty-four acre field back to the barnyard gate. On the way, the kid fell and was dragged along side, so Willard stopped, helped the kid up on his feet again, then told him he could walk or be dragged, his choice. Of course, the kid had walked. Willard cut him loose back at the barn, kicked him in the ass and sent him, by foot, the two miles home without pay.

As Vernon's story went, the kid's father came calling that same night. Willard met him at the door, invited him in for supper, and when the man haughtily refused—aghast with the casual invitation extended to him in light of what Willard had done to his son—Willard went back to the kitchen table, picked up his bowl of ham hock and beans, telling his neighbor if he didn't want to come inside, that was fine, but Willard wanted to finish his supper while they talked. Once he reached the door with the full bowl of soup, he threw it at the guy full-face. Of course, a fight ensued, if it could be called that. The neighbor didn't have time to react in his own defense. According to Vernon, Willard threw the neighbor off the porch, pursued him into the yard and continued to beat the living daylights out of him, while yelling that the farmer and his son didn't—either together or alone—need to show up on his farm again.

So, the story went on, when Sheriff Kiff Reimer showed up at Willard's door the next day, Willard listened to the sheriff's allegations against him patiently, then he told Reimer that in all fairness, he felt his actions with the boy had been justified, as the kid had barely worked up to par even before the milk can problem, that he had tried to be accommodating, but he just couldn't see how this boy was going to ever work for anybody worth a damn if somebody didn't teach him a lesson somewhere along the line. Obviously, Willard had declared, it wasn't going to be the kid's father—anybody could see this from the old man's visit to his farm. The kid was a chip off of the old block, as far as Willard could see, but, what the hell, he could be neighbor-friendly about the whole thing, he guessed. And so, he'd handed the sheriff enough to pay for the kid's employment for that week and extra besides.

Reimer seemed satisfied with this arrangement and evidently the farmer and his son felt the same, as the farmer didn't show up on Willard's farm again nor did he send a negative response to him through the sheriff. To Vernon's mind that should have been the end to the matter.

"Would have been for me."

But the story still wasn't over. The next time Willard saw the neighbor on Main Street in Clearview, he offered the man a couple pints of Missouri whiskey from several bottles he carried around behind the seats of his truck. This offering seemed to heal the wound beyond doubt. When Darlene asked Vern how the boy felt about all of this, he said he didn't know.

"Hell, he's a kid," Vern explained, in a tone too near that of his brother's. "He was high school age. Old enough for him to learned how the world worked."

Darlene asked Vernon where he thought Willard's belligerence came from.

"Willard felt belittled by Reuben when he was growing up," he told her. "He felt ashamed of his size. Reuben was tall and skinny but really strong. He could push himself on others when he wanted to, though he didn't do that much, since he was quiet-natured. But Willard, from the very start, was bent on taking offense, and so occasionally, Reuben obliged him with a fist fight or two.

Didn't last very long, because Willard was no match for the likes of Reuben." Vernon shrugged. "Way of the world."

Darlene was too careful in the days of their courtship to ask Vernon if he saw the parallel between himself and Willard. Willard called him "Shorty" and treated him pretty much as Willard had been treated by Reuben. Very early in her and Vern's relationship, Darlene recognized the pecking order among the Jantz men—actually, the entire Jantz household. So she knew any mention of this to Vern would be a mistake, as he was at the bottom of that order.

None of Willard's behaviors caused Darlene too much thought or trouble, especially once she'd put him in his place. His presence was an annoyance, and, although he put her on guard through his stares and sneers, she found it easy enough to ignore him.

—

Table arrangements at the Jantz homestead were permanent. Vernon's initial seating had been given to him by Hannah when he was old enough to sit at the "big table." Now that she and Vernon were married, Darlene knew they would be seated at their assigned places at this table every visit. She disliked sitting across from Willard and his family, because when she looked up, she too often found him staring at her. She'd talked to Vernon about choosing another place to sit—without mentioning Willard's stares—but he found the idea almost funny.

Why? Was she looking for trouble? It wasn't so much to ask a couple of times a month was it, to just go along for once?

So like so many other times, she remained silent. She longed to sit on the same side of the table as Willard, down the row from him, so he couldn't see her without leaning forward or back in his seat. In her young mind, she had thought others would notice his attentions and with their comments or asides would put a stop to it.

What was she thinking?

Nobody was going to comment on Willard's behavior, openly or in private. But her confrontation with him on the road had given her courage. She was close to speaking out directly to him in front of them all. But she decided to ease into a possible change.

She began by telling Vern she was tired of Willard's stares. Vern had shrugged and told her, first, that he hadn't noticed it that much, and secondly, he thought she was overly sensitive because of 'that trouble she'd had on the road with him' which had long been forgotten by everybody but her. And even if Willard's staring at her were true, even if he was trying to raise her hackles a little, she had one of two choices—she could either ignore him or she could put up with more of the same, because Willard wasn't likely to stop until she showed it didn't matter to her.

"It's how he operates," Vern said with a shrug.

So the seating arrangement drove her secretly to misery until one Sunday—the second Sunday after the confrontation with Willard on the road—she simply let go of it by explaining to herself that chairs at the table were probably assigned in the Jantz household from the time the Jantz kids were old enough to eat at the main table, around twelve. Probably seating was looked on as a time and place of passage into the adult world, so it was sacrosanct in the family. In any case, this explanation made sense to her, so she ceased to struggle against it. She was exhausted with the worry and far too busy to care any longer.

As the early weeks of the 1936 summer of her and Vern's engagement slipped by, they fell into their routines—she helping her mother and father with harvest, canning and getting ready for fall and winter on the farm, and Vernon working as a full-time mechanic in his father's automobile business, phasing out his extra work with his brother on the farms.

During the first summer Darlene had known Vernon, temperatures were some of the hottest on record in Oklahoma so that watering tanks and troughs for farm animals had to be filled by hand from any ponds large enough to hold water or pumped by mills into tanks from aquifers—the streams had long gone dry. The Dust Bowl was continuing its unrelenting drive through the No Man's Lands of the Oklahoma and Texas panhandles into the interior of the state—the location of the Jantzes' and Dirks' farms—and on up into the Midwest.

Vernon had taken time after work to help his brother with the watering of the animals at the Jantz homeplace and on Willard's farm for three days in mid-July when temperatures had reached 110° to 113°. They carried the last of what was left in the pond, and finally what they pumped from windmill-filled galvanized tanks to the barn where cows lay in stalls, some moaning softly in the daytime heat.

Off and on throughout the summer months, Vernon called to tell Darlene that he would go directly home as his work with his brother would run far into the night. He was too exhausted for anything but sleep, especially since he had to rise within three or four hours to begin his next days at the farms and the shop. She had spent much of her time, pumping water into buckets for the chickens, while keeping towels wet that hung over windows to block the sweltering heat and dust from entering the house. Nighttime temperatures fell into the seventies which made house work, ironing, cooking and baking more bearable. Simpler tasks such as sewing and cleaning were usually done during the daylight hours.

———

So it wasn't unusual one evening in mid-July, far past her normal end-of-the-day hours, for her to stay up to clean the kitchen floor before bedtime. She was hoping that by doing this last task, she could sleep in an extra hour the following morning. The day had been tremendously hot, the house a seething, fetid cauldron, especially in the kitchen where she'd been most of the afternoon. When she walked outside, the cooler, steady breeze striking her face felt refreshing, almost a hopeful promise of a good night's sleep. As she carried the bucket of dirty soapy water past the cistern, the high branches of the cedars swayed with small screeches and scrapings in the wind. When she turned the corner into the dark shadows of the back side of the smoke house, she flung the water from the bucket as hard as she could, hearing the soft slushing sound when it hit the dry grass.

It was then that his shoulder slammed her into the wall, the bucket catapulting into the air to the side and front of her, his hands slipping down the sides of her arms, pinning them to her back, a cloth tying her wrists. She attempted to stand, to call out, but her shoulder kept sliding down against the siding of the shed, his strong legs finally pinning her motionless, her knees to hard ground. It was all she could do to concentrate on remaining upright. She knew instinctively she didn't want to fall flat against the earth. While on her knees, a bandana was suddenly around her eyes, knotted with two rapid jerks. Then she was lifted up, like a child, from under her armpits. And before she could gain balance to kick or shove, he had turned her to face him, pushing her into the shed wall, grabbing her by the throat, his strong, stubby fingers tightening the small stream of air sluicing fluid through the hollow chamber of her mouth. His lips were suddenly twisting, screwing hers by mouthfuls, and then he loomed in front of her, close enough for their lips to be intermittently touching. She knew instantly it was Willard from the taste of his mouth, his sweaty, boozy smell, the sound of his gritting teeth, the feel of his unshaven cheek against her face. "Now, bitch, you're gonna know a man for once in your life," he spit in her ear.

She attempted to move, but her shoes were caught in the brittle brambles and vines running along the base of the shed. His body was pressed so hard against hers, she couldn't twist or turn. Spittle fell from her lower lip, and she heard a sound slipping from her throat, passing her ears as a terrifyingly ordinary cry, almost a coo at the soft end of a baby's sigh. The one that followed was a raw, guttural rush of air coming after a blow against her chest with his fist, but the sound was his, not hers, a sound similar to many she remembered herself making during sex with Vern. With his free hand, he lifted her dress, tore her panties away, nearly bringing her down again to her knees, but he righted her with his shoulder and with his fingers spread her opening, the palm of his hand cupping her mound, his fingers sliding hard inside her, with smearing motions from his wrist. Then he began forcing two, three fingers in and out of her vagina, pressing her so hard against the wall, she thought he might break her back or arms. His body was thick, heavy, despite his stature, a man barely half-a-head taller than she was, but concrete, so much more compact than Vern. He was impenetrable, solid, with a head moving, twisting, as though connected to a wall by a swivel joint, his face worming its way into the crease at the base of her neck while his fingers jabbed, stabbed, tore her apart.

When he entered her, he yanked off the bandana from her eyes and stared at her straight on, his tiny, leering eyes finding hers in the moonlight, locking her to him, while her body convulsed in pulsing rhythm to his. She felt herself sliding down, away from him, but he claimed her by thrusts stumbling onto one another so violently she had no chance to resist. In that moment, she knew she was going to die. He would kill her while in the act of sex itself or once the momentum of it stopped, death would come in a smothering embrace of those fingers, tightening ever so slightly, on her throat—they hadn't moved since he began—until she would melt into the numbness beginning to enfold her. She had lost all feeling in her limbs and genitals, her legs shaking so uncontrollably, she knew she would not be standing if Willard's thrusts weren't pinning her upright. He was growing darker before her, not emerging with the night sky, but with her own blackness, her consciousness on the edge of leaving her lifeless, gone. She was falling, giving up and in to the vastness into which he was carrying her. He was fucking her so hard she couldn't breathe, though surely she still was, because she felt the pounding of her heart against his trunk and heard the small air spasms rising and falling out of her in syncopation with his. The hand holding her throat finally slipped down to cover a breast, allowing her to grab air from her chest. He was rutting, heaving an animal's yearning of ecstasy and despair, sounds erupting from his throat so base, yet otherworldly, she thought it might be echoes of some experience emanating from another time and place by people she didn't know. She was floating, falling, trancing, dying. She couldn't let him kill her while he was taking her. She couldn't let the smell of his whiskey and defiance be the last thing she'd ever know.

His attack had been so swift and unexpected she had barely registered friction with his penetration, but now her interior canal began expanding and exploding as though a torch had been thrown into the center of her being. With his climax approaching, he pushed his head once again into the warm shallow of her neck, and it was then, with a slow, incremental shifting of her head, a lifetime in the pulse of one heartbeat, that her mouth found his ear and in a singular jerking movement, she brought her teeth down while pulling her head backward as far as she could. Like a lioness seeking to feed her cubs, she tore raw flesh from the body of her prey—gristle, dripping blood, hanging from her jaws.

She felt him slide out of her, screaming through his teeth, a release so complete that, at first, she thought he had disemboweled her. But she knew now that she was going to live to give birth to her children—hers and Vern's children, all four of them in Vern's vision—and Willard would bear the scars forever for what he had done to her. She spit what she had taken from him into the grass and began to run, swaying back and forth, hands slipping up and down against her buttocks until they were out of their bond, flopping at her sides, and she was back inside the house to her freedom.

—

Nobody was up. The house was as dark as the shadows she had left behind the shed. In the kitchen as she walked toward the dry sink, in the moonlight from the window, she saw the pitcher glistening with water and soap waiting in its dish for the morning wash-up of her father and mother upon rising. She heard a distant starting of an engine, what she knew to be Willard's truck coming from the barnyard, then a lazy, near-silent drifting of the motor as she heard him drive out through the field toward the gate leading to the main road.

She thought in passing that had Whalen kept a dog or two on the property, all that just happened might not have happened. But after Max had died, only a few weeks ago, her father'd decided against getting any more dogs until the dire water and feed situation changed with a restoration of normal weather patterns and the family income improved.

Upon entering the back mud-room, she untied her shoes and carried them to the kitchen counter. There, she lifted her dress over her head, then her slip, dropping them to the floor and began washing herself slowly in careful ritual, using the washcloth as a sponge, until she sensed the smell of him leave her body, her mother's homemade lye soap on her skin. Standing naked, she pumped water over her shoes, scrubbing them clean, then the sink.

As she washed herself and her shoes, she came up with a plan.

She couldn't let what happened to her be known, not even to Josephine, not ever. *Never. Never.* She wondered if Willard was now a dangerous man, perhaps even more dangerous than before. But with his injury especially, she was almost certain he wouldn't risk anybody finding out what had happened any more than she would. He was married, had one child and Mary was near end of term for their second. He was working his father's land, and his own, and had a working relationship with Whalen. Although he'd loaned equipment to her dad after Whalen had lost his to the bank five years earlier, and although Whalen had paid Willard back in a work exchange, they were still on very good terms, seeing each other often, even though Willard had been keeping his distance from her since her confrontation with him several weeks before. When he was at the farm, he didn't come to the house as he used to do. However, he was still seeing Vernon daily as they worked the farms together. What they talked about she, of course, couldn't know, but she detected no signs in Vern that Willard was attempting to win Vernon to his side, against her.

So, she reasoned, Willard could be more frightened of her, than she of him, fearing his working situations could be in jeopardy should she decide to talk. Knowing him the way she thought she did, he would watch closely—especially Vernon—seeking out any clues about how she was reacting to his assault. If she remained silent and calm, she felt he could very well disappear. Since the Smeets incident, Vernon and Willard had reconciled enough for them to share drinks with each other outside the house on Sundays, and Vern had been going to help Willard in his emergencies, but they were not as close as they had been before her confrontation with Willard and the demands she had put on Vernon's drinking.

Lord in heaven, she knew she did not want to put Vern to the test concerning his loyalties to her and to his brother by telling him what had happened. She shuddered to think what Vernon might feel he was obligated to do to protect his manhood. It was one thing to stop his brother from hitting her during a challenge on a country road. It was another for her to accuse him of sexual assault and expect Vernon to retaliate appropriately. He could never take Willard in a fair fight, so his revenge would undoubtedly be covert and murderous. He wasn't the sort of man who would confront Willard with her accusations. He didn't possess the courage to find truth through such direct means.

But then, the opposite could also be true. She played with a scenario in which Vern wouldn't believe her, deny the bruises to be anything but an accident in the house or barn, and blame her for using such a thing to rid their lives of Willard, which could only end in Vern and her breaking up. She couldn't handle the emotional trail that would follow if he accused her of lying—his apologies, his vows of her trustworthiness, his urges to reconcile, his pledges to give his family up, at least his older brother, which might or might not hold over time.

No, the thing to do was to remain silent—utterly, unconditionally silent.

After she was finished at the sink, Darlene wrapped herself in a large dish towel, wadded her clothing under her arm and walked to the stairs to go to her bedroom which was on the other side of the hallway. She doubted that her parents would hear her. It wouldn't matter if they did, as she often was late coming home from times out with Vern.

Before she'd left the kitchen, she'd thought about walking back to the smoke house to retrieve her underwear, but she decided not to bother. Now that she had cleaned the kitchen floor, it wasn't likely anybody would go back there any time soon. She'd look for her panties first chance she had later.

But that chance didn't come for a while. Because of the bruising, she stayed in bed for a couple of days from what, she told her parents and Vernon, was severe "stomach troubles," often a euphemism women used for menstrual discomfort, a condition she'd had with heavy flow since her period began.

The bruises around her neck were her greatest concern, but she covered them with make-up cream and wrapped a scarf loosely around her neck, a scarf she often wore to hold her hair out of her eyes. The bruises were dark, gangrenous-looking, ugly, turning from purple to green and yellow. She was sore for weeks, finding the turning of her head, walking and urinating to be painful. It was as though she had slept in a position that wouldn't right itself during her waking hours. Moving normally was difficult, especially with the bruising on the side of her body that had been pressed against the smoke house wall.

But she worked at the cover-up, especially with her face, delicately applying cosmetics to make the bruises less detectable within days—far less damage showing, considering how long he had kept her in the stranglehold. She did have cut marks on her legs from her entanglement in the dry brambles and vine along the foundation of the smoke house. But nobody seemed to notice her cut marks as these healed rapidly with applications of Pond's vanishing cream. She, Ava, and Josie often had marks and bruises on their legs from work in the fields, gardens and yards.

One day when no one was in the house—her mother in her garden, her father in the barn or field—she left her room and the house to look for her panties in the grass behind the smoke house. She was surprised to discover only a few scuffle marks left from Willard's attack, mainly along the short broken bushes and vines where he had held her. But she was even more surprised to discover—despite a thorough search for over twenty minutes in and around the area, including the barrel where she and Ava often burned trash—her panties were simply nowhere to be found. Nor were the bandanas Willard had used to tie her wrists and to cover her eyes.

She'd thought a lot about why he'd covered her eyes, especially the way he had. She'd come to the conclusion that this had initially left her more disoriented than the surprise attack. And his ripping the bandana off as he began the sex act was his brutish attempt at making her feel exposed and vulnerable. She knew Willard too well by then to suspect he was attempting to hide his identity. She knew he had planned the whole encounter, every move and why. He had used the bandana as a way of letting her know who was teaching her the lesson of keeping to her place and of her realization he had dominance over her in any unguarded moment.

She did find the water bucket and carried it clanging softly at her side back to the house, placing it quietly, without notice, in the mudroom.

Vernon was not easily put off. He couldn't understand why she was withdrawing, why she didn't want to leave her room, let alone the house, her especially not wanting to be touched or kissed. Vern wasn't an openly demonstrative person, but in privacy, despite her "illness," it seemed to him, he should be able to kiss her on the cheek and sit on the bed next to her while they talked. As the days stretched into a week of recovery, he began commenting on her "getting cold feet" about their marriage plans. The more he protested against waiting, the more she felt the need to do as he suggested.

Thinking on it now, she realized that she'd wanted the protection, the cover that being married could bring her, however illusory that might have been. Vernon certainly couldn't save her from every unguarded moment. But, even at the time, she had small worries about this. Willard had made his point. It was a matter after that of how they each would respond to that point. No, at least part of the protection she sought was against exposure. Being married, she reasoned, however irrationally, nobody could imagine such a thing happening to her. It was inconceivable, so she felt her secret was safe.

As she stared at the photograph, she realized she had never used the word "rape," not even in her mind. She called it "the act," when she thought about it, and it had been years since it had fully entered her consciousness. With the talks with Caroline, she understood that this long suppressed memory had become a deeply embodied feeling at the sight, thought or mention of Willard. He didn't represent the "reprehensible deed," so much as he was "it." He was, from that moment on, her mother's *de Beesa*, evil incarnate—Satan, the devil—not just the *man* who had committed the evil act, a person who sometimes acted wrongly, insanely—that was Vernon's view of his brother, that's when Vern mentioned Willard's bad behavior at all, usually having to do with Willard's need to fight and drink. But for her, Willard had morphed into a *pure evil* in the world she'd never known before. And what she wanted most from Vernon, back then, wasn't a shield to protect her—nothing could protect her from that kind of evil. She wanted his comfort while she was buried in an avalanche of numbing cold. Marriage to him could offer her a future, a life-plan with real meaning to offset the haunting bleakness of this memory, but he could never save her from what Willard was. To this, she would feel vulnerable for a lifetime.

And when World War II descended upon them, when she saw the approaching apprehension of people everywhere as the armies of darkness gathered to rape the unguarded and unaware, she understood the force of *de Beesa* and what it could mean in every person's ordinary life. It terrified her, feeling like cold, thin blood in her veins.

Willard's photographed image.

There he was, five years short of half a century from that night behind the smoke house, a devil-man who lived on in her family album even as he lay desiccating in his earthly grave. She wondered if her underwear had been his trophy. It sickened her to think of him possessing her panties, even if he had taken them only to stanch the blood of his partially severed ear. When she lay "sick" in her bed, waiting for her bruises to heal, she imaged them, over and over, being thrown from his truck window back into the night from which they had been stolen from her.

—

One night, after she'd been in bed for a week, Vernon came into her bedroom to visit. He was dressed neatly in carefully pressed khakis and a white shirt despite the heat of the early morning. She noticed small sweat marks around his armpits and a light sheen on his forehead. The summer had seen no rain. The drought wasn't breaking. Darlene wanted to invite him to come closer to her, to sit on the bed, but she needed withdrawal, not just from any notice he might have of her bruises, but from him, from touching of any sort, even though she needed comforting. He stood waiting for a cue. She finally motioned for him to sit in the chair by the bed, but he walked over to her, bent down and kissed her on her forehead. When she didn't respond encouragingly, he took his seat in the chair by the bed and waited. It seemed to her that this was Vernon's whole personality, encapsulated in this one behavior—waiting, always waiting.

He looked at her expectantly and finally said, "How are you?" He took off his hat and placed it over his knee.

Just like that—as though she was anybody he'd meet on the street and was saying 'good day' to. This was his family in him that she wished so often wasn't there.

"Better," she said, without affect. Working to keep the sarcasm out of her voice, she said, "And how are you?"

"Well, I'm not sure." He sighed. "I can't get much done with Willard on the blink as well. He's working, but he's not his whole self yet. Works been heavy at the shop, and now I'm being called on to—"

"Willard's been on the blink? What does that mean?"

"Oh, his dog bit part of his ear off, if you can believe that. In some kind of a tussle with the new German shepherd pup he brought home for the girl. You know how collies are."

She waited. When he didn't continue, she said with exasperation, "For the love of God Almighty, Vernon, just spit it out. I don't know what the heck you're talking about."

"Collies are jealous-natured—"

She burst out in frustration, "I don't mean about collies' natures, Vernon. I mean what actually happened. The *dog* bit Willard's ear off, you're telling me?"

"Yeah, that's what he says. When he went to reach down and show some attention to the pup, Jinks gave an aggressive growl and bit at his ear, grabbing the top and taking it right off."

"Good God," is all she could get out.

So this was the story Willard was going to tell. She felt relief flood through her, together with a sudden quiver erupting from her belly into her throat, and then she was laughing, a high-pitched wail that hung in the air like some weird sound track from a horror movie. She could almost see the sound, her sound, traveling across her bed and hitting the wall.

"It's not funny, Darlene. He shot Jinks, he tells me, saying he can't have a dog doing that outta nowhere."

Her laughter dropped mid-air. *"He shot Jinks?"*

Killed her, shot through her mind. Darlene felt like she was in some surreal dream-play, watching herself say lines, sitting up in bed, while Vernon sat watching from the audience. "When?" She was desperately attempting to follow a sequence from the back of the smoke house to Willard's dog pens. What she saw came far too easily.

"Says it happened when he went out to the dog pens to check on the new pup after he got home late one night last week. He had extra work with his cattle. Julia heard the gunshot and came tearing out the door to see what was going on. Willard told me that she'd shaken for half-an-hour thinking he'd been shot by somebody robbing the place or maybe him taking his own life. Enough people had been mentioned lately in the newspapers about killing themselves, is what Julia'd told him when she gathered herself. In a half-sleep, she thought that might be what was going on with him, I guess. He must've looked a fright to her, blood all over his shirt and the side of his head, holding the rifle in his hand in the middle of the night like that."

Darlene turned her head so he couldn't see the shock and terror in her eyes or what disturbance might be showing there.

"I know. It's not the best thing to hear when you're feeling like you are. I probably shoulda waited even longer to tell ya. I've put it off, not wanting to upset you—right now."

"No, no." She turned back to look at him. "It's hard for me to think that of Jinks. She was such a great dog. I always liked her. He even brought her along sometimes to play with Max when Willard came late to… check on the equipment and such."

"Animals are unpredictable. You never know what can set them off."

"Well, I guess," was all she could squeak out.

Willard had killed his dog to cover what she'd done to him. It was hard not to see this as a message he was sending to her—two messages, really. First, that he wasn't going to reveal what actually happened, well, of course he wasn't. That hardly needed to be confirmed now, did it? The whole incident put him in great jeopardy, as she'd thought before, because it relied on her silence. Nobody would sympathize with what he'd done, regardless of the twist he tried to give it. What could he say? That she'd lured him to it or that his wife was pregnant, and he hadn't had sex in ever so long and that Darlene had been tempting? After her confrontational encounter with him on the road to Smeets's, it was a story that wouldn't be believed. There just weren't any ways he could justify what happened that would make it look good for him with his family, with Vernon, with her family. How could he explain her injuries, if she retaliated and used them in her own defense against such accusations? But the second message overshadowed the first by far. If she didn't keep silence, as he was going to do, she was as dead as the dog.

"How bad was it?" she asked, curiosity creeping in despite herself. She drew her hands under the sheet to keep from touching her jaw which had been tender from the clenching, so tender it hurt, at first, for her to chew her food.

"His ear? Good part of the top of it, but coulda been worse, if Jinks'd gotten a hold of the whole thing or Willard's throat, for that matter. That's probably what she was aiming for. With dogs, it's pure instinct, and it's always for the kill. They don't reason out anything. They just do it."

"Poor Jinks," she whispered.

She felt like crying, something she hadn't done yet over this hideous thing that'd happened to her. She'd not shed one tear. She simply felt weary. Like the dog, maybe she was fated, she thought, from the day she was born to receive this burden over which she'd had no control. But since she'd spent days in this bed, going over and over every detail of the act, she couldn't help but feel she'd had a hand in it, regardless of how wrong what he did to her was. She had *known* Willard's nature. She knew he had blood in his eyes, rage in his veins, heat in his brain, and she'd shown him for the bully he was to all the men on the road to Smeets's that day. And they'd turned their backs on him, including Vernon, by leaving him standing there, choosing *their* lives, *their* homes and *their* women over him and his desires. And she'd felt exhilaration over her triumph. She thought she'd been saving her man for a better marriage in the future, but look now what it had gotten her.

She didn't know how she was going to be the person everybody wanted her to be—Vernon, her family and his—but she would begin by setting her life straight by marrying Vernon as she was supposed to and beginning their family together.

In her bedroom that day, she laid out the plan to Vernon that had come to her, in vague snatches, at the sink a week ago. If he wanted to marry her so badly, well then, they would do that and maybe then he'd see she wasn't putting him off. He would only have to wait, recouping a little while longer, until she was back to her old self.

She wanted him to take her driver's license—and his own too, of course—go to the Wellington, Kansas, courthouse, apply for a marriage license, talk to a judge about performing a ceremony on the day they picked up the license, and get a commitment to a time and place. It would take him an afternoon from his work at the shop, but he could come up with an excuse for leaving.

She convinced him that taking the chance on getting a license in Hopewell wasn't smart, at least not for her. Her Aunt Deana worked in the state clerk's office. She wasn't certain if her aunt worked close to where application for marriage licenses were taken or not, but she wasn't going to take that risk. She wanted this to be an elopement, their marriage to stay a secret until she could talk to her mother under the right circumstances.

Since it would take three days for their application to be processed, she would, in the meantime, get everybody together—Sherman, Nita Jane, Josie and Clifford and Jesse, if he was around and found a girl he wanted to take along—for a day trip to Kansas when the license was available. They wouldn't tell anybody, of course, that would be a sure way for Ava to find out, through Josie, if not Jesse. The trip would simply be a day away from work and the heat of the kitchen and the fields. Since it was a two-hour drive, they could have a few drinks from the whiskey they'd take along, eat some place, and see a movie, and still be home before sunset, so that Josie and Clifford could get their two boys from Ava before it got too late, and nobody would be the wiser.

At least, her mother wouldn't be alerted this way. Ava had been adamant that her only other daughter get married in church properly, since Josephine had been married at the Hopewell courthouse, for which Ava had cried and cried, complaining for weeks.

Vernon was ecstatic that she was deciding to marry him sooner rather than later. And so, Darlene thought now, not without a good deal of sarcasm, it had happened as stated so often in the Scriptures—"and it came to pass". They hadn't let anybody know at the time, but when they got to Wellington, they'd run around the corner to the courthouse and had it all done in less than half an hour while the others sat eating ice cream at the drugstore. Not one soul questioned why they wanted "some time to themselves."

Darlene took the picture she was holding and tore Willard out of it, laying the partial photograph on the table while she literally shredded this dreadful man to pieces. For a moment it came to her that if she placed her and Vernon back together in the album, without Willard, this might absolve the years of mismatch, as if it would make the drive to Wellington a drive to another state-of-mind and into another life, one away from them all—her family and his, just to be themselves, alone, starting their life as she'd hoped in the beginning. But in talking with Caroline as she'd done only this afternoon, she realized that that dream had been hopeless from the start. The mismatch was real, because they were two people caught in circumstances that, had they even been otherwise, could never have been mated forever.

She looked at the part of the photo of her and Vern for a long while, and with a sigh, tore Vernon away from her, placing him in her pocket, out of sight. Then she stood studying herself, holding her oh-so-very-young person between her index finger and thumb. Finally she put herself in the other pocket and decided to wait for some sign as to what to do with these pictures of each of them. Perhaps she would leave them in her apron pockets until they grew old, shriveling into hardly-recognizable remnants of themselves, vestiges of how they were back then that only memory would reconstruct from time to time from what she would be given to gaze upon.

SNAPSHOTS

of

TIMOTHY

1.

Vernon

Tape recording to Caroline—August, 1982

"I don't think I've told you this. Well, hell, I know I haven't, because I've not told anybody—outside of the people in here. As hard as it is to admit, Caroline, I'm lonely. So there, now I've said it. Lord knows, I've had enough practice in detox saying it. Dr. Hyatt, who's my personal psychologist, well, he thinks I should say this to you on the telephone, even though the calls we can make or receive in here are limited. But I told him I wanted to tell you in a letter I'm taping to you, like this. Hyatt and I talked quite a lot about what I might say to answer the questions you're asking me and your mother, while you're in therapy yourself. Could be he's talked to your therapist—he hasn't said, and I haven't asked. I did give him her name and number as you suggested I could do.

"The whole thing's simply ridiculous—how it's bothering me so much to say I'm lonely, I mean. But I've been practicing saying it, in my room, like a child in front of a buncha classmates, for godssakes. We've talked about it in therapy, a-course—Dr. Hyatt and me and in group—but to say it out loud to you, well, that's something else, isn't it? God forbid I'd ever admit such a thing to the boys.

"I know where it comes from. By now, I do. When your mother left me like she did, I experienced the greatest loneliness I think I've ever known. And that's kinda strange, in a way, because I've always thought of myself as being a loner. I'm a to-myself kinda person. I'm sure you've felt that, as the boys must've too. God knows Darlene let me know often enough she did. Toward the end there, she'd say, 'Why does it matter if I stay here anymore, Vernon?

You don't need me. I leave, you'll go right on living just like you always have.' Well, I showed her, didn't I? Nothing like going to pieces to prove her wrong! A-course, she was right, and my drinking myself into trouble didn't make any point except to land me in court with my license suspended indefinitely and my pick-up in the junkyard with me going home to an empty house.

"Well, her leaving woulda happened in any case, I know that now, but it doesn't make me feel any better that I was thrown into detox while she was moving the last of her things outta the house to her own place. She'd been gone for a while by then, as you know, but I figured as long as some of her belongings were still in the house, I had the hope that she might change her mind and come back.

"But the truth is, if I woulda had my way—and what your mother knew about me all along—I probably woulda lived up in the hills somewhere hard to get to, and only come down into town to get supplies once or twice a year like some prospector in one of those black-and-white movies we used to go see, your mother and me—well, anyway, the ones I wanted to see. Your mother liked those screwball romantic pictures. More often than not we'd compromise on some murder mystery. And if we could find one that had some courting in it, that interested Darlene. So we'd look for those. They weren't as easy to find as you'd think, not until Bogart and Bacall came along. But their movies were around too late for us, not while we were still going to the pictures.

"Once we joined the church—had you kids—our movie-going days were over. Mennonites don't go to the movies unless they sneak to do it, which you did, when you were old enough. Can't say I blame you. I saw all of the Bogart and Bacall pictures after we left the church. Re-runs on television. I thought they were good. I like Bogart. *African Queen* is still one of my favorites, and Darlene's, too, if she told you the truth. Kat's named after Katharine Hepburn, but you know that. I think it was Darlene's way of getting back for all those times we gave up the movies for the church. I really do.

"Well, anyhow, as you can see, I've strayed off the mark. I was telling you how I felt deep-down like one of those hermit characters your mother and me saw in the movies. I see myself like that a lot, or I should say I used to, that's before Dr. Hyatt and this program got ahold of me. I'm looking at a lotta things different now, especially how I think I am, when clearly I'm behaving in a way that doesn't fit with the notions I have about myself.

"Hyatt talked to me about what he called my 'self-perception,' and how that got messed up, especially while I was growing up. He said mine is 'misaligned.' In other words, my views about myself and how I act aren't coming together very truthfully.

"He thinks it's mainly because I haven't thought about myself and other people in a studied way very much, probably not ever, until now—not intentionally anyway. So I'm gonna work at being more honest from now on, about how my thoughts and actions fit together. I've learned I can't drink myself into a stupor and still think I'm a responsible person. Lots of misalignments like that need my attention. Enough to keep me busy for a while, I would think. *(soft laughter)*

"So what your mother said to me is right in that I think sometimes I coulda enjoyed being by myself living on a little acreage, making a garden, canning, raising a goat, a cow, maybe having a dog. I see that way of life as coming natural to me, sorta like making yourself outta nothing, since nobody else is there to give you a hand. Hyatt agreed, said I tended to be 'reclusive,' feeling more comfortable keeping away from others. Course, while I'm telling you this, I know I'm really saying it from the comfort of the life I've had with Darlene and you children, so it's easy to look on my being by myself as something I really wanted back then, when I know better. I didn't really want any such thing. I wanted what you all have given me. That's the real truth of it, and it's why I'm lonely now. Because that life is *gone,* and I'm feeling that beyond measure—since I've had it, especially for so long, and it isn't gonna be there anymore, you see?

"Who knows if our lives woulda turned out the way they did if just one or two turns here or there had been different.

"So living hermit-like sounds easier when I imagine it, is all I'm saying. If I've learned anything while I've been in here, it's that I've used drinking—at least, since your mother left me—to escape what I'm gonna be facing up to when I enter that house by myself.

"Having said all this, Caroline, no way do I want sympathy about it. I'm just answering your question in your last letter when you asked me how I was thinking about going back home without Darlene there, after getting clean.

"Well, I'm about to find out, don't you think?"

2.
Evening, the same day

"After listening to what I've taped to you so far, Caroline, the first thought I'm having is—who knows anything really about yourself? I've found out more in here than maybe I'd like to.

"By the way, they're getting ready to release me. Your mother's coming tomorrow to get me and take me home. I told her I wasn't crippled, that I could find my own way, but then she reminded me the ambulance brought me here, and I don't have my truck anymore, so I guess, I can let her do that for me.

"I'm feeling fine, Caroline. Hate like hell to admit it, but I'm feeling better than I have in a good long while. I've sorta gotten used to everybody here, though, being around all the time, so it will be an adjustment when I get back home, not having somebody bumping into me at every turn.

"Dr. Hyatt, the other doctors, the nurses and their assistants have already started in on that big time. They're saying the major concern after you get yourself clean is going back into the situation that was part of the drinking. But I'm not worried so much about that—the temptation to drink, I mean. I can't say I'm cured, that's not how I'm looking at this. I'm just saying I want to live different than before, and the most important part is learning how to be by myself without a crutch, well, and without your mother. It's the missing her that's upsetting to me, doing all the things that you call a life together. But it's finally got through to me how drinking isn't going to make anything better, and it's certainly not going to squash the loneliness. I finally got it in my head that drinking means to be unconscious all the time, and that's not living, is it?

"I had this idea that I couldn't make it without my family, so the drinking would get me through. I felt my life had come down to nothing, that I'd lost everything, everything I'd worked so hard for. But a-course, that's not so, at least not absolutely so. I have you children still, and Darlene hasn't run out the door forever and ever. We'll still see each other, and I'm starting to realize I can do some things in my life I wasn't able to do with her living with me. I have all kinds of freedoms I didn't have when she was there all the time. I can live without hassle, something I've wanted to do all my life. Now I get to see how that feels straight on. If it gets scary, I have some places I can call, including Dr. Hyatt, at least for a little while. I guess we'll just have to find out what kind of nerve I have, huh?

"It's gonna be interesting to see if I lift my arm, pick up the receiver, and call people like I never used to do. I've been practicing a little. I've called Teddy, though I haven't had the guts yet to call you, as you well know. But I'll surprise you one of these days. You haven't done anything to make me afraid of you. It's just my first nature to be fearful.

"In your last letter, you also asked me questions about Timothy, why I thought he left home, why he hasn't called or written, and what I think his problems are about that. First off, Caroline, I'm in a little different position than the rest of you, since Timothy confided in me before he left. I'm not sure that's exactly what he did, but he spent some time with me that I think he saw as a way to let me know he didn't intend to abandon his family. He just needed to separate from us for a while. How he let me know this is still a great mystery to me, but since it has to do with what you've asked me about him, I'll try to let you in on what I think he was trying to tell me.

"I realize my telling you he spent time with me like this might put you off. It's true I've withheld telling you, and the others, until now. But I gave him my word, and I'll not break that with any of you kids until I feel I have to. He's also called me since he's got himself situated—well, I say this, but I really don't know how situated he is. He just sounded that way to me.

"He said he didn't want to talk to anybody else yet, but to tell you he's safe, that he has friends. But he didn't tell me where he's living, and I decided not to pressure him on this point. He didn't mention a job. I figure he'll tell us what he wants to, when he's ready.

"It's how he is.

"We talked for about ten, fifteen minutes, I'd say. This was only days before I had my accident and then went from the hospital into detox, so I haven't had much of an opportunity, really, to let you know—anyway, not without a lot of explanation, and I couldn't do that very well while I was in here. He did tell me that when he gets ready to 'come back home,' as he put it, he'll call.

"So we have that assurance.

"I was relieved that, at least, he's got returning to us in mind, as part of his future, if nothing else but to visit. And it does say, seems to me, that he's not gonna keep himself a secret forever.

"Of all people, you should understand this, Caroline.

"You did it yourself when you were in high school, remember that? Taking off without contacting your mother, pretty much just like Timothy has done, actually. Calling me at work when you felt like you needed to and such. Well, far as I'm concerned, it says loads about how we functioned as a family while you kids were growing up. Not one of you decided to stay close by, except Timothy in Oklahoma City, when he lived there. But we hardly ever heard from him. He could just as easily have been where he is now, for all we knew. He did give me a telephone number a long time ago, telling me it was only for me, nobody else and requesting I be 'discreet,' if I ever decided to use it. He put great stress on these conditions. Well, I never did call, a-course, and I knew better'n ever let Darlene know I had his number.

"So, hell, what is that? *He* called us when he decided to, and it was years he lived in the City like that. Silence is mostly what we got.

"And the rest of you all took off as soon as you could and are living just about as far as you can get from your mother and me. I'm not saying this in a hurtful way. I'm only pointing out that when I look at it—like Dr. Hyatt would in session with me—that's what I come up with. Your mother and me didn't do the best by you children when you were growing up, as hard as that is to own up to.

"So to answer your question about Timothy, you see how it takes in more than just how and why he left? I know you felt close to him in a kind of motherly way, since he was the youngest while Darlene was so sick, and I was working night and day to make ends meet. You shouldered too much of the responsibility with him, Caroline—with both boys—during your young years. You started doing that early, especially with Teddy. It had to've been when you were only eight or nine.

"Timothy was an easy kid, because he wasn't belligerent or hard to manage. But even so, you did far too much, especially with the baby-sitting. He kept to himself a lot—he's always been that way—but when he was a little older, he followed Teddy around. I'm thinking when Teddy was like nine, and Timmy was just starting school. They formed a kind of bond, at least, I think Timothy did. But Teddy didn't soldier up the way you did. He always seemed to see his brother as a tag-along. And why wouldn't he? We all but handed him that notion. Teddy was in the spotlight so goddamned young, which was your mother's doing—with his musical talent, singing the way he did. I don't think he was glad necessarily to be there, but he didn't fight it either. It got him lots of notice. What kid can resist that?

"But I gotta tell you, I was concerned about how much time he was spending practicing his songs and going constantly to sing in all kinds of churches everywhere. He didn't get outside playing with other kids enough, which I thought he shoulda been doing. To me, it makes sense that this not only had a lot to do with how Teddy turned out, but Timothy as well. To me, the amount of attention paid to Teddy in our home was overdone.

"Timmy was a shy kid from the start, while Teddy talked a blue streak, once he got to talking. Timothy, it seemed to me, simply gave up on trying to communicate. I know there's personality in all this, a-course, but the balance with our boys was off. Your mother's attention, at times, wasn't normal. I mean, she worried at one point that both boys were retarded, but in different ways.

"With Teddy, it took him so long to start talking. He was well into his toddler years before he gave any indication that he was going to say a thing. But once he did, you couldn't shut him up. And he came up with sentences that could slay you. People everywhere stared at this kid like he was some kinda genius, and maybe he was. Hell, your mother and me wouldn't've known how to handle real genius, even if we'd been able to recognize it for what it was. We probably should've sent him to college come hell or high water—finding out how to do that at any costs—but that wasn't in our way of thinking back then.

"We thought of life in simpler terms than now, Caroline. To us, you worked, raised your family as best as you could—according to the Scriptures, is how we looked on that—and belonged to your family and a few friends. Ours were mainly from the church. There wasn't much else. And, you know, I say this about sending Teddy to college, but we wouldn't have known how to even begin with that sort of thing. We knew about colleges and universities, a-course, but even if we'd found the means, your mother, especially, would've insisted Teddy go to Goshen, the Mennonite college in Indiana. Any music he woulda studied there would've been with some kind of church work in mind—him becoming a choir director is what Darlene would've planned. In some big church some place. And I'm sure I would've gone along with this as the right thing to do, though, I gotta tell you, there were lots of other ideas Darlene had that didn't exactly fit with what she thought she *shoulda been thinking*, ideas inspired by Hollywood and fame and the like. It ran against everything we were supposed to be practicing as Mennonites, and she knew it, but just couldn't help herself.

"Think about this. She was nineteen when she had you, twenty-two when she had Teddy and twenty-five, twenty-six when she had Timothy. I've looked at this, you see? When you're young—especially a person like your mother—you have dreams. Hell, I was more than any of these ages when I married your mother. I was twenty-seven—though you gotta ask what kinda twenty-seven that was, you know?

"Then too, I guess we weren't so different from a lot of people back on the farms at that time. I heard on the radio the other day that twenty-five percent of Americans lived on farms in the thirties, the years when your mother and me were dating, Caroline. Today it's more like two percent. Back then, it was natural to be secluded, connecting with only family and your neighbors, people in your small town community, people living and doing the same things you were. There were lots of kids in my class that were shy, maybe not as much as me, but backward in social ways, you know? Most of us barely spoke English.

"Darlene tells the story that in her class on the first day of school when John Nightingale's name was called, he didn't say 'present' the way the teacher asked each student to do. He said, '*Nein*, John *Nachtigaul*.' He didn't want to be called by his name in English.

"This kinda backwardness was something that always embarrassed your mother, especially after we moved to the city and started attending Hopewell Mennonite, but, when we dated and were first married, she still had a lot of the old ways about her, even when you kids were little. Hell, we both did.

"Anyway, when I think back on all this—picturing Timothy in it—it was as though, even then, he was trying to disappear from us. No, that's not quite right. It's more like he was always out of focus or range with where our attention was. I'm talking about him being in the middle of what was going on, like the rest of us were, but not really being *there* because—because he wasn't *seen*, you understand? As awful as this sounds, we just didn't pay attention to him as part of what we were doing.

"Well, a-course, he was part of *us*, his family, but he was thought of as a tagalong, and not just by Teddy, but by all of us. It was unconscious, our leaving him out. But looking back, I think that's what we did, as awful as that feels to me now. You'll have to ask your mother how she sees this. We've never talked about it between us. But I can't imagine that by now, after Timmy's leaving us as he's done, she hasn't thought about what's gone on before.

(The tape recorder clicks off, long pause, then clicks back on again.)

"You know, Caroline, there's actually a photograph of Timothy, taken when he was around five or six, before he went to school, before he got sick. It only shows half of him, with the other half out of the frame. It looks like the person taking the picture didn't mean to include him, wasn't aware he was there, didn't register that Timmy was in the view-finder. He's up front in that picture, with his back to the camera, watching what's going on. And now that I'm thinking about it, there's another snapshot somewhere with Timothy, again, standing off to the side, watching Uncle Jesse tease Teddy. Jesse's holding Ted in a headlock like he used to do, rubbing his knuckles against his head. He called Teddy 'Shimps' when he did that.

"You know what 'shimp' means, Caroline? It means 'an idiot,' a person who has a weird look about him and isn't quite right. Why we allowed your uncle to call him this, I don't know, other than with our kind of humor in those days, maybe we thought this was sort of a upside-down twist on how Teddy really was, him being so smart. Plain stupid, is what we were. But it's how we joked then.

"Timothy wasn't treated bad, not openly ridiculed or anything like that, but, he was neglected. Not in a physical way. Darlene and I always gave all you kids what we could, best as we could. It's why I worked so hard, to provide properly for you. You gotta remember, your mother and me met and got married during the depression, the Dust Bowl years, which didn't really let up in

Oklahoma until right before the war started in the early forties. So we sometimes had a real hard time having what we needed. You never went hungry, I can tell you that honestly, but Timothy was neglected in an emotional way, how we went about treating him as a person in his own right. I truly regret this now, because it's what I had done to me by my family, what I've learned a lot about while in here. I wasn't just slighted. I was looked down on as well, though I don't feel we ever did that exactly to Timmy.

"To me, that cut-off photograph says loads about him, though—what the whole family thought about him."

—

"I know it must seem like I've spent a lot of time telling you about Teddy, but as unfortunate as it is, Timmy was looked on as being what Teddy was not. I've never really thought of it as outright as this, but I think that's right, now that I've said it. Darlene dressed the boys alike, especially for church, in the same suits, even the same kind of tie. Teddy sang like a grown-up, so Darlene dressed him like one. He was a child star, really. A boy version of Shirley Temple, only a religious one. There are pictures of our boys together at various ages as they're growing up, and you'll see when you look at them—as I have done lately—that they're 'lookalikes.'

"People told Darlene all the time they looked like twins because Teddy was short and little for his age, and Timothy was taller and bigger for his—so the three and a-half years between them didn't show. If photographs are indications of anything at all, this should've been obvious to us, and, on some level, I think it was. But like the joking around, we just didn't quite get it. What this meant to the boys—each of them—I've never asked. Maybe I've been afraid to."

—

"It makes you wonder about photographs altogether, what they really can tell you, doesn't it? Not so much why we take them, collect them. It doesn't take a lot to figure that one out. We want memories, maybe even to stop time for a little while, so we can remember what's happening later. Of course when

I say this, it's, first of all, about remembering the *appearance* of things. Women in particular point this out when they say how awful they look in pictures, or that they don't look like themselves—whatever that means. I guess it's what you think you look like from notions you have about yourself when you look in the mirror, or maybe even what you *think* you look like by how you see yourself without the mirror. Hell, if I know for sure about any of it.

"The second thing is, I think we take pictures because we want to remember the good times, don't we? We don't see the larger picture, what they might actually stand for, do we? What they could show us about ourselves, deeper than what we look like or what we're doing at the time.

"With your mother and me, it was all about keeping track of this family we were making. When we look at the albums now, we say—well, there we are at this time and this and that one. It's what they call a slideshow now, only, back then, we kept our pictures in albums that we could hold and look at. Albums seem more real to me. It's better than any of these slides we've got in trays today. When you want to see your pictures as slides, you've gotta set up the projector, go to a lot of trouble, while with an album, you can go back in time as you turn the pages. Darlene likes slides because she can sit in a dark room and look at them on a screen, which does make what you're looking at pop to life. Everything seems so alive, bright with color, as though what's in the picture is happening right before your eyes. I get taken in by that, like everybody else.

"But pictures in albums, seems to me, make remembering stories about life in your past more possible. When we watch slides together, Darlene and I make a few comments here and there, but it's like we're in an audience at the movie house, and we don't really talk much about what the pictures remind us of. But when we sit with albums, we spend hours, sometimes, talking about what was happening in our lives at the time the picture was taken. I'm not sure why that is. Maybe it's because albums are like books, you know, you imagine scenes as you read along, turning the pages one by one, you think?

—

"Well, I've had to put a new tape in the recorder. Guess I've got more in me to tell than I thought I might.

"But you know, as I'm thinking and talking to you about your Timothy questions, there was a school picture of him, right before he was hospitalized, that sticks in my mind. He's so damn skinny in that photograph, cheeks sunken in, his eyes seem bright enough but with deep circles around them. My God, what did we think when we looked at that picture? His sickness was showing on his face right there, and we didn't catch it. Or maybe we just didn't want to see it, because it would've meant we weren't feeding him right.

"With us, it was always about food—if we had enough for you kids especially. But, it probably was *what* we were feeding you. We ate heavy, anyway that's what Kat tells me now. 'Dense food,' she says. We poured milk on everything or cream, used gobs of butter. We ate cereal by the box—the biggest you could get—melted cheese sandwiches with tomato soup, lots of beef, hamburgers, roast—well, that's not exactly true. We didn't eat lots of meat of any kind. It was only when we got it from a butcher we shared with Josephine and Clifford, one we did ourselves out on their farm. Chickens we got from them as well, or from Whalen and Ava.

"But Josie, Clifford, and their kids ate with us when they were hard up—'poolin' the food,' we used to say. We ate food that filled you up—macaroni and cheese, vegetable soup with more potatoes and carrots than anything else, weenies—God, we ate tons of weenies on Bond Bread buns with onions and pickles on top, like these were the vegetables for the day! We threw weenies into everything—soup, fried them for breakfast like they were sausage in eggs, wrapped soft bread around them and baked them. But a roast was a special treat for us when you kids were little. Had that only once a month. Usually, it was fried baloney. Obviously, I could go on and on about food.

"So I'm not surprised with Timothy's obstructive bowel problem. Now, I'm not. According to Kat, we probably all shoulda been suffering from it.

"They found a special doctor for Timmy, I've forgotten his name—Dr. Chalmers had an expert on internal medicine called in—and this guy said he thought it might've been a twisted bowel Timothy'd had from infancy which had grown worse through time, and because of all the enemas and suppositories given to him in the hospital, it corrected itself. But when I asked other doctors about this later, they told me that diagnosis wasn't very likely right, since the twisted bowel problem doesn't stay in a person for a long period of time. It's something that has to be corrected when it's discovered or the baby dies from it.

"But for whatever Timothy did have, this special doctor finally came from Tulsa, though he didn't arrive in time to do any good. Timothy got so sick, and then back to normal again so fast, that by the time he showed up, his expert opinion came after the fact. They did watch Timmy for several days before they released him from the hospital to make sure the problem wasn't coming back.

"Well, I'm sure you remember the story of Timmy's cure—putting the medical part of it aside—after all, you were in the middle of it. But you were young. You were around thirteen, maybe just turned fourteen that September. This happened to Timothy in December, close to Christmastime. We haven't talked together about this in years. Probably most of what you remember is from your mother and me telling the story over and over.

"But this I'm sure you do remember. It started with Timothy passing out at the table. He fell from his chair to the floor. I thought he'd choked on something, remember that? Darlene went absolutely hysterical, so much so that at first, I couldn't get to him, with her hovering the way she was. When I finally did, I saw he was unconscious and very pale, his lips were grey. I mean it. He was always a light-complected kid, a tow-head, so he looked pale all the time. He sun-blistered real easy. But there was an ashy tone to his skin that frightened me. I can't say I didn't know what was happening. What I can say, is that I didn't know the exact cause. But Timothy had been complaining off and on about stomachaches for quite a while, and he pushed at his abdomen sometimes when he was at the table.

"But here again, he was a kinda sickly kid, especially about his food. He got real picky and had troubles digesting it. Darlene had taken him to the pediatrician a couple of times, without anything changing, even though we followed what they told us to do—cod liver oil and such. But after a while we stopped taking his complaints as serious as we should've. Darlene kept telling me he was constipated—"he's eating too much sugar," she'd say, or "he never drinks water". And even though that didn't make much sense, we finally came to the conclusion Timothy wasn't eating enough to make bowel movements normal.

"So we got it in our heads he absolutely had to eat, even if it was baby food. First, we smashed everything on his plate, from food off the table. Then we cooked and whipped everything to death, like for an infant. Darlene even bought and made baby formula for him. We finally bought him baby foods, in those little glass jars, mixing it all with a little maple syrup. Well, you can imagine how a six-year-old boy took to baby food or any food different from the rest of us, especially from Teddy's. To this day, I believe what Timmy did eat, he got because of you, Caroline. Because you literally hand-fed him, when the rest of us weren't around. Anyway, that's what Ted told us when he was older.

Finally, we got desperate and insisted Timmy eat cooked prunes to help him go. Well, he'd seen his Grandma Dirks do that and outright refused to eat them—as well as Malt-O-Meal, Cream of Wheat, and Farina. To him, these were foods only old people ate. A-course, knowing what we do now, any eating didn't appeal to him, because he wasn't hungry.

"And so things went from bad to worse until he refused to eat anything. He was losing weight, but we just added it up to stubbornness. Since nothing we did worked, Darlene began saying the situation was hopeless. A-course, we said all this in front of Timothy, sometimes as a threat, to try and get him to eat. You and Teddy heard this too, a-course. But you, Caroline, were old enough to have your own views and fought back with us. You insisted we stop nagging him. And you begged us constantly to call the doctor. Well, we'd done that, and things weren't getting better, and the doctor visits were starting to mount. I couldn't meet the bills.

"And I gotta say, Chalmers didn't seem to know what to do either. We were throwing money down the drain. And, too, by now, we didn't understand why somebody couldn't be called in who knew more than the doctors at Hopewell Memorial. Remember this was still early, before Timothy was in the hospital.

"To this day, I think money was at the bottom of it. We couldn't pay, so they did what they could without even greater hospital bills adding up. Dr. Chalmers had us in mind that way, probably too much since nothing got done until things went terribly wrong.

"So while Timothy was still home, our chiding went on, 'You aren't going to feel better until you eat, Timmy.' 'Not eating isn't natural. Your body needs to have food.' 'Eat even if you don't feel like it.' 'What's it gonna take for you to realize that food is necessary in order for you to live?' Just before he ended up in the hospital, he started vomiting, mainly the dry heaves, just bile coming up.

"I gotta tell you, when Timothy passed out at the table like that, I really thought we were losing him. I yelled at Darlene to start the car and get you and Teddy in it, while I headed out the door with Timmy. You grabbed some coats from the rack—it was winter, in December—and you thought of that. You were always so good during a crisis. Maybe it was all the times you spent taking care of the boys, maybe it was your nature, but your mother and me relied on you to take care of anything we couldn't get to. It was like whatever needed to be done, you understood what that was and did it.

"By the time we got to the hospital emergency, it seemed to me that Timmy was hardly breathing. Darlene was crying so hard, to this day I don't know how she drove us there, but by God, she did. She ran red lights, you name it.

"The hospital staff went into immediate action when they saw how limp Timmy was in my arms. He was skinny to begin with, but showing no signs of life like that, you can imagine. Some attendant grabbed him, and a whole team came running with a gurney. They had him down the hall and into a special room so fast, with all these medical people hovering over him, the four of us were just left standing there in the lobby. I only have vague recollections about how we got taken into a room with some chairs and then once again left to fin for ourselves. It seemed hours before somebody came out to tell us that Dr. Chalmers had been called, he'd ordered in somebody from Tulsa, that Timothy would be undergoing all kinds of tests and we would be taken to a room where he would be assigned as soon as they got done with the first round of testing. At least we knew he was still alive.

"After hours of waiting, they took us into this room, with lots of nurses bustling around, getting us chairs and trying to be comforting. Darlene had a hard time getting ahold of herself. She tried to stay busy talking with Teddy, but he hardly needed that. He was nine, ten years old, but finally she let you two entertain yourselves, reading magazines together, while she sat and cried.

"Finally, after hours and hours, Timothy was wheeled into a room where we were taken to be with him. I was relieved when I saw he was on oxygen, because I was so afraid he'd stopped breathing. He was absolutely motionless. He looked so terribly small on the gurney and in the bed. He was white as the sheets.

"It was around eleven by then, and I couldn't afford to miss work, so I went the next morning even though I hadn't slept at all. It was exhausting, because

Darlene and I took turns staying with him—her during the day, me at night—though most of the time, she didn't leave. I slept as I could in the chair. They put Timothy in a single bed room, whether we could afford it or not, and they offered me a bed, but I couldn't leave the room and go down the hall. I had to be with him. Don't know if you remember any of this, but you kids went with whichever one of us was not in the hospital. I just don't have a clear fix on who was where, when, anymore. Josie kept you. Out on the farm for a night or two.

"God, the waiting was excruciating. Nothing changed for two days. Timothy just laid there like he was already dead. Chalmers told us the expert from Tulsa couldn't get away from his practice until the week-end, because of his emergencies. And Chalmers said he'd done all he could do, that x-rays showed bowel obstruction, but they didn't know the cause for sure. They would have to do exploratory surgery if Timothy didn't move soon. He was going to give it one more day and hope that the doctor from Tulsa could make it before they operated. Exploratory surgery could be long, and, in some cases, fruitless. It was also expensive. If they knew more about what was the actual difficulty, they would have a better chance at success when they went in, Chalmers told us. And they were hoping that this guy from Tulsa could do the operating since he was a special surgeon for this sort of thing.

"Saturday morning Darlene was beside herself. She got in her head we should call Reverend Mastre, who was the pastor after Classen retired. Roger Mastre, was a young fellah with a go-getter attitude, but only in the pulpit a couple years. I liked him a lot. When she told him what was happening and asked him to pray for Timothy, his response came without hesitation. He and his wife would call as many members of the congregation as they could reach, and everybody would gather in the church to pray for Timothy together.

"It was the hope Darlene needed. I was grateful, but, to tell you the truth, I didn't have much hope myself. My faith totally abandoned me, Caroline. When I looked at Timothy—his situation was so utterly bleak—I just readied myself for the worst. I couldn't see anything else.

"Well, you know the rest, a-course. After everybody got together Saturday evening at the church—and there was a church-full of people, which simply amazed me—they began praying around six o'clock. It was dark, because it was the shortest days of the year.

"We'd been invited for a bite to eat at the parsonage. When we got ready to leave for the church and join all the others, Darlene and I took for granted you would join the congregation in prayer since you'd been baptized. You'd participated already in your first washing-of-the-feet service, so you were a full member of the church by then. But you looked at Darlene and told her that you didn't need to go and pray, because God had told you that Timothy was going to be all right. Well, Darlene and I have talked about this many times since, a-course, but at the time, we both just thought you were into wishful thinking, which made sense for your age—you wanted Timothy to get well, so you thought he would. I don't know if you remember what all your mother said to you, but she tried in every way she could think of to let you know things might not turn out the way you were hoping they would, that we had to pray and then rely on God's will to direct what was going to happen next. But you held your ground.

"Reverend Mastre's wife, Sarah, took your side. I wasn't sure she was agreeing with you so much as thinking that any teenager who had this kind of trust in God, needed to be supported and, you know, if it *was* something God was revealing to you, then we definitely needed to honor it. So she offered you a bed for the night, in her daughter's bedroom. Sarah said she'd put Faith up in their big bed, because she would be up all night praying downstairs herself, while staying with you and their two kids. Teddy was invited to sleep in her son's room with him, as Denton had a bunkered bed for him and his friends—they called him Denny, I remember that. He was a mess, that kid, but it's neither here nor there with this story, so it's all I'll say about it.

"At the church, there was a leading prayer by Mastre and then silence. Without being told what to do, somebody stood up and prayed out loud, and when that person was done, another person stood up and prayed. After everyone had their turn—and there were a lot—forty-five, fifty people, is what I'd guess. Well, I didn't pray, because I couldn't. I was in tears, and, I guess, everybody understood. Then we sat in silence, each praying to himself. I have never in my life felt anything like that before or since. If I ever doubted the power of prayer, I don't anymore. But still, you know, maybe it was just people putting themselves together behind something they wanted, believed in. We saw that during World War II, you know. That kinda effort sways things. But whatever's behind it, when everybody's in a concentrated effort toward the same end, it can be very powerful.

"I was told later—'cause I got there after the prayer meeting had started—some were wondering how long they were going to stay and pray—if everybody'd pray the night and then end the meeting or what. The congregation decided that they'd pray until they knew God's will for Timothy, until some definite outcome would show itself, to one or all.

"Rev. Mastre had left his church office telephone number at the nurses' station, so the hospital could call as soon as word was received of any changes with Timothy. That call came at a little past dawn, Sunday morning. Darlene had gone back to the hospital to be at Timothy's side while we prayed. She called Mastre, telling him that Timothy'd had a bowel movement, and the doctor had told her that this was the sign they had been waiting for. It seems that whatever was causing the obstruction had changed or cleared up during the night.

"When I arrived at the hospital, I found Timothy sitting up in bed, eating oatmeal. I had left you and Teddy at the parsonage until morning. Mastre cancelled the Sunday morning service, saying that he would greet anybody who hadn't heard about our prayer meeting at the door, letting them worship briefly if they wanted to.

"But before I left for the hospital, I've never seen such joy in my life as there was that early Sunday morning in our church. It wasn't any glory-hallelujah kinda thing. People simply went from one to the other, crying and embracing each other. I heard it took an hour for everybody to leave, because they stayed, giving thanks to God for saving Timothy's life. If we'd been living in Old Testament times, everybody woulda danced down Randolph Street with drums and tambourines.

"And I gotta tell you, Caroline, I learned something through all this that I've forgotten at various times in my life, I know, but that I sincerely believe is true to this day. *You knew.* Now, *how* you knew, that's a mystery to me. With all my religious ins and outs over the years, I can only say truthfully that if God reveals himself to us as the faithful say He does, then you were His messenger that night.

"But I'll also always believe, whether others agree with this or not, that our prayers were necessary for your faith to be true. I don't know how these things work, or how, or even if, we can explain such miracles, but I do believe all of it was necessary, exactly as it was, and that if any part of it had been missing—if one person's faith that night had been different, if you hadn't stayed away from the congregation, if everybody who was there hadn't been there believing as they did, Timothy wouldn't have been spared, he wouldn't be with us anymore. And even though my faith has worn thin, and I've grown so terribly weary trying to constantly toe the religious line, I will always believe that God did this for us, for our family, whether I'm a believer anymore or not. That night, at least for that night, I must've believed more than I thought I did.

"Well, if you ask me where Timothy was in all of this, I'd have to tell you I don't think he was with us in any of it. He's never said anything about God speaking through him or he himself believing that divine help saved him. I'm talking about later when he was old enough to tell us what he thought happened to him.

"In fact, one time when we were by ourselves, and I asked him about it—I think he was in high school at the time—he laughed and said, 'What do you wanna know, Dad? If I saw 'the light' and thought I was at the pearly gates deciding whether to go in or not, or whether I thought St. Peter was going to walk me over the threshold hand-in-hand? I don't remember a thing from the time I fell to the floor during supper and woke up to eat oatmeal whatever day it was later. It's a total blank. And as far as what I feel myself about it, I honestly don't know what to think. Maybe I was spared by prayer to serve some purpose, but if so, I don't know yet what that is. Maybe I've already done it. I can't imagine this could possibly be so, but you never know how you touch other people, or change things by what you believe, say, or do. If what I've been saved to do is coming up, I guess I'll just find out.'

"Then he told me something I'll remember for the rest of my life.

"'Do I believe in the power of God to heal? Well, I guess I do, because it appears that people get healed in this way. But, you know, Dad, people are healed all the time without prayer. There've been thousands of people as sick as I was, sicker by far, who've been loved and who've had those loved ones hope beyond hope that the sick person would make it, people who haven't uttered a word in prayer, who've seen their loved one live, even miraculously restored. Other people have died like flies, right and left, in war, famine, of disease, all over the world, believers and unbelievers, prayers and no prayers. Most believers call this the 'will of God'. I don't try to put meaning on these things. Seems to me that you and Mother do, and that's fine with me. I respect whatever you believe. But until I myself feel otherwise, I'll simply say I'm glad you got me to the hospital on time, and I made it.'

"This was probably the most I'd heard Timothy say on anything of importance to him until then. And the only reason I remember it so well is that after he'd talked to me, I wrote down—as much as I could remember—his words as he spoke them to me. I thought he was brilliant. I've read that note many, many times, especially now that he's gone away. It gives me hope, as does his telephone call.

"He believes in family, in loved ones, and respect we hold between each other, regardless of our personal beliefs."

"When I think on Timothy, you know—how I think he is as a person— I'd say he's not a leader or a performer, like Teddy is, or even a teacher. How I've come to see him is as a *witness* to what's going on around him. And most people don't view that as much of anything. Person's gotta be *doing* something or they're considered useless. But Timothy spent hours watching us, most of the time not making one comment on what he saw. But I don't think that's useless. It's kinda what the saints and sages do—men of great wisdom—isn't it? Well, and women, too. Kat's made me aware of that.

"Think about how many people have spent their lives in prayer or keeping to themselves about what they see. Sometimes they write down their observations and if we read them and find truth in what they've witnessed, we view them as people of importance, somebody who has something to say worth paying attention to. Sometimes, we believe they've been sent by God to directly tell us something we need to hear. Believers think of the gospel writers this way, especially the Apostle John who wrote *Revelation*. I say this about

Revelation, because it's a message that's so hard to understand. But obviously it's important to us about the world's future.

"Maybe Timothy will turn into something like that, maybe that's what he's doing already, wherever he is. Other times, these kinds of people just sit and think and don't seem to leave behind anything. But is that useless? I feel what Timothy told me is right. You never know when and how you influence others. Maybe these quiet, to-themselves people live lives of silent goodness, helping only themselves find peace, who knows? Jesus wandered around in the desert, even battling Satan in his mind, if not in reality, and look what that gave the world. He ended up preaching, but if he'd just stayed to himself, he'd still woulda done more than a lot of people do who don't think past the ordinary.

"What if Jesus woulda said or done something that brought on his crucifixion, without anybody knowing about it, would he still have been the Son of God who came to save the world? Could he have saved the world without his preaching and any notice? I think so. But there's the Bible with all the fulfillment of the prophesies and such. And who can believe in a savior they don't know about?

"It's these kinds of questions that I ask myself, and I think they're questions worth asking, if only I answer them for myself.

"What all this thinking has lead me to, is that I don't believe we should judge people unless they're hurting us or others. What they do is between themselves and their God, or what I think of as them living what they're called to do. Sometimes that calling is simply how you are. We all have visions, just different kinds, in different ways."

3.

Following day

"Well, I guess you figured out that I started a new tape for this letter, right? I labelled it so you wouldn't get them mixed up. I don't know how long I'll record on this one, though I have plenty of time, actually. I've signed all my release papers and said my goodbyes. The staff knows I'm in here making this tape before Darlene comes to get me, so they can mail it for me. I don't want Darlene doing this. She doesn't need to know when I contact you and such.

The folks here have been good about helping me out, so I'll try to hurry this along since once I get home it'll be a while before I can get to it again. I'll be setting things up for myself in the house.

"You and I should probably talk on the phone for anything we need to pass along in a hurry. I can tell you that talking on these tapes was the smartest idea you've come up with yet. I seem to be able to talk in ways I find hard to do on the phone.

"You know, Caroline, I've been trying to remember where you were when Timothy graduated from high school. Seems to me that woulda been around nineteen sixty-one, sixty-two. You went with him to California around then, and while you two were there, he enlisted in the Navy, ended up in Vietnam, and when he got out of the service, he did some traveling around the States, but only for a bit. He planned to go to Spain sometime, remember that? Just not then. He was partial to Spain, that I know, which had been only a stop on his way to Vietnam. But he had quite the bag of stories to tell when he got home about what he and his buddies did during the stopover there. He loved the people. But when he got back, after his roaming around a while, he went directly to Oklahoma City, got a job bartending and that's what he's done, as far as I know, until he decided to do this recent shuffle off to wherever-in-the-hell he is.

"In the meantime, you moved to New York after your own travels. So unless you've had contact with him that your mother and I don't know about, I'd say what you know is about what we do. It's always been hit-and-miss with him, ever since he came back home, really. I've heard that Vietnam changes a person. Maybe that's what's caught up with him, despite the lapse in time.

"I started this tape by telling you Tim's the kinda person who's to himself, like me. And that's true, but here again, when he was in touch, he seemed to be happy to be with us, completely comfortable at home and in no hurry to leave. It makes me wonder why he didn't come home more.

"I did ask him that once, and he told me he was pretty much like an old scout dog—he tended to follow his nose, and wherever it fell is what got his attention. And that seems to be true about him. I wouldn't say he lacks ambition exactly—though 'shiftless' is what Darlene does call him sometimes. But that suggests he's irresponsible or a bum, which I don't think he's like at all. What he wants has always been intentional. He told me he doesn't want to own a bar or get on in life like a lot of guys do. He wants to make a decent wage, and spend his time off doing what he likes to do. He likes to have a nice enough place where he can burrow in to listen to his jazz and read his books.

"I never asked to see his apartment, but Darlene did—not that it did her any good. I figured if he'd wanted us to know where he lived, he'd have invited us. He did take us out to dinner in the City once, some special eatery, hell, I couldn't tell you where it was if I tried. Snooky's Bar, it was called.

"Everybody knew Timothy there, though it wasn't where he worked which was somewhere closer to Bricktown, that old abandoned, industrial section of Oklahoma City that the politicians have talked moneyed people into renovating for a tourist attraction, so their contractor-friends can make a million. Anyway, I had one of the best steaks I've ever had in my life at that bar. And then he took us straight home.

"But during dinner, Darlene asked him where he *lived*, why he didn't want us to see his bachelor apartment, was it all that disgraceful, she wanted to know? And he smiled—always polite as he is—and said, no, that he shared the rent with a roommate so it was pretty much like she could expect from two guys living together—that is, not a place you'd wanna take your mother. Didn't she remember, he asked her, when he and Teddy lived together in an apartment in Hopewell just before Teddy got married and moved out to California? How shocked she'd been when she first saw their place? Well, it couldn't have been more obvious that he didn't want to share his personal life with us, then or now. And to be fair, Teddy never did either—or maybe he did with your mother. If that's the case, I'll never know.

"Anyway, I tried to figure out what her hang-up with Timothy was over this. And my guess is she didn't want to be excluded from anything having to do with her kids. With you and Teddy—you two talk to her, tell her things—but with Timothy so close to his chest, she felt left out and hurt by it. And I gotta say, when he still lived at home, he never brought anybody around to the house—not his friends, a girlfriend, nobody.

"And that's the other thing. When she had a chance, Darlene badgered him about girls—that was her big interest—girls he might be seeing, and if he ever thought about marriage. Well, his answer was always something like, 'You know, Mom, the kind of marriage you're thinking about is an in-it-for-the-long-haul commitment, and I don't do that. I'm staying put for now, but that doesn't mean I couldn't one day decide to go live somewhere else, just jump in the truck and take off. I never know when that might hit me. It's why I don't keep a pet, even though I love dogs. I try to stay free-and-easy about my life.' And, a-course, this is exactly what he did, didn't he?

"But your mother didn't stop with him there. She started with the whole college question which she chewed to death every time she saw him. Why didn't he take advantage of the GI Bill? Caroline, the government hasn't called it that since the Korean War, but we knew she meant a government-sponsored education program that he qualified for, since he'd served in Vietnam. And he answered her over and over, that it was a government matching fund kinda deal, and it wasn't how he wanted to spend his money. So he turned the tables on her and asked what she thought higher education was, since she thought it was such a good thing. Her answer, a-course, was the one she gave for pretty much everything she wanted you kids to do—about how it prepared you for a real profession, something you could be proud of and would make you some decent money doing.

"Well, he told her, he hadn't done very well in school, which was true, but we all knew that this was mainly because he didn't apply himself, which Darlene didn't let slip past. And she was right about that. He sluffed off his whole high school days. His principal called us once, because they found him in the auditorium, hidden off to the side reading a book instead of going to class like he was supposed to. I asked him at the time—this was after your mother left the room—why, if he found the class so unlivable, he didn't simply leave the goddamned premises? Why sit in the auditorium for godssakes and take the chance of getting caught? He said he'd taken the book from the library without signing it out, and he didn't want to get caught with it outside the building! You figure out that kind of thinking, Caroline! He read the whole book in one day in there, and this without anybody catching him at it, well, until they did, a-course.

"So I asked him, what was it about going to class that bothered him? It was a waste of time, he said. I asked him why he couldn't put up with it until he got through school, and then he could do as he pleased. He didn't want to live for tomorrow, is how he put it to me. He couldn't stand sitting in boredom *now*. Well, I told him there wasn't a way out of this one. He had to go to school until he was sixteen, or until he completed four years of high school, or until we gave him permission to leave—which we weren't going to do. This was the law. Well, that gave him pause.

"So then, true to Timothy's way a-doing things, he said, okay then, that he'd fulfill the portion of the law that he felt like he could. He promised he'd go to classes enough to get him through, because he didn't want to make trouble for us.

"These are his words, Caroline—'Okay, okay, I'll go, but, by God, I better get something special for graduation.'

"We both laughed over that. But he kept his promise. It was always like this with him. Kids his age, they rebel, but it's usually to get back at their parents or authority, you know? Timothy did it because of how he believed, his own kind of honesty, you understand? But you have to've known this about him, because he didn't suddenly get this way in high school. It was how he was from the time he was a little kid. He appeared to be stubborn, like he was trying to get other people's goat, but it really wasn't that. It's not that now. He's got *reasons* for why he does what he does, and he can tell you what they are. But he doesn't let you know until you pull it outta him!

"It's his mild manner that makes him so different. He simply does what he does and then stares at you when you get upset over what he's done. And it takes some figuring out to know why his reasons make sense to him, especially as a parent while he was growing up.

"I thought a lot about why he really wouldn't want to be in that class, what he was calling 'boring,' and, at first, I thought it was because, well, maybe he didn't want to get called on by the teacher since he was shy or maybe he didn't feel comfortable around the kids in there, them being so different from him. But I've come to realize what he told me was really true for him—he was *bored*. He didn't want to spend time listening to all the talk about something he knew better than the others did. He thought you could go read the book on your own, and if you wanted more opinions about it, you could get even more books that told you a helluva lot better what you wanted to know than most of what you'd hear in class.

"I understand something about this, Caroline. I've had to sit through lots of group discussions in detox that didn't have a damn thing to do with my situation, and most of the time, I didn't learn anything. There were endless sessions of people whining and complaining. Dr. Hyatt told me group was an exchange kinda deal, a willingness to be a support to other people's stories, just like they were to me. But I couldn't help thinking it was a two-way street that seemed to get more one-way the longer I was in here. For one thing, I don't think a lot of people want to work on themselves. Not really... ah well, I don't want to get off on this. You get what I'm saying by now, I'm sure.

"Anyway, as to Darlene's definition of higher education being something through which Timothy could gain either money or social importance, he told her that in his view, education was *reading* and understanding what you read. To his mind, what college kids actually learned to do was to listen to their professors. And the professors were more than happy with their little followers, because it taught young people to look up to them for their knowledge instead of finding out how to argue with what they said.

"The other thing was what he called 'efficiency.' He said authorities thought they could get over more information faster if they lectured—their idea being to give off more information than their students could hold in their heads, that way the kids spent all their time taking notes, didn't have time to think it out for feedback. So the profs ended up with all these little groupies running around spouting off what they could put together as fast as possible and the students who could remember more information than the others, were the ones who got all the notice.

"I told him that it sounded a lot like preachers in church to me! Most of the congregation don't read the Bible themselves. They listen to the preachers and then spout off opinions about what they've heard.

"Well, he said, he'd found out the same thing while he was in the service. It taught young people to obey, follow orders, and trust that the people at the top knew what they were doing, so they could get done what they wanted to get done. He snorted, saying, well, by now, we should see how that turned out—Korea and Vietnam, the most recent examples. How many were killed serving that idea? Around fifty-four thousand in Korea—he had these figures in that file-box of a mind of his—and another nearly sixty thousand in Vietnam. That adds up to one-hundred-fourteen thousand who died in these two wars alone.

"He told Darlene he'd gone into the service, not as an honor to his country, but for the same reason he stuck it out with high school—to get something out of the way that would've taken more energy to resist than to simply do it. Now that he was free, he wasn't going to walk back into another situation like high school or Vietnam, if he could help it—meaning marriage along with higher education. Well, that shut Darlene up, at least for a little while.

"So that's Timothy in a nutshell for you, Caroline."

"So Timothy has his own mind about living his life the way he wants to. He quietly goes about doing what he thinks is right for him. And if trouble presents itself, he tries to side-step it if he can. He doesn't go out and buy a megaphone or a gun and start shouting or shooting because of it. Can you picture Timothy in the military as a career? Or as a politician? God in heaven, never.

"Now, I can see Teddy as both of those, as well as an entertainer, a salesman, a popular professor—one standing on the bandbox like Timothy is so against. I'm still amazed those two ever lived together. The only way they coulda made it work was if Timothy shut his mouth and let Teddy ramble on and on. Well, a-course, that's how it was. Always has been."

"Okay, back to Darlene again. Once she'd pounded to death marriage and education with Timothy, your mother's sermon got to be about his health insurance and retirement, if you can believe this. Didn't he feel like saving for the future?—as though this had been her own goal in life, like she and I did that while we were still married. Well, Timothy's response to the insurance question was to go on about keeping yourself fit and healthy, about herbal remedies, good nutrition and the like. He always looked great, like he was in his early thirties, no kidding.

"He totally ignored her plea for him putting something away for retirement. I mean, how ridiculous was that, when she and I barely made ends meet? We never had a savings account in our lives. But maybe that's where she was coming from. You tend to want your children to live better than you do.

"He makes his own clothes, Caroline. I doubt that you know this about him because when you visited, and he came over, or when people were around, other than Darlene and me, he wore jeans.

"It's a stretch to call what he makes for himself 'clothes' really—that's if the definition of 'clothes' is what a person wears to cover their naked body, that's about what he does, in my view, maybe with a little flourish.

"He goes to the Salvation Army stores, flea markets, and yard sales and picks up trousers, sweat pants and the like, and cuts them apart and sews the pieces back together the way he wants. He doesn't even bother most of the time to put the seams on the *inside*. I shouldn't say bother, because he intentionally sews them on the *outside*. I know, because when I asked him why, he told me that if he wears the seams on the inside, they rub against his skin!

"I have to say, he looks a little like a clown, Caroline. Some of the pants have long stripes, some are patchwork, others large sections of various parts he's put together. But he always wears t-shirts that he buys. Most of these have sayings on them—things like 'Bottoms Up,' that's on the first line. On the second is 'Kiss My Fat Ass.' I bet he wears this one at the bar. The one he wore the night he left said 'Pickled Pig's Feet!' He wore it under a homemade vest that looked like some military jacket he'd torn the sleeves out of. Probably got it from the Army-Navy Surplus Store.

"And before you wonder—yes, he's aware that others notice him, but he doesn't care. That's why I'm telling you all this. He saw me looking at his t-shirt every now and then, so he showed me the whole thing, and told me it was a local band that played at the bar where he worked. The letters of the name of the band were all stuffed into a big canning jar.

"*Timothy is thirty-nine years old* now, Caroline. I don't know exactly what to make of him when it comes to stuff like this, but he's somebody worth knowing, don't you think? I'm just not sure what his appearance has to do with his love of books and good music, how everything he is goes together. But I'm so sorry now I didn't insist on seeing more of him. I don't know if it woulda done any good, especially about his leaving. But I really wish I'd insisted on him being closer to us, despite the puzzlement that he was... *is*."

"So there's lots of guilt for me around how Timothy left. I don't see that I could've done anything other than what I did—taking into account where I was at the time. His whole leaving, really, is connected to these feelings of loneliness I've had since your mother's left me.

"I've always liked being quiet this way, especially in the evenings, just by myself, which I haven't had very much of in my life until you kids, and then Darlene, were gone. But when she left for good, the being by myself didn't feel so great anymore. That's when I realized it was final, and the life I had before wasn't going to come back. I was in it by myself, really by myself. It was then that I lost hope.

"But I've learned in here that my hope, back then, was believing what I wanted could still happen. As Dr. Hyatt told me, I was wishing my life away and calling it hope. So I'm learning how to simply be without constantly feeling the loss of my life, my family—I'm meaning, a-course, you, the boys, Kat and Darlene. I could give two figs about the one I was raised in. They can go hang themselves. Haven't seen or heard from them through any of this, not a one. Darlene's family—Clifford and Josephine and occasionally one of their boys—came to visit me once in a while after she'd gone. So I'd have to say, they're the closest to me having family, now, outside of you kids.

"And that's why this time with Timothy was so important. For that night, he belonged to me and me to him. When I talked about what happened with Dr. Hyatt, he helped me feel my way through it, so that even this loss of my son is slowly becoming less a part of the loneliness and more a part of just sitting, being quiet and allowing it to be what it is—not me trying to change it, resist it or handle it. I don't even have to be a father with it, if I don't want to. In other words, I don't constantly have to sort through all the ideas about why this happened, him leaving and me figuring out my part in it.

"I think your mother has a problem with this right now. She's churning through all the ins and outs of his leaving, as well as just about everything else in her life, including me. God forbid that she would approach me with any of it. But then again, that might not be fair, because I can't say I go to her with any of what I'm thinking and feeling about this either.

"God, I gotta admit, I still long for Timothy to call, hoping beyond hope he'll call and say he's coming to visit. He doesn't have to come back to stay, Caroline. You kids all have a right to a life of your own. But Hyatt's tried to show me how I can accept whatever happens. I'm slowly coming to see being by myself as a deeper way of belonging to the people I care about, kind of a way of being there for him and my family in which I just hold them close to me. I can stop wanting everything to be restored.

"And what was it back then, anyway? It's only an idea that what's been—what it was before I lost what I had before—was better."

—

"But after I tell you this story, I think we both will agree that what was, for better or for worse, can't ever be again. We do things, say things that change us forever, and what I'm learning is that this isn't just to be accepted, but understood as how things are from now on, because how they are, is the consequences of the decisions and actions I've made. So, thinking anything else is better, is going against what I've set in motion, isn't it?"

—

"Now before I start this, Caroline, I want you to know that Dr. Hyatt helped me write all of it out, so I'm going to read it to you. It was a very emotional night for me that I'm going to tell you about. And, as I remembered it with Dr. Hyatt, he helped me find the words to put to paper, so I could tell you exactly what I wanted to say about it, especially what Timmy said to me. I wanted to be true to what happened as much as I could, for his sake. Timothy's educated, which I'm not, a-course, especially from all his reading and such, so I wanted to put down his words, not mine, as hard as that was to do.

"So this was really a helpful thing for Dr. Hyatt and me to do together, because now I have what I've written to read any time I want to. And this is a comfort when I'm feeling low. It helps keep the thoughts in my head from circling around and around until I feel like I'm crazy.

"So, here's what happened."

"One night, oh, this was in late summer last year—well, it had to've been, because your mother was still living at home, and she started moving out in October. So it was late August or early September. But this particular night, she wasn't at home. In fact, remembering now, she stayed out the night, because she was getting a room ready to move into soon. We'd been talking for some time about her leaving. This wasn't anything new, but we hadn't talked to any of you kids about it yet.

"Anyway, Timothy called and asked if there was a way for him to see me alone. It was easy enough to say that was fine, so he came around in that beat-up pickup of his, the '50 red Ford I teased him about all the time, me working for the Chrysler Corporation for all those years the way I did, you know. But he'd got it all fixed up— 'vintage-restored,' he called it. He even had me work on it some, but this was before he decided to get it in tip-top shape, so he could take it to car shows. Not to win prizes, he told me, but to meet with other automobile nuts and talk about cars.

"So, he came around and told me he wanted to take me somewhere, and he didn't want a lot of questions surrounding it, just wanted me to come along for the ride—that's if I wanted to, if I didn't have anything else planned. Well, a-course I said yes. All this was enough to make me curious, if nothing else. And he knew I didn't have anything *planned*.

"So he drove us out some ways, out on Highway 9. Then he turned off somewhere, toward the South. It was a beautiful night, there was dew in the air, it was close to dusk. He didn't have on the radio like he usually did. You know he never listened to cowboy music. He was into jazz. But he'd play Western tunes around me, 'cause he knew I liked it. On this night, though, he just smoked and drove, and we drove a long time, him turning here and there. I lost track of where we were completely, and that takes a lot 'cause I have a great sense of direction. But I let go and didn't try to keep track, just stared out the window and let him carry me along. It got quieter and quieter, and when it was totally dark, the stars came out. He drove to some spot he definitely had in mind. But I gotta tell you, I couldn't find it today if somebody had a gun to my head. He stopped, him still not saying a word, but finally leaning over and whispering, 'Come this way.'

"Well, I followed him through some gate into what appeared to be a pasture. I could see after a bit of walking that we were in the middle of a big grazing area. It was still just light enough to make out a group of trees over to our right where some cattle had huddled for the night, because the air was fall-like, but not chilly enough for a jacket, and straight ahead was a pond with the reflection of the moon starting to spread across the water's surface. It wasn't anything I hadn't seen before—seen it a thousand times during the years when I was harvesting with the crews and farming with Willard, when we'd stay out and drink our homebrew after the day's work, and then later on with Whalen. I was in my twenties then but, too, during all you kids' growing up years, with Darlene, our going fishing, staying out by Clanton's and Halstead's ponds and all those county creeks we went to, Turkey Creek near Hopewell in particular. We'd stay out in pastures until it was almost too dark for us to find our way back to the car. You could smell the fish and pond water on our hands on the drive back home, but we didn't care. Remember that?

"But there was something different about this night with Timothy. It could be the memory of it more than what really happened. But in thinking about it so much since, one notion that's stayed with me is that maybe it was different because Timmy and I hadn't spent much time together, by ourselves. Darlene was always around when he did come around, for one thing. But what was different, well, I felt as though Timothy'd waited for a perfect night. He'd chosen it out of all those other nights when he might've done this, so he was *giving it* to me, you see what I mean?

"After walking a little ways, he sat down, and so I did too. Then he laid down on the grass, which I did as well. I was doing what he seemed to be asking me to do, following his lead without questions. We were far enough from the pond so we weren't bothered by bugs so much, but we were close enough to the cows for me to hear them breathe, that slow sputtering noise they make out of their mouths. I could smell them too—cow sweat in their hide, mud and manure mingled with the moist night air. Sounds and smells carry long distances on a night like this.

"I have no idea how much time passed while we laid there like that, just looking at the stars. It was long enough for me to feel a quiet so great that, to me, Timmy and I were one, the way we were breathing together and feeling each other so close but not touching or trying to make each other know we were there together. The only outside thing I sensed was the smell of tobacco on his shirt.

"Then he took one hand and, with his fingers spread, he slowly moved it up in front of him, across the sky. And when he brought it down, he laid it on my arm, lightly touching me. 'Father,' he said, 'Vernon. Daddy. I love you.'

"Well, I burst into sobs. There was something so absolutely true in his voice, in how he said all the names of what I am to him. He didn't reach out to touch me anymore than just having his hand on my arm, and he lay like that, quiet and still, letting me cry. I think he was crying too, but how could I know? I was way too stricken to tell him I loved him too, but when I quieted down, he took his hand off my arm, and he told me this story, the one Dr. Hyatt helped me remember as best I could and to write down.

"'One day,' Timothy said, 'when I was a kid about eleven, twelve years old, a coupla friends and I went out to that open field behind our house and made a fort out of snow. We found branches and sticks under the trees which we used to keep the walls from collapsing. It took us all day, so it must've been during some holiday from school. We even filled one corner of our fort with snowballs in case somebody came by, and we needed to blast them one. After we were done, it was starting to get dark. I'm not sure why any of our parents weren't worried about us, but as I remember it, we didn't have any intrusions or interruptions. Maybe Mother could see us from the kitchen windows, maybe I went back in and let her know where we were, I don't remember, but we stayed out there until dark. And I don't remember if we even had anything to eat, none of those ordinary, daily concerns seem to enter the picture of this for me.

"'After we were done, we didn't say anything to each other, we just lay down on the cold ground inside, and looked at the stars. We couldn't get the roof to stay up over the entire structure, so we left huge gaps we could see through. And as we lay there, it began to snow. In all my life, I'd never felt life so intensely alive as in those moments when the flakes were falling down on us, and there was nothing but the stars.

"'And then a realization came to me, a revelation, a *knowledge*. Life felt so huge, the spirit of being alive so enormous, I was suddenly connected to everything, I mean, *everything*. There was no intense light like people talk about when something like this happens—especially with those who are dying—but I apprehended brightness all around me just the same, in and through everything. I actually felt warmth. I'm sure it only lasted a few minutes, but it seemed as though it went on endlessly. The experience of recognition was so complete, so totally intense, tears began falling from my eyes. I wasn't generating any of this. It was simply happening around and through me.

"'It was snowing hard by that time, and Raymond, the kid down the street I always hung out with, sat up and said we oughta go home. So, all at once, there was great bustling about, getting ourselves out into the night and walking home, which was really only across a lot and our backyard. I do remember there wasn't very much talking, just a lot of trudging sounds, breathing hard, making our way back along the path that was fast being covered up again with snow. I don't remember how we parted. I don't remember if we ever talked again about what we'd experienced that day. I don't know if the other two experienced anything like I did or if they heard me cry and maybe that's why Raymond suddenly suggested that we leave, or if they cried themselves and maybe felt strange about it. I don't remember ever hearing any notions from them about any of this later. I don't even remember if we returned to the fort, played there at later times. All and any of that is a total blank. I can't even picture clearly who the other kid was we were with. Someone we knew well enough to be a part of all this. I only remember Raymond.

"'But this I can tell you, I walked out of that night with a knowledge I didn't have before. I'll never know if I could've had this happen to me while I was alone, if I hadn't been with both of these friends or if Raymond hadn't been there. And if I would've had to explain the means by which I gained that knowledge, I couldn't then. I can't now. But I did learn truths I cannot deny, regardless of a lack of explanation about how I got them.

"'From that day to this, I believe I learned two things. One is that what we call God is so vast, so incomprehensible, yet so absolutely ever present, that to not believe this means that I am bound to everlasting finitude, that I can never know anything beyond reason and sense, beyond the material and that which can be measured and explained. All that is magic, that is wonder-filled, that is limitless, boundless, all that defies words, that which is truly silent—all this can never be known to me if I deny this incomprehensible boundlessness of God-as-Ultimate-Presence. Perhaps it's only in a name, but I haven't a clue as to what else to call it. It doesn't feel right to call it imagination or creativity or some such, because it didn't emanate from me.

"'The other thing I learned is that I can trust a kind of inner light, a faith within myself about what I can know about my life and how to live it. I also have come to understand that I must do certain things to stay in touch with whatever that is. I see all of this as a kind of self-identity, but a kind of higher knowing beyond the self. In this sense, I believe I can know myself. I am simply a spirit as a 'being-alive-presence' in this world, completely a mystery at the same time that I'm material, finite, explainable to me and everybody else.

"'In other words, I'm a contradiction by simply being.

"'I haven't always remembered this, nor lived it in my life—not knowingly. In fact, I've spent some real time denying it, usually doing that as loudly as I can in order to convince myself that what happened to me wasn't actually what I experienced. But there it is. And I wanted you to know the truth of it. I've not told another soul what I've truly felt about this, not one. I haven't even written it in my journal.'"

—

"Well, all at once, Timothy stopped talking out there in that field. After what seemed to be hours, with us lying there in the grass, he said, 'We need to go home, Dad.'

"And I gotta tell you, Caroline, I don't remember a whole lot after that. I do remember standing up, him reaching over to make sure I was steady on my feet after lying in the night air so long, but I don't remember much about driving home or after.

"He got outta the truck, walked me to the door and hugged me under the porch light, June bugs flying all around, hitting the door and us. And then he said goodbye, walked back to his truck, waved and drove off into the Wild Blue Yonder. He said 'goodbye,' Caroline, not 'good night.' I'm remembering that right, because it struck me at the time.

"And he musta meant it, because I didn't see him again. But as he turned from the front door to go to his truck, he said, *'komm vada.'* This means, "Come again," in Plattdeutsch. It's what we said to relatives when we said goodbye but knew we'd see them again sometime soon. These two words give me hope. And that one telephone call.

"There's another strange thing though. When I turned to go into the house, I was overcome by the thought that he was older than I was. I felt shriveled, almost tiny by what I'd experienced with him. But, at the same time, I felt as forceful, bigger, better than I'd ever been. I went into the living room without turning on the light and sat in the dark. Your mother wasn't home and, to be truthful, I didn't even think about her. It was like I was already living alone.

"So I sat in the dark and smoked. I would've wept, but I was too overcome."

———

"Now here's what's so hard for me to accept, Caroline. Timothy was gone for weeks—no, more. He was gone for *months* before I received the call from him to let me know he had left and was okay where he was—he wouldn't say where. And there've been no calls since. As far away as you and Teddy are, your mother and I know where you live and expect to know if things change with how you are, because you respect us enough to let us know, for godssakes.

"I'm trying to think how long it actually was before I received his telephone call. Well, I can tell you. It was from early September to late November is what it was. You and Teddy had both called several times during those months, and you had both let us know you were coming to visit soon. Nothing from Timothy, not a word, not during that entire time. And, you know, this is something that both your mother and me have conditioned ourselves to accept.

"I think we've been scared to let him know that this wasn't acceptable, because we've been afraid he'd disappear altogether if we did. Well, look what that's got us. So all our trying to consider his feelings, at the expense of our own, netted us damn near nothing, is how I see it."

———

"But since you've asked, I'm telling you how it was and is with Tim and us, and why I think he left. While I've been in here, I've given this a lot of attention to how all these fragments of Timothy's life—actually, how all of our lives as a family—come together. And what I've figured out so far is, first off, there's not a whole lot of easy 'coming together' to life, period. The remembered events don't lead one to the other the way we think they do. We search for purpose or meaning among all the bits and pieces, or, at the very least, look for something that makes sense of all of it. But when you step back and look at your life, really look, you get a whole picture only if you *build* those bits and pieces into a history, something you can tell as your life story.

"Dr. Hyatt was big on one's story, what we put together to tell ourselves about what's happening, what's happened, who we are. And we all look for that thread, don't we? But, with Timothy, the part that's him as family, well, it seems his pieces aren't all out there to see, so we can't put him together with us very well. Anyway, I can't see how they fit into the picture of him in my life. What kind of a picture would that need to be for me to truly understand who he is, especially who he is to me and me to him? You can't tell a story about a picture that's only partly there, can you?

"And second, what scares me to think about, but what I can't get out of my mind is—what if Timothy's purpose has been met, and he's drawn some conclusions about that, feels he doesn't have much to live for anymore? I know how absolutely crazy this must sound, but, remember, he and I discussed this, and I keep thinking, what if he gave me this gift from his childhood, the story he told me about his vision out in that fort with his friends, passing it on to me in another field, where I had my own similar vision of sorts—well, I just don't know. Could be I'm totally losing it over him. But I keep feeling he gave me something that's supposed to explain him to me, and, goddammit, I can't figure it out. It's scaring me, Caroline. There's something almost final about it that's scaring me a lot."

4.

Two days later

"I'm at home, now, Caroline. Darlene helped me grocery shop, and after seeing everything was in place here for the next few days, took off. So I thought I'd wind up this tape tonight and get it in the mail tomorrow myself.

It's strange being all alone. It's the silence, mainly. Detox wasn't noisy, but there were people sounds around here and there. Dr. Hyatt has called already, just to check in. I'm fine. I want you to know that right off.

"When Darlene brought me home, she stayed long enough for us to have a little talk about Timothy. I wanted to know where she was with him, and after our talk, I've made some decisions about how I'm going to respond when he gets in touch with us—if he ever does.

"First I'll bring you up to speed about our visit to his place in OK City.

"When Darlene and I went to inquire at his apartment about three days after I tried to reach him—yes, this once I did call him, because the night I'd spent with him had been so special—even shocking—I felt a real urge, desperate even, to get in touch with him again. Remember, I had his phone number that he'd passed to me earlier, a long time ago. I knew not to use it unless it was an emergency, but if this didn't fit that definition, I can't imagine what would.

"Can you imagine what I felt when I heard this electric voice on the other end of the line telling me his phone was disconnected? I kept hearing him in my head saying goodbye instead of good night. It's the message suicides give sometimes, you know? I've learned that from Darlene's Tough Love work. Well, I didn't know what to do, so in a panic, I called your mother. Now this was tricky, because I didn't want her to know I'd had his number all along, and I certainly wasn't going to tell her about my special night with him, but I needed to run things past her. After all, she was, is, his mother. I just felt so strong that something was wrong, or at least not right.

"So I gave in and owned up to having his number. Darlene wasn't the happiest mother on the planet, let me tell you, but after hearing me out, we both put that aside and decided to call Snooky to get the number where Tim worked. We got him right away, using the number in the OK City telephone directory, and found out that Timothy'd quit his job, had told his boss that he was moving to Spain. Snooky assumed we knew. Can you imagine? Out of nowhere, we hear, 'Spain.'

"So then, we got his landlady's phone number from Snooky, and from her, Tim's apartment address. We went out to see her since she lived right next door to his place. Talking with her, we found out that Timothy never came home the night he and I'd been together. He'd paid her the rent up to date early that morning. All his things were gone, so he'd cleaned out, evidently taking with him what he wanted. His belongings were in his truck the night he said goodbye to me, and I simply didn't see them. Knowing Timothy, it probably was about enough to put in a suitcase and a coupla boxes, if that— though I haven't any idea what he did with the records and books he's so fond of.

"Now I'm finding there're secrets everywhere you look around this. I still haven't told your mother about Timmy and my night together, and I'm asking you to honor that. It would only hurt her. She never came home that night. I say 'home.' She didn't come back to our house that night. She stayed in the apartment she'd rented and was moving into— our separation Timothy didn't know about.

"You can see how I was left sitting squarely in the middle of two impossible secrets.

"She had called and left a message on the answering machine, so I wouldn't worry, though I didn't catch it until very late.

―

"So here's where I am with it all, Caroline. I'm angry, *very* angry at Timothy. I've decided to stop putting anymore of myself into him. I mean, I'm not going to think any more about him, try to find him, worry about where the hell he is or anything else concerning him—not even discussing or trying to figure out his past anymore with you or anybody else, especially Darlene. And if he calls me, I'm going to tell him right away, up front, that if he wants a conversation with me he can stop playing all these goddamned cat-and-mouse games and say what he really thinks of his family, and whether he's going to be a member in it or not.

"If he wants to be, then there are some responsibilities. Whatever in the world he thinks he's doing with us, I don't know, and at this point, I don't care, unless he steps forward and commits himself to us. Everything I felt on the night of his special evening with me, well, I've just shelved that. It's not in the trash, but I'm not thinking on it—not now anyway, and maybe not ever again.

"It feels shoddy, what he's done. I've been betrayed, is how I'm seeing this.

"He *knew*, Caroline, the whole time he was in the field with me what he had in mind, and he chose not to share his intentions with me. All that passed between us— what was that? In light of what I know now? *What was it?*

"Okay, he's called me, but, in this, here he was, up to his old tricks of being in touch but not in touch. Here I am, again, left dangling on a line, waiting for him to decide when and where he wants to come back home.

"So I'm done until he shows himself properly to us. I know that families are supposed to love unconditionally. Well, hell with that. My view is when you get to be an adult you don't expect to be loved regardless of what you do. You may be loved out of a sense of belonging—after all he's our child—but real grown-up love has adult responsibilities attached to it. It's what I've learned in detox, and it's what Darlene talks about with Tough Love. She was so troubled by him leaving the way he did, that she went to extra meetings and got some understanding about what to say and do if and when Timothy reappears, if he ever does.

"She joined this organization when she worked and ran into some troubles with co-workers on her job, but she saw it could help her with upset feelings concerning her kids, especially Timothy. And a lot of what she's told me makes absolute sense. If he contacts you, I want you to keep it to yourself, Caroline. I mean it. I'm done with him until he straightens up and acts like our grown-up son."

5.

Vernon
Tape recording to Caroline—Mid-May, 1991

"I hope you aren't too awfully surprised by this tape. I'm the last one who would ever've believed I'd find this more comfortable than talking on the phone, but it's true. I guess I feel I have time to gather my thoughts before I begin, and if I say something I feel isn't the right thing, I can erase it and begin again. With that assurance, I don't seem to be making as many mistakes in what I want to say. The phone gives you no room for errors. You say it, it's said! And tapes're better too, because if there's anything I want to tell of any length at all, I can stop and then get back to it when I'm able or when I'm up to it. You can't very well hang-up the phone like that and pick it up again later and keep your thoughts going from one time to the next, can you? Well, I guess you could, but thoughts leave me on the phone. This way, I really get to say what I mean.

"And with all the tapes you and I've made back some time ago, I feel somewhat at home with this way of talking to you. I'm thinking about when you were in therapy, asking me all those questions about your childhood and about various members of the family. It was a good thing to do. It sorted out a lot of my own thoughts and feelings about each of us. But it's been awhile, and I'm wondering what you'll make of my getting in touch with you like this again. You'll have to let me know.

"Well, your mother and me have heard from Timothy. Of course, you know this already. Darlene has shared with me some of what you've exchanged on the phone.

She did tell me that you haven't heard 'the news' from him yourself. I suspect he wants to wait until he's heard our answer about whether he'll be coming home or not before he tells you, Teddy and Kat. I can see why he'd not want lots of discussion milling around about whether he should have asked this of us, what you three think about our taking it on, especially with the dangers.

"I hear from Darlene that you do have some concerns, but you must know we can't say no, Caroline. That's just not within our power. He's our child however old he is—just as you all are—and we aren't going to abandon him to a lonely fate. I also know from your mother that she did not take the time to read you his whole letter. In fact, she said she told you only the gist of it, whatever that is to her. Although it might be hard for me to get through it, I would like to not only read it to you now, but let you know that as you requested of her, we are getting the letter and the pictures copied he sent, so you can have them. As soon as the photo shop calls, we will send it all, and you can decide how and when you want to inform Teddy and Kat. This isn't going to be the easiest thing for me to do—to read the letter. But I want you to know what it says in his words.

"Timothy did not tell us we couldn't share the letter with you and the others, so I'm doing it this way. I do think that the package I send you should not be shared outside our family, at least until Timothy gives us the go ahead on it. So here it is. It's lengthy, and then there are my comments, so there are several tapes, as you can see.

"May 2, 1991
"He just starts out. He doesn't give a greeting.

"This letter is by way of introduction. That might sound formal and a bit strange, but I feel I have withheld myself from you for many years, probably, in some ways, for my entire life—most certainly since I left Oklahoma and came to California. I am living in Pacific Palisades, Los Angeles, in a house that I've inherited from a close friend, Maxim Sheller (oh yes, that's his name, and not to be confused with the Austrian actor Maximilian Schell, though Maxim was at least as good-looking!) My friend just recently died from AIDS thus my acquisition of his property. All this is a long story, so I hope you will be patient with me. But it is a story far too lengthy to tell you on the phone, and one I don't have the strength to put on tape. Writing this, too, might enable me to gather my thoughts, sort and arrange them before I put them down, and in this way, tell you what I need to in order for you to make your decision about whether or not you want to accept what I will be proposing. Writing will also give me a chance to tell my story progressively, if not in sequence.

"I'm not well, and it takes effort to finish anything that requires endurance, especially writing a letter such as this—which isn't the easiest thing in the world for me to do under any circumstances. I feel more comfortable with writing (as versus talking)—no surprise there for you, I'm sure—though what I have to say throws any comfort I might ordinarily have, right out the window. I'm not meaning to be mysterious, but I need to tell you my story in a certain way. I hope to answer most of your questions by the time I finish with the telling. If not, I've left numbers where you can reach me day or night. In any case, I want to begin conversations with you both after you've read this. You will find my current address and those numbers at the bottom of the last page of this letter. The only request I make is that you read together what I'm sending and discuss it thoroughly before contacting me. The packet of photographs I've enclosed should be opened after you've read everything. It's why I've sealed the envelope securely with a note—to help you wait!

"My leaving Oklahoma so abruptly had to have been a shock. And though it was unfair to you, I needed to go as I did, because if I'd taken the time to leave appropriately—especially regarding your feelings—I would never have gone. My nature is to be sluggish. I think I know myself pretty well. I've spent a lot of time in solitude, and I feel I've accepted who I am. I know it's an American trait to constantly be reinventing oneself, but I can't seem to muster the energy to go through what's required to do such a thing—if I could even envision what that might look like for me. I've always felt comfortable in my person—as conceited as that might be—and have spent my time attempting to develop, use and be with who I feel that is, rather than to be in the state of constant reconstruction. I've had some difficulties trying to sidestep what other people, at times, have designed for me, but on the whole, I've managed to compromise—if you want to call it that—just enough to feel I still have kept "myself" intact.

"I have very few interests, really. I like to read, listen to music and write and be connected to a few close (very close) friends. But I'm not hopelessly lost in my own self-indulgences. I do have some small visions that propel me out of my reclusive inclinations—well, one of them actually turned out to be not so small, but I'll get to more about that.

"I've always wanted to play the trumpet, which I thought was only a fantasy, a vision of sorts. I am a Louie Armstrong and early jazz fan and have collected over the years early recordings of his and other musicians that I don't need to list here, for heaven's sakes. I have fine speakers and a turntable that I play these old 78s on, at various sizes—some I've found in the most obscure places, others from collectors who have charged me far too much, and still others (the most obscure recordings) I've located in searches through word of mouth with people who are as crazy as I am about these things. For a while, this preoccupation was all consuming and brought me into contact with some extraordinary people—a couple whom I became more than just friends with, characters who will enter my story as I go along here.

"I knew that my trumpet playing was going to take some real discipline and given my laid-back disposition, I wasn't certain I would be up to what it would take to master the instrument. But I found a good teacher, practiced religiously and in several years, discovered I had a genuine feel for it. It took me some time, but about three years ago, I was playing with a couple of loosely put-together groups that performed in small, private clubs around the L.A. area—that's when I found the time. I knew quite a few of these clubs since my bartending brought me into contact with other guys doing what I did, well, truthfully, I sought them out, because I went to other bars to see what and how they did successfully (or not) what they did. It was through this search that I ran into musicians and got some soft playing gigs. I didn't make a lot of money on the trumpet, but it supplemented my income enough for me to add to the savings I'd brought with me from Oklahoma.

"The other vision I had, the one that took me to California in the first place, really, was that of living in Spain. As you know I was stationed there during my duty in the Navy. I simply fell in love with the country and its people, at least the people I came into contact with, though at the time (something just short of two weeks) I didn't truthfully meet that many. I was in Cadiz, a port station for Naval Forces working in missiles and radar. And my unit and I were involved in reconnaissance—the details of which I've not told you as our missions were classified—so we were flown out of there to carriers in the South China Sea. I'm sure Cadiz at the time wasn't the greatest view of Spain, especially since foreign troops aren't going to bring out the best in the natives. But I was there long enough to understand that this place felt familiar to me, and I wanted to return some day. Why I didn't act on this earlier, I guess I have to attribute, again, to my sluggishness. Seems I follow through on some visions, others not. As you will see, I've come to view motivation less about conscious decision-making than about fate, almost in the classic sense. The nearest explanation to what I mean is the Biblical teaching of "the will of God," I suppose. But be that as it may, part of my California journey was the hope that I'd pick up some money, and then travel often to (if not live) in Spain.

"You might wonder why in the heck—especially you, Dad, with your love of geography—I didn't go east since that's the usual, and shortest, travel route to Europe. But I've heard that it's easier for Midwesterners or Southwesterners (whichever way you view Oklahomans) to transfer to the West Coast than the East, which is probably true as the melting-pot nature of the West is more conducive to the easygoing, sprawling culture of where I was born and raised. But remember I also went through Navy boot camp in San Diego and stayed there a while before coming back to Oklahoma with Caroline, as I'm sure you remember. She had gone to California with me after I graduated from high school. We'd had this grand plan about living and working in California where everybody went who wanted to do anything with their young lives! So that's where I headed back again. It seemed less intimidating to me than, say, New York City, despite the long gap between the back-then sixties and then present-day California of the eighties.

"How I ended up in L.A. was a fluke but so was my stay in Las Vegas. I decided I wanted to see the Grand Canyon—you remember how you drove around it once on our vacation West, Dad, when I was about eight or nine. And we all wanted to kill you for not going there? Well, I saw my chance, so I went from Oklahoma through the Texas panhandle to Albuquerque, over and up into Northern Arizona to see part of the Canyon and then further down, around and up North again to Las Vegas. Once there, I stayed to gamble, of course. Bartenders are known for their gambling—if you don't already know this. I thought I'd stay for no more than a couple of days but after doing well for myself—in fact, very well for myself, far better than the averages—I decided to make it a few months. So I found a bar to tend—I thought very temporarily—and gambled with the hope of adding to my resources for Spain beyond my Oklahoma City savings. I ended up staying for almost two years, twenty months to be exact.

"I finally left Las Vegas in the summer of '83. Now, Las Vegas has a hot climate, as it's in the desert, of course, but the day I left it was a nasty 103°! And, driving along at a good clip, baking alive, I saw this hitchhiker on Interstate 15 where nobody's supposed to hitchhike, but there he was in the blistering heat, cowboy hat and boots and a jacket on, if you can believe that. This young lad—well, not so awfully young maybe, but a decade short of my years—turned out to be named Cheroot Chéreau. Of course, this wasn't his real name—he was Native American, for God's Sake. I went along with his little name-charade—he did smoke cheroots and, believe it or not, loved opera. He was a fan of Patrice Chéreau, who was known for his productions of Wagner in the 1970s and experimental theater. Cheroot knew an awfully lot about the guy. Chéreau was gay and chain-smoked, so Cheroot thought he'd die of lung cancer, if AIDS didn't get him first. I hadn't a clue what he was talking about, but I let it pass—Cheroot was inclined toward monologue.

"When I asked if he was a relative of Patrice Chéreau's, Cheroot grinned and shook a hard Kentucky pack of cigars at me, telling me to have a smoke, his treat.

"What I did learn on that trip though—he never would reveal his real name—was that Cheroot was (or claimed to be) descended from the Mashantucket Pequot tribe, one with a long, interesting history—as they all do, don't they? But the Pequot met near extinction under the British, but survived, and were now striving to financially revive themselves so that the government, according to law, would not inherit their lands. His family was embroiled in all kinds of legal battles in an effort to keep tribal lands in the family. He was investigating casino halls as a possible means for their financial solvency—it's why he'd been to Vegas and was going to California. It seems various tribes across the country had taken state governments to court in an attempt to gain sovereignty over gaming rights on their lands, which started out as bingo and pool halls.

"At the time of this letter, the tribes, one by one, are winning slowly, in baby steps, to control their own gaming establishments, it seems. You may know some of this yourselves from situations there in Oklahoma.

"Anyway, I found all this fascinating and don't see how Cheroot could have invented much of it, even though I thought it odd that once we got to L.A., I learned he was also very involved in the movie-making business. Maybe he saw that as another possibility for his tribe. And it could be how he came in contact with Patrice Chéreau—through film-making. Who knows? I have kept up a little with him during the past seven, eight years, off and on, but the last I heard, he'd left California to move to Connecticut where he claimed his family was getting ready to establish a casino in Ledyard. He told me if it gelled, he would be managing some aspect of the business. He wasn't clear about what exactly that would be. And I haven't heard from him since.

"I got off a bit on a tangent with this, but it was through Chéreau that I met Maxim Sheller. Well, that's not exactly accurate either, but I'll get to it. I guess I want you to see how the dots across the map of my life have lead toward a destiny that I never planned nor envisioned, let alone would have known how to manipulate, into reality. It's as though, when I do make plans, they are derailed or sidetracked by an invisible hand pushing me along as "it" sees fit. So much of my life up to now has been an unfolding—a propulsion from one place, event, person to another over which I feel I haven't had much control. A lot of what has happened to me in important times in my life seem fated, or, at the very least, seem to emanate from magical, if not divine, sources. I've come to accept those forces, and how they play in our lives if we step out of the way and let them arise.

"But in all of my vision-making, the most central one (if not the biggest) is that of "home"—in both its conceptual and conventional meanings. I like to nest—to stay put. (I can see you nodding—hopefully smiling—at this not so surprising revelation.) I moved to Oklahoma City and didn't budge for how many years? For two adult decades, really—which brings me back to the question of why, if I wanted to live in Spain so much, did I go to California instead of moving immediately and directly to Madrid or wherever in that country? There are planes that go out of Oklahoma City to the east coast and on to Europe, for heaven's sake.

"So why did I end up staying in California? And why, for that matter, did I dally around in Las Vegas?

"The most immediate answer is I needed money, at least, I told myself I needed more money. But the truth is, what I needed was the courage to make the leap to such a dream after waiting so long. I had my desire, my passport, my suitcase and my trumpet—music is universal, right? I reasoned that I could learn to play and join in the musicians community in Spain, well, that was the idea anyway. All were packed to go, together with some savings—but not enough to live on without working. I knew I could bartend because it's universal, but without speaking the language and without knowing much about the culture, I wasn't sure what to expect right away.

"But, of course, all of these concerns became history, as they say, because I never made it past Los Angeles. It wasn't ennui that held me this time though. It was necessity. What I didn't realize was that I was walking into a pandemic of HIV-AIDS. And if this were true of L.A., I knew it had to be more so in other metro areas with large gay populations across the country—well, and I was to learn, in Europe as well.

"The first bar I considered for work—an ad placed in the newspaper—was a gay bar. Of course, there were plenty of other bars in L.A. I could have found work just about anywhere, because as the disease spread, gays and Haitians, especially, (however unjustified) were being fired from their jobs—many in the food and entertainment industry. And lots of these folks did not work just in openly gay establishments. There was a bias against non-European immigrants on the whole because of the widespread misperception of their involvement with the infiltration of drugs into the country.

"But there were two reasons for my staying with the bar in Silver Lake in central L.A., which was named Changeable Assets, by the way—I know, I know, far too cheeky and maybe even cheesy, but a very popular spot nonetheless—where a lot of both the famous and infamous mixtures of indie musicians and film makers hung out. When I interviewed for the job, I saw right away that this was an atmosphere where I could make a living and get music into my life the way I wanted. So that was the first reason. The second was that the bar had become a haven for people who were confused, desperate, and victims to a situation over which they had no control. I didn't feel I could turn my back on that. A lot of people were running as fast as they could from this state-of-affair, because it was high risk and dangerous. I didn't see it that way. I saw it as an opportunity to help.

"My first years there were heady, filled with fresh emerging cultural ideas from all over, including the Latino influence right there in the neighborhood, despite some hostility from many residents in the area. The bar became known as a hub for lively social activity. But then AIDS became everyone's concern and Changeable Assets truly changed, but for the time that it lasted, it remained an asset for those in the gay community.

"It was during these early days that I first ran into Maxim Sheller. I didn't know at first who he was, only that he was a "crazy-as-I-was" early jazz record collector. We spent that first evening talking off and on about 1920s jazz—he was into ragtime, I was into blues—while I made drinks and delivered them to the waiters who were screaming their bloody heads off that I wasn't getting to their orders fast enough. Course they were worried about their tips! In my schizophrenic haste between Maxim—I didn't even get his name then—and the waiters, I lost him to the crowd, and after my shift, found he had left without offering a goodbye or possible connection for contact at a later time. I was disappointed, as he really knew a lot more than I did about the music I was interested in, and I thought I was pretty much at the top-of-the-game with this stuff. I didn't see him again until… well, I'll get to that soon enough.

"You might wonder why I continued working at this bar that became increasingly risky to me health-wise. With my reference from Oklahoma City, the manager of the bar hired me on the spot, so I knew I could go anywhere and get a job. But I felt comfortable at Assets from the get-go, mainly because I could be myself, especially dressing as I do, and the place had a huge flow of musicians by the time I was playing trumpet myself. Also, bars and especially bath houses were fighting mandated closures, and it wasn't long before Changeable Assets felt like home, so I wanted to stay and help fight for its right to be there. Many bars were hubs for information and for fermenting actionable support for the gay community.

"I have no idea where you both are with this issue, but personally, I couldn't do anything but empathize. The need was so great—people were dying at staggering rates, and there were no medical therapies to offer them in the early eighties. It wasn't until 1987 that the Drug and Food Administration approved AZT! And it wasn't until then that ACT UP started and more aggressive and effective organizations to support those with the disease and work for its cure.

"I don't know how much you know about AIDS. National news finally started *carrying more information after Rock Hudson died. But back when I first came to California, I walked into this situation because information about it wasn't readily available outside the gay community in Oklahoma City at the time. I had heard talk while still in OKCity of cases of some strange "gay cancer" inflicting that community and IV drug users in California, especially San Francisco, and in metro areas such as New York City, but it seemed remote, having nothing to do with any of the rest of us, especially us way out in the Mid-and-Southwest! By now, of course, there are gay organizations in Oklahoma City with some political activity going on.*

"I knew with startling quickness that some of the people I'd just met, some I considered friends, at least friends-in-the-making, were being diagnosed. But it took a while to discover that the incubation period for the disease was on average eleven years. So all at once, gay men, who'd had a life of easy sexuality before this, were getting sick—and some with not so promiscuous a lifestyle. The problem, of course, was that the latent period is from three to six weeks, when the disease can't be detected, so even one encounter with an exposed person to the virus could mean infection without immediate detection (even if tested right away) and then the "person with AIDS" (PWA) wouldn't know for years, infecting others along the way.

"It was all so damn crazy. We couldn't figure out the pattern. I knew guys at the bar who had been promiscuous earlier in their lives, say in the seventies, and when finally tested didn't have the disease while their current partners, who'd had only another partner before the present one, were laid low very rapidly with full-blown AIDS. In fact, this was the case with Maxim and Trotter (his partner), at least initially. It took years before Maxim succumbed to the disease, while Trotter went very quickly.

"To say that the gay community at our bar, well, the community as a whole, was terrified, doesn't begin to describe the hysteria. And Reagan's government, the FDA, and Americans at large didn't seem concerned. The FDA should've been looking for a cure and wasn't. When they finally did, it was too late. The numbers began to mount.

"In the early 80s, there were three to four thousand cases of AIDS in the U.S. By 1988, there were 83,000, over half of whom had died and a year later, it was 100,000. The only drug sanctioned in the U.S.—AZT which you may have heard a lot about on the news by now—was tremendously expensive. People without insurance couldn't afford it—it was something like $8K a year when the average annual income was around $25K—and that's people with jobs! Gay *people were losing theirs, so it wasn't just their income, it was often their health benefits as well. You had to qualify for Medicaid which wasn't always possible for people who didn't work. And I have to say, when Trotter's insurance capped in what they'd pay, if he hadn't had other means—especially Maxim's help—he wouldn't have lived as long as he did.*

"*What Maxim was able to do was get him into a Suramin drug trial, which unfortunately didn't help. The drug proved ineffectual and the trial was abandoned. But the point I'm making is Maxim had connections inside the medical establishment which helped. It's how the whole corrupt thing worked—you knew somebody who knew somebody, and you were "in" for the latest treatments or trials.*

"*It was a wild ride for a while, but later, after Trotter succumbed to the disease, and Maxim was diagnosed, he was able finally to procure some illegal drugs through a buyer's club in L.A. which, at least, helped him with his symptoms, allowing him for a time to feel better, though not leading toward a cure.*

"*My role in all of this is, first, to tell you how I got involved and, secondly, why it's so important to me still. I'm a laid-back guy so getting active in the ways I have is an amazing story even to me. Since Reagan's conservative government gave no support or funding to this horrific state-of-affairs, the gay community took the situation into their own hands. Changeable Assets became a central meeting house for gays wanting to make a difference. There were also the gay presses that began to generate and disseminate information to the community and to the public at large— that's when the public cared to look.*

"*In the mid-eighties, when I saw how many of my regular customers at the bar were dying, I decided to do something. This was my being only a couple of years into the situation. But selfishly—because I still had dreams of going to Spain—I wanted that contributing "something" to also earn me some real money.*

"*I first considered becoming an RN because it pays so well, but it takes from four to six years to complete a nursing degree and certification. Then I thought about becoming an Emergency Room Techie. Because of the broken week on such a job—three long days on and four off—I could supplement my bartending income or I could give up bartending altogether for the ERT work full-time. Unfortunately, this would've been a considerable drop in pay. I did exceptionally well at the bar.*

"*In the meantime, I was also considering going the Emergency Medical Technician route, which is first responder work and has similar hours to those of ERTs.*

"I was figuring I could begin school for a degree in nursing on my off hours and ultimately become a PA in a hospital or in a doctor's practice, which could be done perhaps in less time. My idea was to find a way to earn enough for living in Spain, while I was helping my friends and the community during this crisis. It would not be easy, and with the trumpet playing on the side—heavens, I didn't want to give that up!—well, it all seemed daunting. I was in a state of constant confusion about what to do.

"As it turned out, just as I was looking into how to proceed, Cheroot showed up at the bar one day with the same fellow I'd met earlier, the jazz enthusiast who'd slipped by me without my getting his name or number. This was Maxim Sheller. I was at a distinct disadvantage, because Cheroot had informed him about me—what there was to tell—but I didn't know anything about Sheller at all. I was embarrassed to learn he was a well-known indie movie producer who'd scored several awards, the major one for a documentary at Sundance. He'd get a BAFTA award in 1987, but that was down the road, after I knew him well. These recognitions probably don't mean anything to you, but out here, it gives a person enormous credibility, which translates into a way of getting money to do your work.

"Cheroot had found out my desire for possible nursing positions in the future. I thought I'd been pretty discrete about my search into this. But who knows the guy's resources? Sheller told me his partner had HIV and at present was battling a bad case of PCP, which, if you haven't heard of it, is a lung infection—basically, pneumonia. Over half of AIDS patients get it, sometimes more than once, and in the early years—at the time I met Maxim—half of AIDS deaths in the United States were caused by this infection.

"So Maxim was simply terrified for his partner's future, and said he was seeking a full-time aide for him. Cheroot had told him of my career aspirations and, since Maxim had met me and seemed to have much in common with me (his notion), he said that if I'd be his partner's "spotter" and respite sitter, he'd pay me what I was making at the bar plus room and board, if I'd live-in. A spotter, by the way, is a person who helps with all the daily routines and spots for the trained partner or other person who is qualified to change bandages, care for lesions, wounds, administer some medication and injections. These trained people have to be certified to do specific tasks, and they are expensive as hell. Some doctors look the other way when guys like me extend past what they should, others are scared they'll lose their licenses, so they keep a close eye on who does what.

"Maxim said his difficulty was not with money but time. He had to continue to work in order to keep appropriate medical care for Trotter for one thing. I was to learn that it was an endearingly shortened nickname for Trotsky, as Trotter was a Russian history major at university with leftist leanings. His real name was James Madison (if you can believe this), which doesn't help much in this regard, does it? He was even a "junior" as the fourth president had been, though, unfortunately, the president is not one of Trotter's ancestors. Sometimes you have to wonder about celebrity and its seepage into our ordinary lives, don't you?

"Well, as you can gather, I did ultimately leave my job and went to be Trotter's live-in spotter and respite sitter for Maxim's sake. Because of Sheller's generosity, later I was able to become a licensed vocational nurse (LVN) so that I could legally assist in every way, except give medication, injections and such. For this, Maxim hired an RN to come three times a week or as needed. When Trotter was on AZT toward the end, he was taking it in such large amounts—dozen or more bottles a day— that this became enormously expensive, not just the drug, but the legal administering of it. He finally found a doctor who allowed me to hand Trotter the bottles, for God's sake, and take care of him while Maxim was away. You had to be so careful, because a nurse did have to come in every now and then to "monitor" the situation, and that person could be a snitch.

"But we managed to escape the legal bind, and Maxim told me my living with them gave him comfort and support, an ability for him to leave for work without so much guilt. Sometimes he was gone several days, weeks even, and sometimes out of the country. As it was—despite Trotter's own personal financial contribution—Trotter's illness was costing Maxim between $30,000 and $40,000 a year. Insurance and federal and state agencies were covering treatments for a few of his conditions, but he and Maxim were still left with tens of thousands of dollars in medical bills. I don't know what the national figures were for PWAs then, but now it is, on average, $32,000 annually with a lifetime cost at $85,000. Compare this with the average for a person without AIDS at $5,150 per year, and you can see why insurance companies and the government aren't receptive to a more inclusive treatment for this disease. I shudder to think how many without insurance, who've lost their jobs, are attempting to find ways to help themselves. No wonder they grasp at any trial or any smuggled-in drug to stop their suffering.

"It took me little over a year to become licensed as an LVN. Shortly after this,

Trotter died, but then Maxim was diagnosed the next year with HIV. He helped me through scheduling and some financial assistance to complete my nursing degree, graduating early at LAC Medical Center School of Nursing in 1989. So I'm a RN now and pretty much know what's going on with this disease currently.

"I nursed Maxim for two-and- a-half years (some of that while I was still in school), and since he was estranged from his family—they had disowned him years before for his being gay—he bequeathed all of his earthly possessions to me, with the exception of some donations to Cheroot and a few other fellow workers, earlier friends, and to various AIDS relief organizations.

"The Pacific Palisades house and grounds are lovely, though not close to being a mansion with the gardens of Versailles! The packet of photographs will give you a look at me through some of the years and of us together and apart (all four, that's including Cheroot) and the place where I'm living now. I've labeled them so you can see who is who, and what is what. I hunted for a shot of the bar but couldn't locate any. It's still there although it closed its doors a year ago because of dwindling customers and gay shops and bars that began to fade off Hyperion Avenue and throughout the Silver Lake District.

"And so, as you have undoubtedly gathered by now, I have AIDS. Actually, I'm still medically viewed as HIV but am in the ARC stage of the virus.

"There are four stages: the carrier stage where there aren't demonstrable symptoms; the enlarged lymph node stage, where the body is attempting to handle the virus, so the symptoms are beginning to show but allow for normal functioning; the ARC stage, which stands for "AIDS-related complex," in which the person feels like they have a chronic illness and their activity is limited to some degree; and finally full-blown AIDS. At present, there are some PWAs who, with rigorous treatment, have slowed down the progress of their HIV. I have done this, but as I will explain, I'm tired of being poked, prodded and living with the side-effects of the medications and sick to death of the disease itself, living in constant vigilance the way you have to, worrying at every turn if this or that means "the end." So I'm making some decisions about what I want to do next.

"I know this is a shock, but there it is. I was diagnosed with HIV in late summer of 1989, right before graduating from nursing school and just before Maxim died. He told me that his decision to give me the house and a good deal of his investments was to help me through what I'd done for him and Trotter. The property *already has a potential buyer—all I have to say is the word and the realtor will proceed on the sale. And although this would afford me income to see the disease through—who knows for certain where the experimental trials for new drugs will lead?—I'm emotionally coming to the end of it all. At some point the struggle to stay alive isn't worth the life that's struggled for.*

"I have a few close friends, but these have changed, as I've lost so many of my earlier buddies to AIDS, or, as with Cheroot, they've left the area. And I'm not so sure anymore how living alone agrees with me—with or without AIDS. I've learned to live with companionship, especially in greatly troubled times, and I have a longing to come home—I'm using the term not just to mean where you are living, literally in your house (I take it the house is still both of yours in the important sense), but also I mean "home" as being back where my life began and in many ways, where my heart still longs to be. I miss that familiar smell of the earth after it's been disturbed by storm, that feel of the red dirt between my toes, and the taste of hamburgers cooked on an outdoor charcoal grill. (They don't know what hamburgers are out here. They think they're meat loaf, I swear, with their catsup, lettuce and tomato instead of mustard, onion and pickles!)

"I do have to say, eating is a problem for me these days. Nothing tastes good and my appetite is gone much of the time. I have to work at keeping the pounds on. And that's part of the reason I'm writing and sending the photographs so that when you see me—that's if this works out for you—you won't be so stunned by my appearance. I've never been buff, but now I'm about as close to the bone as I want to get and still look in the mirror!

"So here is my proposal. Lord knows, I can understand if you have doubts and refuse my suggestion. I'll accept without question any uncertainties you may have. AIDS is a daunting task—far too much for me to ask of you—but I feel I have to give it a try. And on my behalf, I can tell you that I'm taking drugs that are extending my life, lessening my symptoms. I am still up and around and plan on driving myself in my pick-up—with a fellow going to Kansas City by my side to help me with the driving and hotel necessities. (Remember the red 1950 vintage pick-up, Dad? Never could give it up.) Also, I am financially able to hire helpers (though I can still do much of this myself as I'm certified), but that which I can't do, if and when the time comes, I can hire help to come in, until that also becomes too burdensome.

"I'm a Vietnam vet, so I get some healthcare through that agency, and it's my understanding, after talking to folks in the office in Oklahoma City, hospice services are going to be available soon for us vets. I will financially insist on contributing to my living expenses, including allowances for rent and board with you + any other out of pocket necessities.

"I've already contacted a doctor in OK City (through mine here), and I've consulted my lawyer who has drawn up legal bindings for all of this. At first, I thought I'd look into getting an apartment on my own, but if you can find the space—I was thinking the back couple of rooms that are used for guests and storage when I last visited—I'd prefer the company, the nearness of somebody around. I should be speaking specifically to you, Dad, about the companionship part of this, I guess.

"I found out about your divorce in a most unusual way. Snooky sent me a clipping from the paper with your divorce listed in it. And I did this sneaky little thing by having him look into where Caroline was living and giving her a call. In this roundabout way, she was enticed to give him information of all sorts for her finding out about me—my living in L.A. and how things were with me—not my current state-of-affairs, but where I was at that time. There was this stipulation in all of this, though—I was to make the first contact, before she let you know of my little subterfuge. Unfair, but done out of curiosity and what I thought at the time was self-protection, both yours and mine. And in fairness, Snooky did not give her specific information about me, with the directive that she wasn't to contact me. I just imagine where she is with me now in all of this.

"So I realize that legally you own the house, Mom, therefore, you have both an emotional part in this, and legal concerns as well, such as insurance. Like I say, I've located a doctor in Oklahoma City which I can then use to connect to others more locally—depending on what my needs are. If you'd like to draw up any legal papers through a lawyer to cover any iffy situations, that can be arranged as well.

"I'm primarily on AZT with an immune booster. Trotter and Maxim were on what I am. My booster, Isoprinosine, has been purchased through a L.A. buyer's club who get their drugs from Tijuana. I called the number I knew through Maxim and connected with some of the most ambitious, respected people you'd ever want to meet. Some of these organizers and workers in these drug "warehouses" give freely of their time and own money to help PWAs in their areas. There's an annual fee but it's dirt cheap and only helps with distribution. If I come to Oklahoma, my *buyer's club will be through Dallas as it is closest to the City, just over three hours driving. You need to know these drugs are illegal, but after some of the gay organizations brought pressure on the FDA, the agency lightened their rules to allow three months supplies of illegal drugs brought from countries where they are still legal. It's how I've survived without such awful symptoms—at least up until now. Without the drugs, the symptoms are extensive as the disease advances—bouts of diarrhea, coughing, night sweats, fever, disturbed sight, and the list goes on and on, depending on what infections you contract. But I want you to know my situation is under control, at least for now, and I have all the right people and drugs I need in place. But I cannot guarantee what the future will look like.*

"I know I'm playing the "child card," and, as a grown man, it's not the most responsible thing to do. I hope you will forgive me for this and will find it possible to call me and help me make some decisions about what to do next. There is the option of my getting an apartment in the OK City area so that we can exchange visits. There's also the choice of my remaining where I am, and you coming to visit here, which, of course, I'd pay for. And there are others, of course, but I'll leave them for when we talk.

"I look forward to hearing from you,

"Your son, Timothy Michael

"P.S. I've attached a list of resources for more information about HIV/AIDS. You can get most of this from the library. If they don't have the sources on their shelves, you can ask for them through inter-library loan for a small fee. It can give you more about what you're walking into. But I can explain any of your questions, too, when we talk on the phone. My numbers are 310-313-4579 and 424-858-3456. My mailing address is P.O. Box 645, Pacific Palisades, California, 90272."

—

"So there it is, Caroline. I'm not sure how I feel about your knowing certain reassuring information about Timothy before he contacted us. On the surface, it makes me not just a little bit angry, but now, given the present circumstances, I'll forgo that until we meet and can talk it out. Darlene is a totally different matter and that's strictly up to you two to settle.

"I have to tell you that I did hear your conversation with her the other day, that is, until I couldn't stand to listen anymore and went into the garden. I figured you two could work through it without me. Lord knows, I've heard it word-for-word since. And I do understand that once you knew about Timothy and his condition, of course, you felt Teddy and Kat had to be told. Your mother has let me know you are doing that, and I'm glad you convinced her that this was how it should be handled. She's not in the best shape to be introducing all this to them, that's for sure, and neither am I.

"Of course, after we'd read the letter together, she was beside herself because uppermost—other than that he has a terminal disease—she's viewing it like it's cancer, and I think she pretty much plans on telling others that's what he has. Other than the dying part of this, her main concern is that he's gay. Never mind that there are other ways he might've gotten the disease—through blood transfusions, for one thing. I don't know all the ins and outs of this AIDS situation, but maybe there are all kinds of transmissions I don't know about. I do know that you can get it by injections, but, God-a-mighty, that could mean he was a drug user which would throw her into cardiac arrest. To her, it's easier to deal with him being gay! I've about sold her on the idea that he's gotten it by contamination through his AIDS work with his friends.

"But she just can't bring herself to accept outright that fact yet. It's not going to keep her from tending him, of course. But she won't leave him alone, either, until he spills the whole truth to her. When we called him and told him to sell his house and start packing, she couldn't let things remain as they were. She asked him if he was leaving anybody *close to him* behind. Well, of course, he understood immediately what she meant. He'd already told us in his letter that he'd lost all his friends, and my feeling was that if he *did* have somebody he was living with, it probably was Maxim after Trotter died. But you know your mother. I have to say, I thought Tim was very interesting about how he answered her. He said that he had lost all of his close friends—he thought he'd made that clear in his letter—and though there were people who he considered part of his love-family, he had already told them of his desire to come back to Oklahoma. A lot of PWAs, as he calls them, are doing that—leaving to return to families, anyway, the families who will receive them. He feels very fortunate that we are accepting of his request to return. That's all he would say.

"Well, she made much of his calling the people close to him, his "love-family"—not to him, you understand, but to me. She saw this as a complete admission that he had given himself to *that* community. She could read between the lines, she said. She's no dummy. But Timothy sounds like he can handle anything she throws at him. He's been through so much, I'm sure anything Darlene springs on him must seem like child's play.

"But your mother has always been a surprising woman, Caroline. For all her sputtering and carrying on in the beginning, she's completely reconciled herself to his coming home. She's told me already that she's moving back in, but she hasn't decided whether she's keeping her apartment or not. For the time being, however, she wants to be as close to him as she can—that's when she's not working. I've talked to her about that as well. I've told her that our social security checks together can be enough to get us through this situation, especially with what Timothy wants to throw in, and, I think, she's actually considering giving up her work.

"She's watching the telephone like crazy now, trying to keep the lines open for him—if and when he might want to call, either to her apartment or here. She's worried about his phone bill, telling him to call her only at night when the rates are cheaper, so he can use all his resources for him being at home with us. Money worry is a primary instinct with her."

"Well, Darlene's already started getting the rooms ready. We had to re-paper—no joke—the back bedroom which is going to be Timothy's living quarters. I spent all last week cutting and getting the paper ready, and then she came over during her time off, and we papered the whole thing in an afternoon. We've had good weather, thank God, because the smell of wheat paste was enough to asphyxiate an elephant. But by the time Tim arrives, in the next two weeks or so, the smell should be down to normal. She's leaving the windows open, even at night, and since we've had hot, dry weather, it seems to be working.

"She's also redone a room for herself. Thanks be to the Almighty, she didn't want to redo the walls in that one. She's even had a kid she works with help her move several pieces from her apartment into the room. It's going to be so jam-packed in there I don't see how she'll make it out of bed at night to get to the toilet. But that's her worry, right? We've given Timothy the larger bedroom, the one with the bath. I'm sleeping in the bedroom just off the hallway near the living room, the one I've slept in since she left, so I'm all set. She's got Tim all the things he might need, two phone jacks—one for his computer, the other for a phone—and she's made sure there's enough room for a wheelchair to move around to the bathroom and out the door and down the hall when it comes to that. It's gonna be snug, some of his maneuvering around, but think it'll work.

"I have to tell you, Caroline, I'm thankful for her ambitions sometimes. I'm overwhelmed by what needs to be considered, and Darlene's taking it head-on. I don't know what Tim's going to think about the framed sign she's put up over his bed—a Scripture from John 14:27, *'Peace I leave with you, my peace I give unto you: not as the world giveth, give I unto you. Let not your heart be troubled, neither let it be afraid.'* She had an old Mennonite woman embroider it for her, somebody who knew her mother, a long time back when this sewing woman was a young girl out on a farm in Shirly. She's living in Hopewell now. Darlene located her through Josephine, I think it was, and it looks nice, I have to say. Knowing Timothy, he'll leave it right where she's placed it."

6.

Vernon

Tape recording to Caroline—Early Winter, 1992

"Well, this taping thing may just be getting out of hand. *(light laughter)* You'll think so when I tell you the latest development, I'm sure. I asked Timothy how he'd feel if I recorded some of our conversations—not all of them by any means, but just a few, now and again. He could decide which ones, a-course. I reassured him that I'd respect any conditions he wanted to make.

"He actually laughed, and then asked me, how come? You know, why I wanted our conversations on tape. Well, I said I wasn't so swift anymore at remembering, for one thing. Would be a way to sorta keep track of what we'd said. I explained that I'd done this with Dr. Hyatt, at times—I'd played him some of the thoughts I'd put on tape between sessions since I don't write worth a damn. And I mentioned about how the doctor and me listened to a few of your tapes as well—the ones Darlene and I made answering questions while you were in therapy. I explained about how I got into the whole taping business. Well, after all that, Timothy asked me—he was grinning while he said this—if another reason was so I could hear his voice after he was gone?

"I told him I wasn't so sure I could bring myself to listen later, really. It was a consoling thought, but I wasn't sure it would work that way when it came right down to it. When Timothy talks like this, Caroline—about his dying—I don't try to get him to stop, because I can tell when he talks to Darlene and people who show up here—which aren't many anymore, I can tell you—but when they do come 'round, they try to shush him or tell him reassuring things like Clifford and Josephine did the last time they visited, saying, 'Oh now, you got lots of life left in you, Timmy. Don't you give up on yourself just yet.'

"Well, you know how it is with those two, especially. They have to get in how we don't always know God's plan, and we have to allow what He has in mind, however and whenever that is. I've noticed even though Timothy doesn't try to stop them, he doesn't appreciate this way of dealing with what's happening to him. You can see it in his face, plain as day. But then they aren't looking at him when they say it. They're paying attention to what they're wanting him to hear. They—and Darlene too, I gotta tell you—don't keep in mind that this very sick man is practically a doctor himself. Well okay, if not that, he certainly knows more about his illness than all of us put together. They think it's cancer, and why wouldn't they? It's what Darlene's told them. So they say things like, 'You know they're discovering cures every day.' Timothy didn't correct them, because I'm sure he doesn't want to show Darlene as being dishonest.

"Well, what does it matter anyway? What point would he prove by telling them the truth? But here again, I gotta say, Darlene's a little different. She does read and even comes to Timothy with questions. But then she can't just leave it there, either. She tries to tie it all up in a neat bow by throwing God's divine intervention into it, not quite like Cliff and Josie do, but still, it's to make sure

Timothy's getting *The Word* as she interprets it. Darlene doesn't exactly say that God is directing the doctors in this according to our prayers, or even that they don't have the last word on matters always, but it's in there.

"As hard as it is sometimes, I try to keep away from correcting or fixing anything Timothy wants to express about his illness and where it's headed. I just feel that allowing all of us to talk openly about how sick he really is, it's good. Not only for him, but for us—anyhow, for me it is. Denying that he's dying isn't the truth anymore. He's wasting away before our eyes, and this time around, I'm not sure he's gonna be spared like before. I'm just not.

"And my way of feeling about this has given me some pause, don't think it hasn't. First off, this is exactly what I did before, remember, when he was six. I had my doubts while everybody else seemed to believe. So once again, I'm wondering if it's my 'unbelief'—if you want to call it that—that's making me think in this negative way about his future. But if I'm honest with myself and with him, I can't deny what's happening.

"What we say and how we are together right now is how it's gonna be… well, I almost said, 'be remembered'. For him, there will be no remembering, will there? And that's the point, isn't it? What's going on right now is how it is for always for him, because always is now, this very minute, minute by minute. It's no longer about the future. I want him to be at peace. I'm talking about every single moment and not having to worry about anything as he goes along here. Tending his soul is between him and God. It's not for me to worry him to death about it, you understand?

"The remembering part of this is about us, who're left behind. We *will* remember how we acted. You wanna know the truth, I think that's Darlene's biggest concern. Despite all her changes—leaving the church and trying to find her way in the larger world—she's still worried about her place in the hereafter. She's terrified about what God's going to hold her accountable for—did she try to save her son as she believes she's supposed to?

"She wonders how she can be a testimony in the world to others if she can't help her own kids in their religious destiny. It isn't as simple for her as it might appear. She flip-flops back and forth all the time—you know, whether she should press others in their relationship to the Almighty or not. And a-course, it's not something she feels she can talk about with me, because she's still trying to keep me from abandoning the ship. What she can't or doesn't want to see is that I'm adrift at sea, farther from the shore than she can ever imagine.

"Anyhow, I started this by telling you I asked Timothy about taping him while we talked, and he said, 'sure, why not', as long as we have private talking time as well.

"He did ask me not to bring the whole taping venture up with Darlene. She'll only get upset, worrying about what it might do to his emotions and attitude, but, also, he feels she'll get in knots about what we're doing behind her back, deliberately keeping her out of it, which we are, aren't we?

"So your mother is off-limits about this one. I asked him if I could share some of our tapes with you. He hesitated a minute, but said okay after I reminded him again about you and me having this long-standing arrangement of taping to each other, and how we understood about keeping it to ourselves.

"So here's what I thought I'd do. First, I'll talk to you a little bit about your visits while you were all here—well, yours and Teddy's together, and then Kat's, who, a-course, came a little later. And then I was thinking I'd like to record some of my ideas about Timothy's present situation, as well as sending a separate tape with one or two of the conversations I've had with him. That's the plan, but, we'll have to see how it goes.

"I'm not so sure Teddy and Kat are ready for this right now, though, Caroline. Timothy didn't say I couldn't include them in what I'm sending you, but after your visits here together, I'd hold Teddy and Kat off a little before sharing some of this with them. Beyond doubt, I would with Theodore. Like Darlene, Teddy might find it upsetting that Timothy is talking to me on tape when he wasn't forthcoming with him when he was visiting.

"And the acceptance of what's happening is difficult for all of us. When you watch one of your children die, it's too enormous to take in, because it just doesn't make sense. Timothy's dying is not the natural order of things. He's the youngest, if anything he should die last in our family. But as a parent, I see this a little different. It's more like, you brought a living being into the world, cared for it in the best way you could, watched it grow to adulthood, and then suddenly somebody else, something else, takes it away from you. Of course, we know our days are numbered, because we are part of creation's birth and death cycles. It's just that some people's number is a whole lot smaller than others, isn't it? Timothy is going to die at 46 or 47, Caroline. And it's just too horrible to contemplate.

"I know it was awfully hard getting away to come here like you did, so sudden. But Timothy has told me many times how much it meant to him. He knows that probably the next time you are summoned home, he won't be doing the asking or telling on much of anything.

"First off, I'm sure by now you know that despite all the help and drugs, Timothy's going downhill pretty fast. He's no longer in the ARC stage of the disease. He's moved into full-blown AIDS. At the most, they are giving him twelve, eighteen months. I think it's closer than that, but that's only because I saw how he didn't pop back after his last bout with PCP. You know it's his third, and, Caroline, he just can't take much more of this. His doctor is telling him some PWAs survive through more of these than he has, but Timothy's tired, he doesn't much care anymore. I feel he's staying hopeful for us more than anything. And I wonder if this isn't one of the reasons why he came home. His tendency before was just to stay to himself. It was why he kept away from us, almost like he felt he'd disappear or get lost if he got too close to somebody. But then he tells me that he changed, because of his few close friends in Oklahoma City, though mainly because of the ones he lived with in California. But lately he's been sliding back into himself. We have these great conversations, and then he goes silent in between."

"Timothy told me that you've been in touch on the phone now and again, so I know you have somewhat of a fix on what's going on with him. But there's a good part of what we're seeing here I'm sure he isn't imparting to you, Teddy and Kat. With Darlene still working—you know she's not given that up yet, and I think that's because she can't look constantly on what's here. So I'm alone a lot with him. As a result, I've learned to know him pretty well. And what I see is that he wants to spend time talking about things that matter to him, and his illness is a way to enable him to do this, even though he tires now easily. But about his illness and anything having to do with it, he's not saying much, which is leaving anybody hanging who's wanting to know anything beyond the most practical care. And he's not picking up on people's frustration, not even when it's coming at him full force, which is what happened during Teddy's visit. Just before Ted left, let me tell you, he let Timothy have it with both barrels.

"I don't know how much of this you know since you left a couple of days before Teddy did, though I'm sure you've heard Darlene's version. But mine is that Teddy's outburst didn't change anything far as Timothy was concerned. They patched things up, best as they could, before Ted walked out the door, but Timothy remained just like he's always been with his brother—*stoic*. Actually, that's what Teddy called it to Timmy's face. I don't know what Ted was hoping to see or hear, but it was easy enough to see he wasn't going to get it.

"He's so much like Darlene.

"And you know, while I watched this happen, I didn't intervene, though after it was over, I ask Ted what he thought he was doing, because, after all, this could be the last time he might see his brother alive. He waved that aside, and said he thought that should make it all the clearer to Tim how he needs to open up to his parents and siblings and stop what he called Tim's 'incessant impenetrable personality.' He said he was sick of Timothy's 'long-suffering' in silence, this said with not just a little sarcasm—as though Tim was reacting with this stiff upper lip toward what he was facing, so he could be the cool one, leaving the rest of us to twist and turn in the wind with our feelings. Teddy sees Timothy as a manipulative, conniving bastard, really. He asked him outright how he thought we could feel comfortable with showing our feelings when he isn't willing to show his? This was after Ted'd had a long cry in front of him, while Timothy was resting in his bed, turning his head to the side, waiting it out. And, I have to say, there's a side to Teddy's argument that's not totally unfair.

"But on Timothy's side, his times are getting longer and longer in bed because getting up and attempting to move around when he's in 'his downs'—as he calls the days when he finds it hard to function— are exhausting. And it's equally exhausting to watch him try to walk, to move at all, even when he's helped. While Teddy was going off on Timothy, I could see those old brothers' differences that made for such battles so often a long time ago, when they were kids, and here again, I did get Teddy's point. We've all felt Tim's retreats. But as I see it, it's Timothy's time, you know? Teddy will have his day. We all will. But this's Timothy's now, and we need to honor that.

"When I got Ted alone, I asked him what he was trying to get Timothy to do, you know, to satisfy him? In that way of his—like everything going on is so damned obvious to everybody—he said to me, 'Oh, he knows. And if you don't think so, he's got you buffaloed.' That's pretty much how the conversation went from then on.

"I said to him, 'Ted, he's not trying to put something over on any of us. He's exhausted with being sick'.

"'You do know how he operates, sick or not, if you just take a minute and think about it, Dad,' he told me. 'He's kept himself apart all along, with his big well-read, above-it-all fix on everything. He left you and Mother high and dry and was the same when I left and when Kat did as well. I don't know what his relationship is with Caroline. He seems to be partial to her, so maybe he's talking to her, but if he is, how would we know? She's as mum about him, as he is about himself. Neither one of them gives any of the rest of us an inch, and all I'm wanting is some intimate time with him, since it seems the right time for it.

"'Don't tell me you don't feel this in him, Dad,' he said to me. 'Or maybe I'm barking up the wrong tree here about you as well. Maybe he's talking to you, and that's why you're close to the chest with what's going on around here, too.' He was thoroughly disgusted with you and me, I'll tell you that. 'I'm not sure I'd know anything if it weren't for Mother,' he said. 'What is it with you and him, Dad? You think the rest of us are the plebs or something?'

"I had no idea what he was talking about.

"The *what?*" I asked him.

"His answer was, 'Never mind. Just answer the question. What is it with you and him and your withdrawal from the world, the way you both do? I'm coming to think it's a gene. One I didn't get.'

"'Is that really what you think it is, son? That we feel better or special from the rest of the family by how we are? Well, if you think that, I guess you think we feel superior to everybody else as well? That right?'

"'It feels that way. I haven't heard one word of closeness from him since I got here,' he said to me.

"'Have you been close with him?' I asked.

"'I've tried,' he said, hanging his head to the side the way he does, like he's listening instead of talking. 'And he just shrugs or stares at me and changes the subject. He's spent his time with me, and with Caroline—when she was with him when I was around— talking about his life as an antique record collector, as a bartender, skipping past the hard-to-admit parts, is my guess. When I asked him point-blank where he got AIDS, he said it was an occupational hazard, and then smiled, implying he got it from his personal life as an extension from the gay bar he worked in, I guess. Or maybe he was hinting about the medical career he's had and somehow that was involved. How would I know? What I do know I've learned from Mother, at least some of his story—well, however much she knows, which doesn't seem like a helluva a lot given that she's his mother. But he's never wanted to share any of it with me, and, when I press him for more details, he side-steps all over creation to keep from revealing any of his secrets—the important stuff he keeps from me. And that makes me not just a little angry. I get anything personal second-hand from Mother.'

"'Why can't you just give him that privacy and enjoy what you can with him, *while you can*, Ted? There's got to be lots of things you can talk about. Why not memories? You two lived together for a while. Darlene still talks about those times. Just enjoy what you *have had* together, if he doesn't want to go into his present situation with you.' It's what you did, Caroline.

"Well, I tried to get him to see that since Tim got AIDS from his life in California—at this point, who cares how—and now that he's dying from it, he's come home to get away from all the suffering he's experienced. He simply wants to be with us here as he goes, so why can't Ted simply be with him? I think he's wanting something from his brother that Timothy can't or doesn't want to give. So why can't Teddy leave that as is and take what he can and be satisfied with it?

"'Well,' he said, 'that's what he was having to do regardless of what he felt or wanted, wasn't it?' He left like that, Caroline, can you imagine? After unloading on Timothy the night before. But they settled things well enough, I guess. I wasn't in the room when they talked it out. Teddy did his own shrugging toward me as he got out of the car at the airport—guess he sees me as an extension of Timothy. Darlene drove us there, a-course, so I got to hear the sermon all the way home about pretty much the same things as Teddy had expressed about his brother. I asked Darlene to drop it, especially when we got home, because Timothy'd been battered enough by what Teddy had to say to him, and, thank God, she agreed."

—

"But, about Kat, that's a whole other story. This woman is interesting. She was here by herself with him, a-course. I always think of Timothy as the youngest child of ours, because Kat was raised so different from the rest of you kids, being so much younger. Your mother and me were different people by the time she was born. We were out of the Mennonite church—out of church altogether—and knowing more about how to be in the world with people not like ourselves. So in most ways, Kat was an only child.

"But there seems to be a feeling between her and Timothy that's almost envious. Lots of laughter from those two, to the point where Darlene came more than once and told them to cool their jets, because Timothy was coughing too much. He finds Kat funny, and, God knows, she is. And for all of Darlene's admonishments, it didn't stop her from bringing in her camera—she's bought herself a new Canon—and taking pictures of us all laughing our heads off. Timothy brought the house down by stopping her photo-taking a couple of times, telling her, first, she had the camera aimed backwards, and, another time, she had her finger over the lens! We don't have the pictures back yet, so I don't know if she got any good shots or not. Half the time her pictures are blurry, because she's moved the camera, or her fingertip shows in a corner of the shot.

"But Kat's a great storyteller. She has a way of bringing up subjects that have funny twists to them. And she's quick, so she says things before she thinks, which can be funny as all get out.

"She's into her regular teaching in her own class room now, I mean, she's past her student teaching days. But the stories she tells about her master teachers, I think she called them—those who taught her directly in their classroom—are hilarious. She had us laughing all over the place about some of the things they did with their students, and what some of their students said.

"One of the stories she told was about this teacher who—when she was a kid in Catholic school—tied the tassels of a nun's robe to the leg of her desk, you know those long rope-like belts that they wear. Well, she was sitting on the front row and the nun was talking to the class and was so involved in her lesson, she didn't notice that her tassels were tied. So when she turned and started walking toward the blackboard, she fell. She didn't get hurt, but her pride was injured.

"Evidently, this teacher told Kat that the head nun called in her parents to discuss her punishment, and her parents got so angry over the head nun's lack of understanding, they pulled their daughter out of the school. Well a-course, we all laughed, but then Kat said this teacher had been called on the carpet again, because when she taught in a school herself, years later, she had this unruly kid who was really big and hard to manage and a good bit on the mentally deficient side. He wouldn't stay in his seat. He kept getting up and walking around so with the help of her classroom aide, she tied this kid to a piano leg, you know, just loosely, nothing hurtful—why she had a piano in the room, who knows? Anyhow, she went back to her teaching and all at once she heard this terrible racket, with all the kids laughing, pointing and shouting. And when she turned around and looked, this kid had pulled the piano all the way across the room and was trying to drag it through the door. I guess she didn't last very long in that school either! Sounds to me like she had an issue, as Dr. Hyatt would say, about tying people up. And Kat did tell Timothy , "Well, it makes you wonder about her sex life, don't you think?" And Timothy almost fell outta the bed laughing. *(laughs)*

"This was pretty much Kat throughout her entire visit. I just wish Teddy, and you too, could've been here at the same time she was, because I think Ted's attitude would've been different. Darlene was transformed. She lost herself in the fun, and that's how I think it should be—if that's what Timothy wants and needs.

"I'm so glad Kat came last, because, as a result, Timothy ended you all's visits with a feeling of happiness instead of the upset that Teddy left him with."

—

"Here's the thing, Caroline. Timothy has been just about as uncomplaining and pleasant as anybody could, under his circumstances. Basically, he's a good-natured person. You can see that from the way he talks about his life in California, even when it was hard. He tries to find solutions to problems, but he doesn't make a big show of it. And he believes and lives for something bigger than himself now, even if it's only ideas. I'm not sure I can say that about Teddy, despite his active participation in his church and all his civic endeavors. I don't want to speak about him with hostility or anything like that, but I'm just telling you that what I observed here wasn't the best side of him at all. I don't know if there's some jealousy there—you know how boys in a family can be. If it's this, I guess I don't understand what he has to be jealous about, unless it's because he feels Timothy did us all dirt, and he wants him to eat it, because Tim isn't bending over backwards to explain himself. But that's not jealousy exactly, is it?

"Okay, I have this gut-level feeling that Ted feels he can't measure up, that he feels Timothy's in the world in a way that he'd like to be, especially about his dying, you know, like how he's doing it. And instead, Ted's attracted to making money, and he's told himself this makes him happy. Actually, it's more than even this. Underneath it all, I do believe, he's convinced himself that this is what everybody should want, even worse, he believes that people's natures are satisfied only in this way, and if they aren't making money, out there ahead of everybody else, they're just making excuses for their failures. He really believes we all want to be successful as he thinks he is. And he is. Right now he's selling projects to the state government through the company he's built from scratch. And he's good at it. He could talk his way into hell and back out again, and, on his job, I'm sure he does. He manages multi-million dollar contracts.

"Hell, I'm certainly impressed.

"But Timothy isn't, you can tell. He's happy for Ted, since that's what Teddy's decided for himself, but it's not what Timothy is about in this world. And down deep Ted senses this, so I think he goes after Timothy over everything he feels his brother has value for, labeling it irresponsible, or what he labels do-gooder-ism—otherwise, to his mind, why would a grown man work as a bartender to support himself and then turn to nursing as a substantial profession?

"And I have to admit that's even a leap for me, sometimes. I can't imagine wanting to do it, especially being around all those women in that kinda work. But that's Timothy, for you. He just doesn't care what people think about him, and that's pretty much everything that Theodore *does* care about.

"If you want to know my opinion about this comparison in a nutshell, it's the difference between Darlene and me. She's like Teddy's wife, Sarah. She wants what the majority of people want—the job, the car, the looking-up-to-you for what you have. She's always been like this. Unfortunately for your mother, I wasn't Teddy. I tried, but it just didn't work. Our circumstances simply didn't allow it, and it's taken me a lifetime to understand I really didn't have to kill myself for her the way I did. I thought it was love—what I was trying so hard to give her. And it was simply its substitute. I learned this in detox therapy. I hope Teddy discovers this. I really do. But there's no way you can tell him. Back then, nobody coulda told me."

7.

Vernon
Conversation with Timothy—Winter, 1992
Tape #1

"I have some things I want to say, Dad. And I don't know how long I've got, and how long it's going to take to say them, so I suggest we get to it. I'm saying 'we' because you're more than just a listener in this, and, God knows, you're more than the subject, though it may sound like that at times. I'd like for this recording to be a conversation, but I may forget that. You'll have to bear with me, okay?"

"Sure. I'd rather you'd do the talking any day." *(laughter together)*

"First, I want to talk about time. Have you ever lost all trace of it?"

"A-course. If you're meaning getting lost in what you're doing to the point of looking up at the clock and suddenly noticing that hours've passed by, and it's only seemed like a few minutes. I pretty much still work like this most of the time. On my job, everybody told me I was fast getting the job done, and that's because I didn't think about anything but what I was doing."

"Yeah, I think everybody gets lost in what they're doing off and on, especially if it's their vocation or regular chores, especially when you're in situations where your attention is totally diverted off of yourself. And even more if what you're attending to is something you enjoy. Psychologists call this 'flow,' at least, there's one psychologist who does—Mihaly Csikszentmihalyi, who coined the phrase, as I remember. He studied people who are totally absorbed in an immediate task, especially if it's highly demanding, technical, athletic or creative. And what he found—he states this in a book he wrote recently—that people are happiest when they're in this 'flow'."

"Well, hell, I'd agree with that. It's what sent me to work every morning. I can't imagine people working at something they don't get caught up in like that."

"I feel the same way. Even when I was taking care of Trotter and Maxim—as hard as that was—I was totally into it. But I want to talk about this whole time thing a little bit differently. I'm thinking about an experience where you *transcend* time, a transcendental state in which your consciousness exceeds ordinary experience, going beyond even the ones we just mentioned about work and creative endeavors."

"You mean like the experience you had when you were a kid?"

"You talking about when I was six or twelve?"

"I was thinking about the one you had at six, I guess, because I was actually there."

"Well, I didn't really have a transcendental experience myself at that time. But now that you've mentioned it, I've always wondered if you did? Or Mother?"

"You'll have to ask your mother, but I don't think so, not either of us, because we were just praying for your survival, concentrating on that real hard. I guess you could say, our attention was heavenward, but, far as I'm concerned, nothing extraordinary happened to me. Darlene was at the hospital, watching over you while the rest of us prayed at the church. But I didn't ever leave the reality of the sanctuary. If anything, I think I was there *too much*."

"Too much? I'm not sure I understand."

"Well, I've wondered if I was too much into my concern, you know, into what was going on at the hospital and right there in the church and wasn't leaving enough to God. Mainly I was worried you were going to die, and it was impossible to get out of that state of mind, praying to God or not."

"You mean your state of worry?"

"Yeah. That's why I've always felt it was by God's mercy you were spared. I didn't have anything to do with it, if you talking about having faith enough to make a miracle happen—which to me, is a kind of transcendence, as you call it. Could be others who were there experienced that, but not your dad.

I've always believed they did—at least, as much as a mustard seed—because God did answer our prayers."

"A mustard seed? Oh, you mean according to the Scripture that states if you have faith as little as a mustard seed your prayers will be answered."

"Well, that's not quite it. It's in Luke somewhere, I remember it because God knows I've referred to it often enough since then. I got it marked so I can find it. It says something like—I'll speak it now outside King James, in everyday English—*If you have faith as a grain of mustard seed, you can say to this sycamine tree, Be uprooted and be planted in the sea, and it should obey you.* And in another gospel—think it's Mark, maybe it's Matthew—Jesus said that you can move a mountain by faith and cast it into the sea. In that one He tells us what true faith is—that you can't doubt, you have to believe what you say will happen, then it will. I have that one marked as well. Got lots of places to go to find faith in the Bible, but I'm not always able to believe as complete as it says to."

"I thought maybe you had some moment of recognition in the church that night, some...."

"The recognition was very real for me, Tim, because it came with a telephone call. Can't get more real than that. Came to the church office, from your mother. If you mean, did I see a light or have a vision or know something inside beyond doubt and hope? No, I didn't. You told me that you didn't have that either. Remember when we spoke about this when you were in high school? Well I do.

"But Caroline had that kind of faith, as young as she was. You had to be there, see her and hear what she had to say in order to understand that she knew beyond doubt that you'd be saved, Timothy.

"You know, when people talk about faith, most of the time it just sounds like hope to me, like they're wishing hard for what they want. It's what we thought at the time, but I saw something else in Caroline's face. It was *complete knowing*, total trust in what she was seeing as what was gonna happen. You want to know about that kind of recognition, you need to talk to her, not me."

"I've seen so much hope and listened to so many prayers these past few years that I'm like you, Dad. I find it hard to believe in the way you're describing. I've seen so many prayers go unanswered or, I should say—looking on it from the standpoint of faith—were answered in the negative. Not one of my friends who contracted HIV has been spared. Of the people I've met who had the virus, a few have been given an extension of life, but none have been 'saved,' if you want to put it in the language we're using here. So faith isn't something in my life. Anyway, I just wondered if you observed any transcendental experiences during this meeting by others, if not yourself."

"You mean like a vision or being in a trance, something like that? If anybody was, they kept it quiet, to themselves. That's for the holy-rollers, I suspect, where they speak in tongues and see all sort of things. I'm not sure what all that means, how it happens exactly. I just know I've never felt any of that revival sort of stuff. But I've had visions before, just not at that time, or since, for that matter. Or maybe they weren't visions like you're talking about."

"I didn't know this, Dad. When did you have visions?"

"Oh, I used to get them off and on. *(laughs)* I make it sound like they came and went regular, don't I? Well, that's simply not true. I've only had two, three that I remember, and I put it like this because, I think, you can have visions and not notice. You simply don't pay them any mind, because it feels like you're in a dream, or coming out of one."

"Like daydreaming."

"Pretty much, yeah. The one I remember most was like that. I was in the middle of a field, working for Willard on our homeplace, and, all at once, I saw a spot in the distance that was burning. It wasn't exactly a burning bush, but, it was sort of like that, so I started walking up to where it was. It was burning so hot, I couldn't get close enough to really see, and, anyway, a voice told me to stop, that coming any closer was hallowed ground. I knew that voice immediately, but wasn't sure where it came from. It seemed like it was coming from the bush, but it could've been so deep inside me that it was coming from my own head, my own mind—don't misunderstand, it wasn't *me*, even if it was coming *from* me. I was so paralyzed I never thought to run or doubt what was happening. I knew it was God. And He told me I would marry your mother and have four children by her, two boys and two girls. I was dating her at the time but hadn't asked her to marry me yet. That was all there was to it, but it was so clear I couldn't deny it'd happened.

"Your mother has taken exception to this—though she's had her own vision about God promising to make her well from her sickness. I was there when she had hers. This was after we were married. I think you and Teddy were actually born by then. And with Darlene—just like with Caroline—there was no doubt that something was going on beyond herself. But about my vision, Darlene's told me it was too much like Moses and the burning bush from Exodus. Well, my answer to that was, even if her idea was right, maybe God chose to tell me something important by using a burning bush, because He knew I'd accept it, being an image I'd recognize from the Bible.

"Regardless, I've decided to stand by what I saw, Moses's bush or not."

"How did you know you weren't hallucinating? That's what I've come to question about experiences like this."

"Why would I be hallucinating? I hadn't even had a beer or anything."

(Timothy laughs) "Maybe from the heat? I don't know. I'm just asking."

"Well, I'll answer this by asking you one. That time you told me about when you were twelve—you took me to this field, the night you left and told me all about it—were you hallucinating when you had that experience in your homemade fort in the snow?"

"I'm not sure. How would I know? Maybe I was having hypothermia, how would I have known? But it's been hard for me to believe it coulda been anything but supernatural, because I was in a natural, ordinary state when out of nowhere it came upon me. It just suddenly happened. And I've believed since then that something close to what we define as God was involved. I think I told you this at the time I described it to you. I do know that shaman and sorcerers in other cultures have transcendental experiences like this, but they usually do something to make them occur—go without sleep, take hallucinogenic herbs or plants, beat drums, chant. Often they use repetitive behaviors over a long period of time—a kind of sensory deprivation or narrowing of the perceptual field. And they usually use plants, herbal drugs that transport them to other realms. I've read all of Carlos Castaneda's books where peyote and other hallucinogens are involved in Don Juan Matus's teachings—that's Castaneda's sorcerer-teacher from Mexico.

"But with me, I was a kid, a normal kid, well, okay a book-reading, genuine nerd, even that young, but unlike you, I can't say it was God. Its character was divine, or maybe 'sacred' would be a better word for how I think about it, especially from what I've read about others' similar experiences."

"You were pretty definite when you told me about it, Tim. You called it an incomprehensible presence, no, you said it was God-as-Ultimate-Presence, that's how you put it."

"But that's not exactly God in the sense that most people think of Him in our society. I have no idea where my experience came from, really."

"Are you asking me about this because you've had some revelation or vision lately? Is this what you're leading to?"

"No, not really. I've just always wondered about my 'miracle,' as you call it, and then about my experience at twelve. But in answer to your question, I did have a strange happening shortly after Maxim died. It wasn't a transcendental experience exactly, but I saw it perhaps as a sign, something that I never quite understood, especially if there was a message, and if so, what the message was. I have to admit, I did feel there might be something I was supposed to understand from it."

"A sign? I didn't know you believed in signs—they come from someone, you know."

"Yeah, I know. Let's call it a mystery, then."

"Okay." *(Timothy laughs lightly)*

"You want me to go on or not?"

"Sure. A-course." *(pause)*

"I was in the hallway, maybe a week after Maxim died, in the house he bequeathed to me. All of his possessions—what he'd left behind—were all around me. It was as though he was still down the hall as he'd been for months while he was bedridden. When I stepped out of the bathroom, walking down the hall and was not far from my bedroom—this was after I'd been sleeping, you understand, and I'd awaken, realizing I needed to urinate. Something brushed against my arm. I turned to follow the movement past me, looking up, and saw a dark shadow floating across the room, near the ceiling. I'd turned the overhead light off so the hallway was only illuminated by a small night light coming from the bathroom. My vision wasn't the best, as you can imagine, and I saw whatever it was for only a second. I expected it to be a bird that somehow got in or perhaps a bat, though we'd never had either in the house, and the shadow didn't flap the way a bat does, or even fly in a straight line like a bird. It *floated*. Ghost-like.

"There's that old wives' tale about a flying bird in the house indicating a death. Since Maxim had just died, that's what entered my mind, as unlike me as such a thought was. What held my interest, though, was that whatever brushed past me had a shadow larger than either of those creatures, and it didn't come back out of the bathroom. So I went in there and looked around, *everywhere*, turning on all the lights, even in the hallway, investigating behind the curtains at the windows and the shower. Nothing.

"I barricaded myself in my bedroom that night, and the next morning I fully expected to find a dead something or other on the floor of the bathroom, if only a large moth or some such. Again, nothing. And it never showed itself. You know, Dad, I've never told anybody and barely admitted this to myself, but there was something *recognizable* in the presence that brushed against me. It had a familiarity about it that I couldn't grasp, hold onto. I *knew* it but didn't *understand* it, as crazy as that sounds. Perhaps that's what a transcendental experience is. It's simply too complex, too rich or deep to absorb, but on some level beyond usual knowability, it's *real*.

"I thought about this a very long time—what it could've been. And when I was diagnosed with AIDS—only a short time after this—it occurred to me the message was for me and not one about Maxim. You know, I'm not a superstitious person, but there are more things in heaven and earth than we can dream up in our philosophies—using a Shakespearean line I'm appropriating to fit my point. I've battled with these seemingly supernatural or transcendental experiences since I was very young. I know that the religion of yours and Mother's upbringing was based on revelation as a means of ascertaining important truths in your lives. I was curious enough about what was happening to me to go back and read a bit about Holdemanism, if you want to call our people's brand of Mennonitism that."

"Not your mother and mine, but our people's, yeah."

"Well, as I'm sure you know, John Holdeman, who founded that church, had a vision telling him to go back and revisit the Bible, interpreting it differently than other branches of Mennonites were doing at the time. The Holdeman Mennonite people choose their preachers through a sign from God, so divine intervention is a deeply embedded means of accepting answers to questions in their practices. The major religions all espouse a belief in an individual's 'being called,' which seems to me to mean, 'being called to some destiny or service' by God. I'm not committed to this kind of trust, or faith, if you will, but I do believe in these experiences in some way, because I can't deny they've happened to me. My problem is less about believing they occur than in figuring out what they mean exactly.

"I have a friend who uses them as devices for paying attention to whatever is going on in her life at the time—the thing she's focusing on the most, a kind of heads-up. She hasn't told me whether she thinks we tell ourselves these things or if she thinks they come from a sacred or divine source or even if the source is important to her. It seems to me, this sort of experience has something in common with dreams and their interpretation. Or perhaps interpretation of anything, really.

"In other words, on what grounds, with what kind of proof, do we say a thing like this is real or even validly experienced? But then, if we accept some source for it—or even if we put that aside—how do we know what the 'revelation' or 'sign' means?"

"Well, unless the meaning comes with the message."

"You mean made clear from the messenger? Like from the voice of God or some such? Hmmm. In any case, I've always been deeply intrigued by such experiences."

"I see what you're saying, but in your case, with your illness and our praying for your getting well, there's something in those two things coming together like they did, that's meaningful, don't you think? I mean, we were praying in the church, right when you had a bowel movement." *(sudden laughter from them both)*

"Synchronicity. When two things are close together in time or space, they're thought to be contiguous—we tend to see them as belonging together. Doesn't mean they do."

"So those two things, our praying and you getting well, might not belong together, that what you're saying?"

"I don't think we know for sure if those things have some causal relationship—yeah, that they belong together in the sense that one *causes* the other to happen. If you strike a match, the flame that flares is caused by the phosphorous surface on the match box igniting the potassium chlorate in the match head through friction. So that kind of association has a causal connection, a knowable 'proof.' About these seemingly, non-casual relationships, well, that's something else. I've always thought because they have personal significance in our lives, we tend to imbue them with a power that they don't truly have."

"Well, I think... no, we really did believe there in the church that night that if God chose to answer our prayers, it was Him who caused you to be spared. I'll always believe that, son."

"Anything's pretty hard to refute, when you throw down the God card, Dad. But an atheist would probably tell you the experience in the church was coincidental. Okay, let's take it out of personal context, having to do with me directly back then. Let's say, you're walking across a bridge, and just as you become parallel with a person about to jump—a man, say, you didn't see until you were parallel to him—he jumps. Do you believe you caused that to happen? And don't say, well, if I push this person over the edge, yeah. *(laughter)* You know what I'm getting at, right?"

"Sure. I don't know about this, though, because there's all kind of things that might cause that to happen right then. The person could have seen me and decided to jump so I wouldn't stop him. And if that's so, then yeah, I caused him to jump in a way, didn't I? On the other hand, the person might not have seen me at all, because he was thinking all these terrible thoughts, and so he jumps when it just so happens I'm even with him."

"That's what I'm talking about, Dad. See? Coulda been coincidence." *(Pause for a beat.)* "You know what we're doing now, don't you?"

"I have a good idea, but what do you have in mind?"

(Timothy laughing) "We're talking philosophy, Dad. And religious philosophy at that! Didn't know you had it in you, did you?"

"You bring out the best in me, son." *(Laughter as the tape clicks off)*

8.

Vernon

Conversation with Timothy—Two days later, early evening
Tape #2

"That was a great supper, Dad."

"You didn't eat much, I noticed. You okay?"

"Gotta quit asking me that. Just slightly nauseated. It's hard to know if it's the condition or the side effects of the medications. I take something for the upset stomach, but it doesn't always work."

"I noticed they've stopped coming to the door with your 'extras.' That package you're getting every now and again in the mail?"

"Yeah. I'm having them shipped from the warehouse, since I'm ordering them so far in advance. No need to alert the neighbors."

"Oh, they're not gonna be that curious, and anyway if they are, Johnny'll set 'em straight. He's the watch-dog of the block, so he's big on people minding their own business. Everybody thinks you've got cancer anyway. Darlene and I don't talk to anybody except Johnny, and if it's anybody else in the neighborhood, it's niceties—as your mother says, 'from across the fence.' You aren't getting a package often enough for them to notice anyhow."

"Well, I was also concerned about the delivery people. What they're doing is illegal. No use making their presence any more noticeable than necessary." *(pause)* "This daily routine of mine must be on overload for you both, especially Mom since she gets up early to help before leaving for work. I want to say I'm sorry, but I know you'll only admonish me for it. So just let me tell you—as I did her this morning—that I appreciate all this. It was a lot to ask, but we're doing it well, don't you think? At least, I'm staying out of the hospital, and so far PCP hasn't raised its nasty head again. Knock. Knock."

"Who's there?' *(laughter)*

"No joke, Dad. No joke."

"When you start rapping me on my head, then I'll know you're serious!"

(more laughter)

"You're hardly a blockhead, Dad. You know, despite my inquiries into transcendental experiences and such, it's the ordinary ones that I've come to respect lately. Illness does that. It demands you focus whether you want to or not, mainly on the body, but that expands to other things when you live with being sick a while. Especially since I can't just up and leave, can't even walk out the door anymore. I think a lot about people who live their lives in wheelchairs, who've lived the majority, if not the whole, of their lives restricted like this. In the past, I've spent a lot to time literally 'out there' searching, for records and sheet music and such, and playing at various gigs here and there. It seems now like a space itch, constantly wanting to go beyond myself. But when I did stay put, I realize reading and music were a means of escaping the present as well, wanting to expand but not wanting to leave the nest.

"I still read, but I'm not finding it as enjoyable. It's the drugs—which are a different take on being transported and escape, for sure—but most of it's my condition. The narrowing of my perspective through confinement is a completely new experience. Perhaps it's because I know my situation is determined, but I'm catching myself wanting to notice the little things. I'm seeing them now with a narrowed vision, a new focus.

"I see each object of my attention for itself.

"It's so easy, in normal daily life, to become beguiled by the extraordinary. Before AIDS, I looked forward to experiences which were complicated or different. Most of us are drawn to the dynamic—maybe the nature of all life is about movement. It's a little like that famous Woody Allen line from *Annie Hall* about a relationship being like a shark. It has to keep moving forward or it dies. Maybe that's true about life as a whole. We tend to fall into routines or patterns, so we turn the ordinary into drama, just to escape the boredom. It's what nosey neighbors are doing. And reporters who rev up single, simple incidents for headline grabs. Conflict's in our nature—we notice what moves, threatens.

"Music moves, of course, and I've noticed when I give the horn my full concentration, proceeding from sound to sound, this, more than anything else, makes it live. I don't mean playing for fidelity to the notes, but playing for what each sound brings to the whole—the flow. The same is true in the best performances in sports. I've heard baseball players say, when they're asked what went wrong with a drop they made in the outfield, 'I took my eye off the ball.' Runners will tell you they visualize the course ahead and take themselves mentally through it, step by step, before the race, but they also tell us when they're actually running, they're concentrating on the positions of their body in space, how they're extending themselves with each thrust of their leg and so forth. There's a kind of freedom in that, when you've practiced this kind of concentration so intensely. I see myself practicing alertness, attentiveness quite like this, in the tiniest perceptions I'm encountering now.

"Mother asks me sometimes what I'm thinking about. It's hard to get this concentration across to others. I think I'm practicing how to let each experience unfold, how to not anticipate what's ahead, but enabling myself to be totally in the moment as it arises. And this goes for death as well as life. In this, the Buddhists are right, maybe—living and dying are the same. It's our tendency to think of experience in terms of concepts, emanating from our minds, but in truth this only interferes with the flow."

"You mean when we're told we're thinking too much."

"Exactly."

(pause)

"You know, you ask me to think of a question to ask you, Tim, something we could record, 'for posterity,' you said, though maybe you said this as a joke. I have a lot of questions I could and want to ask you, but this one you probably can answer pretty easy. I've been wondering about it, but I've hesitated to ask, because I thought it might be a touchy subject."

"Go ahead and ask. At this point, not much is too touchy anymore, really."

"What happened to your record collection?"

(Timothy's loud burst of laughter)

"Omigod, out of all the questions, you ask this one? *Why?*"

"You seemed to be so into collecting, but we haven't really talked about it much, anyway you haven't to me. I thought what you told Teddy and Caroline about it was especially interesting. It seems to be a very competitive business, collecting these rare albums. They aren't that easy to find anymore, I take it."

"Oh, if you know what you're looking for, you can still find some at yard sales and flea markets. But people in general—and store owners of collectibles in particular—are becoming aware they're valued, so it's harder and harder to find them for a dollar apiece like some collectors say they did back in the sixties and seventies. Today, there's a huge network of folks who bargain with *each other*, feeding each other information as to what records are where or where they aren't, can't be, and such. It's an interesting venture to get into. I was never a real contender by authentic collector standards, because I wasn't a highly selective one. I didn't have an agenda. I'd take almost anything I found in early 78s or LPs whether I liked it or not and a wide spectrum of 45s as well. I'd snap them all up. I'd play them, and if I didn't like them, I'd give them away or sell them for next to nothing. I've had a few yard sales myself. Some of the records I got rid of, I found out later were worth something. But investment was never my game."

"You were always big on Louis Armstrong. You talked about him even to me and Darlene when you were in high school. You wanted to play the trumpet, and we couldn't afford to get you one or the lessons."

"I dreamed of playing, Dixieland especially, but I was too lazy to put into it then what was required to learn. I've done that since, though, and it's been rewarding, but looking back, I would've disappointed you both. This I can say with assurance, because right after I moved to Oklahoma City, I did buy a trumpet. It sat on the shelf in my apartment's living room for years and years. I never sought out a teacher to learn to play. I'd pick it up and tinker with it, while I played a Louie recording every now and then—trying to play along, you know. But the thought of all those lessons and all that practice was daunting. I took the trumpet with me, of course, to California. It wasn't much more than student grade, but I learned to play on it, before I invested in something better. To this day, though,—and I had a great teacher and practiced religiously for several years—I'm not an artful player. I can loosen up with a band, but I don't really have that feel great players have. I'm too serious. I play too safe. I don't take risks, mainly because I don't quite know the risks to take. That make sense? Dad, you can't nod at the recorder, you have to say something."

"Oh. Sure." *(laughter)* "But you did play in some bands, you say. So you were good enough for that."

"Sure but these bands hired out for practically nothing, in small bars here and there. God, in L.A., there are bazillions of bands like the ones I played in. Every now and then I'd play with an inspired player in a band, so I knew what that felt like, but for the most part, these band guys did what I did. Played for enjoyment. I eventually got some money out of it, but nothing like I'd hoped to do."

"So what was your record collection like?"

"It was a hodge-podge really. Altogether I had about five thousand records—which isn't a huge collection by most standards. Unless these smaller collections are specialized, they aren't worth much. A 78 record collection of two thousand can be impressive, if the recordings are primarily from a narrow period of time in which not a lot of records by one artist are still available.

Most collectors aren't into the music, oddly enough. They're interested in the rarity and quality of the record and the authenticity of their collection.

"'Authenticity' is the big buzzword with these people. 'Authenticity' doesn't allow for 45s or CDs—forget that! And you aren't *authentic*, a real, bona fide collector, if you don't specialize or have a focused view of a genre, like say, country or jazz. And it's not a cheap hobby, if you want to call it that. It's a vocation for most of the collectors I've known. And a lot of the personal collections I've seen or heard about are in basements, because when you have thousands of vinyls, they weigh a lot and upper floors have to be fortified to hold them. And these guys are downright paranoid about their collections, because one rare record can cost tens of thousands of dollars. But it's not so much the monetary value of them as it is finding and possessing the right records—which usually means those that everybody else is seeking. Many of these guys are obnoxiously possessive. I keep saying guys, because it really is all guys, unless a woman is married to a collector and has been bitten by the bug herself. But even then, she really has to be backed by him, and I might add, it's almost *totally* white guys, at that, despite the large number of blacks who created the music.

"Anyway, most authentic collectors will play any record you want to hear from their collection, but that's once you pass muster, and they've let you into their house. It's not the easiest thing getting introduced, unless you have another respected collector vouching for you. It's a closed circuit, a very exclusive club."

"You got in mainly through Maxim, then?"

"Yeah. But I'd already started collecting without realizing, so to speak, even as early as Oklahoma City. I'd go to garage sales and flea markets and get some that way. It takes time, and I had it in Oklahoma City. But in California, I did a lot of it before I met Maxim, especially before I was hired to take care of Trotter. After that, I had work and nursing school. Had to squeeze it in, just like with the trumpet. And Maxim was gone a great deal, so I had to stay close to Trotter. There was a time between Trotter's death and before Maxim was in the ARC stage, that we went out searching together, but that was short-lived. Only a few months, but it was intense. I got a lot of good stuff then."

"What did you do with all your records?"

"Well, that was a long, hard decision. It intrigues me how possessive you can get about something like this. For a while, it was fun taking people down into my basement, playing old records with them. Most of the people I let down there were buddy band players. And then I started getting worried about break-ins, especially when I was away at night so much. I didn't know some of these people all that well, and after a while, they started bringing friends, then it was friends of friends, and it was hard to say no. My collection wasn't all that great of an investment money-wise, not compared to collections up to fifteen, twenty thousand choice records. I'd seen a couple of those. Had to drive up to Omaha once and into Michigan another time, but they were impressive. It was worth it to hear vintage songs on shellac though—that's what 78s were originally pressed on, shellac discs. I came out of those collections with a couple of choice sides of Louie, one with King Oliver, but it cost me an arm and a leg, and I really didn't want to get into it quite that rich, you know?

"I have to say, it was the Louie part of my collection I found the hardest to give up. Louie made his first recording when he was twenty-three years old, with King Oliver's Creole Jazz Band—he was on cornet. And from the very beginning he showed an improvisation that's never been equaled. He could play with a traditional orchestra as well as with a band of his own, where he had the undisputed lead. He had an intuitive sense for all jazz, but especially for the blues. He accompanied all of the greats, Bessie Smith, Ma Rainey, Ella Fitzgerald, you name them. I only had a few of his vintage records on Okeh and Gennett labels, which were some of the first shellac pressings, and are prized. Mine were in what's known as 'V' condition.

"There's a Record Grading System, VJM, from the early fifties that collectors use. I won't go into details, but 'V' means the surface is crackly and there's wear, but the record is still playable, that even though there are noises from the surface, they don't intrude to the point of making the record unenjoyable.

"Most of my collection were vintage LPs—vintage meaning, they were originals at the time of their release. And my LPs were often re-issues of selected pieces of the original works which were borrowed from collectors for these recordings or the recordings were ones in which the collectors acted in a supervisory capacity. In other words, my LPs were as authentic as you could get without being shellac or the originals.

"But the thing for me and my Louie collection was that academia was looking for a comprehensive spread of his work. My collection wasn't definitive—not even close to being everything he did—but it was very representative of the full range of his development, styles and venues.

"I didn't want to break them up, as it was a sequential, chronological spread, and I knew I could find an old-time jazz collector who would snap them up for a good price. But I wasn't sure, once in a collector's hands, they'd ever be available for people to hear—especially people in general, who weren't into scholarship or collecting.

"So I took my collection to the University of Wisconsin at Madison's Mills Music Library and asked which recordings they would take, which turned out to be almost everything. Their music library has all formats, and it's open stacks so people can take records and sheet music and listen, look at it, or play it themselves right there. I considered The University of Oklahoma's music college library, but it didn't look like much was there for the public, and I also considered the University of North Carolina at Chapel Hill which has a large authentic library of Americana, jazz, folk music and so forth. But the way things were set up, I wasn't sure about accessibility there as well—a lot of these places you can only listen if some librarian played it for you and the like.

"I only had my impression of these places to go on. So I traveled to several others, looked and asked around. In the end, I settled on Wisconsin because it was available to the public in a way I liked. Mills looked at everything I had and called me about returning only a few items which I told them to donate to some charity or school library."

"I wish you'd saved back some and brought them with you. I woulda liked to've heard them."

"Do you have a turntable, Dad?"

"That old seventies console of Darlene's here in the living room. It has a turntable and built in radio and speakers. I don't imagine the sound's worth a damn to your ears, but it would've given me enough of an idea."

"I didn't realize. I just assumed that you might not like the music I did, for one thing. I was pretty sure Mother wouldn't."

"Maybe not, but it would've been interesting to me anyhow. I like what Darlene calls 'cowboy music,' Western songs is what I'd call them. Gene Autry, Roy Rogers, Roy Acuff, Hank Williams, those guys. I guess they call that Country Music now. When *Hee Haw* came on television, I liked Buck Owens and his Buckaroos. Well, you can imagine what your mother made of this. She was into all her high-falootin' sopranos from the movies, so my music was cheap noise to her. I never put music on, until she left the house, and then when I did, I'd listen for her car in the drive."

"Oh it couldn't've been that bad, Dad."

"She could be pretty snotty, and I didn't wanna hear it."

"I wondered why there never was any music in the house."

"Well, now you know. She likes her music, and I like mine, and the two don't mix. I like Roy Acuff in particular—Roy Acuff and his Smokey Mountain Boys. It was no never mind to Darlene that he was called the 'King of Country Music' and had all these hits on the charts, and he's in the Country Music Hall of Fame. Roy Acuff sings off key, she says. Mostly, to her, though, it's because he came from Tennessee and played his hoedown in the Grand Ole Opry. To her mind, the hicks couldn't even say the word 'opera' right. Well, she got shut up when it was announced on the news that John Kennedy's Arts Center—or whatever it's called—gave Acuff a national metal for his lifetime achievement in country music. That was just last year, came on the news. Acuff's still alive, though he doesn't, a-course, sing anymore. I loved that her criticisms blew up in her face! When I heard the announcement, I put a tape of his on in the house after the six o'clock news. You were here then, I'm sure. Don't know how you missed it."

"I probably thought it was the radio on for a change. Couldn't have been too loud."

"She left the house with a bang, came back with groceries. I had the tape off by then, a-course. I just wanted to rub it in that once, is all. We put the groceries away together and nothing more was said.

"Well, I'm glad you put your records in a safe place, but, still, I wish I'd heard some of them."

"I have a tape or two of Louie's, Dad, we could play, if you want. You could bring out your Roy Acuff, and we could have a little party."

"Well, let's put 'em on. We don't have all night. I'll play Acuff first, since she'll be home by six, and she doesn't mind jazz so much. In any case, she'll not say anything to you about your tastes, that's for sure."

9.

Vernon
Conversation with Timothy—Later that evening
Tape #3

"Sounds like this collecting business was a good part of your life, Tim."

"Well, it was, and it wasn't. I found out fast that the down side to collecting is the collector's preoccupation with it. Some of these guys have given up their jobs to do nothing but search for records. Their wives work, or they've left them. The wives who stay are usually sympathetic. Have to be. But I only met one who looked for records with her husband. For one thing, part of this collecting venture is about uniqueness—being the *only* guy in town who knows what he does, and how much of it he does, and why he's looking for what he's looking for. Most serious collectors don't think women are 'good enough,' that they don't have the aggressiveness to stay with it and do it well. What it amounts to, really, is they don't think women are single-minded and territorial enough for it. It's very misogynous. At the very least, they're very protective of their male insider game with each other. It boils down to their thinking women will lessen the seriousness of their game.

(pause)

"Most of the collectors who I've met don't think of themselves as preservationists of American history or music. They're too selfish for this. They're in it for themselves, what they can get that the other guy wants. But selfish or not, they are actually preserving American music history. Shellac discs are extremely vulnerable. They're breakable, susceptible to moisture, light, heat and cold. Dragging them out of their storage holes—out of attics and basements where people who aren't collectors have stored them—is saving recordings that are fast disappearing. Some of these records are 'one of a kind,' because the metal masters the songs were originally recorded on are long corroded or gone. Most were thrown away after the records were pressed. 78 collectors are aware of all this, of course, because that's why some records are so rare. In most cases, there were only a limited number of them made to begin with, and then only a few have survived, anyway only a few that can be accounted for. There's always the hope that a great discovery will be made somewhere from the rumors as to where they might be that float around from time to time. And I'm here to tell you, collectors go to extreme lengths to find them. Sure, these guys are glad to contribute to history, but that's not their aim as much as possessing the discs themselves. It's like owning a Rembrandt, even if it means getting it on the black market and hiding it so well it can't be found. It's that kinda thinking. Sometimes I see collecting as a downright evil activity—narcissistic, possessive, engendering jealousy, aggressive competitiveness—much like professional sports, really.

"I have to tell you, I was very aware of the historical value of what I found, but that wasn't my aim either. I wanted to hear certain of Louie's songs that I'd read or heard about, but had never listened to. So I'd ask around and try to see what I could find out, then I'd go on a search and see where it would lead. I wrote a lot of letters and got some records by mail this way."

"Sounds like you had a pretty active social life doing this."

"Not really. Not if you mean forming friendship where you go places together, have dinners and such. You've brought up an important point though. I tend to be a loner, and by bartending, I was forced to give up some of those tendencies. It was good for me, even if I saw the worse in people some of the time. But people were out for a good time, and after a few drinks, they talked, sometimes to the bartender. When serving times were low, I'd have conversations with them. I've met lots of people this way, and, of course, it's how I met Maxim, who, by the way, did not pass his collection on to me. He gave it to Wisconsin. It's why I looked into Mills, as he'd done. Maxim's collection wasn't all that large, maybe only a thousand records, but his were choice. He was into ragtime, which was mostly too early for shellac by originals such as Scott Joplin, though there are some rare recordings from the late 1800s, a few of the banjoist, Vess L. Ossman.

"Ragtime wasn't all piano, as Maxim informed me. He searched for anything that was ragtime-inspired, even going back to John Philip Sousa, whose marches were seminal to the genre. So he collected recordings of works that influenced this music— artists not necessarily specializing in it. And he collected sheet music. So his stuff was a whole historical compilation of this musicology."

"I like that music."

"Yeah, me, too. It's happy music, like some of the best early New Orleans jazz, the street-parade stuff especially. So anyway, I felt like my job and my trumpet-playing and this collecting that came out of it, kept me from becoming a total recluse. Had I worked a job that isolated me from others, I would've been in a shitload of trouble, I think."

"What do you think would have happened?"

"I've reflected on the question of my collecting quite a bit, Dad. And not getting too therapeutic about it, I see how it reaffirmed my notion of nesting, having a place of my own where I was secure. Part of collecting is about order. You're sort of a librarian, looking after something archival, meant to be both accessible to others but protected.

"Mom's illness had a great impact on me during my childhood. I saw how out of control she was, really not able, at times, to manage herself in her environment, and then when I got so sick and almost died myself, I began to really not trust life. I felt you just never knew what the hell was going to knock you down. It made me feel lonely, but also terribly isolated. For me, collecting was realizing something as emotional and transient as music has an historical context. In other words, it has substantial importance in everyday life. So despite its impermanent character, it is *there*, for everybody anytime, especially as recordings.

"But with collecting, rare records especially, that public quality can be claimed personally, held from others if you want to, particularly if these recordings are few of a kind and almost impossible to find. So I fell for the security of it and the possessiveness of it, even though I enjoyed sharing it with others—as long as I was in control of when they came to hear it, when I could give it to the world in a particular rendering."

"But you were spared by God, Timothy. Doesn't that make you trust Him for your life? Why would you need something like this to feel safe?"

"What I got from that sparing, was that God—if you want to put this in those terms—is the *giver* of life but the *taker* of it as well. What if I didn't do His bidding? The testaments are full of people who earned His wrath for disobedience. We seem to be at His beck and call, don't you think? Why would God allow such troubles into my life, and then rush to save me, was my question. What kind of a God is that? It felt like God had Munchausen Syndrome. I couldn't have labeled it this when I was six, of course, but it's how I grew to view God's nature—anyway, the nature of the God we've created. As the story goes, He creates us and then puts us in jeopardy or allows us to put ourselves there, and then watches to see if we will let Him save us through our promise to love Him. I ask you again, what kind of God is this who plays with us and played with Abraham, Job and the other 'heroes' of the Bible like this? He even allowed His own son to be killed. What am I saying? We're *all* supposedly His children, as we're told, right? You feel He can toy with us, if He likes? That's okay with you?"

"But He's God, Timothy. In Romans it says that everything can be clearly seen by all of us, the earth, the sky, everything that's been made by God, so that we don't have an excuse for not believing. God has made all of it, Timothy, and He made it out of nothing. *Nothing.* He took nothing and made it all. That kind of power, well, yeah, I guess I'd say there's no way we as finite creatures who are called by His breath into being, aren't at His beck and call. A hurricane rips through your house, you don't argue with it."

"Hell, Dad, a hurricane rips through my house, I'd run, or, at least protect myself best I can. A hurricane *has* ripped through my house. It's ripped my house apart! I don't buy it. You can see the light in this if you want. All I see is darkness."

"I know I'm talking a bit out of both sides of my mouth right now, Timothy, because my faith hasn't always been what it should be. And your mother worries about this with me. But under it all, I do believe. God has made promises to man. And He can't break them, or He wouldn't be perfect. So God's word is trustworthy."

"What about the times He's changed his mind, when He's said he's going to do something and then has taken it back? He promised to make the Israelites a great nation, but He got angry at them during their wanderings in the wilderness for their idolatry and was going to abandon and punish them. Moses interceded for them, so God spared them."

"But the Israelites made their troubles. God didn't. It was by His mercy that He spared them. He had made laws for them to follow, which was His word as well, you know."

"So you're saying that my life was in jeopardy because of something I did against God, because I didn't follow his 'laws'? At six, Dad? Really?"

"Well, no. But maybe your mother and me—"

"C'mon, Dad! Is this your answer for why I have AIDS?"

"I don't know how these things work, son. But no, I don't blame people for their illnesses. There are germs and—"

"Dad, I think we should just leave this one up in the air, don't you?"

"Maybe that's a good idea." *(pause)* "Hey, Timothy, have we just done some more of that religious philosophy?" *(pause, then scattered laughter)*

(long pause)

"Guess so, Pop."

(long pause)

"Is this why you didn't come around much, to visit your mother and me, when you were living in Oklahoma City? You were into your collecting? We got so we didn't want to bother you. This was especially hard on your mother, because she'd had that business with Caroline moving out and away, so she was especially careful not to tread on your toes. She was afraid she would lose you like that."

"No, it wasn't the collecting that kept me away. I didn't think about my 'not keeping in touch' like you and mother did—which says a lot about me, doesn't it? I worked, like we all do, and then went home and read and listened to music. And on my off days, I went searching for records. I wasn't present for much of anything or anybody else. I dated for a while in there, but it fell through."

"Oh, don't look so surprised. I told you I'd fallen in love once, but it didn't last."

"Well, I guess I shouldn't be surprised, since you didn't share with us much about your personal life. You coulda been married, and we wouldn't've known."

"I didn't share my life with anybody, really. I'm hoping my being here now is making up for that a little bit, maybe."

"Your mother and me are glad you came home, Timothy. That you've decided to come home and be close to us now."

10.

Vernon
Conversation with Timothy—Early Spring, 1993
Tape #4

"I know you want to ask me what my life has been to me, Dad. Yes, you do, because by analogy you want to know what *your* life has been to you. It's why most people are uncomfortable around me right now.

"We all tell ourselves—anyway, I used to before the whole AIDS thing hit me in California—that we don't know what to say to the dying. But it's really about hiding the fact we're relieved that it's not us. There's a lot of guilt in this. Of course, we're all hard-wired to survive, but in order for us higher forms of life to feel above the level of the animals, we want our existence to *mean* something, something more than just living in order to be living. And what a terminal illness does is make you very conscious of that.

"I grew exhausted watching my friends—Trotter and then Maxim, in particular— struggle to just stay alive, and then it was me. Suddenly, I wasn't privileged, protected, sheltered anymore, as though any of us ever are at any time. But, all at once, I found myself going through the same emotional and mental progression my friends had gone through. First it was the hope to be restored to normal, then it was simply to feel better, and finally it was to survive—to do about anything not to die.

"When I got to the ARC stage, I asked myself what I was surviving for. Just to be alive, instinctually, like animals do? What was I fighting so hard for?

"The first thing I did was go back over my life. It actually became that thing where I saw my life flash before my eyes. But, of course, it wasn't quite in a flash, because with AIDS you don't die right on the spot. Most of the time, not even rapidly—not these days. You have time—even in your feeling-awful moments— to reflect on why you want to live, because you feel that in what has gone on before, surely there must have been a clue—there has to have been *something* in all that history that kept you going, laid claim to your life, other than just living it day after day. Maybe it was somebody to love, something to do, something to hope for. Remember that famous saying from that guy who's spokesman for Motel 6, on the radio spots, you know, the one who says, 'We'll leave the light on for you.' That guy? Remember him? No, well, I'm remembering now. His name was Bodett. Tom Bodett. And far as I'm concerned, he had it pegged.

"I don't want to go into this right now, Dad, but I did love somebody once, and it didn't work out—oh boy, did it not ever. I don't want to dismiss it, because it was important to me, and I did have something to do. I liked bartending and being with people who were trying to find happiness, or, at least, some pleasure in their lives. I liked the people I worked with and the regulars around the bar, and when I met up with Trotter and Maxim that became central in my life.

"My focus has always been very simple.

"And I loved playing the trumpet, the people I met in the bands and audiences. Maybe this will strike you as odd, but in California, especially, I grew to enjoy the feeling of community and belonging to other people. This was very different from how I'd been before, I know. But I changed, or I found another self, perhaps.

"The other part of meaning in one's life, the 'hope for' part, is a little harder to compute for me. In the abstract, I'd say I longed for security. I wanted something permanent, solid, foundational. I've always relied on myself for this, but that wasn't working so well anymore. So when I reached the level of survival in California, that's when I wrote you and Mother the letter.

"I can see the same question in your eyes, now that I'm here with you, and dying is so close. You're in your eighties, Pop, am I right?"

"Yeah, I'm eighty-two."

"Well, I would think that this what-do-you-hope-for question would be one for you, even if I weren't here now, because you've come to the time in your life when wanting to know that would be natural."

"You mean, what do I hope for *now?*"

"Yeah. Isn't that so?

"Dad, you gotta say, you can't just nod on tape!" *(laughter)*

(very loud) "Yeah, you're right." *(more laughter)*

"Anyway, because I *am* here and in the circumstances I'm in, I can see it's not just the question of what your life has meant in the past, but what it *could* mean for you, because you aren't dying, not yet. You've got to be studying on why you're so much happier now that Mother is here in the house, even if it is to care for me, and your knowing that chances are good she'll leave again after I'm gone.

"You want to know about family, what it is that binds us to each other like this, at least what it means at present and has meant to you, right? Why that has been everything to you, why you've invested your life in it, lost it and still long for it.

(waits, silence)

"I know because I puzzle on this too, you know. I came back home to die, didn't I? Why is that, when I seemed to not care all that much to participate in what our family was when I was—well, when I was alive."

(shaky voice) "You aren't dead yet either, Timothy."

"No, and I'm as alive or dead as I've ever been, I suppose. It's just a change in my body we're all adjusting to. I keep telling myself that."

"Well, it's a helluva lot more than that for me. And despite what you seem to think, it's not just you in relation to me I'm looking at about this."

"This?"

"You know what I mean."

"Say it, Dad."

"Okay, your dying, my dying."

"It's okay, if you cry, you know. God knows I do."

"That's different."

"Oh, really. Why is that?"

"Lots of reasons. Why are you snorting at me?"

"Well, I'm not allowed anything because I'm dying, Dad. You can allow all you like, but I don't want to, because if I do, I'm going to miss out on what I came here for—the honest truth for once in my life, without evasion and subterfuge, without any attempt to undercut what's really going on. I came home to face dying *without denial,* as much as possible. And, in California, I think, it would have been easy for me to feel sorry for myself because of all the suffering going on around me there. That may sound odd, but after a while, everything gets to be only suffering, and the fatalism makes you feel helpless, which is only a step from self-pity. I wanted to know, for one thing, if, as I was dying, I could see the life that would go on after me. It's why people have kids, don't you think?

(pause)

"I'm not sure I know what truth I'm looking for exactly, but one of the most important aspects of imminent dying is the discovery of respect, even devotion, for, what I'll call 'ordinary experiences.' I want to surrender the last of my time to noticing the little things, giving them affection and care, because it's so easy to seek out what seems complicated or different. I think I mentioned this before. But now I've come home to it, in the sense that I don't want to manufacture drama, which is something we often do in order to have conflict in our lives—something to become invested in.

"I watched it around me all the time, especially at the bar. People used to tell me I was stoic. It's what Teddy called me in his anger. But invented conflict and drama move us away from ordinary life experiences which we begin viewing as irrelevant, insignificant, banal."

"I have less of a problem with this than your Mother, I think."

"Oh, I think we all have this problem, Dad. Mother tends to express her drama openly is all. She rails against her boredom. She detests the idea of life without intention. She perceives that as 'drifting along'. Life without goals is terrifying to her. Mother knows you have goals, Dad. They just aren't big enough for her. She wants to live life bigger than it is."

"I'm not sure I understand that."

"Well, to me, she wants a magnifier put on her ordinary life, hoping to see something unique, that's exclusively hers and isn't like everybody else. She wants to be a person of value rather than one who sinks into the background, can be easily overlooked. A lot of human behavior is about that, don't you think? We all do things to be noticed—things we feel have value to others and ourselves.

"The other day, when we were talking about your work, you said you'd received a call from a man who traveled three hundred miles to bring his car to you to be repaired. Because you'd been so highly recommended, he was willing to take the chance on his car breaking down to travel that distance. For men, it's easier to accept pride in one's work, maybe, because women's work is devalued, especially housework and childrearing. And since our society places great importance on material possessions, Mother wants her life to reflect clearly that she's a person to be noticed by how she dresses and what she owns."

11.

Vernon

Tape to Caroline—Summer, 1993

"It's hard to realize that he's gone, Caroline, even after you girls, the boys, everybody's been here and left—what is it? two weeks now—and even after all the memories were discussed for hours, the crying, the funeral and all. I don't know what has been explained to you. It's a blur, so if I repeat myself, forgive me.

"We kept everything small, no memorial in Oklahoma City, because we just couldn't handle it, but we did put it in the paper as Tim had asked us to do, in case anybody from there wanted to come to the funeral, but nobody did.

(pause)

"It's still seems like he's in the back room, and I keep wanting to go back there to check on him, you know? I promised I wouldn't tape this until I could get a grip on myself. We'll just have to see if I do."

(pause, clicking off, then back on)

"Well, this tape is going to be different from the rest, probably. I have something particular to tell you that's happened concerning Timothy. Surely he told you he kept a journal and wrote some personal essays about what mattered to him. I found a manila folder with notes and several of his writings in it, which I've shared with Darlene. You'll find copies inside. I sent these to Teddy and Kat as well. Some he wrote when he'd just arrived at home, others while he was in California, and still others during his stay here, a few after his handwriting had become shaky and harder to read.

"But two weeks ago Saturday, I got a call from a woman from Oklahoma City who knew him. Right away, I felt she was the one he'd mentioned a couple of times in passing to me. She asked if she could see me, that Timothy had given her our number. Anyhow, this woman introduced herself as Angelina Hart and after talking to me a bit, said she had several packages of Timothy's he'd asked her to pass on to me—exclusively to me—and she wondered when she could do that. She said she was willing to come to where I was. I didn't need to drive to Oklahoma City. Well, I told her I'd appreciate her meeting me here, because I couldn't drive to the City, let alone drive in it very well, that I only drive around town these days, and out to a few surrounding smaller towns in the country.

"Well, we made arrangements to meet in Clover. Remember that diner where you and I used to meet up every now and then to talk without your mother knowing it, after you'd moved away from home? It's where we went to discuss your Uncle Jesse once, remember that? Well, that diner is still operating, though the name's changed. It's called, ah, let me think—it's—

The Prairie Chicken House now. Anyway, we decided to meet on the following Saturday, which we did.

"I gotta tell you, Caroline, my curiosity was up about as high as it could go. And I'm not sure what I expected, but when I entered the café I looked around to find this man sitting in a booth. He seemed to know who I was, because he waved me over. I wondered what the devil this was all about, you know? This couldn't be the woman I'd talked to on the phone, no way. He stood up and introduced himself, telling me he was the driver for Angelina, and the packages she was to deliver were in the car with her. He paid for his coffee, and we went out to this black Lincoln, black interior, even she was dressed partly in black. Well, she was sitting in the back seat, and he opened the door to let me in.

"I can't remember the driver's name, but he was very polite. He told me to sit down with Angelina, which, a-course, I did, while he stayed some distance away, leaning against the back of the car, waiting. She had long brown hair, though it was thinned out and brown eyes, a dark-complexion. Even in her sick state, I could see she'd been a beautiful woman, like some film star when your mother and I used to go to the movies, only a little on the Mexican side, maybe. She wasn't elaborate with her clothes. Wore a simple dark blouse, black jeans, loafers. I knew right away she probably had AIDS. She had that look about her.

"She introduced herself again as Angelina Hart. She didn't hold out her hand, so I did mine, and she smiled as we shook hands. She said that she didn't initiate contact with people, because some didn't want that. She seemed exhausted, so she got down to business right away. She was real easy to talk to, very natural. She said she'd known Timothy from the days when he bartended in Oklahoma City, that they'd become… she said, 'intimate,' and she'd been married at the time. I was amazed at her honesty. She'd chosen to stay with her husband, she told me, because they had two children, and she knew he would make her life miserable concerning the kids if she ever left him. Her children were nine and twelve at the time. When Timothy saw that she couldn't leave her marriage, he left for California. She was undecided about going with him for a time, but she knew it wouldn't've had a good ending, that she and Timothy could never have been happy knowing she couldn't see her children or have a decent share in their lives. She wasn't sure she was totally the motive for Tim moving away, but she felt she undoubtedly had a hand in it. So she must've been the person Timothy had mentioned in one of the taped conversations I sent to you—when he said he'd loved somebody once, but it hadn't worked out.

"It was after he'd been living in California for a few years that Angelina discovered she was HIV positive. Her husband had been infected and didn't tell her, passing it on to her. He might not have known, as he claimed, but she doubted that was so, but regardless, when she was diagnosed, she separated from him, but didn't divorce him as he promised to provide for her and their children if she remained his wife to the end. He died two years ago. Her children are now seventeen and twenty-one. She came from a close-knit family, so her children would be well taken care of, as they went through college on the trust fund she was leaving them. She could die content, knowing they would always have a family beyond her death. She'd recently been given the prognosis of less than a year.

"She had immediately contacted Timothy upon learning of her diagnosis. At first, she hadn't tested positive for HIV, her gestation period for the disease was uncharacteristically long, and it took a little while to locate Tim. Over a year, she said, but once she finally found him, Tim was open to communication, especially after she told him her situation. He was working as a helper to Trotter Madison and Maxim Sheller by then. So Timothy knew before he was diagnosed that the likelihood of him getting AIDS was high. It was uncanny, but, evidently, he didn't get symptoms quickly either, because when she talked to him, she said, he didn't have any signs of the disease. And whether he chose to get tested right away or not, he never told her, and she chose not to ask. She said she felt like it was her job to inform him, and he could do as he wanted with the information.

"For a while they kept in touch, usually by short phone calls, but, in time, she found it hard to manage everything, especially her work—she did volunteer work in AIDS-related foundations she had established—but that together with her illness and being with her kids was too much. And Timothy was very involved in nursing school and taking care of his friends. She also knew he played trumpet in bands. So they just let their relationship drift into silence, is how she put it.

"I could see she was having a hard time maintaining energy to tell me what she needed to. But she sat with me, while her driver put Tim's packages in my truck, using my keys. She said Timothy had asked her to hand-deliver the packages to me upon his passing. She had kept up with the obituaries in the *Daily Oklahoman*, so she saw the notice we'd put there and knew he'd died. Anyway, he'd called her not too long before he passed. Evidently, he had mailed packages from California off and on to her for safe-keeping, after he was diagnosed with AIDS. She wasn't sure why he'd chosen to do this the way he did, but he always had his reasons. He had been very specific about her giving them to me and *only me*. She'd promised him if she became so ill she couldn't deliver the packages herself, her driver, who was faithful to her, would see it through. So when Timothy moved back to Oklahoma, he got in touch with her again. But with their respective diseases, they found it hard to keep communication steady. I'm not sure how he did this, but we allowed him his privacy, and he did use our telephone.

"Well, if I'd been curious before, I was even more so by this time—about his writings, I mean. Now I had the problem of getting the boxes into the house and keeping them away from Darlene, with her living with me again. They weren't light, but I managed with ropes to pull them up the ladder to the attic over the garage where I knew she'd never go. For one thing, she hates ladders.

"So when she'd gone to work the next day, I crawled up there with them. I remembered him telling me how he was so unsure about leaving the boxes of records in his truck. Well, I got a little of that feeling myself when I left his boxes in my truck overnight with a blanket thrown over them, hoping and praying Darlene wouldn't have reason to look in the window of my pickup and ask what the heck I had in there.

"Anyway, I open them up in the garage attic to find this huge amount of writings, some in his hand, some typed. And there was a good share done on a computer, on long, folded sheets with perforated pages. The handwritten ones were mainly in notebooks, but there were others in bound books that were poems. I knew I'd never be able to read all of it unless I spent hours and hours doing nothing else while Darlene was away at work. The boxes were in order, numbered with a marker, and, in the first one, I found this note that told me to send them to you when I was done with them. I've read quite a bit, actually.

But I'm overwhelmed by the amount of thinking and expression Timothy has in writing. He could've published a book, I'm sure of it.

"He talks about all kinds of things—forever seeking answers to the questions he had, mostly, about religion, politics and his ideas about what he read. And in the notebooks and journals, he recorded his own experiences, often every day. It wasn't so much what he'd done, like a list of doing this and that, but of his thoughts about what hit him as unusual, special. Or a serious question he wanted to think about. He'd marked a few with those colored, plastic stick-ons and dots. I never saw so many different thoughts together in one place in my life, outside a library.

"He sent Angelina all of the boxes from California but one—connecting with her again in order to do this. The last box came from when he was living at home with us. He must've kept this one under the bed or some place in the closet. I have no idea how he got it mailed, with proper stamps and all. Maybe there's some service that comes to the door to do this—I suppose there is. And he must've arranged to have them given to the carrier when Darlene and I were both out of the house.

"I can't imagine where he'd hidden them, where Darlene wouldn't have found them when she was cleaning. But then Timothy was in the house or backyard all of the time, especially toward the last, before he was bedridden. He never left the house, so he knew pretty much where she was most of the time. He could've kept them in a locked suitcase in the closet—that's probably how he did it. He could get away with that, but I never could've. She would've snooped into my stuff, but not his, anyway, not in a suitcase.

"I've copied at Kinko's a few of the writings that I especially like and have them in my desk, in a locked box. I'll share them with Darlene sometime—maybe, or maybe not. So far, she hasn't asked me about that box. I've put everything of his in the mail and sent it to you. The post office guy said you should get them in a week to ten days. All I can tell you is there's a helluva lot of them. The journals remind me of the conversations that he and I had—similar to the ones I sent you on the tapes, only him talking to himself. But in a way, it sounds like he's talking to somebody else, because he questions himself constantly. He doesn't talk about family and friends or what's going on every day or anything like that. He writes about what he believes and feels concerning different subjects, topics, his experiences. I think if you read them all, you'll know him better than almost anybody. Maybe some time I could visit, and we could talk about a few of the ones you find especially interesting. We could enjoy them together. I'd like that.

"So, here's the thing, Caroline. Chances are very good that Timothy got his AIDS from this married woman, and not what your mother finds so hard to accept, that he was homosexual. Maybe that's not fair to your mother, because by the time Tim died, and we had seen both the suffering and the tremendous spirit he showed us, I think she changed her opinion about this. She didn't say, but I could tell. So in the larger scheme of things, I, myself, am not a hundred percent sure where he got his disease, because he never told me outright, but he did tell me in a roundabout way.

"One day when we were talking about his California experiences with AIDS, he told me about this scene in the movie, *Spartacus*. The Romans are trying to find out which man is Spartacus among the group of prisoners they'd taken from the revolt against them. And just as Kirk Douglas, who played Spartacus, starts to tell them it was him, Tony Curtis, his best friend, stands up and says that he's Spartacus, and then the next guy says that he's Spartacus, and one by one each of the men stand up declaring they're Spartacus until the Romans have no idea who Spartacus really is.

"Timothy called this the 'I-Spartacus-stand.' He told me that him being silent about where he got AIDS is intentional in this I-Spartacus way. He doesn't want anybody 'to exempt him from their prejudice about gay men'—that's exactly what he said. If he told people he got it from a woman, he felt that then they wouldn't blame him like they do homosexuals and, in his view, that's just plain wrong. And, I gotta tell you, I've just about come around to his way of thinking. Whether he slept with Maxim or not is none of our business, or if he slept with anybody else, for that matter."

12.

Vernon

Tape to Caroline—Almost two weeks later

"Well, we've talked on the phone, brief as that was, and I was happy to hear you've received Timothy's boxes, that his writings are safe and in your hands. I've put off sending this tape to you, because I needed to add something important to it, and I couldn't bring myself to do it until now.

"Watching Timothy die wasn't the easiest thing I've ever done or the hardest either. By the time he was actually dying, the hospice nurse was here, and I was with him in the bedroom. She asked if I wanted her with me and Timothy, and I told her that if she was in the living room that would be fine. If Tim needed her, I'd call for her. Darlene was in the backyard on the swing, just sitting there, waiting. She had taken care of him that morning before her work, and when the hospice gal called her, she came home. It had been days of him in and out of consciousness, so she felt she couldn't stay home anymore or lose her job. I don't know if they woulda fired her, out and out, but she needed a reason to not stick around, I think.

"She came into the room and sat with him a while. I left them alone, but I could hear her talking to him from the living room, though I couldn't make out what she said. The hospice woman and I talked together. She told me exactly what to expect, what his last moments would be like, so I wouldn't be surprised or worried. When Darlene came out, she was crying. She said she needed to be outside, that she'd wait for me out there. She didn't say she would wait until I notified her of his passing, but I knew that's what she meant. She'd told me earlier that when the time came, she might not be able to be in the room, and I'd reassured her that this was okay. I'd stay with him, so she could be where she needed to.

"It happened so fast, Caroline. Before this day, it seemed to me that so much of dying was waiting. They'd taken his ventilator and IVs and all that away some days before, because hospice doesn't require that. Well, I hadn't been seated but a little while, when he opened his eyes and smiled a little, so I went to the bed and bent down to listen if he wanted to say something to me. In a really weak, dry voice but looking right at me, his eyes so bright—I swear, I saw a grin with mischief in them—he said, 'I see the light, Dad. Thank you.' And he closed his eyes and was gone. I wasn't sure he'd died, but he had the last rattle in his throat that the nurse told me I'd hear. I waited a few minutes by his side before I got her from the living room. I followed her into his room and watched as she checked his heart. She turned around and nodded that he'd passed away.

"I walked out of his room, down the hall to the kitchen and out the back door into the backyard. The minute Darlene saw me, she waved her hand back and forth in the air in front of her. I couldn't see her face, so it was like she was waving me 'hello,' but when she kept it up I knew it was her way of trying to wipe away what had just happened. When I got next to her, she stood, the swing hitting her in the legs, and she slumped forward into my chest and arms, sobbing. It's the first time we'd hugged in years. I cried with her then, and we sat on the swing for a while before going inside. She stayed in the living room with a cup of tea I'd made for her, while the ambulance came and took his body. Then she went into the bedroom, and I heard her weeping. I cried my heart out in the kitchen. And just like that, it was over.

"I've had a wish all my life. It's been for one person to love me just for who I am, before I die. I wanted it to be a choice, not an obligation or for being a father. And as hard as it might be for you to hear, Caroline, I believe I got that wish, because I believe Timothy did."

THREE PICTURES
of
TEDDY

1.
Teddy's First Words

My brother Theodore was born—well, I want to say he was born speaking in sentences, but, of course, that couldn't be true. He was actually born in a deep silence that lasted almost until the end of his second year. My parents were afraid, at least Mother was. She took him to the doctor for his regular checkups, but nothing was said about his lack of babbling or cooing. He did cry, that he did. He cried until he turned blue, and my parents had to blow or throw water on his face. Mother became concerned almost to the point of hysteria, which undoubtedly didn't help my brother one bit. Dad did his blowing and throwing on Teddy to pacify Mother, and since he wasn't the kind of man to speak his mind—he always had this way of pushing everything into oblivion—he said, "Oh, Darlene, now settle down. He'll talk when he gets good and ready." But Mother didn't let up until she got her way and, despite the tight money, finally took him to the pediatrician for a special visit.

But Mother was too terrified to tell the doctor the whole truth. She had her own ways of denial. At home, she showed all sorts of panic over Teddy's incomprehensible silence, but to the world—to others beyond our family—she simply declared him "a good baby". Her face would twist up tight when people at church bent down to Teddy and tried to get him to talk. Everybody noticed, of course—well, *of course,* they noticed— and since they did, they commented, "He's a small little guy isn't he? Well, he'll come around," or, "Nothing wrong with him. He's a bit on the stubborn side, like my Davie." Mother would tremble on the way home Sundays, turning Teddy on her lap to face her and staring into his eyes. "Nothing wrong with him," she'd mutter in the voice of somebody else. "What's the matter with people?" But it sounded to me more like, "What's the matter with Teddy?" She'd look at Daddy and me as though we were keeping the answer from her.

At the doctor's office, she began by telling Dr. Hildebrand that Teddy was "really such a good baby," not saying a word about Teddy's lack of jabber and first word-forming. Nothing about his silence or even his hysterical crying. Mother was worried he was retarded. But even to suggest such a thing to the doctor would mean casting shadows on the family she didn't want to try and see through. Instead, she suggested that Teddy might have some chronic throat problem, that he found it hard to swallow his food and that he was spitting up more than babies should be doing at his age, so would the doctor take a good look at his throat and lungs for obstructions? Maybe check his diaphragm for any malfunctioning? Whether Dr. Hildebrand guessed at Mother's worries through his investigations—mostly consisted of a bit of thumping Teddy on the chest, running his fingers along the sides his neck, getting Teddy to say "ah" and forcing him to gag and cry—he didn't say. He told her that the little guy showed a hefty set of lungs, and there were no obvious obstructions or growths that he could see in the upper passages of the throat, but he could do an x-ray if this would put her mind at rest.

Mother gave me a quick glance which I knew meant to keep my mouth tightly sealed. She was about to reply—I'll never know what she was going to say, because she was too proud to tell him we didn't have health insurance or money to pay for anything like x-rays—when Hildebrand suggested we just observe Teddy for a month or two and do a follow-up visit at that time. If the problem wasn't resolved by then, she and my father could decide if more conclusive testing was warranted.

"He is cutting teeth," Dr. Hildebrand stated as he walked us to the door. "It can express itself in more ways than crying." When Mother simply nodded, the doctor didn't elaborate. He simply closed the door quietly behind our leaving.

In the following months, Teddy's silence continued, and she began voicing her suspicions of his retardation to me, beyond earshot of Dad. Sometimes she'd mumble comments with him hanging on the periphery, as though she was half hoping he could—if God permitted him to—catch a word or two of her worries. If my father heard enough to make sense of it, he never showed us he did. He and Mother may have talked together when they were alone in their bedroom— I can't imagine my mother holding this away from him altogether—but if they ever spoke about it in private, it never spilled out to where I could hear. Dad acted as though he knew nothing of her suspicions, and Mother never mentioned Teddy's possible disability when Daddy and I were together. Dad got so he referred of this odd state-of-affairs as "Teddy's procrastination," smiling while he did, proud that he was carrying a vocabulary over from the newspapers he read in the living room before and after supper every evening, while Mother prodded Teddy on the floor to speak by tickling his stomach or changing his diaper gruffly.

She could get him to cry, but couldn't get another thing out of him.

"His eyes are so bright," she'd say to me while I stood off to the side watching and waiting and wondering with a strange and different anxiety than any other I knew under different circumstances. "He knows more than all of us put together, don't you think?" she'd ask me, not wanting an answer, only agreement. My face probably told her I thought he was mute out of spite. I never would have had the courage to come out with such an insight, even if I'd been able to articulate it then. But I did feel this. When I looked down at Teddy in his cradle, later in his playpen, sometimes when we'd walk shakily along the couch together—me the big sister showing him the way, only a little more certain than he was in the walking—I'd see the stealth in his eyes. Then I'd think, "*You don't come right out and show it, little man, and although it's probably not the most successful way to get back at them, you're finding your own way to do it, aren't you?*" It wasn't the message I told myself in exactly those words, of course, but it was one along those lines, I'm sure of it.

When I watched Teddy's silence, I began to wonder if *I'd* gotten started on the wrong foot. I crawled out of the womb telling them what I thought. It was what she'd given birth to me for, I came to realize after I was an adult and had been through several therapies. I was something to bounce her thoughts off of, something to throw out at my father to catch, something to heave onto her shoulder, another chip to carry around for others to see. To her mind, she was too proud, so she was cursed with all three of us. But, to my mind, it was Teddy's problem, because it really was *his* problem, despite the weight it carried in the house. If he would just be normal like every other baby, then this all would end. But, as I grew older, I was to learn that Teddy's not talking was, for her, another hassle life with our father had given her, and by extension, my problem of too much talking was another given to her, as well. She loved, hated us. She wanted me to tell her what I thought but wanted it to be what she thought. It's what she was wanting from Teddy too, but he had decided, evidently, to not join her in the conflict she had with our father.

But then miraculously, without hesitation or preparation, Teddy uttered his first words in the form of a sentence, "Put me down." There it was, spoken to Daddy while in his lap, Teddy kicking him in the leg, grasping the table top, moving all our supper dishes about. It went unattended for a stretch. Daddy started lowering him to the floor, grinning vaguely, not looking up or giving his full attention to what Teddy wanted in that moment, just fulfilling his demand. I see this still, Daddy's release of Teddy's weight, shifting him from his leg toward the floor, as though Teddy could walk without support—which he could do pretty well by now.

Then in a burst, a door flew open as Mother rushed toward Daddy and Teddy from the kitchen with such force, I thought she'd knock the wind out of them when she got to where they were. "He said something," she declared.

"Wha—un?" Dad stuttered, choking his food down, his fork a clatter on the plate. He grabbed my brother and held him up eye-level, searching for danger. Mother was reaching for him past Dad's arms—Teddy flailing, a fish on a string. His face was odd, uncertainty clouding his eyes, which darted back and forth from Momma to Daddy, Daddy to Momma. His mouth, opening to a smile, possibly a scream, then all at once clamping shut, his face becoming suddenly lifeless. What I saw was an unforgiving defiance that, had I had prophetic vision, would have revealed how Teddy was to carry himself into adulthood—a defiance of leaving, constantly running away, from them and anybody trying to hold him close. Because once he was theirs, he knew instinctively he'd remain forever a fish on a string, unable to disconnect. I can't say how hard he tried to keep his resistance of them going. All I remember is his fall from defiance to resignation and his subsequent self-loss. Of course, I didn't know any of this then. I only saw him running from the table that evening. Running from them. Away.

"Tell Mommy again, Teddy," Momma said, her voice overly sweet, her hands on him, pulling him from Daddy, up into her arms.

"You're scaring anything he has to say right outta him," Daddy said toward the table, placing his napkin to the side of his plate, not yet fully emptied, and scooting his chair back, shifting his legs to the side.

As Teddy began to squirm in her arms, Dad left, walking slowly toward the living room. Mother pulled Teddy closer to her.

Suddenly his hands were on her face, pushing. His fingers, splayed out, were gouging her lips, distorting her expressions of her surprise and rising anger. He smashed into her, twisting side to side, his head bumping her forehead as he flung himself back and forth, screaming.

"Stop it, stop it right now," she said, lowering him to the floor. "There. You wanted down, now you're down. So what're you gonna do with it?" She asked, releasing him to his own support. He almost lost his balance in his haste to get past her. He grabbed her skirt, holding on, then stepped out, seizing the seat of a chair to steady himself, his back to her. Mother sat down next to him, leaned over and kissed his hair. He instantly let go of the seat and took off, a rocket shot from a cannon.

"Why don't you want to talk so we can hear?" she whispered. In one, smoothly executed movement, Momma turned and reached for her Kodak Brownie on the sideboard behind her, its flash with bulb attached seemingly waiting for this exact moment. While Teddy stood waiting, as though he knew what was coming for the rest of his life, he turned his face toward her and her camera, smiling, with both bottom teeth showing.

2.

Momma's Song

The summer of my junior year in high school, I moved away from home—really, away from Mother. I was working at a short order restaurant only a couple of blocks from the school. On week-end football nights, the place was packed, because hamburgers sold for $2 a dozen, which was a penny a hamburger over what McDonald charged, but since the nearest McDonald's was in Oklahoma City, we were the best deal in town. But mostly we packed in crowds because Stern's Stop-and-Go was the first place in Hopewell to introduce soft serve ice cream—called "frozen custard" back then. Aaron Stern, the man who owned the place, was an old, tough-speaking, cigar-toting sort who attempted to snap our bras when waitresses were gathering supplies from the store room. He was surprisingly supportive of us with the customers though. Once, he ordered a woman out of his restaurant who was spitting expletives at me after I accidentally poured a chocolate malt on her white linen suit. He offered to have her stained outfit dry-cleaned, but when she continued with her tirade, he pointed to the door, saying politely, "Leave, don't come back and take your party with you!"

We all—minus Stern—ate their order in a booth after closing hours while he sat on one of the counter stools, spooning and swilling coffee, reading *The Hopewell Herald*, with a cigar pinched between his thumb and index finger, a Cheshire cat grin on his face. He let us chase down the warmed-up cuisine with medium-sized cokes and a soft-service cone for dessert, all on the house.

But there were tough years before I moved out and away from Mother. I sought refuge in my job, school, especially art class, and finally, after leaving, in an attic room that I rented from an eighty-one year old woman I worked with at Stern's restaurant. I was fifteen, allowed to pass for sixteen, so I could work without my parents' permission. It wasn't easy since I was a short, gangly, socially unsavvy kid without a clue as to what went into just about anything. I did know how to work and was willing to learn what was necessary to get ahead, at least to keep my job. It must have been this that convinced Stern's store manager, Mildred Cartwright, to hire me. It was my saving grace, because I was able to afford Ruth Gifford's room at fifteen dollars a month on a salary of seventeen dollars a week.

The garret apartment—which is what I called it, undoubtedly from some art book describing the abode of a nineteenth-century European starving artist—was one big room with a bed and a small side table and with bathroom-and-kitchen privileges downstairs. My closet was a long pipe suspended from two wires at the foot of the bed where I hung my clothes on wire hangers. I supplied little else because the rest of my money went for food, books and art supplies.

It was in this room that I taught myself to paint, borrowing books on art from the local library from which I studied the paintings of Van Gogh, Gauguin, Matisse, and the Impressionists. I purchased a small magnifying glass so that I could scrutinize the layers of color and shapes of the illustrations of their works. Not realizing that the colors of those printed illustrations were not those in the paintings themselves, my work from that time—had I become famous—would have been known as my "Muddied Blue Period," with dirtied oranges, yellows and reds and white for all light, black for the shadows. I still have two paintings I did from those years. One is a large pitcher of Van Goghesque sunflowers for which I won a blue ribbon at the county fair. It hangs over my computer monitor and reminds me of the years of hope and disappointment before I went to college and majored in art and literature. The other is on my dining room wall, a lively picture of a poinsettia with light streaming from behind, flooding two chairs and the table with Titanium White acrylic. It was the impasto application of just such white light in other paintings in college that earned me a number of humiliating critiques from a grad student who won the Gold Metal of Art several years before I did. I stood my ground, continued the technique and sold two paintings before graduation, both in blacks with white bursting from the bottom layers like light from the entrance of a cave.

But even though painting got its start in that garret room, it will always remain as the place where I fell in love with opera. I listened after work every Saturday afternoon during the season to the Texaco opera broadcast from the Met with intermissions filled with the opera quiz. The only music played in our house had been popular tunes and instrumentals on the radio during the evening after Mother's soap operas in the late afternoon. As a young girl brought up in a Mennonite home even with our mixed messages about radio, theater and music, this love of opera was a mystery I couldn't quite explain to others. But I had a pretty good idea where it came from.

My mother had a marvelously light, melodic singing voice with a range from the upper notes of a soprano to the lower notes of a mezzo. She found this out from Miss Hartel, my piano teacher, who listened to Mother's singing voice one afternoon when Momma came to pick me up after my lesson. At the time, I already understood that Miss Hartel's comprehension of such things as voice range and timbre—words she used to describe my mother's talent—was because she was a devoted fan of the operas of Wagner.

Mother often sang along with the radio and would have purchased the recordings of Jeanette MacDonald if her religion would have permitted it. In fact, she had seen most of MacDonald's movies with Maurice Chevalier and Nelson Eddy while she was dating my father, before they joined the church after their marriage. She told me the scripts of those movies as though she were reading me bedtime stories. I knew the plots of *The Merry Widow* and *Naughty Marietta* by heart, although Mother stumbled through the European aristocratic names of the principle characters. To her, they were staples of the court and officialdom, so she called them the King, Duke, Princess, the Governor and such. When she got to the scene in the movie where a song was part of the script, she would sing it to me. Her favorite of the four principal songs in *Naughty Marietta* was "Oh, Sweet Mystery of Life," although she always sang "I'm Falling in Love with Someone" with lingering dreaminess. I was enthralled with the plot of this movie in particular which involved a journey from France to the United States by a princess in disguise, who encounters mercenaries and pirates, marionettes and gypsies, and a finale at a Governor's ball where MacDonald and Eddy, as the mercenary captain who saved her from the pirates earlier, dance and sing together before they escape to the American Wild, Wild West. I was always left with the unspoken notion that Jeanette MacDonald could be living next door without any of us knowing. After all, in the movie, she was a noblewoman in disguise, because she'd made the run for land in Oklahoma with Nelson Eddy during the Cherokee Strip.

I saw my first movie when I was eleven years old, *The Babe Ruth Story,* starring William Bendix. I went with my boyfriend after his father came to the house and met my mother, and they agreed we could go to a Saturday afternoon matinee without chaperone. Perhaps my mother was slowly giving in to her yearnings to become part of the larger, secular world—which did eventually happen—or perhaps she simply was too sick with her undiagnosed bipolar condition by then to explain why I shouldn't go. I didn't question it, because I had been begging to go to the movies and football games with my friends at school for over a year.

But I was to be surprised at my own depth of fear and guilt. Halfway through the movie I insisted that my boyfriend and I leave because I was afraid that Jesus would come back to claim his own while I was in the movie house, and I would be cast into the fiery pit forever and ever. It wasn't until I was fourteen—and if not fully recovered from that view of sinning was ready to pay the wage for it—that I saw my second movie with a girlfriend, Sara Hopkins, secreted from Mother's tightening rules on my teenage behavior. We held hands, ventured a careful kiss or two in the back rows so far in darkness not even the projectionist could catch what we were doing. By this time, I understood clearly the laws of God and church and knew that what resonant pleasures any of us had during our short life on earth came with a terrible price if we gave into them. This time, I wasn't about to leave the movie house or Sara's embrace, so I knew my soul hung in the balance and could be flung into eternal damnation at any given moment.

But back when I was eight and my brother was four, our lives were dominated by our mother's desire that Teddy should "reach his full potential with the talent that God had given him." He had been blessed with a clear high-soprano singing voice since he could talk. And for this, he spent hours practicing new songs a cappella in our living room ready for any chance to perform should the opportunity present itself. It wasn't long before Momma came up with an extended plan. Noticing the handicap of no accompaniment for him, she decided to give me piano lessons so that, at the very least, I could help him while he practiced, evidently not realizing that even if God had given me musical talent to the degree He had my brother, it would take some years before I could play any of the songs she was teaching him. But I trudged on to my piano lessons, by way of bus and walked across town, beginner's sheet music to "Ten Little Indians," "Three Blind Mice," and "Itsy Bitsy Spider" in hand, and a year later *The Beginner's Book of Piano Classics* firmly in my grip, the sheet music to church songs that Mennonites rarely sang or even knew. After a year of spurts and starts at the piano, mother began buying music that I could play well enough—after rote practice day in, day out—for Teddy to sing along, with him slowing and gaining speed in an attempt to stay with my accompaniment.

One Saturday, Momma called me away from the jigsaw puzzle I'd set up on a make-shift folding table in the living room, brief respites from Teddy's and my grueling practice schedule. My brother by this time had completely abandoned the defiance of his early years for that of notice and acceptance from his audiences. The only teeth he bared to Momma now—and any and all other listeners—were those set in the perfect rows of a smile. He had become the fish he had feared, dangling from our mother's string. In other words, he was hooked.

"It's unnatural the way you are so crazy about those jigsaw puzzles," she said to me, not turning around from the sink. "Now, take down these dishes from this cabinet after you're done with the drying." Her hand held out a dish towel for me to take, her eyes still toward her dish washing. I wanted to argue that these shelves had been done only a few days ago and the newspapers that she used as shelf paper could testify to that fact, but I knew it would be useless. She said even before I started my comeback, "I don't want to hear it. Your brother is going to see Spec Petticott this Saturday, and this has to get done before that happens." What the cleaning had to do with my brother's next singing engagement was beyond me. But I'd learned to not point out such inconsistencies in Momma's reasoning. It would take years of reading and learning to love language before I'd know about non-sequiturs. For this day, it was a matter of hacking my way through Momma's jungle of intentions as best as I could.

"He's coming here?" I said in disbelief.

"Of course not. Don't be silly," she said, with a flip of her hand, finally glancing my way. "Mr. Spec Petticott doesn't interview in people's homes, Shike. Your brother is going to the radio station for his interview, and then the movie house for the audition like everybody else." Everyone in my house called me Shike, a contraction of "Shypoke," that my Uncle Clifford had given me years before, but none of my family or relatives used it at church or school under strict orders from Momma. People in "the larger world" were to call me by my given name, Caroline Louise.

Upon hearing about the Petticott interview, I almost dropped the dish I was drying. "The movie house? Teddy's going to the *movie house?*" I knew all about the years before I was born she'd spent in theaters, sitting with my father in those seats dreaming about her future, what it would be like to really live out the stories the stars were acting out on screen. She'd told me this more times than I could count, but that was before she joined the Mennonite church with Daddy—the church they were both brought up in—when she found out I was coming into the world. Since she reconsecrated her life to Jesus, she had not seen one single movie, and that translated into *my* never seeing one, either. Not ever. Well, at least, not as long as I was living under her roof. She would renege on this later, of course, but I wouldn't know this until then.

Most of the time, my brother and I weren't even allowed to walk on the street near either The Big Chief or The Cherokee motion picture theaters, because Momma didn't want us to be curious by what she called, "The Temptations of the Devil." She would even look away—like the Amish do when they passed us in their buggies on the road as we whizzed by in our car. When Momma was of this mind, she walked faster past those theaters, jerking Teddy by the hand, expecting me to keep up. When we were far enough away from the posters in the large show cases on both sides of the ticket booth, she'd straighten her hat and hair and sigh. Walking past the movies at night left a great impression on me because of the flashing neon lights spelling out their common fate, arrows pointing the way to sin. I knew Momma slipped glances at those theater posters and looked at the stars in the magazines Vivian Davis kept for waiting customers at her beauty shop. I grew up knowing Momma wanted more than she let on. Her concern was that we'd want more too. So she had "a big job to do" with Teddy and me, she said. Keeping my brother and me on "the straight and narrow" meant that, as our mother, she was "held accountable" for more than just food, shelter and clothing. She was guardian of our souls.

"It's fantasy, Caroline. All of these pictures are lies that nobody actual lives by," she'd say, squeezing my hand gently against her coat as we walked away from temptation as fast as Teddy's legs would allow us to go. To my mother, the rich and the tales of their matinee up and downs were scarcely of this world, or, perhaps, more correctly, too much of this world, this wicked, wicked, world. When she was swinging in this direction, she would say, "See how the rich live? The price they have to pay for it is too high." I knew she meant they couldn't buy their way out of hell any more than we could buy the coats they wore on their backs. But I wasn't sure how she reconciled this view with those evenings when we snuggled together in my bed, and she told me the movie scripts for *It Happened One Night, Show Boat, Pennies From Heaven,* and *Rose Marie*. The way she told them, they seemed like grown-up fairytales rather than stories from actual movies that had shown on the other side of town.

"Why, yes," she said this morning about going to one of those very movie houses. "Your brother is likely to be singing on KSRC."

Despite the fact that Spec Petticott was the target of jokes around town—he was called the Speckled Petticoat by the sixth grade boys at school—Petticott had the most widely listened to program on the local radio station. He had based his show on Major Bowes's *The Original Amateur Hour* on CBS radio, only without the gong that Bowes had used to send bad performers packing. Coming live from The Cherokee Theater stage, Petticott's Saturday morning variety show had filled in the gap in local radio since Bowes had died and his show had been dropped. Petticott had hit on a successful run, even snuffing out the rival station's talent program.

But the "audience of the airways," as he liked to call his radio listeners—inspired, no doubt, by the fact that the station was located next to the local airport from which airplanes roar over the very airway his audience was listening to—were the folks that make the show "fly," as he told us over and over again in his sing-songy voice. For his talent show he needed us badly, listening every Saturday morning, because it was our phoned-in responses that were the ticket to the state "Championship of Stars" in Oklahoma City, a smaller version of Bowes's vaudeville contestant tours. Spec Petticott remained judiciously silent on where the winner went from there, which was just as well. No one, least of all Momma, could possibly have imagined the actual route from KSRC's talent show to the dancers and crooners on the movie screen running nightly in our hometown. For Momma, Oklahoma City was the end of the line any way we wanted to look at it. For her, Hollywood was totally out of the picture, a flight from real life. Real life meant a life dedicated to God, living His picture of our lives, His images in our minds, His will carried out daily without padding or excuse. So where this new flight-of-fancy was taking Teddy and me we knew not, but we had a bit of an idea, since we'd been here before—not in a movie house, of course—but in a big revival tent with an all-city chorus called

"The Voices of God." Teddy had sung a solo once while Momma had sung in the soprano section of that chorus. He got a standing ovation while Momma got to say she was his mother—in front of the microphone while everybody clapped, and "whooped and hollered," as Daddy would say on the way home in the car. It was the last city-wide revival Momma could get him to go to.

The preparation for the interview with Spec Petticott was not any more unusual than the preparation I'd gone through hundreds of times for church. Momma polished all of our shoes with liquid shoe polish, washed the shoe strings—mine in Clorox—and laid out dry-cleaned, well-laundered and stiffly ironed dress clothes the night before in the extra bedroom upstairs.

—

The Saturday morning of the interview and audition, I shook impatiently as she dropped my dress over my uplifted arms and tied the dark bow in back with two short jerks. The puffed sleeves scratched my cheeks when I turned to the left and right. My brother stood motionless with steaming washrags on top of his head. These were intended to sear his crown and double cowlick to his head. Although Teddy was the star of this show, Momma had spent more time on me. He would put on his suit and tie just before we slipped out the door to the car, his hat slightly askew, a miniature Gable or Bogart, exactly like they were in the posters Momma claimed she detested so much. And I would be what I'd been since I was four, Shirley Temple, as gangly and outgrown as the real one was now becoming at our ages. It would not be long before Momma would drift permanently into mental darkness and both Teddy and I would look suddenly only like ourselves, facing the world without image or protection. But on this day, we knew only that we were getting dressed up for a role we were about to play, and it'd be Momma who'd show us the way through what we had to do.

She had spent days making her own preparations, most of which had been on her knees. At the time, I felt—though never would've been able to articulate—that there was some terrible contradiction with which she was wrestling but seemed equally determined to resolve. The conflict centered by the end of the week on what my brother would sing at the talent show. She was determined to convince Spec Petticott that my brother's voice was devoted entirely to God, and he would sing only God's songs.

In the car on the way to the radio station, she practiced aloud to Teddy and me the speech she planned for Petticott. "Hollywood does not need more songs about falling in love, unless it's songs about falling in love with Jesus," she said with an especially tight grip on the steering wheel and looking only straight ahead through the windshield as though Petticott were riding on the hood facing her.

What I made out of this was that if Spec Petticott agreed to let my brother sing Momma's song, the one she had already picked for him, Teddy was ready to go directly to The Cherokee stage this very morning after the interview and audition and do his song for Jesus and the "audience of the airways." I had no idea which song she had in mind, but my brother knew about as many religious songs as any boy five years old could remember. In fact, Teddy probably knew more, because he had an amazing memory. And his memory was what Momma called his singing "style." She could teach him songs in several hours, very difficult songs like "The Holy City," with key changes into the minor and back into major and with complicated vocabulary, words in them like "Hosanna" that she never bothered to explain to either of us and which I'd stopped asking her to tell us their meanings—songs such as "The Holy City" and "My God and I" that lasted three to five minutes, just like songs on fast-selling 78 records. But Teddy also knew dozens of choruses, short tunes with uplifting messages like Rufus H. McDaniel's, "Since Jesus Came Into My Heart." My brother could sing these on the spot, without a pitch harp to get him started.

"He's got perfect pitch," Momma said proudly. She could play any note, black keys or white, on the piano, and he could sing it, and after he memorized the keyboard, could tell her its letter-name. She and Teddy had turned his perfect pitch into a game. She would call out the name of a chorus when she was working around the house or we were driving somewhere in the car, and Teddy would sing the first line before she named another song that he'd sing just as quick. After a few weeks of this, she would call out "G major" and Teddy would begin the song he knew in that key. Teddy could begin singing each chorus on the right note every time. He knew dozens and dozens of these, all verses, all stanzas. He could sing any amount you asked for. He never seemed to mind. But his wife would tell me many years later that she begged him to sing for her since she knew he had a great voice, but she couldn't get him to hum a line. She told me that every now and then she'd hear him singing softly in the shower, but the minute he heard her footsteps he'd stop without her hearing another note. When he sang with the congregation in church—forget about his ever joining the choir—he would make sure his voice was lower than most, so that he wouldn't stand out and be noticed.

Now I was wondering what Momma would do if Spec Petticott didn't agree to her song. But Teddy and I were kept in the dark on this score, because Momma hadn't bothered to tell us what terms she and God had worked out concerning Teddy's debut in the movie theaters.

In the small waiting room, on the tenth floor of the tall building where Mr. Petticott had his office, I sat flipping through magazines Teddy and I were never allowed to see. Smoke drifted up from a cigarette smudged out only minutes before in a nearby ashtray. The woman who left it there came out of Spec Petticott's office before my brother went in. She was holding her gloves and a poodle's leash, the dog lurching for spaces under the coffee table and chairs. Her daughter followed after her, humming a ditty and looking defiant. Her eyes met mine, grinning with condescension. She wore tap dancing shoes that clicked loudly, the laced-on bows swaying from side to side as she walked past.

It wasn't ten minutes after Momma went into Mr. Petticott's office, that she emerged, her hand slipping from his double grip. Teddy's red curly hair shown with oil and his freckled face smiled at me as Momma took my hand and steered Teddy and me out of the waiting room and down the stairs. Momma didn't wait for the elevator.

"What did he say, Momma?" I asked in a whisper, catching up from behind. Why she didn't allow me to go in with them, I'd never know, but she left me to sit out in the waiting room where god-only-knew-who could've shown up. I would learn soon that it was because of my guilelessness, my terrible ability to let just about anything fly out of my mouth regardless of the audience or venue—family secrets, hidden agendas, forbidden desires. But at the time, it was a mystery to me, a kind of interior understanding I'd come to about Momma's mood swings and her wishy-washy rules about my behavior and Teddy's.

Her hat was trembling, and I saw her eyes were watering. "Can't you wait till we get out the door and to the car?" she hissed without turning around, bounding down the steps until I thought Teddy would fall. He was hanging from her hand like some doll she's just picked up on the way to the toy bin. "I don't want Mr. Petticoat—Petticott to hear you." I stifled a giggle even though I knew I was in trouble. When she had jerked Teddy down a couple of floors with her, me close behind, we got in an elevator to descend the final eight floors. As our elevator car began moving downward, she glared at me and said with another hiss, *"Mien jauma! Kaunst dü dit festone?"* For goodness sakes, didn't I understand this? She was so surprised by her sudden outburst in Plattdeutsch that her fingers flew over her mouth, and she began to cry, almost in sobs. The small plume on her hat pulsed up and down all the way through the parking lot.

Inside the car, with all doors slammed tightly closed and my brother sitting alone in the back seat, Momma gathered herself with a deep sigh and a wad of handkerchief to each eye, finally telling us, in that churchy voice she could pull out of nowhere, "Mr. Petticott is of the mind that no religious songs will be sung on his show. He listened to a couple of choruses, and it was clear he wanted your brother to sing, but he said it was the strictest policy that religious songs would not be allowed on the talent show. I made it plain as I could that my son could not sing love songs at his age, I would not have it, and he said perhaps I could compromise. Why didn't I select something somewhere in between?"

Momma paused, wiping her upper lip with her linen hanky and starting the engine. She placed her hanky in her lap, its monogrammed "J" hanging over her leg, before she shifted and said, "I wasn't sure what he meant by that, but he suggested that Teddy sing something like 'Somewhere Over the Rainbow,' or maybe even, the number one song on the charts right now, 'Chickery-Chick.' Well, I told him that these were Hollywood songs, part of the whole business of Hollywood. I would not permit it because God would not permit it. He looked at me a long time, and I thought for sure he was going to give in, but finally he just said again that it was 'the station's policy' to not play religious songs except for religious programming. He kept saying 'policy' over and over, that the *station policy* couldn't be changed." When Momma said "station policy" she used her snotty, high-toned voice. "'Written in indelible ink,' he said," Momma continued in the same voice, only louder, through the windshield at the make-believe Spec Petticott still seated on the hood.

She backed the car out of the lot and into the traffic on squealing wheels. At the light, she stopped with a jerk and looked at me, suddenly smiling and giving me an emphatic nod. Then she took off with her foot heavy on the accelerator. Some idea had come to light, but only she and God knew what it was.

Then suddenly at the next light she had a change of heart and decided to tell me. "It occurs to me, Caroline, that if I was to go through sheet music at Hinkle's Music Store, God might provide something suitable for Teddy to sing. If that happens, your brother will sing on the radio. If it doesn't, that will be a clear message to me that Teddy is not supposed to sing on Spec Petticott's talent show."

Momma parked our '38 Plymouth behind Hinkle's and ordered us both out of the car. I walked with Teddy to the counter of sheet music, where lined in rows were all the pictures of the Hollywood stars, some exactly like those in the posters at The Big Chief and The Cherokee theaters.

My brother was named after Theodore Eck, the choirmaster of the great Mennonite *a cappella* choir in Omaha, Nebraska. Momma had an interview with and auditioned for Theodore Eck before Teddy was born. She didn't know it at the time of the audition, but two weeks after she received her letter of acceptance from Eck, she found out she was pregnant. It was true that she also realized no amount of scheming could make my father leave his job and follow her to Nebraska even before she told him she was going to have a baby.

"Your Daddy said he would not leave Oklahoma and move to Omaha if the angels asked me to sing for God Himself," she had told me many times. So she took her revenge by naming her first-born son after the choirmaster and not after my father as he would have liked. She told him at the time—when he accused her of what she'd actually done— that Teddy's name didn't have anything to do with Eck at all. It was because Theodore was the English version of Theodosius from the Bible, which meant "a messenger of God." So Teddy's name, she told us, was a reminder that he had been God's message to her that she was supposed to stay put and wasn't to move and sing in Eck's choir regardless of my father's position on the matter. How my mother knew that Theodosius meant "a messenger of God," remains a mystery. But Mother's sister, Josephine, had her own ideas about all this naming-of-Teddy business.

"Ever consider that she might have made this whole thing up?" was Aunt Josie's suggestion when I asked her years later. She told me this with a laugh, then added, "Truth be told, Darlene probably got it from our dad. He had all kinds of Biblical trivia stashed away on the creaky shelves of his mind." What I found out still later on my own and probably what Grampa Dirks knew but didn't tell my mother, was that Theodosius wasn't in the Bible at all, but was a Roman *Catholic* emperor, who was the last to rule over both eastern and western sectors of the Roman Empire and who had a great deal to do with early Christian history, anyway the one that was in the textbooks.

Undoubtedly, Grampa Dirks was grinning to himself over these unrevealed details every time Teddy came into his view. Anything Catholic was located right after Cancer in my mother's dictionary.

Aunt Josephine added, "She took it as a sign from God that your brother was born with a photographic memory and the aptitude for music because she named him after Eck—which she never admitted openly, of course, especially to your dad, though I can't imagine that he didn't actually *know*, for heaven's sakes. But nobody, not even your mother, could have predicted the talent that boy would have."

By three, Teddy was singing in all the local Protestant churches, Mother forgetting completely the scriptural arguments concerning denominations and their ill-fated destiny with hell, the same forgetfulness she had when we went to the inter-faith revivals, and she sent us to The Assembly of God Daily Vacation Bible School. At these times, she must have been thinking that if a little religion was a good thing, more of it was even better. By four, Teddy had a regular itinerary he went through each year, singing almost every night in churches the two weeks before Christmas and Easter. "What Mennonites do things like this?" Aunt Josie would ask me, when mother wasn't around. "We Baptists do it all the time and the Pentecostals do it right in their churches, but *Mennonites?* I was raised in a Mennonite home, too, remember, and I do not know one Mennonite, not one, that talks about going to hell on one side of their mouth while they talk about Hollywood on the other."

"It's not Hollywood—" I tried to explain.

"It's Hollywood, honey, anyway you cut it. Your mother's religious veneer doesn't cover her desire for glamour. Put this bee in your bonnet and let it buzz around. Your mother's star-crazy, always has been. It's why she decided to become a Mennonite, you want my opinion—though she knows better than to ask me about this one." I didn't understand very much about any of this until later, when I was in high school and separated from her, especially about the Mennonite part of it, but Aunt Josie supplied the answer before I asked, like she often did.

"Darlene bought enough of our mother's old country Mennonite religion to know that she loved far, far too much of all this gaudy, ritzy, showy life she saw in the movies and magazines. I doubt that she dreamed when she was a young star-struck girl, you know, even before she was dating your father, that she'd make it to Hollywood. I don't think she dreamed that far, but maybe she did, who'll ever know? After marrying your dad, though, forget it, she wasn't even going to Nebraska, kiddo. Your dad was an excuse. I think joining the church, becoming a Mennonite, was her way of making herself settle down and behave, resigning herself to the life she had in front of her. Your mother...." Aunt Josie stopped and tapped her chin, pointed her finger at me—only a little—then smiled and said, "She had a flapper in her that she just couldn't let show or she wouldn't have been able to stop where she went and what she did."

"What's a flapper?" I asked her.

"A holy roller at a dance hall," she said, laughing. Then she became serious so I'd understand. Squatting down next to me, she said, "It's a woman who loved life, who liked to dress up, dance all night and have fun all day. Flappers lived around the time that your mother and I were born. They were something else, Shike. They did things that other people thought were too... well, not nice for women to do."

"Not lady-like," I said.

"Exactly," Aunt Josie exclaimed. "They said what they thought and acted like they could do as they wanted. A flapper smoked, drove cars at a time when women didn't do that so much, and she didn't always wait on a man to accompany her everywhere she went. She was a new, very modern kind of woman. Just about the opposite of what your momma became and what she and I both ended up doing with our lives. We made our families first." Aunt Josie pulled me to her and gave me a hug, then held me out from her, her hands on my arms, and added, "But you can't ever say any of this about your mother to her or anybody else, because it's just my idea, and if your mother got wind of what I've just told you, she and I might not be good friends very long. She's a proud woman, Shike. She always makes the most of whatever she decides to do, and you and Teddy are *it*, you understand?"

I nodded.

"Good, because 'flapper' wouldn't be one of her favorite words, not now—probably not ever. You can trust me on this. So be a good girl and keep this between you, me, and the bee in your bonnet, okay?"

I put Aunt Josie's bee in my bonnet, and it did buzz around and around, pretty much like she said it would. A dimension was added to how I viewed my mother I couldn't have figured out on my own. And in all the troubles I had with Mother that followed, I never betrayed my aunt's trust in me. Even when I was furious beyond reason with my mother, I never told her about the flapper Aunt Josie thought she kept inside.

"Teddy's talent is very, very special," Momma would say when I grew tired of all the nights of singing, piano playing, and church-going. "It's not meant to be hoarded or hidden under a bushel." During the summer, tent meetings and revivals were jammed in between daily vacation Bible schools.

I had not been born with my brother's gift, but Momma saw early the advantage in a brother-sister team. So at nine, after almost two years of piano lessons, I became part of his act. Since God had not smiled so amiably on my fingers as he had on my brother's voice, I studied piano with Miss Hartel in her home across town. I caught a bus every Saturday at our corner and was deposited two houses from where Hartel's pianos sat waiting for my unexercised hands. The austere portrait of Wagner hung over the Kimball keys where I labored year in and out for Teddy and for God. The piano that sat silently at home in our living room was a Jenkins. It cost $25 to just get it tuned every year. I had to grow older before I understood that this was totally unnecessary since I didn't play it enough for this kind of maintenance.

The sheet music Momma bought for me came from Hinkle's Music Store and was, according to Miss Hartel's instructions, of the classical variety, an educated version, to Momma, of her own religious music, especially after she discovered a song I was learning by Mendelssohn in our hymnal. When I turned thirteen, Momma finally stopped paying empty money to the woman who worshipped opera, but this was not before Teddy and I had made a long career of religious performance in our town.

For this new musical venue, Spec Petticott disqualified me from his talent show before I even touched a key. His secretary did this on the phone when Momma made the appointment for my brother's audition. It was the *station's policy*, she told Momma in a nasal tone that our mother would use for days when she told anybody about this call, to have its own pianist for the live broadcast from The Cherokee. That was so everybody could have the same chance. This accompanist was in every meaning of the word, 'a professional,' and needed any sheet music only seconds before the live performance.

When my brother walked across the stage the following Saturday morning—his initial audition had been waived because Petticott had made up his mind in his office to have Teddy sing, he told Mother—Petticott adjusted the mike, stooping to announce him from Teddy's height, no one in the audience paid much attention to him. The piano could barely be heard above the noise of the kids waiting for the movie following the talent show, but within minutes of his singing, a hush fell over the auditorium, and Teddy held them captive as he always did. He sang from memory, "When the Red, Red Robin Comes Bob, Bob, Bobbin' Along." His head bobbed, his eyes sobbed, and he throbbed his way to the listener phones, four on pedestals, ringing from the time it took the audience of the airways to get through to the operators of Spec Petticott and his Receivers. Teddy hit *live* and *love* in the lyrics hard as Momma had taught him, then a softer *laugh* and *happy*, which he sang with a smile, bringing his fist down in the palm of his other hand.

At the end of the song Harry M. Woods had written and Momma and Jesus had picked for him, Teddy had received more calls during a performance than any other talent on Petticott's shows. Calls for him continued through the taps and chirps of six other contestants. At the end of the show, he sang an encore, "The Little Dutch Boy and the Little Dutch Girl," who were sleeping on a hill. Momma debated a long time whether this song should come first. "The boy and girl could be awakened by the robin," she said, knowing there would be two songs for Teddy, not just one like everybody else.

It was the day of this contest that my true competition began for me with my brother. Within months, I had won $6 at a prayer contest in a Nazarene tent meeting and had recited a poem for another $10 at a nearby Assembly of God revival. Momma took a second look at my talent and began planning some acts for me aside from the accompaniment to my brother's songs. From the time of my winning $16 for praying and reciting, I became the flannel-graph storyteller throughout our growing church community. I did "The Creation," "The Crucifixion and the Ascension," and "The Christmas Story," at appointed times of the year. "Noah's Ark" was my favorite. I did this for Children's Storytime before the major sermon at the evening worship hour, and at Sunday Schools, and mid-week prayer meetings. Sometimes I took up the entire hour of Christian Endeavor, every fourth Wednesday night prayer meeting time at our church.

Once a month, regular as clock work, I traced and colored pictures Momma copied from books that I would use for the stories I'd tell. After these were finished, I laid them down on flannel and cut out the backing which Momma helped me glue on. Afternoon after school, I memorized lines and practiced putting the flannel backgrounds and pictures together for my stories. This was when I wasn't practicing songs with Teddy.

My career outlived my brother's because after Teddy's KSRC win, Momma came to grips with her conscience. She told us she would not be driving us to Oklahoma City to Spec Petticott's big state contest, and did not allow Teddy to sing anymore, even "non-sexual tunes"—it's what Mother called them—because she knew Hollywood still produced, distributed, and profited from the sheet music she bought at Hinkle's Music Store. In a dramatic gesture for God, she struck a match to "The Red, Red Robin" and "The Little Dutch Boy and The Little Dutch Girl" in our backyard trash barrel.

She gave a flat "no" to Petticott's secretary when she called to make arrangements for the Oklahoma City talent show and did not answer the phone for weeks during the day for fear Petticott himself would tempt her into the devil's business. A $100 war bond was at stake and four cases of Royal Crown Cola. Teddy couldn't have drunk the cola, Momma said, since it contained drugs way too strong for little kids.

"Anyway, what kind of silly advertising is this station sponsoring anyway?" she asked Daddy at supper the night after she'd said no to Petticott's secretary. "KSRC translates to *Cases of RC?* What kind of twisted language is that, all in the name of money?" The station sent a letter of acceptance for Teddy to join the contest in Oklahoma City if Momma changed her mind. She only needed to sign and send in the form the note attached had stated in well-written cursive. Petticott had enclosed a picture of Teddy on stage, in front of the mike, while he was on the air. Momma put it in the top drawer of the sideboard and tore up the letter on the way to the kitchen, throwing it in the tall trash can under the sink. I was surprised she hadn't torn up the picture along with it.

Later that evening when she thought I was setting the table, I opened the drawer carefully and took out the photograph of Teddy singing. The photographer had taken the shot from some distance, because it was grainy and the light and dark contrast had been flattened out to grays, but Teddy stood, as he always did with utter confidence, this time in front of a microphone, singing his heart out. I stared at it a long time, wondering what was to become of him and his talent once he grew a little older.

But my brother didn't seem to mind giving up the state contest. He dressed with me for church the same as he always had the next Sunday morning after his radio success. He never mentioned the win. He didn't even hum the tunes. He knew about acceptance and non-acceptance just like I did.

—

But Teddy was as surprised as I was when shortly after her refusal to let him sing in Oklahoma City, Momma announced a new act for us that very Sunday at the Hope and Grace Baptist Church.

I had always thought that Hope and Grace were two Negro sisters who had the money to build a church and name it after themselves and did not allow white people to go there. The church was located across the street and down a block from the Negro swimming pool. I had only seen the church once, except in passing, when Momma drove my brother and me past it slowly after dark as people were coming out into the night after Sunday evening service, bundled up against the winter wind.

"Look," she said in a whisper, "I want you to look at them. They are people just like you and me, and God loves them just the same."

Our '38 Plymouth was moving so slowly past the open doors, the entire congregation spilling out onto the sidewalk turned and faced us, suddenly, motionless, their hands up over their eyes, shading them from the glare of the church porch light and looking to make out what white folks were driving past their church at that time of night. There was only one street light at the corner of the block, and I felt sudden panic at the thought that this was not our place. We did not belong here. We had our own service and our own way of coming to Jesus. What was Momma trying to tell us?

But she had found a way to get us to the Hope and Grace Baptist church without audition or compromise. We could, she said with great assurance, sing whatever we liked and to an audience in need of our message, though she admitted that most of these black souls were already within the arms of the Savior. "Praising God in all His majesty means crossing the road to do that sometimes," she told Teddy and me solemnly.

The few days after my brother's radio broadcast, "a caring white man for the Negroes"—Momma called him—had telephoned her to say he'd heard my brother sing on the radio and felt he'd heard a special voice from God. He told her that arrangements had been made for him to record the Hope and Grace Baptist Church choir on site and if Momma could bring my brother to the church the following Sunday morning for the service, he would record him as well. This was free and in no way obligated us to commercial offers. He was a distributor from Oklahoma City who loved Jesus and wanted local talent to "witness" in local stores. The records were mostly sold through church meetings and tent revivals for now, but it was his vision for God that Hinkle's Music Store would one day have a section of religious offerings from local talent right alongside "The Row of Stars." Momma saw this opportunity as a direct response from the Almighty for her doing the right thing about Spec Petticott's state competition.

However, the Hope and Grace Baptists were not Momma's kind of people. She'd taught my brother and me to conduct ourselves during our acts like the great choirmasters conducted their talents. Clapping, swaying and amen-ing during the singing of songs were not in keeping with that tradition. My brother stood in sedate contrast to the hymn singing that had been recorded before he walked up to the microphone. But his young voice and stature hushed this crowd and once "The Holy City" began, the audience sat motionless and silent except for some small bench sways and fan waves.

Teddy sang the story in Revelation about how the Apostle John had envisioned a new world arising from the Jerusalem back then and the Jerusalem now. "Jerusalem, Ja—rooh—sah—lemm," Teddy sang, and then the encore, "Hosanna" on the highest sweet notes of Jesus—just as he had been taught—with a joy that would last forever and ever.

There was a slight pause as I attempted to catch up with Teddy's final notes. Much of my brother's phrasing depended on the accuracy of my fingers to the keys. The church members gave random amens and polite applause while the distributor walked on tiptoes to my mother and talked in her ear. She nodded, and he returned to his machine and turned it off.

He walked to the mike and said, "Because of the length of the selections this young songster for God has chosen today, his mother has agreed to record his voice after the services. This seems fitting and leaves us all free to sing God's praises this morning as we choose." I wondered about the microphone, because in most the places where I'd seen them used, there had been huge audiences, in the enormous sanctuaries at the Assembly of God church or outdoor tent meetings. This was a church no bigger than Hopewell Mennonite. Teddy could have sung without any microphone and been heard all the way to the back pews. He knew how to extend his voice plenty, as Momma had taught him. But maybe these people wanted to reach the hard-of-hearing or help everybody hear the music above all the amens going on—that's all I could figure out.

After the Caring-White-Man made this little speech, there was a decided ruffling of fans and feet. "Teddy's mother tells me he knows lots of choruses," he went on, shouting in the mike to the audience, his voice so loud I wanted to cover my ears. "And I bet anything that you know some he knows. Why don't we start out with 'Heavenly Sunshine'?"

I sat motionless at the keys, very pale and alone. I didn't know how to play 'Heavenly Sunshine.' Teddy could easily sing without my accompaniment, or anybody else's. He usually did for the choruses anyway, but I wasn't sure what to do about walking back to where Momma sat. Suddenly, before I had a chance to stand, a Negro woman scooted me aside after giving me a hug and began using all white and black keys at once. The entire congregation stood and sang with Teddy in unison, filling the church with heavenly sunshine and glory divine.

The clapping was thunderous. I wanted to go back and sit by Momma but there seemed like nothing to do but wait until I'd been given permission by this woman in her church to leave. She stood up then, as though reading my thoughts and walked me back to Momma, hands on my shoulders, an enormous smile engulfing her face. In my relief, I had not realized that the congregation was beginning to file down the aisles singing *a cappella* in their own style and version of "Heavenly Sunshine." My brother started to sway and clap his hands to the glory of God and the crowd, acting like he'd been doing this with every chorus he'd ever sung.

The volume now ascended past the ceiling and the walls. A large Negro man, with eyebrows like great tails and eyes shiny black as marbles, picked up Teddy and straddled him behind his head on his shoulders. My brother hung on to this man's ears like a rider on a bucking bronco. He seemed to be enjoying himself, smiling and laughing, but every now and then, he'd glance at Momma to make sure everything was all right. The man was singing and swaying so that my brother fell backwards and forwards, feet clamped to the man's underarms, heels to ribs. I knew Teddy was riding for all Negroes everywhere and for Jesus in particular.

I looked up at Momma's face, hoping to find some reassurance that we would be leaving this place soon in order to be restored to our former selves. Her face was white as death itself. She swayed stiffly in keeping with the music, clapping her hands clumsily back and forth, as though she needed to keep up with what was going on, but didn't know the melody. It was true that "Heavenly Sunshine" had long evaporated into some musical cascade that had little likeness to what my brother had started ten minutes before. I looked at the piano player, who was standing now, pounding the keys at arm's length, jumping for emphasis, her fat behind rippling up and down for the Lord. She motioned to the distributor to move parts of his equipment to the window sills, hoping in that way to ensure it didn't get smashed in the steady march of the congregation to the altar and stage. Momma and I were the only ones left in the pews, except for a few young children jumping on them while pouring out their smaller messages for Jesus.

Clearly my mother was not prepared for the intensity and length of this service. At final prayer, her head bowed but eyes open, she took my hand in hers, cold and damp, and whispered that we would get Teddy and exit at the first opportunity as our daddy would be waiting for his Sunday dinner at home with Timothy. Teddy's recording session could wait.

But it was two-thirty in the afternoon before we sat in our car waving goodbyes to the crowd. I had counted no less than fifteen offers for Sunday dinner which Momma had graciously refused. And she held in her hands an agreement for my brother and me to record for Living Soul Records in Brother Gibson's home within the month. She also took with her two small 78-speed phonograph records which Gibson had given her. One was of Teddy singing "The Holy City" with my accompaniment, and "Heavenly Sunshine" by himself *a cappella*. The other was of Momma herself singing "God Understands."

The record agreement was never fulfilled, because ten days after Momma and Brother Gibson signed it, he died of a coronary at Hopewell Memorial Hospital. She read his obituary in *The Hopewell Herald,* silently and with pursed lips after Daddy had pointed it out to her.

We returned to the Hope and Grace Baptist Church after that but never to sing. Momma gathered up clothes from the white congregation and took them there on occasional Sunday nights, sometimes after our evening service, leaving them with the pastor who smiled benignly and accepted these gifts from his sisters and brothers from "across the way."

Two of Teddy's new songs did have clapping in them. These were picked by Momma for "congregational singing" which he lead at Hopewell Mennonite for Christian Endeavor, rocking left and right like a metronome, the audience as straight as bean poles in their seats as they'd always been.

That winter, mother's manic-depression worsened. She spent a great deal of her time in bed, for days, never getting out of her house dress. When she called me from the kitchen I knew it wasn't for her singing as she used to do, to ask me about the lyrics or if her notes sounded "off key." She had stopped singing months before and the radio was rarely on, the house silent of human voices, tomb-like, with green shades—left over from the war—remaining down unless I pulled them up. I knew the music I was hearing this afternoon, rare as it was, was her recording. Momma was standing in a housecoat and slippers, looking at me like she didn't know me. It had been a long, long time since our record-making concert at the Hope and Grace Baptist Church and news of Brother Gibson's passing. Teddy was in second grade, and I'd just turned eleven. Timothy was three.

"Caroline?" she asked.

"Yes, Momma," I said, not moving from the doorway.

She walked past me to the phonograph player in the dining room where she checked the speed, then turned the knob to the "off" switch. The record made a smearing noise of her high soprano notes. She sighed, walked to Daddy's sofa chair and fell into it, farther from the kitchen still, into the living room.

"Is Teddy all right? Where's Timmy?"

I didn't move, just stood where I was and waited. "They're with Aunt Josephine, remember?" Momma didn't acknowledge what I'd said, but she didn't ask more about the boys, so I knew she'd heard me.

Her breathing was erratic and her hands moved to her throat as though she might choke. "I'm not feeling so well today," she said absently, her hands now in her lap. "You'll have to help your daddy with supper."

I looked at the empty counter and walked to the refrigerator. There were no preparations for dinner. It would be canned vegetable soup again. My brothers would return with Aunt Josephine and Uncle Clifford on Sunday when they came for dinner, the dinner Aunt Josie would bring and finish cooking with Gramma Dirks while Momma did little things next to them to add some contribution to the chores. My uncle and Daddy would sit on the porch, talk politics or news stories, and smoke while they waited to be called in to eat. I'd tend to Timmy, while Teddy played cars or games in his bedroom with my boy cousins, who would ultimately spill out into the rest of the house, running around, jumping on the furniture. Then after they were gone, life would return to normal, the normal that was silence.

"Your brother will be singing at the Bible Baptist Church next Sunday,

Caroline. I don't think I have the energy to teach him a new song." She paused, started to go on, but words failed. Finally, she said in a whisper, "I'm so tired."

"Teddy's singing at the Baptist church was cancelled, Momma," I reminded her carefully. "You don't need to worry. Teddy doesn't want to sing there anyway." I didn't tell her that he didn't want to sing at all, anywhere. She fell in the habit of making engagements for Teddy, and then cancelling them. That was until this past fall when word had spread that her commitments with her son weren't reliable, and when Teddy did show up, the sweet voice he once had was gone, along with his earlier enthusiasm. Nobody invited Teddy to sing and when Momma attempted arrangements for even a sing-a-long, nobody committed to Teddy's appearance on their programs.

Momma would hang up asking, "How can all these churches have schedules this full?" Then she'd say to Teddy and me, "It's a brush-off, is what it is. They think I don't see it, but I do."

So when Hope and Grace Baptist turned her down, she went to bed, not getting up for two days, except to tend to Timmy. I pulled him around the house in a wagon, as I had Teddy before him, and when weather permitted, down the back porch ramp into the yard and sidewalk, going back and forth, up and down the block until he wanted to return inside. Sometimes he pedaled up the street and back on his hand-me-down tricycle, while I walked slowly alongside.

My piano lessons continued even though I abandoned practice every chance I could, and Teddy didn't sing except when Momma asked him to—for her. He became truculent or sullen when she suggested he learn something new. That was on the days when she was up and around for a few hours.

About Teddy's singing, Daddy finally informed her, "Well, times have changed, Darlene. People're into their church lives different than they used to be. Even Hope and Grace Baptist Church. Looks like they're building an extension, and I think they've started live radio spots, just like some of the other churches in town. Church congregations can tune in now without bothering to put on their Sunday best and getting out in the rain to attend normal worship services, don't you know that? They mail their offerings in pledge envelops these days. And before you say anything, no, Teddy will not sing on the air. I'm putting my foot down on this. You aren't up to it, and neither is he.

He's telling you—if you're caring to listen—that he's done with all that, and you need to bring your attention to your life here, especially with Timmy. We can't keep asking Josephine to fill in for us. She's got a house full of her own kids, plus the whole farm to help look after. I'm asking you to pull yourself together and concentrate on what needs to be done right here and now." Daddy was saying "here and now" every time he talked to Momma lately. She sat silently staring at him when he talked to her like this.

She had spurts of what Daddy referred to as her "get-up-and-go," by which he meant she'd make a pot of soup, a roast on Sunday, or she'd mop the floor, do the laundry. She'd be "up and at it"—another of his phrases—especially after he'd nagged her for a while, then she'd fall back into bed and complain when she got up that she was "dizzy," or "things were hopelessly foggy," or "people sounded like they were in tunnels."

Today she was daydreaming again, but I knew it wouldn't last. Nothing lasted, though she never stayed up for long. She was in bed more than she wasn't.

"Best to just humor her along," Daddy told me. But he was losing patience with her. He'd come home exhausted and forever hopeful she'd "spin out of it," and sometimes she would. He'd find her baking, cooking, and cleaning again. For a little while, he called me after he knew I was home from school and asked how things were before he left work at Davenport Motors. But for the past several months, he didn't bother with my news. It usually wasn't what he wanted to hear.

"I'm embarrassed to call so often from the secretary's phone," he said to me, one evening when Mother was in bed, the door closed as usual. "It shames a man when he has to hang out around the corner until the secretary leaves for the bank, so he can use the phone without her listening in."

These past couple of years, Momma had fallen in and out of trances several times a month. The episodes were getting more frequent, and they were lasting longer. When she came out of one, she had boundless energy, but she was very hard to satisfy. Her demands increased during these times, and when Teddy and I could not meet them, she was vicious to us. She would slap my face, tell me to clean a closet, rearrange a shelf, mop and wax a floor, none of which I could complete alone, so they often remain half done, if done at all. She'd see me set a pail of soapy water on the kitchen floor, and when I returned with the mop, she'd be standing there waiting. After beginning the task, she'd sigh, take the mop from me, place it in the bathroom tub, empty the water down the toilet and return to the couch or the bed. It was easier when she was lost to herself and to us. For a while, I prayed she'd get better until my prayers not only weren't answered, but she got worse. After a while, I found myself encouraging her to not get up. I tried to fill in with my brothers until Daddy came home. Some days, she sat listening endlessly to the records Brother Gibson had given her.

"Why did you turn the record player off, Caroline?" she said this afternoon, sitting in the sofa chair, studying her hands as she spoke.

"I didn't, Momma. You did." I said carefully.

"I don't remember that. Would you put it back on, please? Put on Teddy this time."

I went to the phonograph player, put on the record and dropped the needle down that brought Teddy's grainy voice into the room—the record was becoming worn from overuse. She sighed and leaned her head back against the white doily on the headrest. She looked like a disheveled angel with a crocheted halo. I wasn't supposed to play these records, Daddy's instructions. But this afternoon I didn't want her upset.

"Theodore Eck retired a year ago, Caroline, did you know that?"

"Yes, Momma. Aunt Josephine told us, remember? Gramma told her."

I went to her side, sitting on the arm of the chair. I hugged her neck, but she sat stiffly alone. "It's okay, Momma," I said, moving away, standing. "You'll get better. Remember the record *God Understands?* You sing that God understands your sorrow, that He understands your fears."

"You're right, Caroline," she said with unconvincing resolve. "I do listen to the words. I'm just not sure they're getting through."

I walked to the record player and took us out of Teddy's Holy City and put us into God's Understanding. Momma stood up, walked into the kitchen and began washing the dishes she'd left untouched for two days.

"Goodness," she said, overly loud. "These dishes haven't been done for ever so long, Caroline. Where have you and your father been?"

I watched her cautiously from the kitchen doorway. "We let things go to pieces, I guess, when you don't help us, Momma," I said, using the words she often used on us when she was exasperated about the house chores not being done.

"Well, get out the vegetables, and we'll tend to supper the best we can."

I walked quickly to the refrigerator. I knew that Momma would probably disappear halfway through the making of dinner, but I was hopeful there might be a shred of reality with which she could identify some potential in us that could meet her everyday expectations. She needed hope, I knew, and Teddy and I couldn't generate this for her any longer.

I did not know it then, of course, but what Momma needed was the movies. She needed to sit with abandon and without guilt while she watched Bette Davis tear someone's eyes out, as she did in *Jezebel*, when I was one year old, after Momma had found Jesus once again and didn't go to the movies anymore. She needed to watch Olivia de Havilland sit stiff-necked and willful against the pounding fists of Montgomery Clift at her door in *The Heiress*, when I was twelve, and Momma had forgotten how to dream and fly to an unreal heaven, when Teddy and I could no longer rescue her from the life given to her by her mother's claustrophobic religion.

3.
Random Objects

My breath was coming out in spasmodic little spurts, a sound from my throat I didn't recognize as my own breathing. It frightened me a little, but I told myself I needed this agony. I was running too hard, at a pace faster than I could maintain, but I pressed on, telling myself I'd hold out for as long as I could. My body was heavy, uncoordinated. It felt wrong. I had been a high school athlete and even two years ago had taken second place in a USATF younger-end veteran class race. Now I was boy-scouting up the hills and walking more than running on the last half of the hour out. But I'd only started up again two weeks ago. It would take time.

The air was cooler than it had been in days. Temperatures had been soaring, setting records. Yesterday's paper had reported the hottest day in 98 years. I slowed, then stopped, spotting a piece of broken asphalt in my path. I picked it up and examined it. I felt lucky to have found it. It had the texture and appearance I'd been trying to get in a drawing I started several days earlier. I smiled remembering how many times I'd raced from my drawing table to the apartment driveway, up and down the stairs in the last week, looking at the asphalt there in an attempt to remember its texture and transfer it onto paper. Why hadn't I snapped a picture of it with my camera? Who knew? But then, I did know. It was the hassle—the taking of the picture, then the wait for the development and then the likely disappointment with the picture's resolution and detail.

I put my find in the burlap bag with the trowel I'd brought to dig out a scarred rock I'd seen on my run one day last week. I pictured myself suddenly a bag lady. Would I be gathering textured stuff from the roadside years from now, no longer distinguishing the artist I took myself to be from the other demented souls who collected such garbage? I had talked to one of these women once in passing. I'd met her on one of my runs, and I'd asked her about the substance of her fortunes.

Surprisingly she had talked with me at length about what she carried home and even about her family who came to see her from time to time. She had been strange, but hardly crazy. It was an image that haunted me. She'd had a preference for broken fragments of shiny objects. Some were extraordinary, having unusual shapes and textures. Others didn't seem to belong, finding a place in some extreme category in the woman's head. The whole act of collecting struck me at the time as arbitrary and personalizing, as though objects could be possessed through any claim at all and thereby made precious enough to protect, giving them a power far beyond what they seemed, at other times, to have. Why did this woman and I long for them? They were inert things, having no life, unable to respond, as an animal, a cat or a dog could. I thought now perhaps I collected them a whole lot like the woman I'd met, through some belief that objects, random as my attention to them might be, made me less lonely. They drew me into the world, while I thought I was drawing them out. I slung the burlap bag with my tool and treasure over my head, adjusting the shoulder strap across my chest and began once more to run.

There was a distant rumble and the sunlight grew dim. I had some distance to go before my hour was up, but I couldn't see the sky clearly for the trees. I decided to run ahead to a clearing. If it was a storm, I'd have time from the sound of the thunder to turn around and make it home before it broke. When I reached the clearing, I realized the decision to come out at all had been a mistake. Lightning cracked behind me and another flashed to the side. I had no place to stop. The road was bounded by power lines and trees. I decided to dash for it. Maybe I could get to the houses some distance up the road and wait it out on a porch. But by the time I was there, I was soaked, my new running shoes sloshing water up the sides of my legs. A man leaned over his porch railing and told me to stop. From the looks of him, I decided against it. I inanely wiped the water pouring down my face with the bandana I untied from around my neck.

"Too late now," I shouted to him. His poodle snarled as I passed and startled me from my path. Out of the corner of my eye, I saw the man swat at it and miss.

A garbage truck splashed me as I ran alongside the curb, leaving a trail of ooze on the pavement. My over-a-hundred-dollar running shoes were damaged, if not gone. But the rain had almost stopped by the time I was on my way up the back driveway to the apartment complex. Suddenly the smell of the gravel mixed with dirt and heat filled me with wonder. I was jerked back to a long-time-ago place of enjoyment, of promise and surprise. Red dirt flowed in my mind like rivulets cutting deep scars into the memory of childhood, of growing up on a farm in Oklahoma playing unfettered for hours.

In the apartment, I flung my clothes into the tub and standing in the bathroom naked, I tended immediately to my shoes. Staring at them without laces, their tongues up and out, they reminded me of those Sunday mornings with my mother, those times when my brother and I had waited for the polish to dry—in my case, white. In his, brown—and the shoestrings to be inserted so that we all would make church on time. More than once I had tied them in the shoes, pulling tight, the strings still wet, and in that act bound myself prematurely, it occurred to me now, to intentions of going where I had not wanted to go but did out of a terrible sense of commitment I had not understood. Sometimes, back then, I had cried and hadn't known why.

Now I looked down at my empty feet and naked legs, up to my mound of pubic hair and stomach, breasts sloping down, and I began to sob. A vague emptiness filled my chest as I reached for a towel and slumped to the toilet seat, giving way to the indefinable hurt. And then, unbidden, the image of my brother, Theodore, came bounding out of the past and stood before me, his head a little to the side, wistful face turned up to me. *'Why are you crying, Sis?'*

he seemed to be asking. *'You know nothing ever changes unless you do what's asked of you in order for it to change.'*

I had received Teddy's wedding invitation in the mail and hadn't answered its requested RSVP. It lay under a stack of unopened solicitations of an altogether impersonal kind. I couldn't make up my mind what to do and now as I studied this image of him in my mind—him, at four or five, his dress suit trousers hanging over his high-topped Buster Brown wing-toe shoes, his oh-so-starched white shirt under his oversized jacket, the jacket 'he can wear next year,' Momma had said, and a boy's version of a grown-up tie, dressed for his performance Momma had committed him to—I felt my enormous betrayal. We had all left him, abandoned him at nine to his life without armor or defenses he could use. How he'd found himself in that overlooked, left-behind dump-heap was a miracle, and I needed to honor that. But I couldn't seem to pull myself out of our bond to the past to do it.

Finally, his fiancée, Sarah, had called and asked in a flat, stiff voice if they could "count on my being there." I had told her in a helpless reply that, of course, I'd be there, I'd just not found the moment to let them know. She did need to know, however, that I wouldn't be attending the temple part of the ceremony, only the reception, as though this wasn't a given. An enclosed note had made this remote option available. Anybody wanting to be a part of the ceremony who was not a member of the church would have to get a recommendation card in order to do so, and in order to get that, would need to contact the number at the bottom of the letter for guidelines and instructions. The number had a Salt Lake City area code which I'd looked up but had no intention of calling. The alternative option was to wait "on the quiet grounds in meditation or prayer," while the "sealing ceremony" was being conducted, which would take around half an hour. Family photographs would follow in front of the temple.

So now I was locked into a scenario I neither had the desire, time, nor money to walk into. It would be a flight to Salt Lake and then a ride with Sarah's family or friends to the reception at a Ramada Inn on the other side of the city after the wedding, followed the next morning by a trip to the terminal via taxi or airport limo and the flight back home. It would cost me close to a half to three-quarters of a grand—that's if I played it close—and I'd have to secure a quick-term loan to make it happen. But I kept seeing Teddy's high-topped brown shoes on the bathroom floor waiting for him to step into, which would walk him to the performance he had been so well-trained to do.

—

The day of Teddy's wedding will be etched in my memory for the rest of my life. Mother wanted to go, but her resources were minimal. She had "spent her wad," as she put it, on a trip to see Kat five days in California the summer before. She was still working for minimal wages at Red Lobster as a food preparer, with only ten-cents-an-hour raises for the past few years. Groceries, the rent and utilities on her apartment, and gas for the car ate up most of what she earned. Dad was retired with no extra money to speak of. They sent Teddy and his bride best wishes, a gift of a Kitchen Aid mixer from both of them, despite their divorce and living apart, with apologies for their not being at the wedding—this after returning a high-end ceramic tea serving set for six which Mother thought was "so fine," before remembering that Mormons don't drink caffeine.

I sat in the sunny gardens outside the Salt Lake Temple, watching the long lines of brides and grooms waiting to enter to be married. I only found out years later about the ceremony which I researched online. The whole affair was impersonal, with only members of the Church of Jesus Christ of Latter Day Saints in attendance, which in Sarah and Teddy's case was exclusively her family. Since Sarah had been raised in the church from birth, it was obvious she knew what was expected of her by way of dress and behavior. She wore a simple tailored suit, though some of the brides in line were in wedding dresses without trains and made of non-sheer fabric, covering the bodice to the neck and with long-sleeves. There were no decorations inside the room where the wedding took place and the ceremony lasted only about twenty minutes.

There was a continuous flow of weddings through the day of Sarah and Teddy's, as it was gloriously pleasant weather. The only time Teddy and Sarah recognized my presence after coming out of the church was when the official wedding photographs were taken in front of the Temple. Teddy stepped over to me quickly, thanking me for coming, saying he would see me at the reception, while Sarah waved half-heartedly from the center bottom of the riser, waiting for Teddy to return. Two pictures were taken, the bride and groom with all their friends and family and the other with them alone. There were no groomsmen or bridesmaids. I found a 5"x 7" glossy photograph of the wedding party in my mail box three weeks after it was taken, no note, only the photo in a sedately decorated cardboard frame.

The reception was a primarily family affair. Hers. I sat on the periphery waiting to be invited in, and when that didn't happen, I walked to where the group was, received a perfunctory greeting with smiles as they turned, introduced themselves, shook my hand, and resumed talking to each other as though I weren't there. Many were Sarah's friends, graduates of Brigham Young University where she attended and expected to graduate in the fall with a certification in teaching. It was an endlessly long affair, during which, after talking briefly with Teddy about their honeymoon, I sat down to chat vacuously with a young couple next to me who asked intrusive questions about where I had been raised, what religion I proclaimed, and why my family wasn't with me.

The only information I gathered during the entire reception was that Teddy and Sarah weren't taking a honeymoon until vacation time the following spring, to Hawaii where they would go to Oahu, visit the Laie Temple on the island and stay in a nearby resort. The Mormons had occupied the island from the mid-to-late nineteenth century so they wanted to check out the LDS Church history there. This was their hope, Teddy had told me during a brief conversation we had away from the group, if Sarah's spring break came when he could leave his new administrative position at West-Southwest Construction Corporation. He handed me some syrupy punch and a small sandwich on a dipping paper plate and returned to his bride and her family.

His honeymoon would be fated to happen five years beyond his and Sarah's best laid plans. I was to learn that most events in Teddy's life—from his honeymoon plans, to the birth of his two children, to the jobs he sought to gain—were all "postponed." They came late in his life—even his marriage to Sarah, whom he claimed was the love of his life, was his second. His first, well after his service in the Navy, had been to a woman named Margy, which ended after five years.

But I was still surprised when thirty years later I received a call from Sarah telling me that Theodore has suddenly passed away from cardiac arrest, on his way out their front door to work. She had tried to resuscitate him without success. He was dead before the ambulance arrived less than ten minutes later.

She did not ask me if I'd attend the funeral, and I did not go. I had lost touch with Teddy after our brother Timothy had passed away. I had attempted at first to reach him at home from time to time, but Sarah seemed to always monitor these calls, or perhaps he simply didn't want the contact, especially in front of his wife. In any case, he was either not home or not available to take my calls. Occasionally he would call me back, his voice filled with anxiety, wanting to know if everything "at home" was all right, and once he was reassured, his conversation was terse, with an obvious desire to get off the line. We rarely exchanged anything except the most practical information. And after our parents died—within weeks of each other—three years earlier, I hadn't seen or heard from him since their funerals.

When I'd hung up the phone, after Sarah's last call, I had an urge to locate pictures of him among the scattered photographs that I had recently been putting together in albums. I'd been the beneficiary of the archival boxes in which Mother had put collected photographs through the years, while Kat kept most of the albums. In a portable file, I found a manila envelope labeled 1940s and pulled out a handful of photographs, laying them on the table. The picture of Teddy sent from the KSRC radio station slipped into view. I separated it from the pack, putting the others back in the envelope and returning it to the file.

Looking at the photograph of Teddy taken while he sang for the Pepsi contest on The Cherokee Theater stage, I saw how very small he was in the space he occupied, the whole theater curtain behind him, pedestals with the telephones and the volunteers taking calls to his left. I walked with the picture to the back porch, holding it in my hand as I sat down on the top back porch step and stared out into the yard.

It had been on this step I sat one Saturday afternoon three years before, talking to Teddy, his phone call coming out of the blue. From the start, his tone had been different. As he inquired through the pleasantries, I tried to get a feel for what this call might be about. The thought had crossed my mind—call it hope—that Theodore had found the light and was leaving Sarah and her way of life. But the thought that followed on its heels, like a lost, hungry puppy, was that he'd never leave his children to her fate. Suddenly, he said, in a voice so exhausted and haunted from a long time ago, it left me breathless, "I'm so tired."

"Are you ill?" I asked, expecting the worst of diagnostic news.

"No, no more than usual." His words were on the edge of sarcasm. The statement seemed to be directed at some vague presence in his life beyond our conversation.

"What does that mean, Bro?"

He paused and laughed lightly, possibly over the "Bro." I hadn't called him that since I visited him in San Diego when he was stationed and living there while in the Navy. Time seemed to be rushing by at incredible speed back then, and we were glad for it, that's the wonder. I'd gone earlier to California with Timothy who had joined the Navy ahead of his brother, for once not being the tagalong to Teddy's lead.

"My life is not well, or, I should say, not all is well in my life," he said, breaking through my thoughts.

He obviously wanted to talk about it but I wasn't sure I had the know-how after our long absences of being in touch. Would I be able to come up with what he needed to invite him into a meaningful conversation? To ask, as the therapist in me might, *"Do you want to talk about it?"* seemed vacuous and chilly.

"Where's the sore spot?" I tried.

"Well put, Sis." He gave another light laugh. "It is sore." A pause, then, "I just don't know when it will ever be my turn."

Ah, I breathed, he is aware. "Breathing space needed, huh?"

"Oh, it's more than that. I've given up on normal breathing. I've been surviving on shallow, panicked breath for years, maybe my whole adult life. Well, if we wanted to go back, it was long before I left home. You have to know this."

I was astonished by his insight. "I've been in six therapies, Teddy. They all have been breathing lessons."

He was delighted. He laughed openly. "And did you learn anything?"

"Never learned to breathe under water. When you're drowning, it's impossible to suddenly become a fish regardless of how many affirmations and deep meditative visions you attempt, you know?"

"Oh, God, do I! You've put it perfectly. I'm working my butt off and making such little progress."

"Are you talking about your new house, the one you're building in the mountains, outside Ramona?" How did I even know about this? Must have gotten it from my sister, but she never kept up with him either, or did she?

"Yeah, about an hour northeast of where I work in San Diego. It's a little over an hour's drive if the traffic is reasonable but twenty-five miles of it is on rural roads not always plowed promptly during the winter season up there. The roads're little more than trails. It's truly beautiful but getting the supplies up the mountain and finishing off everything by the end of the summer is pushing me to the limits."

"It sounds like it. You aren't doing this alone, are you?"

"A lot of it now, I am, since the frame is up and my contractor connections are also pushed to the limits—so is our budget. It's hard getting this through to Sarah. I just feel sometimes like… I don't know. That I can't go on this way."

"Can you clarify a little bit more what you mean by that, Ted?" Now I was sounding like one of *my* therapists, the one that I'd liked the least, so I added hastily, "It's got me a little nervous." So I personalized it, risky as that was. "I'm not sure about the vague way you're putting it."

"Just about every way it sounds like, Caroline."

A huge hollow feeling spread through my chest, up my throat. I thought nothing but a squeak could possibly come out if I tried to speak. But I found my voice. "I know this must feel like your whole life, but it isn't. It can't be. You're more than this."

"I don't know. I've been doing what you're calling 'this,' maybe for a lifetime. I gotta have a turn."

"And what would that look like? Can you describe it, even a little?"

"That's the strange part. I've been pushing like this so long, and…I'm not sure what's on the other side anymore. It's why I keep pushing."

"You know, I'm going to take a chance here, Teddy, and reiterate an image given to me by my first therapist, who by the way was the best of the whole lot. She said that when you let go of the life you're into—the one based on a modus operandi we've used up until it doesn't work anymore—it's like you're a trapeze artist hanging in the air between letting go of the bar you've been on and the one you're reaching for. You're totally suspended, and the reason most people don't let go of the bar they're grasping and reach for that new one is because that feeling of suspension is utterly terrifying. For a while, you're groundless.

"We're creatures of security as much as adventure and how much insecurity any of us has had in our childhood or our lives up until this trapeze act, can tip that balance one way or the other." When I heard only his breathing on the other end of the line, I wondered for a moment if he was smoking. But it didn't seem likely. I wasn't sure what he did exactly in his LDS ministry, but I knew it was up there somewhere with the bishops. "You're having a case of nerves, it sounds like, about whether you want to jump or not." I wasn't sure about the image here. It was dangerously close to cliff-jumping without the bungee cord.

"Oh, I want to jump, but there are certain…. *conditions* holding me back." I didn't want to press, especially about Sarah. It could be the death knell for our ever communicating again.

"You've got your faith, Teddy. That's got to give you assurance, a foundation to depend on," I said, searching. I sounded like Dad talking to Timothy on one of the tapes he'd sent me of their conversations—this when Timothy was dying, and Dad was trying to help him hang on to the end.

"Yeah, there's that—for sure," but his voice sounded weak. The pause was so long I was afraid he was going to end the call.

"Do you have anybody you can talk to, Ted?" I asked, and then realized it might sound as though I was trying to push him away. "I mean, somebody you're especially close to? From the church?"

"Yeah, sure. I have a friend who's as tight-lipped as anybody I know. But…." He seemed on the edge of telling me something he'd regret, like *the church was the problem?* But he suddenly changed direction. "Yeah, I could talk to Jeffery, sure I could. I just thought that you…." He trailed off and I told myself that I had no idea what he might be alluding to. But I knew. There was that back then bond we had, the shoes, the strings, the walk to the mike and the piano. But what could I do for him now? I hardly knew what to do for myself.

"I'm glad you called me," I said, feeling this was another wrong move. It felt as though I was closing him off. Was I? I told myself I was out of my depth, overwhelmed, stunned by his confession, this sudden intimacy. "It just seems that you might need to get into areas of discussion that I don't have the current knowledge to help you with."

It was the church, it was Sarah.

"Of course, you're right. It would take far too much time to get at this to any depth at all. I guess I want a quick fix on how to stop... my MO, as you say. It's killing me."

We finished off the conversation with some vague reassurances and promises to connect again soon. He could call me anytime, I told him. Yes, we could talk about anything he needed to talk about, even the past, if that's where he needed to go. It was fine. He left me with his business number, saying he didn't want to worry Sarah with this. I told him that anything he had to say to me, anytime, would be heard in the strictest confidence.

But time had slipped by, and we didn't connect again. When I made several follow-up calls soon after our conversation, he wasn't in his office or didn't pick up the phone. After a time of leaving unanswered messages, I quit calling.

And now I was sitting on my back door step, holding a picture of the young Teddy in my hand, longing for that time that we both knew so well, the time we were talking about three years earlier when neither of us seemed able to reclaim it to help us both.

VERNON'S ALBUM

Summer 1984

"Well, when I got out there, a-course, nothing was left. That's no surprise. I didn't even go into the house first. Why the hell would I? I knew there wasn't anything left behind, and when I did go inside, I was right. Nothing. Not a single goddamn anything. They'd moved Mother into town with Hannah a month before, so they had time to clear everything out before they even let me know. When I went into the car shed, I found one of Dad's shovels and a coupla old tools laying on a work table to the back. They weren't worth anything, and I'm telling you they were Dad's, but I'm not sure. They could just as soon have been Willard's or Reuben's."

My father gets up from his lawn chair and tries to move the sprinkler by twisting on the hose from the patio. When it falls over, he mumbles to it, "Oh come on," and then louder, "Hell, get on over there," and finally with an especially hard yank on the hose, he says, almost with surprise, but exasperation too, "I'll be damned. Why won't you get on over there?"

He walks through the wet grass, letting the sprinkler spray him as he reaches to turn it over. "Now stay. Right like that," he grunts, slamming it down into place. A small shudder goes through me. It's hard not to see him from a long time ago. He begins to run back as though he's dodging the spray but watching the grass in front of him as though that's where the water's coming from. I laugh because he's thoroughly soaked, partly from not dodging before, and both of us see there's been no point to his dodging around now. He looks up at me. "Consarned things never do what they're guaranteed they will."

"You mean it's supposed to roll over when you tell it to?" I ask him. He sits down, glances at me and looks quickly away.

He watches the water jerk around awhile, its spray curdling, coming out in wobbly spurts as though it has a kink in the line. He says, "Well, no, nothing that gol-darned fancy. I just expect it to turn, to spray from all sides and to stay on its legs instead of tipping over when you turn on the water. Isn't that what sprinklers are supposed to do?" We sit silently both watching it settle itself on the grass, a little tipsy to the left but spewing out enough water evenly for him to be satisfied. He nods in its direction, "The dang thing's too top heavy's the problem. Anybody can see that." He takes a swallow of iced tea from a tinted glass that's been setting on the crinkle-topped picnic table. Each time he lifts his glass and sets it back down, it makes a tiny, musical clink. He runs the cold water from outside the glass over his already dampened hair with both hands. After wiping them on his pants, he leans back and sighs.

I look at his handiwork, where he must spend most of his days from dawn into twilight, here in the backyard that he's turned into a verdant, pruned jungle of deliberately entangled vines and undergrowth running along decorative fences to beds of flowers blooming despite the heat, something like planted fireworks aimed overwhelming at an audience who's come to see them. Who comes here? But I know. He does it for Mother, a way of both pleasing her and getting back at her for leaving him. She lives in a cramped three-room apartment with no yard for gardening, even taking her cat for walks around the court on a leash, "just to get out," she says.

Last week on the phone she finally admitted to me that she does her laundry at "his place," the house they lived in from the time Kat was six until her graduation from high school, when my sister moved out and away from home, to settle into teaching at a special elementary school in California. About the laundry, Mother told me, it's a way for her to check up on how Dad's "looking after things," that is, keeping things up on the house—after all, her name alone is on the deed, although with the terms of the divorce, he can live in it until he dies or remarries.

When I asked her if she does his laundry when she does her own, washing his clothes with hers while they eat their supper, she grew silent, and I stood with the receiver in hand picturing their underwear tumbling together in the dryer while they are eating their evening meal, forks lifting and lowering to and from dinnerware they used to share daily. I didn't ask—can't bring myself to ever ask—what it must be like to divorce a man just four years shy of their golden wedding anniversary. But she's busy now with her new life. My visit with her this time around went well, minus the introduction of the new man in her new life.

"Too early to make him think it's something it's not," she explained as though this new man was already pressing her to become a part of the family. Well, maybe he was. Who's to know? I did spent several evenings with my parents together over a supper they cooked for me, as I watched them move around the kitchen as though they weren't ever going to do otherwise.

But things have changed, irrevocably, it seems. I've been left to spend the last days of my visit with my father alone, as Mother's taken some days from work, "to go out of town with Donald." Of course, my father knows. I grimace at the thought.

"Anyway, I took what was left, and that was nothing." At first I don't realize Dad's talking about his inheritance and not the settlement of his divorce. "You think they'd bother themselves to call me when they were reading the will and settling the estate?" he asks. I think he might be tearing up, but I can't see his face as he turns to look out over the neighbor's hedge.

"The farm, you mean?" I ask carefully. I'm wondering if he's referring to the estate as the Jantz's home place, the house especially, thinking that each of the living members of his family at the time of his father's death were to receive a share once it was sold and, once again, he didn't get his, which is, and always has been, what's galling to him. I know his brother Willard owned and worked the homestead land, giving part of the proceeds to his parents at harvest time. But I'm not sure how not giving my father a share of the house could even have been managed without a glaring oversight to everyone, especially the lawyer, but stranger things have happened between Dad and his family. Marriages, births, and deaths came and went—extended entries in the Jantz's genealogical record—without his knowing, at least not until months later. To my mind, it's always been a deliberate, evil-spirited omission. I haven't a clue as to why he's the family's black sheep, but, to Mother, these dismissals were and are clear. They're the Jantz's revenge for her entry into their family—an overt sign of how money shows contempt for poverty.

"Your father is the only one they overlook in this way," she has told me from the time I was a child. "It's toward me they're aiming their meanness." But this doesn't explain to me why my father has felt their rejection since he was a little boy in a house with three brothers and five sisters.

"The farm? God no, not the farm." My father eyes me with a squint from the rays of the sun streaming into a magnified mirror he's placed near the rain gauge, so he can read it from the kitchen window. "Willard owned that for the last fifteen years. I thought you knew that. He just let Mother and Dad live there. Well, in all fairness that's not quite right, either. That was part of the terms of the agreement—of him getting the farm in the first place." He hesitates a minute, searching my face to see if I understand. "When he got it, he agreed to two things. That he'd keep up the place—which in his case meant planting and harvesting a hundred and forty-four acres of wheat—and him letting our parents live in the house until they both died." If he sees the parallel between this state-of-affairs and his own divorce agreement, he doesn't show it. I become aware that I'm sitting with my mouth hanging open, getting ready to comment on this, but I don't. I decide wisely to listen.

"No, no, the household goods are what I'm talking about, though I've got my say about the house and land as well." He remains silent for a couple of minutes before picking up the thread of this idea. "Thing about the house and land, Caroline, well, I gave up on that a long time ago. The reality is, Willard wasn't the only one who'd worked the homestead land. As the only boy who hadn't married yet, me still living at home and working at Dad's dealership, I helped Willard for years before I left. I'm talking about, with the planting, the harvest, storage of the wheat. I worked the same hours as he did—hell, he had his own place to farm, plus he got married and started a family. And working the land was just half of it. I helped take care of the livestock, the chickens, and the upkeep on the property. I put in my share, believe that. It's true, I married and left Willard with it after that, but I had as much right as any of them of getting my share back.

"Dad's will had to've had *something* in it. My God, that's what wills do. They list things and state who gets what. Dad sought legal advice all the time. For godsakes, he owned a car dealership and gave away three farms to three of his sons! I'm sure he left everything in the house to Mother, but after that, well, it's hard to know. At retirement, Dad sold a successful business, and he had investments. Plus there were enormous amounts of stuff in sheds, the barn, the granary. There was a huge attic full of.... Well, who knows what all." He pauses and swipes the table with his hand, fast and hard as though he's erasing everything he's ever thought and said about each and every member of his family, a long and tired litany of grievances from a long and tired history of personal slight. When he brings his hands to rest on the table top, he reaches for his glass, lifts it without drinking and sets it back down, holding it loosely as he taps his fingers one by one over its surface. The tea inside ripples.

He studies the yard before he says, "Elizabeth was a little upset about this, because she saw Orland Ray come in and take the cuckoo clock off the wall, while the deacons of Mother's church walked through the front door to see Dad in the bedroom. She told me she saw Orland do it, because she'd come to the door to greet the preachers, to let them in. But why in the hell she allowed him to take it like that, right off the wall, I don't know! For chrissakes, she knew Momma was still gonna live in the house, with Willard and Julia looking in on her. *Mother* wasn't gone yet!" He waits a beat. "Well, okay, she was gonna be moved real soon, to Hannah's. I get that. But the clock was still *hers.*" He trails off, shrugs and studies the far end of the yard again.

He's arguing his case, as always, to a host of devils or angels somewhere beyond the horizon, sitting in judgment listening and waiting for the conclusion of his defense.

My question would have been why Elizabeth bothered to tell my father this cuckoo clock story when she didn't bother to call him at the time of the reading of the will. And the more exasperating question, why Dad didn't confront her over this dismissal as well as the one concerning the will, or any of his other brothers or sisters, for that matter.

But I let this slide. Instead I say, "You're kidding. When Grandma was going to continue living there, at least until she moved to Hannah's?" I know this story. Mother has told me more than once. I'm just delivering my lines. But he is truly upset, still, after all this time. He's not working at it. He's genuinely furious to the bone.

"Why would I kid you?" he looks at me, eye brows quivering, eyes icy blue, fingers slipping up and down on his tea glass. "Elizabeth told me about it, you see, but she wasn't upset enough to stop it, or she simply didn't have the guts to do anything, take your pick. At any rate, Orland Ray's got the clock hanging in his living room right now, while we were having this little talk, and he didn't even know my father. I doubt that he ever talked to him. He's not even the oldest grandson." He looks at me and corrects himself, "grandchild."

"How'd he get it, then?" I am meaning, how did he get away with this, not just with Elizabeth, but with everybody else, but my father has a more literal take on my question.

His disgust is instant and rabid. "How'd he get it? Hell, he was the one who went and took it off the hook. His mother said something like, 'Orland, you always liked that clock when you were a boy. Why don't you go take that as a keepsake,' and he went and took it off the wall. It's that fuckin' simple." His chin is jutting out, his eyes are small and he is clinching his teeth, his jaw pulsing. I don't recall my father ever using the f-word in my life.

I shake my head, more to comfort him than for anything I'm feeling about what's happened. This is his side of this story. I've never known him to show anger toward his family, not with this directness. "Guess it wasn't an item on the list!" I say, looking at him, but after seeing his face, I think it best to hurry on. "He did this as the deacons were coming through the door, with Elizabeth right there? Somethin'!"

"About lists," my father says, calming down only a little, "it wouldn't matter, not with them, not even with wills. They never paid any attention to such things before. Unless you're there to protect your own, you can forget it. And once they got what they've taken, put it in their house or their bank account, hell, how's the one who's got the right to it gonna get it back without a lot of legal pushing and shoving?"

I watch the sprinkler shower the backyard, while my father rocks for a while, the springs of his lawn chair catapulting him in a small oblique arc of despair. I know the answer to the question I'm going to ask, but he doesn't know I do, so I ask him in order to find out what he thinks, "What were the deacons doing there, Dad? I thought Grandpa was an atheist."

"Oh he was, right to the end. They came because Mother had Elizabeth call them, a-course. Elizabeth stayed in the room, she said, when they...." he hesitates, almost grins, "...*visited.*" Then he does grin hugely, almost laughs. "Elizabeth said he looked up at them, as soon as they all were in the room—

there were three, she said, as though they thought numbers would make the difference. Dad just looked up at all three of them, smiled and said, 'The answer is no,' and died."

Now my father does start laughing, a loud pop that breaks open and then fades quickly as he wipes his eyes fast with the heels of his hands. "But, by God, he was buried in the church cemetery just the same. Mother said she'd pull her membership if he wasn't buried in the plots she'd bought for them both. She'd contributed a fair amount of money to the church over the years, and they knew she had her share of his inheritance. So they buried him like he was a true believer, sins and all. Money still counts for something with the Almighty, I guess." He's smiling at me when he tells me this, but he lets his hand fall lightly on the picnic table. "Well, not totally, I suppose. He didn't get the church funeral, but he got the plot next to her and not off to the side by the fence that they reserve for *distant* relatives." We both know that distant in this case means relatives that never were members of the church, their church, the one true one.

"Where was the service? I don't remember. We went, didn't we?" I'm not sure how old I was, though I remember being told he'd died. I've seen a picture sometime, somewhere of the entire family with all the children to the whatever-numbered generation when the old man retired. I was four or five. But I haven't a clue when he died and how old I was then.

He nods his head. "The funeral home." He lifts his hand slightly and waves his fingers back and forth before placing them down on the table. "Elizabeth wanted it in the house, but she got outvoted. They were being contentious for the sake of it. All about who got the final say. It didn't have anything to do with anything more than that. Hannah won! 'Course she did. Who else? She was top dog, always was. I didn't even know, a-course, till I got there where the service was gonna be held." He leaves the fact that he wasn't called to vote on this in the air between us, silent.

"Dad?" I ask, never really knowing or not remembering. "Why didn't they read the will while y'all were there? Aren't wills normally read soon after...."

He snorts, interrupting me, his contempt for them jumping out before he can rein it in. He directs his disgust and anger for them out toward me. "Caroline, you know the answer to that if you just think for a minute." He doesn't give me time to reflect or respond. "We *were* all there, and then I wasn't, couldn't be. I had my job that I had to go back to. You think they didn't know it would be hard for me to return for the reading of the will? I couldn't just take off whenever I wanted to, like they could, as farmers I mean."

I start to reply to this, say that surely it could have been part of his bereavement leave, but he continues without looking at me. "It was intentional." He slurs, "intenshnal," like a drunk. He's breathing hard, attempting to stifle how close he is to being out of control. I don't know if he's near tears or the rage that can erupt into the breaking of things. His nearly-bald head gleams in the wet, slowly sinking sunlight. He suddenly looks like a disheveled bum disappointed in the mission's room and board, the low life he's sunken to. He's truly upset but obviously wants to talk about it. There's something he wants to tell me now that Mother isn't by our side. I've a feeling this is the lead-in to something much larger, deeper, underneath.

I watch the sprinkler shoot out unevenly like a clogged fountain. The version of this story I've heard from Mother through the years has become truncated, without much detail or enthusiasm. She's not mentioned any details of my grandfather's funeral that I remember. Her stories are edited, no doubt, pivoting around her personally chosen times of my father's rejection by his family. She's mentioned the will, of course, but very little about either of my grandparents' deaths. Surely I attended Grandfather Jantz's funeral with my family, or did I? I must've at least been in high school. Why can't I remember any of this? I'm attempting to compare what I know to what my father is telling now when he says, "Goddamned bastards!"

"It was a cheap trick," I say. "But your family's always left you out, Dad. It's the same old story with them."

"Oh, that!" he says as though he hasn't just been near rage in the retelling of this to me. "Naw, that wasn't new, a-course. I'm the last one that's called even for reunions." He nods and sets his glass down with a louder clink. "Well, that's not true anymore, now that there's only four of us left. Elizabeth calls when there's a get-together. They know if we, well, it used to be your mother and me, if *I* don't show up, a lot of the reunion won't be there!" His laughter is a rumble in his chest that never quite comes to surface. "What I'm talking about are *Mother's preachers*. It's bad enough when the family lays claim to things they feel is theirs, that's family. But when the church members do it, that's somethin' else. I hate to admit it but Orland's taking the clock may've saved it. It was hand-carved from Munich. Grandfather Jantz probably got it from his mother, though his family never lived in the southern part of Germany, so she may have received it as a gift or somebody in her family did, and she inherited it. Who knows how old it was... *is.*"

I'm trying to follow this new direction he's taking suddenly. "Preachers? Wait a minute. Are you telling me Grandmother's church people came in and took stuff out of the house? I don't understand. Why would they do that?"

"Well, they did it all the time, even when I was a kid. Sometimes they'd rip up, smash and burn stuff right in the yard while we watched."

"What kinda stuff?"

"Mainly table cloths with lacy edges or tea towels with embroidery, a guitar, sheet music, monthly magazines, photographs. Sometimes they put it in boxes and took it away—not wanting to wait it out with a fire—especially if it wasn't all that much. They were collecting it from all their members to destroy it later. Supposedly, what was carried to their buggies—well, they drove Model As too, you know—this was the best stuff or stuff that couldn't be destroyed by the fire—like something made outta hard metal, that kinda thing. Or things that could explode, were highly flammable. Some of it took too long to burn, like pieces of heavy furniture. They said they were gonna bury or burn all the stuff they took away, make a bonfire at another site after they'd collect more. Right! Sure! I learned in later years that they had big arguments among themselves about whether the items they carried off should be thrown in the dump or not. Hey, big bonfires are a lot of trouble, you know. You have to watch them for hours. They argued about what to do with it. Supposedly some of the preachers thought if they dumped it, the goods could be looked for and taken back.

"Picture a church meeting like that, Caroline. Elders standing up in their pews saying things like, 'Throwing these objects of the devil in the dump, well, that leaves it open for the owners to come get it, take it back, or worst still, what if, by doing this, we lead unbelievers to sin by their finding it and taking it home?' Can you picture that? We're talking about what? A side table? Maybe with a broken leg?" My father's nostrils flare, as he sighs through his long, fine nose. I know the religion of which he speaks, the ultra-conservative Mennonite country church my Grandmother attended from the time of her arrival in Oklahoma, newly married to Grandfather Jantz, after being converted and baptized by the reformist preacher himself—John Holdeman—in Kansas.

My father continues, near hyperventilation. "But there was also what they called 'costly furniture.' Now that was a big one! God better not catch you with a high-back rocker with too much padding or a dresser with tiger oak veneer or a lavatory with fancy faucets or probably even indoor toilets when they first started to be used out on farms. God only knows what all they saw fit to claim as sin. And this changed almost yearly, no joke, well, okay, often enough.

"Caroline, they held conferences where all this stuff was discussed and decided as to, you know, whether it was sin or not, would be allowed—everything from insurance policies, birth control, paying taxes, even marriage and certainly divorce." He glances at me with a weak smile. "And you can imagine the clothing items—everything from rick-rack on dresses to what kind of underwear was okay in God's eyes. Mother actually told me once that at one of these conferences, the powers that be decided that men's shorts were sinful!"

"You mean cut-off overalls?" I question, smiling at him, knowing this isn't what he's talking about.

"Oh, sure." He laughs. "You know I'm meaning underwear, right?" He studies my face a minute, grins. He knows I've been Sunday-schooled in the rules of Mennonite sin. After all, he's one of the ones who did the schooling. "I don't know if they specified what brand or whether it was *all* shorts of any kind, shape, or color. Lord only knows how any of that was done. How do you tell people this kinda thing with a straight face? Can you see the elders standing up before the congregation saying,"—Dad takes on a supercilious tone—"'men's underwear that come down the leg to the knees are acceptable to God, but shorts that're higher up, lightweight, too close to the skin, or have elastic are sinful to Him?'

"Most of their lists of prohibitions—their fancy word for sin—were about behavior, a-course, but their suspicions about anything fancy or shiny knew no bounds—all of it labeled 'ungodly.'" He stops that line of thought, switching tracks back to the bonfires. "I guess they didn't want to spend the time trying to destroy by fire the hard stuff—well, things made outta iron, steel, or aluminum. That would be kinda difficult. How do you get rid of well-built sin, huh?" He laughs. "What a crock a-shit! 'Removin' sin like a mite from the eye,' they'd say as they carried a blanket chest with curly-cues carved on it out the door. Oh yeah. *Beautiful hand-crafted furniture."*

"How did they know what belonged to whom—keep the belongings straight, I mean? You and your brothers weren't church members so how did they know what was only your mother's?" I answer my own question, "She told them, I guess. But what about your brothers and sisters and your things?"

"I was a kid when they did this. I did what my mother told me to do. My brothers weren't there a lot of the time, or if they were, they simply told my mother what they didn't want taken, I guess—probably some things did get destroyed, and they got mad over it. Hell, maybe they went out there to the church and talked to the preachers, even to their farms. I can see Willard doing that, with his temper. My sisters? They probably closed off their bedroom doors and told mother not to let these guys go in." He waits a minute, then says, "The answer to your why-they-did-it question is that whatever they took was not supposed to be a part of a believer's life, and they, by God, were helping you decide what that was. It was mainly to keep the church 'pure,' and that meant keeping the church members from temptation. Vanity and pride were the ultimate evils to them and were the reasons at the bottom of a lot of this. But I'm here to tell you, there was more than just the hard-to-destroy items in the back of those carriages and trucks, you can believe that! More than just iron goods and heavy furniture didn't make it to the fires."

I knew about the prohibitions Holdeman, Amish, and other conservative Mennonite churches established as soon as our ancestors came to this country and began meeting together to decide what was considered acceptable or not in the new society they had immigrated into, but I hadn't known the elders searched homes and took out and destroyed items they considered sin.

"Are you telling me they *kept* some of this stuff? What they considered to be *sinful* stuff?" I don't have a hard time seeing these men in their dark suits going through the house, gathering and carrying temptation out the door, their lips pulled tight across their teeth, and I can even see the smashing of objects, the bonfires and maybe some scriptural chanting here and there, but *keeping items?* Putting boxes filled with lace, fine goods, possibly magazines, in the back of their old panel trucks, Model As, and horse-drawn carriages to what purpose, what end? It's hard for me to picture them actually *stealing*, keeping some of the items for their own. But my father doesn't seem to have a problem with this view.

"Where the hell else do you think they'd take it, if not to keep it? He leans back in his lawn chair and rocks gently back and forth some more. "They're all a buncha greedy, self-righteous hypocrites," he says, the fire back in his eyes that I know so well. I think of the Salem witch trials, the now-known lust for land buried in the righteous purge of sin and sinners among the Puritans in seventeenth-century colonial America. As though summarizing my thoughts, my father says, "They take what they want, when they want it." I can't picture the lace doilies, colorful table cloths and embroidered tea towels in their own homes where other church members could see, would visit.

Dad's angry exaggerations have always confused me from the time I was a little girl. When I was older, I grew to understand he was a grand storyteller, entertaining as much as informing others as he went along. But I also knew he had an insider's view of all of this that I could only see through his and Mother's eyes. They'd grown up with it, lived it and had ultimately given up their practicing version of it. They knew more than I could ever imagine about any and all of it.

"I guess I don't understand, Dad," I say. "How'd they get away with destroying these things, let alone taking them? I understand why Grandma might let them. It was her religion, right? She couldn't or wouldn't defy their authority. But Grandpa, I don't understand why he'd allow it. Some of that stuff had to've been precious, valued by the family. And if your dad didn't do anything about it, why didn't Willard or Reuben step in?"

My father doesn't answer my question. He continues the flow of his thoughts. "They'd come after revivals, see, and go through the house, and anything they thought was a sin—something they might have missed before but struck them as sin now— they'd have it carried to the yard. Hell, as a young boy I'd help them carry it out there, because my mother told me to."

"I can't see your father allowing this to happen. Why did he?" It's hard for me to take this in. Grandpa Jantz was such a patriarch. His sons did his bidding before he even told them what to do or not do.

"He never, never once, interfered with Mother's religion," he says with such forthrightness, I feel as though I've been struck. It's almost as though he's challenging me, that long-ago look of defiance in his eyes that sends a small, quick shock to the pit of my stomach. "As for Willard and Reuben, they knew better than cross Dad when it came to this," my father tells me, lighter now, looking away. "Hell, our dad lived his whole adult life without electricity, because Mother wouldn't have it. She thought it was wrong. Electricity was never presented at church conferences among her people for consideration as a prohibition that I know of. Other members of her church had electricity. *Entertainment* that used *electricity* like radios or television was considered sinful but even farm equipment that ran on electricity like milking machines and the like, these weren't prohibited, when they came into usage.

"But Mother leaned toward the narrowest interpretation of what was wrongdoing. In lots of ways, she was Amish about all this. There's a reason that intermarriage was allowed sometimes with the Amish among our ancestors. The Old Mennonites and Holdemans intermarried with them is what I was told. I didn't ever see that myself, but it makes sense. There's a desire in these really conservative branches to keep the church pure by erring on the side of narrow-mindedness. They wouldn't call it 'purity,' a-course. They have a literal interpretation of the Scriptures, is how I see it. But with our people, hey, nothing like sin should get in the way of earning a good living! That's how they think. And some of the Amish aren't exactly poor, you know.

"Caroline, after all I've told you about this, I wanna say that I don't think these prohibitions are looked on as a list of sins exactly. They're probably thought of more like rules to help keep the church as free from worldly influence as possible. The sin is when members of the church don't abide by them. The elders are big on obedience once the rules have been agreed upon. But finding the agreements isn't always so easy. If you look at the prohibitions through the years, which I've gone to the trouble to do, because I got real curious at one point over this—and I've had cause, I can tell you that story sometime if you want—but when a person looks at these prohibitions, you can see how the elders kept going back during their conferences to items they viewed as troubling, studying on them over and over, sometimes allowing them, sometimes not."

"You think making money had anything to do with this?"

"Sure, undoubtedly. It gets harder and harder to stay in the market when you have more and more modern ways of doing things coming into the picture. These Mennonite farmers had to sell their goods to outsiders if they were going to make it. It wasn't just a matter of feeding themselves. You've got maintenance of your farm and such. You have to replenish your crops and livestock. Somewhere in all that, you gotta compete with others out there in the selling and buying."

He waits a minute to see if I'm going to comment or ask more. When I don't, he picks up the thread of his earlier story. "Mother was very spotty in all of this prohibition business too, just like the policymakers were. She wouldn't have electricity or running water in the house even though these were not a problem with her church. But then, she'd turn around and take her rides in the car to the grocery market and church even during those times that it had been outlawed. She never learned to drive herself, a-course, but she loved to take even leisure drives around the countryside in the evening sometimes." He waits a moment, smiles at me. "If I'm remembering correctly, when I was a kid, there was a time there when the conferences didn't permit automobiles or were considering it. They'd do that kinda thing, you know, say yes and then say no. That's what I'm trying to tell ya."

"You mean, like off and on about what was good or bad behavior? They'd decide what their people could actually do at one time but not another? How the heck did the membership keep up?"

"Well, hell, that's what the preachers are for, don't you know that? They get to tell you what's what." He stops, then starts rocking again. "Somewhere along the way, they decided driving cars and trucks was acceptable and held to it. They had a big thing about lightning rods, I remember this. Thing is, if you put them on your house and barn, well, that's sort of like preventing the will of God—a little like life insurance which they don't believe in either, or contraception, a-course. Same thing. A Christian doesn't interfere with God's will. If your house's gonna get hit by lightning, it's meant to get hit—divinely-ordained fate, just like if you lose your wheat to a hailstorm, have a child, or you die. *Willagod!*" He smiles at me like he's made up a new swear word.

And then he adds, "Like not shaving under your arms!" And we both burst out laughing. "If God'd meant for you not to have hair there, He either woulda not made hair in your armpits or created you with some kind of a built-in razor!" I'm picturing Norelco's rotary blades fitted into my armpit, automatically coming on as my underarm hair begins to grow—the robotics of *Star Trek* sanctioned by God! When I tell my father this, he begins describing his own inventions for the daily shave, and it takes us a while to calm down.

"Is that why men grow beards?"

"Well, has to be. Nowhere in Scripture does it say a man's gotta wear one."

"What if a woman grows one?"

He laughs. "Well, I dunno, Caroline. You'll have to ask an elder about that. I've never seen a Mennonite woman with one, so she's either doing some scissor work in the bathroom when no one's looking, or God's seen fit to just not grace Mennonite women with facial hair! Maybe they got enough on their legs," he says, laughing. He knows Mother had movie-star perfect legs when she was young, legs that she shaved most of the time with his razor. I remember the fuss he made over it. After this frivolity about the sins of the Mennonites, we sit, lost to ourselves for a time.

"You know here's something else to think about, about my dad's part in this," he says, breaking the silence. "He never joined the church, but he never called himself an atheist exactly either. He just stayed mum on all that religious stuff and didn't join the church. But he was raised in the old Mennonite ways, and once you have that preached to you from the time you're a kid, maybe it never quite leaves you." He clears his throat, turning very serious. He looks my way. "What I'm saying is, maybe he was more to Momma's way of thinking than he wanted to show his boys."

"Are you're telling me that *not* being religious was considered a demonstration of *manhood?*"

"No," he says as though I haven't understood him at all, but then his tone changes. "Well, actually, maybe that's right in a way. When I was a kid, it was me who went to church with Mother. And when I got to driving as a teenager, I took her to the service. None of my brothers took her or my sisters either, come to think of it, unless I couldn't go. And when any of them did take her, they just dropped her off at the door and either waited outside or went back to get her when services were over. None of them ever attended church with her or joined her church or became Mennonites, for that matter, except me. Bennie joined a church after he was married, but that was considered his wife's doing, you know?

My brothers thought it was so he could have peace at home. Bennie became a strict fundamentalist. Church of the Living Reformers, it was called, a little like a cult, as I remember, an offshoot of some Southern Baptist group somewhere in the South—Louisiana, I think. Shreveport. That's right. They branched out to several missions in Texas and Oklahoma. They were really to themselves, spoke in tongues and had holy-roller kinda ways, lots of revivals, but it was more for themselves than a call to outsiders like most evangelicals do. I guess that does tell you something. Bennie and I were the outsiders, the short guys, the unmanly ones, the henpecked ones, the.... not quite right ones. Stupid." I don't know if he's referring to his brothers and their ideas about them or to him and Bennie.

"So in your family, most of the men didn't join a church? Not just your Mother's church but church of any kind, you're saying?"

"That's very interesting, isn't it? They all didn't go to church except Bennie and me, and they thought Bennie was a halfwit, though not so much a halfwit that he wasn't included in their brotherly get-togethers and, well, the will."

I'm remembering too, that Bennie was one of the brothers who got a farm.

"Why didn't you join, Dad?"

"Momma's church?" He knows this is what I mean.

He looks at me and smiles. "Maybe Whalen got that part right when he told Ava he wouldn't join because he didn't wanna wear a beard." He chuckles. I know this story by heart. He's talking about Mother's parents and how Grandma Dirks wanted to live the conservative Mennonite life and Grandpa Dirks wouldn't have it. When I don't respond, my father says, "I didn't join, because I didn't want that way a-life. You don't just kinda do what these people do, you know. It's an all or nothing proposition, and I didn't want to live with all those prohibitions. I don't think there's any call for it—so many limits to things. I don't think the Scriptures ask for that."

I wonder how much his drinking played a part in this decision. I know from Mother that he started drinking with Willard when he was very young and continued into his dating years—when she tells me, now to her regret, she tolerated it. But when he carried it into their marriage, despite her initial threats of leaving him, it drifted into a nagging contention between them, especially after we children were born—to Mother's mind, the leprous spot spreading contagion through the life of our family. There were other secrets, but his sneaky drinks and the outright binges were loathsome to her, which she bore with what I now view as an insufferable self-righteousness.

How my father got past the Mennonite sensors, I'll never know, because he was a deacon in the church as far back as I can remember, until we left the Mennonites altogether. Other deacons from our church visited often, but then one in particular, Karl Toews, often drank a beer with Dad during evenings when the men listened to "the fights" on the radio—another Mennonite sin—and the women drank coffee and gossiped about church members in the kitchen—not an altogether righteous act in itself.

Dad waits a minute, says, "It's a constant brow-beating kind of life they lead, Caroline. They spend so much time working so hard to be good." He waits, shakes his head and says, "Working hard to be perfect like Jesus is what it is, with each one trying to sit closer to Him than the next guy." He doesn't pause before quoting, "Be ye perfect even as your Father which is in heaven is perfect." He smacks his lips, sets them in a near smirk. "Well, I guess it's really trying to be as perfect as God, is what it amounts to. Full-time job for finite souls." *Finite souls?*

His speech is still sprinkled with the expressions and talk surrounding the Scriptures that I heard while standing by his side in the parking lot at the church of my childhood, while I waited for him to finish discussions with the other deacons so we could go home.

He speaks out toward the back of the yard. "Matthew 5:48. You don't think I know that one, guess again. Your mother quoted it at me, and at you kids too, often enough. I'd be surprised if you don't have it in the back of your mind somewhere. Well, just look at her now." He's thinking of the man she's seeing, sleeping with outside marriage, no doubt. If Mother hasn't outright told him, he's found out from my sister, Katharine, who could never keep anything from him about Mother. Since their divorce is final, he's pushing the point that Mother too has left the church—the churches, any and all of them—seeking another life in the secular world apart from him, after all the grief and hell of the insider's life together.

But I've discussed Mother's spiritual life with her. She's still a believer, as I'm assuming he is, just not of the same kind of faith—if that's what you'd call it. It's Christian, but beyond that, I don't know much about either of them and their religious views.

I ignore his just-look-at-her-now comment and ask, "What do you think all this is about, Dad?" I'm meaning the desire for all that purity within the church—his mother's church especially—and the brow-beating in order to get it. But again, he takes my question differently than I intend.

"I think they thought I was a Momma's boy."

Something goes very still inside me. My breathing becomes suddenly erratic. I'm sensing the approach of something entirely new from him.

"Because you went to church with your Mother?" I finally ask, amazed.

"Well, that and the fact that...." He starts again. "The way they see it, I've never been a man. I liked being with my Mother and sisters in a way they never did... no, more than that. They actually thought this was... strange, I guess. From the time I was little, I was close to my Mother and my sisters, especially Elizabeth. I spent a lot of time in the kitchen, even helping the women clean up, and I eventually learned to cook, bake bread and the like. They didn't think men should do that. I already told you they didn't respect Bennie because he joined his wife's church. They thought he was henpecked." He brushes the table with his hand again, not looking at me. "They thought I was a sissy. Worse. They thought I was... like a girl, you understand?" He hangs his head away from me, to the side as though he's looking for something on the ground by his lawn chair.

"That you were homosexual?" I can't believe I'm asking him this.

"Oh, not *that*," he says very fast, as though this is a new idea to him, his eyes darting my way and then looking out into the backyard. "They wouldn't go that far, probably, though I think it crossed Willard's mind, and could be he was acting on their behalf when he tried to save me by becoming such a drinking buddy and taking me with him to western Kansas to help with harvest out there, and I was still a kid. It's more like they were embarrassed that one of their own brothers was womanish, did womanly things. They didn't know quite what to make of it. And it didn't help that I was little to boot and the youngest boy."

"You mean they thought being *short* was girlish?"

"Something like that. Little stature is girlish to them, yeah. Your mother was embarrassed about it too, you wanna know. She hated that they and people at my work called me 'Shorty.' She always said it was a cowboy name, and that's what got her about it, but I knew."

"What about Bennie, you said he was short, and they thought he was henpecked. Did they think he was girlish too?"

"I said that we were *shorter*. He wasn't so small, overall, as me. I don't know what they thought about him for sure. One of the things on his side was that our father showed his approval of him, didn't he? He gave him a farm, like the others."

"Being short and thin isn't the same thing as little stature, Dad. To me, the word 'stature' implies a person's character more than size. I don't think talking about yourself like that is helpful, and it certainly isn't truthful."

My father sits and thinks this over while he rocks silently. He finally says, "Oh well," to himself as he rubs the ends of the arms of his lawn chair. He adds, "You gotta remember they only knew their narrow little world, mainly the farming and small town kinda life in Oklahoma. They never went much of any place outside Oklahoma, Kansas, and Nebraska, maybe a trip to Colorado to see the Rocky Mountains, take pictures of the Royal Gorge, Garden of the Gods, and come home.

"It would never occur to them that some of the world's great chefs in fancy restaurants are mostly men. Inconceivable to them. They saw Bobby Talbert from school days cooking at the local diner in Clearview, but that's not like baking bread with your mother in her kitchen, I guess. Bobby's cooking was a *job*, not exactly real work like theirs, more like making a living flapping the jacks. But also more like being a cook for cowboys out on the trails, so it was acceptable. Hell, they probably think diner food's honest people's food, *tough food*, for godssakes! Who knows how they think, exactly. I just know they didn't see me as one of them."

"Speaking of the world's great chefs, you're a better cook than Mom," I tell him and mean it, attempting to ease the serious place we've just gone. I'm surprised he even uses the word, "chef."

He squints across at me. "You think so, do ya?"

"I do," I say. "Well, you have a tendency to pour milk and cream all over everything, but outside of that…."

"I always add butter," he interrupts me in a mockingly serious tone and laughs. "Must be the number of cows we milked. We were practically a dairy farm and had to be, keeping all eleven of us in food, counting Mom and Dad."

He taps me on the arm, leaving his finger there for a minute, then dropped the others as though he's taking my pulse. It surprises me, this contact and his need to return to the seriousness of our earlier discussion. It's not like him.

"I coulda pointed out to them that Pretty Boy Floyd, who was raised in the eastern hills of Oklahoma, killer of I'm not sure how many men, and who was constantly featured in those detective magazines they all loved to read so much, well, ole Pretty Boy, when he tried to quit crime for a little while, he'd hide out in a relative's kitchen baking pies. It was his favorite thing to do." He laughs softly and grins at me. "Hell, John Dillinger always helped the ladies with the dishes and was known to even vacuum the floors in the places where he hid out. He was no pansy. He knew how to win over the women."

"How do you come up with this stuff?" I'm always amazed at his vast range of trivia. I've never seen him read much of anything but the newspaper and his Bible, or maybe the *Saturday Evening Post* and *Life Magazine* when I was growing up as Mother kept a handful of those in a basket by the toilet. She presently has a white wicker bicycle basket, complete with plastic flowers attached to the wall, arm's length from her toilet in her apartment bathroom. A question flashes through my mind as to whether my father ever goes to her apartment to visit as she comes to his house.

"There was a film on television not too long ago about all those gangsters back in the thirties," my father continues with his story. "Bonnie and Clyde, Machine Gun Kelly, Ma Barker and her boys, the lot, and they told this stuff about Floyd and Dillinger. I had a big laugh over some of it." He pauses and then says, with a shrug, "But given the way my brothers thought back then, had they known this about these gangsters, they woulda just pointed out that's why Floyd was called 'Pretty Boy.' I haven't a clue how they woulda explained Dillinger's wifely ways." When I look at him a while, he becomes uncomfortable and adds, "They'd think he was domesticated, I guess."

Domesticated? He's a marvel to me. His new vocabulary has to be the detox program's influence. And perhaps his new interest in reading. Have I not been paying attention?

I don't tell Dad this, but I happen to know Dillinger had sex with men while he was in prison and not because he was forced to—a piece of trivia I'd picked up from reading or television viewing or maybe even therapy. I say instead, "You're cute, Dad, but nobody is going to mistake you for being pretty under any circumstances!" We both laugh, and I add, "And Dillinger was ambushed by G-men outside a movie theater with his date, who was dressed in red—well, really in orange, but nobody remembers it that way, because the newspaper accounts stated 'red.' Anyway, I guess getting killed by the Feds next to your girlfriend, who looks like a prostitute, lets you off the hook. Who remembers Dillinger swept the living room floor, right?"

Dad grins, nods his head. "So there!" And we laugh again.

"I watch the TV cook shows sometimes, you know," he admits. "I don't tell anybody, a-course, and they're a bit fancy for me... too much gourmet this and that but I've learned some tricks."

Gourmet? I'm fast becoming the insufferable self-righteous highbrow, leaving Mother far behind. Why do I have this biased view of him as uninformed?

"I'm a terrible cook, Dad," I say honestly. "I should watch the shows and see if I can get turned on." He jerks his head around and looks at me puzzled, and then laughs a little as I join him.

We sit silently for a long time, both looking out over the yard, the late afternoon light drifting slowly, even tranquilly, toward sunset. Barely rocking in his chair, he seems more relaxed, at ease. After some silence between us, he gets up, turns the water off and sits back down. The sprinkler stops spinning, a large water drop hanging from one arm as though by a string. I have the urge to pick the thing up and shake it dry. I'm glad the whole sprinkling ordeal is over.

I finally ask what I tried to ask before. "So what do you think all that fire-burning, church-going purity was about?"

"What *'all'?*" he asks with disgust, not waiting for me to answer. "It was about my mother's religion—her following the old religion...."

"I think that's what I'm trying to understand. What is that about—the old religion, the old ways? Are they still trying to destroy sin out of their believers' lives like that?"

"If you mean the bonfires and searching for sin through their houses, I don't think so. Anyway, not as severe as back then, because things've changed. People don't put up with that kinda invasion into their personal lives the way they used to, but some forms of it are there, I'm sure. I know they still question their members about their wayward behaviors, those they find out about.

They've always preached real heavy about what's sin. They'll always do that. But to answer your question, I'm not sure what they do anymore, actually. I've lost touch with all those people."

"What do you think the preachers want, really want when they're doing this kind of thing? What are they thinking, Dad? I guess I know what they're doing, but I'm not sure I can grasp what they're believing when they do it. The idea that they could be purifying everybody's lives in this way, shocks me. It shocks me in the same way the Salem witch trials do. It's when beliefs have gone on such a destructive course that they can't be stopped until it stuns even the people who're doing these crazy things, forcing them to finally look at the havoc they're creating in other people's lives. Many of them, of course, never quite recognize that. But it's, well, I don't know, a kind of madness, isn't it? I have a hard time understanding what they're wanting." When I look at him, he seems oddly to himself, involved in his own thoughts. The silence is so long I think he isn't going to answer.

"They want *you*, Caroline, don't you see that? That's what they're after—*us*." When he says this, it sounds astonishingly paranoid, like some nut case who climbs into a tower and starts shooting at everybody in sight. He tells it in a whispered rush, a restrained release of spittle through the teeth, and then suddenly he stops as though he's surprised even himself, but gathering his thoughts again, he goes on in disgust. "Hell, they won't let up until they have it all. You wanna know what 'all' means? That's what it means. They want *all* of us, each and every one of us, as many *you's* as they can get." When I look up he's pointing his finger straight at me like the famous war posters of Uncle Sam. Suddenly he retreats, rocking and glaring out at the yard.

I've not heard my father talk like this, at least not recently. Despite the paranoia in it, an unfamiliar and sudden warmth flows out of me toward him, a feeling I haven't had for a very long time, perhaps since I was a little girl. This tenderness sits, though, behind a cautious screen, peering out at him, like a small bird attempting to read a hawk not looking its way.

"Why? Why do they want to own us all?" I have my own idea about this, but I want him to answer what I'm not sure I'm asking of him. My inquiry is deeper than any family history I might be trying to grasp or any ethical discussion I'm seeking. It's clothed in layers of subtle meanings, like the Scriptures themselves. I want something I've never had with him and feel as though it's suddenly possible, close, even tangibly between us.

He's taken his fingers from my arm some time ago, but now he places them on the table near mine. They are curled slightly as though he's about to play the piano, or, with a small lifting, place them over mine gently as he did when I was a child.

"What does it get them? To claim us?" I prompt, wanting the answer only he can give.

"I used to think they wanted to do the right thing, you know, they really were trying to be 'good,' like God wanted them to be good—wanting all of us to be good. They were just trying to please Him and make sure others were being helped along. But then, I began to realize that with all this talk about The One, True Church that they insist they're creating on earth, they mean something not so much like *doing the right thing* as *being right,* like they're the only people who know what that is, and everybody else is wrong who doesn't see it their way. So when they catch you in what they consider to be wrong, they feel they have the right to hold you to account, by their claim that you should want what they do. They feel it's their duty to guide you to the one true way, and then keep you on that straight and narrow path. If they don't, they think they fail in their duty toward you as a fellow human being and toward God." His voice is shaking as he says, "But I think even more different now about what they want."

His voice is stronger when he says, "The whole thing that's just come out on the news about this Jim Jones fellah they're all talking about on television again, the one who had his followers drink poison, when was that? I know it's five, six years ago, because the anniversary's coming up in the fall, when they all killed themselves. There's a new book out on it, that's why it's in the news. Well, the preachers I'm talking about—Momma's preachers—they want what this Jones fellah wanted. He was the one who got to say, you see, the one who got to tell everybody what to do, even to die, if it came to that, and with these guys more often than not, that's what it comes to in the end. It's just not actual murder like it was with Jones. It's more like shunning or excommunicating you, which, to these guys' way of thinking, is damning you to hell fire forever and ever. It's murdering your *soul.*" He stares at me. "You lose your *soul*, Caroline. It's not just an idea or teaching. It's more like a battle between *them* or *you* with your eternal life on the line. If you don't belong to them, they mean to kill you spiritually—pure and simple."

His features are animated, alive, his voice spirited, impassioned in a way I haven't seen in him since he's been out of the hospital. I'm ashamed to wonder where he's getting these ideas, as though he's incapable of coming up with them from reflecting on his own experience. Are these thoughts emanating from the recent news broadcasts about Jonestown he's been mulling over? Well, of course, but they're broader than this one topic. This new reflective bent is undoubtedly the results of his detox therapy with his doctors and others in the program, which unquestionably included hours and hours of speculation about his life—especially his life with Mother and her leaving him.

He had drunk heavily after their separation, the drinking culminating in blackout binges that frightened his neighbor, who contacted Mother, who attempted to get him help—help that didn't come in time to save him from the accident that almost cost him his life.

But is this an alternate, obsessive avenue of escape coming from living alone with so much time on his hands, his sitting around and brooding? Or are these reflections emanating from a new church life—though, with this kind of questioning, embracing another church doesn't seem likely. I'm embarrassed to realize I don't know if he has a religious connection now. Our closeness in the past couple of years has been sporadic at best. He's better at letting me know more about himself when I'm visiting than on the telephone, which makes sense, given his penchant for self-protection. And the tape recordings we have made and shared have opened avenues of communication not available until then.

But I'm not sure what he's trying to reveal in this description of his mother's religion and its consequences. Whatever it is, I'm grateful for it. I want the intimacy of his revelations, even if the heart of these stories feel known, familiar. I sit, waiting. Maybe with enough silence, he will fill it. Finally he does.

"I mean, when we're told to possibly die, let's say in war, by a general, we're *glorified* into it, aren't we? They make up this big buncha nonsense—well, some of it's nonsense anyhow—downright lies they tell us if they need to, in order to convince us to make what they call 'sacrifice.' They make up this whole thing they tell us, so we'll believe it and do what they want, don't they?" I'm nervous about where this might be leading, but he's thinking as he's going along, so I play along.

"You mean they sell us a story," I say.

"Exactly!" He slaps the table, grabs his glass before it falls over, and brings it up to his lips, draining the last drops as though that's what he'd intended before he accidentally knocked it over. "Yes, yes, exactly, exactly." His eyes are on me steadily as he sets down the empty glass. "They give us a story to believe in. So much so, we work hard to make it.... we make it *real."*

"But the story can be true, sometimes," I say. "You believed the World War II story, didn't you? That there was a real threat?"

"Well, a-course, sometimes the story's true, but even then, even in that case, there was lots about it we believed, and then found out later, it wasn't so, or, at the very least, gave us room for doubts. We still don't know for sure if Truman had to drop the atomic bombs, killing all those people in one terrible instant, leaving the population in such horrendous agony. It's hard to believe that was necessary, that there was no other way out of the situation." He waits in the silence he's created and says all at once, "To end the war, I mean."

He's so intense, he looks mad. He thinks I'm arguing with him. He's lived alone long enough to have these conversations with phantoms from his past, present, and future. I see him talking to the stove, the dresser, the empty space between him and the television set he sits in front of every evening on his rocker.

"I mean," he goes on, heat seeming to rise from his glowing skin in the shimmering twilight. "What kinda goddamned story do you have to give people in order to drop a bomb so mighty it threatens to destroy the whole world? Was the need to drop that a true story or not?"

"I guess I'm losing my way here, Dad. Are you talking just about what happened in World War II? You're not, right? You're saying it's about other things as well, like you were saying about Grandmother's preachers?" I can see a thread between the A-bomb and the Holdeman Mennonite preachers' bonfires in the driveway of his childhood home, the extreme extension of authority. But when I attempt to connect all he seems to be trying to tell me, I'm getting lost. Is this some kind of pilgrimage he's making in order to structure what he wants to finally say? Or is it simply a meandering through his daily woods, where moral lessons are being illustrated like Dante's *Inferno?*

He interrupts my thoughts in a burst. "It's about *everything.*" His tone suggests I'm somewhat of an idiot for not getting his point. "It's especially true about religion. I wonder now why I believed what I did, well, that's the real question, isn't it? How much of it did I really believe, now that I think on it?" He's looking off into the distance as though he's reading some complicated cipher on an ancient tomb only by the light of a match. He glances at me and then out toward a distant star just starting to appear above the hedge framing the back neighbor's yard.

"They tell you these unbelievable stories, and then they *sanctify* them, so you'll believe them. They tell you they're *holy,* sacred beyond anything you can reason out for yourself, well, you'll just have to believe it on faith, won't you? That's what faith is—to believe what's beyond anything reasonable, isn't it? That's what the virgin birth is about, and all Jesus' miracles. But they make it easier to believe these stories by saying it's coming from a real history, from things that have really, really happened, and this history has been preserved and passed down to us through the mighty hand of God. You wanna take God on in an actual fight, like Jacob wrestled the angel? Better still, spend some time reading the Book of Job if you wanna know what taking on God in battle is like! He made a pact with the damn devil before Job knew what hit him. That was the point, wasn't it?"

"So you're talking about Biblical stories, too?" I'm so stunned by the possibility that this could be what he's aiming for that I want desperately to understand clearly what he's saying. I want him to commit to his meaning. I want to ask him—Is this a 'yes, I believe' Dad, or a 'no, not anymore?' It feels as though my childhood—all those days and nights in church—is at stake. Of course, I no longer believe these stories myself, at least not as they were told to me, but Dad—*my father*—giving his faith up on the altar of... what? Disillusionment? Possibly even clear-eyed reflection? Is this possible?

"What else would I be talking about?" he says, forging ahead. He's so angry, I'm afraid he won't continue. He's breathing hard out of his nose and mouth. I feel the weight of saying something to give him time to collect, or maybe even correct, himself. As I watch him, though, I realize this isn't anger so much as a kind of passionate nervousness. He's hacking his way through a jungle of possibilities to a revelation he wants to share.

I ask him quietly, hopefully to hasten this disclosure, "Am I hearing you right, Dad? Are you saying that you don't believe these stories from the Bible anymore? What are you telling me?" I can't imagine this could be his conclusion. From the time I was a little girl, I've seen my father open his Bible before he went to sleep, and read it under a light, even with Mother lying by his side. Now in this house without her, he still has the open Bible on his desk, a goose-necked lamp hanging over it, his glasses folded by its side. I can hear the thin India-paper pages crinkling in the air as he turns them at night, alone.

My parents were religious throughout my childhood. Some kind of agreement was struck between them, when we children were born, to join the church of their ancestors. I knew both of their mothers were ultra-conservative, church-going Mennonites who had taken their youngest to church with them until they were old enough to resist the tagalong. The church we had belonged to when my brothers and I were growing up was liberal compared to those our parents attended as children, but we had grave restrictions that haunted us for much of our early adult lives, even though we'd abandoned their religion—all three of us—never looking back.

When my brothers and I were gone, our parents left church life entirely, phasing themselves through a couple of Baptist memberships—conservative to moderately liberal—and then out into the secular world. I view this now a little like when one quits smoking. The smoker often goes from non-filters to filters and then to menthols, a pack a day, then a week, then a month and then the final half-smoked pack to the trash can. They had slowly given up the insular, religious community life for one without church in the larger world, but they both had remained Christian in outlook, attending some nearby church occasionally, though not together. I saw them, each in his or her way, keeping the half-smoked pack in their pocket—in my father's case, literally.

Kat had never experienced what my brothers and I had, because she'd come late into the family, after our parents had left the religious life—my sister more than two decades younger than I am. I'm shocked by my own conflict over their religious life, the realization of how much I want to be free of it on the one hand, but, on the other, how much I want my parents to remain committed to some semblance of the religious past into which I'd been brought up.

"I'm telling you something I want you to know about me," my father interjects stubbornly, ripping me back to his storytelling. I have an unbidden, sharp intake of breath. I am falling into a strange well of uncertainty. "First off, I'm still a believer, a Christian. I can't see that much of anything is ever gonna change that, okay? But I'm coming to understand some things about these stories we read and believe in," he says, evening out his voice, taking his time, rocking in the dimming light of our day. "We're told they're holy in a way I don't trust anymore. I've spent most of my life believing every single word in the Bible is holy like that, you understand?"

"You mean beyond doubt in the sense that you feel wrong if you question any part of it? Yeah, I was taught that. You taught me that, Dad."

He sighs in exasperation. "Yeah, this whole notion, you know, that there wasn't any mistakes made along the way, like what's in the Scriptures just as they are—even in English translation—every single word—that's God's doing, that's what I'm not believing anymore. The Word as unerringly, perfectly given to us. But when I ask why I believed that it was, I can only say that the Scriptures themselves tell us they're perfect, and it never occurred to me —not once—to ever not believe that. I didn't *behave* like I believed it, at times, but down deep, even when I was going off half-cocked in a worldly way, I thought I still *believed*. I was just missing the mark. Or the devil tempted me to do it, and I succumbed."

There it is again. The reckoning, the calling into account he's been talking about, the underbelly of the holy—sin. My heart is racing uncontrollably.

"But somewhere along the way, maybe it was when your mother and me left the Mennonite church, maybe it was because I worked out at the Air Force base, and I saw how much I wanted to participate in something I'd been taught my whole life was wrong, very, very wrong, but I couldn't help myself, wrong or not. I *wanted* to be a real part of it, with the other fellows, fighting for *what I believed in,* and not what was the church's idea. Or maybe it was because I saw you kids wanting to be a part of the world outside the church like I—and your mother too—started feeling. And both of us not being able to stop wanting it. Maybe it was this continual battle night and day about what was right and what was wrong. Maybe it was joining another church, and then another, and, finally, finding that didn't make things any better, didn't make me feel any righter.

"I don't know when or how it started, but somewhere along this path, I began to ask questions about why I believed the Bible was straight from God, no questions asked—I'm talking about every single word, without any questions about how *man* could've had a part in what're our Scriptures. I'm not talking about the *inspired* Word, okay?" He looks down, and I think he might stop. He wrings his hands several times compulsively, then looks at them as though examining the veins. He starts rocking again, looks up and says, "But more, for me anyhow, was why the *interpretation* of what's said has to be from some preacher who's supposed to be the mouthpiece of God Almighty. You think Mother's preachers were getting the Scriptures right when they did what they did, taking sin outta our house, burning our fine furniture and heirlooms?"

"Of course not, Dad."

He continues as though he hasn't heard me. "I never mentioned this to your mother, a-course. She woulda been terrified, especially since she had her own doubts about what to do next, church-wise, well, hell, any-wise. I just know that since I've made this break...." He stops and searches for me in the twilight air, starting again when he's looking directly at me. "You know in AA, they talked about 'stinkin' thinkin'' about alcohol. Well, I've stopped my 'church-thinking,' about my religion, you know? And since I have, I feel, all at once, free to ask some questions, which I'm now doing. Boy howdy, am I ever! And my questions are taking me to places I never expected to go."

"Sounds like you're doing some real soul-searching," I manage to get out. I sound so much like a therapist, it sickens me, but I can't form a single original thought.

"You could say that. Yeah." He seems not to mind my comment, perhaps falling right into the rhythm of his therapy from his detox program. He lifts his chin and nods to himself and then over to me. He rocks gently in his lawn chair, viewing his yard and beds like a great caretaker of the Gardens at Versailles.

—

The night is beginning to fall against the sky in a dark billowing bank with jagged edges, floating beyond my father's shoulder and over the neighbor's fence to the brilliantly fading horizon. The last of evening's light trickles through the large black oak leaves and loblolly pine, scattering shadows in splotches across the glass-topped table, our faces and arms, and beyond to the bushes, flowers and grass near the vegetable garden gate. The air is thick with the fragrance of flowers in the beds around the yard, but the breeze is light, dry, keeping the gnats and mosquitoes away. It's a warm, gentle night. We both look up to see the stars shining through the fading light. I listen to June bugs hitting the back screen door, sticking for a time, then taking flight in a buzz. Verbena, hibiscus, lilies, honeysuckle, roses nod gently against the dimming sunset. Catching the shimmering coral rays along the vegetable garden fence are zinnias, columbine, marigolds, black-eyed susans—it's an overwhelming display of my father's labors from dawn until dusk.

I decide to let him take the lead in what he wants to tell me next. I'm lost in confusion, not able to form a single offering about what he's just told me. I have questions, but these will take time for me to order into any tactful inquiry.

He breaks our silence. "You've gotta have questions," he says, as though reading my thoughts. "But before you ask, I have to tell you some things."

So here it finally comes. 'Tis the gloaming, the bewitching hour. In this approaching darkness, he's about to reveal his hiding places, and what's buried there. I see how he must've been in his detox circle, listening, drinking his coffee. But it's harder for me to picture him talking and participating in the group about his interior life, even his history. He's good at telling his stories, but they're usually about 'the other fella' as he calls his relatives, church people, neighbors, and a few acquaintances he used to work with as a mechanic, then in semi-retirement as porter, the guy who gets the used cars ready for show.

"Okay," he begins again. "Just so you understand where this's coming from, it's not me sitting around all by myself moping and festering that's got all these ideas percolating. You know...." He pauses, frowning at my face. "Just me in an empty house without your mother and only the TV to keep me company, and no drink to slow everything down.

"Here's the thing, Caroline. Bottom line is that detox changed me. Maybe time will tell in what ways and how much. We'll just have to wait and see on this, but it was constant therapy in there, I kid you not." He breathes in the twilight, staring straight ahead with his hands lying across his stomach as he rocks slowly like a pregnant woman only weeks from delivery, though his stomach is flat, not at all distended. Still he has that remarkably ethereal glow, as though the body knows what the mind hasn't quite grasped. He's kept himself fit since his weight loss in the detoxification program. He's learning to take care of himself. He looks healthier than he did my last visit, when the strain of his recovery was still on his face and in his carriage. His skin is clearer, his movements quicker, he's more alive.

He wears a new undershirt that spreads easily across his narrow chest, but he's brought a long-sleeved flannel shirt with him. He stands up again to put it on, looks over at me and asks if I need something to wear against the chilling air.

I shake my head and tell him I'm fine. So he sits down and continues.

"You know how the Christians say they've been 'born again'?"

The Christians? He makes it sound like a foreign group he's not ever been a part of, a secret forces agent gone into a protective witness program. I grin to myself. An ex-Mennonite in hiding as a CIA operative? Now there's a picture for me to ponder.

"Well, that's a little how it all felt, feels even yet. I'm so new that about half-a what I'm thinking these days feels downright silly. Well, no, 'crazy' is more like it. Sometimes I sit in my backyard here, right where I am now, and shake, literally shake so bad, I feel like I'm gonna fall outta my chair and disintegrate to dust, scatter like so much chaff in the wind. It's not the DTs, I want you to know. I'm way past that, Caroline, and anyhow, I wasn't that bad off during withdrawal, not really. Well, it was the DTs, actually, regardless of how bad off any of us were one way or another... in there." I think he's about to say 'in the tank' but then thinks better of it.

"We all laughed and called the DTs—the 'downtroddens'. What I've learned to do when the downtroddens come over me is wait them out." He makes a little sound, a kind of "ah," but softer, coming from deep in his gut, up through his throat, a sound I used to hear him make when I was a kid, but now it has less resignation in it. It's more like a gasping for breath, needing space around his talk in order for him to go on. "I sit with these victim-thoughts until they're gone. And that's not such an easy thing to do. But I gotta tell ya, even though I shake like I've got the DTs sometimes, I'm not nearly as scared as I used to be. I can sit around back here for hours drinking tea by myself and not be terrified of everything in sight." He looks over at me, then quickly away, a habitual gesture he seems to have with me. He's wary but extending himself. We are a lot alike, I'm thinking. "Well, I've congratulated myself about this enough, haven't I?"

"You *should* congratulate yourself," I tell him, attempting to impede his inclination towards self-deprecation. "You've earned it. I can't do what you're doing. I'm all ears. I want to learn."

"Learn, huh?" There is a real sadness in his voice. I wonder if he believes me. I want to reassure him, and suddenly I know how to do that in a way he can accept.

"Dad, would you like a smoke?" I ask. He already has his caffeine down, maybe not quite the amount he used to drink in AA—the gallons of coffee-buzz I know the ex-drunks seek during meetings—but he smokes back here while he has his coffee, I'm sure, even though he's cleaned up every trace in the house and patio.

He eyes me and grins. "I would," he says, that after-sound coming again, from his depths, a small wind in a cave. He stands up and walks inside, slamming the screen door behind him, but not closing the inside door, so that I hear his soft, flat footsteps leaving the kitchen, no doubt going down the hall toward his bedroom. I wonder where he's hidden his smokes. Much like his liquor before, he's probably stashed them in the recesses of his clothes closet even when he knows I wouldn't—nor anybody else—go into his bedroom without his permission. Perhaps it's still Mother he fears?

More wind in the cave, as he opens the closet door, I imagine, and reaches to find his treasure, just as I did as a kid, in the rafters of the garage from the ladder against the wall to secure my cigar box where I kept my marbles and other secrets from battles and collections only I knew, together with the older neighbor kid who would steal his mother's boyfriend's cigarette papers, so we could roll our own, and smoke while we assessed our treasures.

Now my father is by the screen door, his cigarette already burning between his fingers. He takes a drag, not caring that he's leaving a little smoke in the kitchen as he steps out onto the patio, his cigarette dangling from his lips, looking a little like the older, but a more clean-shaven and sober Bogie from *The African Queen*. He doesn't look at me as he takes another long drag—drags he's been doing like this awhile, nothing new, quite practiced actually—and lets the smoke out into the darkening air.

"Ah," he says. "Thanks."

I nod my head, nothing more.

He hands me a flannel shirt and tells me to put it on. I won't be sorry, he says. I do as he instructs, the material smelling faintly of Clorox, tobacco and the all-too-definable odor I recognize as only my father—sweat, grime, automobile grease and exhaust. He has to be still tinkering with his car, and maybe a neighbor's as well, here and there. As I push my arms through the sleeves, images and sensations stir through my body—the indefensible heaviness of his approach, the rapid footsteps on socking feet, the fists and fight to escape, the unbearable shock of assault, regardless of how many times it's been, and then the weeping. He flicks his cigarette a little to the side of his chair, letting it rest between his thumb and finger as he watches the fire, licking his teeth and lips. He hasn't brought an ashtray. Maybe that would be admission of habit.

"I never know when the DTs will get me," he continues after another inhale. "But whether they come a bunch together, or one every now and again, they still come. I'm talking about the 'downtroddens,' with the shakes like the real ones, you know, the body ones. Dr. Hyatt—you remember him, you know, my detox doctor—he told us their name, in Latin, but a-course I don't remember it anymore. It had delirium in it, I remember that. When mine come—these are in my mind now, you know—I just sit with myself back here or if the weather's bad, it's in the kitchen, looking out across the yard, because there's nothing else to do with my life but sit with it, do you understand?" He's told me this before, but I'm simply listening. He needs whatever he needs in the telling and retelling.

He doesn't wait for me to answer, so I nod my head toward the garden. The air feels faintly cool despite the flannel against my skin.

"I'm alone, but as I know now, we always are. There isn't ever anybody else, not really. Nobody can save us, even if we want it so bad we can taste it. And that's literally what I did, a-course."

Oh, yes, I do get this. But how could my father know? I've sat silent during his recovery stories, not venturing to disclose my own struggles with alcohol. I squirm in the secrecy—my deliberately keeping myself apart from him in this—but I feel great kinship in what he's saying. It's why we're called alkies. We're like street alcoholics who drink rubbing alcohol toward the end—it's not just for the lack of money they ultimately drink so cheaply and with such risk. It's for the love of the raw, alcohol-y taste that sears the nose and throat as it spreads heat on its way to the belly. It erases the confrontations in the head by concentration on the burn in the gut.

The smoke eases out of his mouth, fogging up his face for a moment. The patio light from behind is casting him in great shadow. "We get lost in the notion that we can be saved by our marriage, our children, our friends, our work, our possessions." He waves his hand around the yard. "You know, what we think we have. But in the end, all that fades away, we lose it one way or another. These things give out, people die, they leave, our house gets lost, we can't do our job anymore, we get sick, and we're alone whether we want it or not, well, who the hell wants to accept any of this happening to them?

"But here's the thing, if we aren't aware of it, we live in a trance. I went through the motions, Caroline. I was never awake. I was scared to death of everything. Terrified it was all going to disappear, because I didn't deserve it. Your mother was doing me a favor, I thought, ever' day of my life by staying with me. When she left, hell, I wasn't *surprised*, I was just more *terrified*, afraid to the bone that it was true, that I wasn't dreaming, that she wasn't ever coming back. That's how deep into terror I'd gone. Well, self-loathing is what it really was. Fear was just a cover-up for how much disgust I had about myself. It's what I found out while I was in there." He waves his hand toward the east part of town where I know the hospital is located, his burning cigarette leaving an arc of light in the air.

He pauses a moment, adds, "I make it sound like I slowly went into this fear and disgust, like a person descends into dementia or something. Hell, I was in it all my life. I didn't know how to be any other way. Well, you can see what that kinda thinking produces. Now here I am...." I'm stunned by his admissions, but his articulation makes me feel I'm in the presence of a father I don't know, perhaps never knew. Why am constantly being surprised? I feel a small shuddering inside as though he's telling me he has a terminal illness, that he's slipping away from me before my eyes. Picking up his talk, he jerks me back to listening,

"We spent most of our time in detox facing reality, looking our worse fears right in the eye and finding out why we had them. But that was nothing compared to what followed. The hard part was accepting them." He takes in a jerky breath. I'm not sure he can continue speaking, but he adds, "Whatever in the hell that means. What does it mean to accept your fears? Most of the time, we, well, I, at least, spent my time trying to get rid of them, hide that I even had them, is what I did, for a lifetime. I'm trying now to stop hiding, and that's no small potatoes." He says, "puh-tay-duhs." He shrugs, grins not to me but toward the ground, letting his fingers dangling down, his arms on his knees.

"This," he holds up his cigarette that now has ashes he looks at, a little amazed, flicks them off and takes a long drag, the last of the tobacco before the filter. The fire's got to be frying his lungs. "This here's a distraction. I know this, sure as anything. But Hyatt reassured me that it was okay to be a little distracted every now and then. It just can't be booze. I've used it too much to cover everything up. Distraction burnout." He's pleased with his creative word joke and laughs a little, nodding his chin in my direction. He too can sound clever and educated, he seems to be telling me.

It strikes me how deeply embedded this childlike need for permission is. I picture his father, rarely leaving his rocker after retirement, still commanding his household through his two oldest sons—his consigliere carrying out his orders like a great mafia don.

While I watch and wait, Dad smashes out the stub of his cigarette on the patio cement, twisting it gently with the toe of his shoe and picking it up, laying the butt carefully on the table in front of him. He squints at me, says, smiling, "That's so I keep count!"

He picks up where he left off. "I didn't get a lot of what Hyatt told us, me in particular—I'm talking about in our group sessions. In the private ones, he took the time to explain. But even then, he had to spell everything out to me in bold letters, especially at first, as you can imagine. It took me the whole time I was in there, but eventually I got most of what he was trying to get across. He had me read books. Well, I've never been able to read worth a damn, so this was pulling hen's teeth when I first started, but he assured me it didn't matter how slow I did it, even if I had to go back and read some places again and again. There wasn't anybody looking over my shoulder with a stick this time, he said."

"What have you read, Dad?" I'm thinking it can't be much. I've not seen a book in the house when I've visited. Was he hiding his books like his smokes?

And from whom? The men he worked with or Johnny from across the street who might drop by? Was this another "unmanly" thing he thought he was doing? Was he afraid of the discussions his books might bring with me? If so, I've put him on the spot. But, if anything, he seems excited.

"Oh, quite a few." There is pride in his smile. "You'd be surprised how reading picks up the more you do of it. I gotta use the dictionary all the time, have it right there by my side, but I'm getting better at it. I'm reading *Fried Green Tomatoes* right now." He says "tuh-may-duhs." Frowning, he rubs his empty glass. "It's got a longer name than that... *At the Whistle Stop Café*, that's it. Saw it at the library on a table, some kind of display, and decided to read it. Now, there's a first, don't you think? Me picking up a book at the library. I astonished myself, well, for even going, let alone getting a card." When he looks over at me, I'm assuming he's searching for my approval, so I tell him next to a driver's license, a library card is absolutely necessary to be a citizen of these United States. Too late, I realize how touchy the loss of his driver's license has been to him as his DWI precipitated his entry into detox with license restoration coming only after he went through a test as he left the program.

He grins and says, "Well, now I have both so guess I'm red, white, and blue these days, you think?"

I grin back at him, and he goes on with his library tale. "This Fried Tomatoes one is about a buncha women in this small town trying to find themselves—anyway, that's what it says on the back description. It makes me laugh right out loud, but it's sad too. Dr. Hyatt gave me a long list of books to read when I left therapy, which I'm working my way through one at a time. I decided with *Fried Tomatoes* to get away from his list for a while, because his are all pretty serious. Let's see, I've read some hard ones. *Lord of the Flies*. And oh, I read the man's book who was in the concentration camp, Wiesel. *Night*, that one." He says "weasel" for "Wiesel."

"*Night* took some doing, not because of the words, but because of the story—it was horrible what this man suffered in that camp. But I read it. Makes my troubles seem downright silly by comparison." His voice changes when he talks about reading. He becomes hesitant, walking around words, possessing a limited expression, as though talking about reading is as difficult as the reading itself. "I can't remember anymore, but I've read quite a few. You can look at the list. I've got it on my desk. I check off and date the ones I've finished."

So this list is now next to his Bible.

"How long have you been out of therapy, Dad. Two years, isn't it?"

"I've stopped seeing Dr. Hyatt now for a few months. But I tapered outta the program. I think you know that though. It's been a year and a half, since I was released." He makes it sounds like prison, but I know he stayed an extra thirty days at his doctor's request in order to be a special mentor to those newly entering the program.

"I had contact with him for a while after I left the hospital," he tells me about Hyatt. "I still have his number if I need it, but I've done all right." He lights the citronella candle, tipping the glass to start the flame with a match he's taken from his pocket and struck across the matchbook. "I've learned a lot about how hard it is to stare at your life without blinking." He laughs that airy little laugh he has, the sound falling out of his mouth like a sigh.

"One of the most interesting things I learned in therapy was that I'm afraid of you, just about more than anybody else." His voice is strong, and he's looking at me directly, but then, his self-confidence evaporates, leaving his body in silent heaves, while he attempts to gather himself by rocking and looking toward the flower beds on his side of the yard. I am as stunned as he is by this declaration, my heartbeat quickening, my breathing rapid, shallow, erratic. Once again he's talking far beyond any part of him I know.

Obviously, he's given this some thought. I try to wait. But it comes like a slap, one of those sudden accusations from the past.

"Me?" I hear myself saying, no little amount of defense in the tone. "Why would you be afraid of me, if anything...."

"No, hear me out, Caroline. I'm not blaming you. It's nothing like that." The deep up-from-the-belly sound again. He throws his hands in the air. "I'm sorry. I'll get back to this, okay? There's a lot in it about—back then." Struggling to breathe, he's working to keep control of his voice. He wipes his face with his hand, then does that quick glance at me and away. "It has a lot to do with how I came to believe you were your mother's child and not mine. Well, a-course, you were our child by blood, together. What I'm saying is that I spent so much time trying to win her over by using you to do it, that it felt like...." He pauses and swats the night air with his hand, his voice close to breaking. "It wasn't right."

He can't look at me, so he says in a wavering voice to the garden at the far end of the yard, "Can you let me tell you this my own way, in my own time?" He isn't demanding anything. He's making a solemn request. I want to tell him it's not me who brought this up, and, therefore, it can't be me holding him back, but he may not see it that way—my comment could sound defensive to him.

I nod in reply. He's staring at me in what I take to be anticipation, but then I realize he may not be seeing me nod in the shadowy light.

"Of course, Dad," I tell him. What was he going to say? Using me to win Mother felt to him like what? He's said that it felt as though I wasn't his, but what does that mean to him exactly? I know well what it meant to me, or, at least, how I see it now— the use he made of me for himself. But even in the shelter of the dim light, I sense he doesn't want me to ask him anything, so I remain still and silent. He looks up at the night sky full of stars. Clearing his throat, he asks, "Do you think we should go in? Are you getting hungry?"

He doesn't wait for me to reply. He stands, blows out the candle and starts walking to the door like he would if I weren't there.

—

After supper, he waves his hand when I ask if I can help with dishes. "I could dry like old times," I say. He made us potato pancakes, eggs with onions, that we smeared with catsup, and toast—a country breakfast without the bacon, exactly like he knows I like it. He had baked the bread, pulling a frozen loaf out of the freezer at the beginning of the day, warming it in the oven minutes before we ate, and he made cocoa from scratch, topping it off with Reddi-wip, squirting the foam down from the can over my cup.

"Very old times," he says, adding quickly, "Well, okay then."

He nods toward a small rack where several tea towels are hanging neatly in a row, towels Mother had embroidered with cats in hats washing and drying the dishes, going to market, or ironing their way through the days of the week. But he suddenly changes his mind again, before I get to a towel.

"How about a compromise? How about in the morning?" I think he might want to go on with his talk so I agree. He runs water over the dishes, utensils and cookware then leads me into the living room. He takes his soft pack of Marlboros that he'd left on the table during supper and walks them into his bedroom. He's back faster than it would take him to put them in his closet. Are they lying next to his Bible with the list of books given to him by his therapist, an inventory of his life's development away from The Good Book and the church?

"Decided to leave them out so I can see them?" I ask, curious, smiling at him. I've taken a seat on the couch somewhat across but still close to his glider-rocker. When I first arrived, he's told me that his glider was the one new piece of furniture he allowed himself after his return home from detox. He said that he needed something he could sit in that moved and bought this to replace his stationary recliner which still sits on the other side of the room facing the TV. I wonder if he ever thinks it will be filled again with Mother's return. Maybe it's where she sits when she comes to do her laundry and after supper, as they watch "a show" together. In grave philosophical tones, he told me rocking was something to relieve the tension, adding, there was a reason mothers rocked their newborns. "It quiets the demons whispering in your ears," he told me.

"What? You think I hid them from you before?" He's talking about the cigarettes he's carried to his bedroom. "Naw, I had them in my desk drawer is all. Just outta sight, so I'm not easily tempted. I get two a day, that's my limit. But now you know where they are in case you want one. You haven't taken it up again, have you?"

"Nope. When I gave it up, I gave it up. But I saw dragons on the wall before I did! Pall Malls without filters were my drags of choice."

"Well, how long ago was *that?*" he asks, smiling hugely.

"At least twenty years. They still sell them without filters, actually. But they're hard to find in most places, have to go to a tobacco shop. God, I loved the taste of Pall Malls. No other brand tasted so good to me."

"We pick our brand of sin, for sure," he says. I swallow but look steadily at him. Is he searching, I wonder, but I think not. He's still talking about cigarettes and playing with the notion of nicotine sin.

There is silence for a while. He rocks, says finally, out of the blue, as though he's starting where he stopped, but the sentence he comes up with isn't where we were, and it surprises the hell out of me.

"I would never tell you that your mother was a wonderful woman. But then, I've never used the word 'wonderful' to describe anything in my life." He laughs cheerfully. "At least I never used it until I went through detox. In therapy I learned to talk all kinda ways I didn't before." He squints at me with that squint of his, head cocked to the side with a long frozen wink. His cheerfulness seems new—not so terribly unlike the man I've known all my life—but something's different. It's the articulation about his emotions, despite the word fumbles. He's alive, animated, even if his edges are still a bit ragged. He's leaving himself exposed, vulnerable to me.

Gliding steadily in his chair, he continues. "When I did say things like beautiful—and your mother was that, too, to me, she was beautiful, even when she was at her worst—and I used words like wonderful, ah well, I might as well tell you. Dr. Hyatt made me say them. I'm talking about actually saying the words out loud that he seemed to know I wasn't wanting to say. But when he finally goaded me into saying them, my God, Caroline, it was like taking my clothes off and standing naked in front of him. When I finally could bring myself to say them loud enough, he told me, 'Okay, that's better.'

"But he snorted, saying, 'bew-*tee*-ful? Vernon, you make it rhyme with pew and spew! You should see your face. It's like you're either smelling something very bad or are embarrassed you've been caught pickin' around in the trash. And won-*dur*-ful? What language is that?'

"He said the words the way I had, which I took to be mocking me, which it was, especially, my Okie accent. But I knew what he was getting at. I knew way down deep I was saying the words cockeyed, because I was embarrassed to say them outright, serious-like. But having him catch me at what I was doing, before I even knew it, well, my feelings were somewhere between wanting to kill him and wanting to burst into tears while running behind the couch to hide. Dr. Hyatt seemed to know right where to go with me—with all of us—to make us feel two feet tall. A-course, I learned, in time, he was deliberately taking us back to when we were kids, back to those places where we felt shame or resentment or anger over situations we were still feeling as adults. At first, it didn't take much to send me back there. But I learned to say lots of things out loud I was holding inside. And I learned to cry, not trying to hide it. Hell, I didn't have to learn, what am I talking about? I'd just fall apart in front of him and anybody else who was there. I was so embarrassed the first times. It seemed like I couldn't feel anything but sorry for myself, and then I got mad, my God, I got so mad I thought I'd explode or have a heart attack. But I couldn't bring myself to show him that right away either, a-course. So I'd literally fall down on the couch and turn my body in such a knot my head was at my knees.

"One of those times, Dr. Hyatt pointed out that this was the way a baby lays in a mother's womb. Boy, oh, boy! Can you imagine how *that* made me feel? My God, I was going back so far, I was acting like—like a *fetus!* By the time I left the hospital, I felt as though I had been born again. Here I'd heard about being reborn all my life in church, and I was really doing it on a shrink's couch!"

He stops moving, gazes off toward the kitchen door, then back at the wall, then down at his hands. He massages them as though he's attempting to rub off the grease and grime of years of labor. I think of Lady Macbeth. I ask him if he'd like some more coffee, thinking this would keep him busy during the telling, but he shakes his head. He'd just pee all night, he says.

"Anyway, what I'm trying to tell you is that Darlene was somebody special to me and I loved her, best as I could love anybody. But I've come to wonder about everything, what it means to actually feel what I do about anything. When I tell you I loved her, I'm not sure I know to this day exactly what I mean. I'm trying to find things like that out now."

"I never doubted that, Dad, as a kid, I mean. Despite everything, I knew you loved Mother." I don't tell him I know he still does, even if he doesn't fully understand his feelings toward her. It crosses my mind to tell him despite its being an old tired line, love truly is incomprehensible. It's what all the songs are about, that most of us don't know why we pick who we love, at least not until we examine it for some reason, and that I understand what he's attempting to do.

"Most of the time now I think she was something I made up that I called 'Darlene.' She was like a story, a story I believed in back then, when you and the boys were children, but, for all I know, it might still be true. Maybe I don't really know her at all, even yet. It feels like that's so a lot of the time, especially now that she's gone. She's changed, you know."

The confession is rolling out of him so fast, I'm not sure he could stop it if he wanted to. He needs to tell what he's kept hidden from me so long, gathering the courage to speak it.

I want to tell him, of course Mother has changed. My God, she's left you, is all but living with another man, and is earning money and spending it on her own. But I find out soon enough, he isn't meaning that she has changed so much as *his perception of her* has.

"People change, a-course. I know I'm not the same person that went into detox in the hospital. But I'm not talking about a normal kinda change in people, because things happen to them, and they react to that, or they grow older and become different. I mean, when I really looked close at who your mother and me were when you kids were little, when I studied on it with my doctors, I started seeing that there were different ways of 'knowing' her."

He pauses as though I might not understand who the woman is he's referring to. "Darlene, your mother," he clarifies, as though I've asked. "One was this sorta fantasy I had in my head of who she was—the woman I wanted her to be, needed her to be. It was the person I kept thinking she was when I met her, before all our troubles." He means before her mental illness, his drinking, and the constant struggles with money. "But I'm not sure that woman ever really existed.

"And another Darlene was this woman I lived and dealt with every minute of every day." He says "dealt with" as though his endless efforts became his life. "When I was with the "more real Darlene," the one I lived with every day, I didn't have time to think about anything but how to get to the next thing. I just lived one situation after another." He sighs. "Maybe we never know anything but these made-up stories about our lives, anyway."

"You mean everything feels unreal?" I ask carefully. Does he think that everything's a lie, a kind of dream-story?

"Yeah, maybe. Well, not everything, but then again, in a way, yeah. I think that's true, but for everybody, not just me." He runs his hands over his knees. Is he talking about life as an illusion, an ungraspable experience, or does he see life-as-experience as false, a lie in its very nature, absurdly against what we attempt to make real through our daily struggles?

"Your mother used to say that to me all the time when she was sick with her depression, do you remember that? She'd say everything looked so far away. Everybody else was living in a world she couldn't get into—a world she could only pretend she was in, or watch at a distance, like she was looking through a window out on what everybody else was doing.

"That must be what it feels like to be crazy. Sometimes she'd beg me to put her in an asylum." He glances at me and rushes on, "But this isn't exactly what I'm meaning when I say our made-up stories aren't real, we only think they are, and that gives us a feeling that we are crazy. I mean, we can't see things as they really are, we each just have our own story going on in our heads, and, all at once, *we know this."*

"You mean you realize it's a story going on in each of our heads?"

He nods.

I want to reassure him that the alienation of self produces this, but when I start to speak, he holds up his hand to stop me, and continues with his idea. "And when you're in recovery, Caroline, this gets more intense. Dr. Hyatt called it, 'living life in a hyper-state of reality,' because you notice everything you're doing and what's going on around you constantly, and your separation from it. Part of it is getting the alcohol out of your system, both in your body and your mind.

"'You're gonna feel foggy, then everything will seem very clear, almost too clear,' he told me, when I got shaky after I left the hospital. 'That comes,' he said, 'from looking at ourselves closer than we're used to doing.'

"You know, with your mother, I never really got this when she talked about how crazy reality seemed to her. I *believed* her, because I could tell by just looking at her that she wasn't *right*. Well, and she acted crazy, too, sometimes."

Images come to mind of Mother hurling objects across the room, of her stomping her feet on the floor or kicking furniture, of her slamming her hands against her head, against the wall or table, of her throwing herself down on the floor or furniture while Dad attempted to subdue her, her limbs flailing about. Her screaming. Her terrible screams.

"Anyway, in recovery, I started to understand what she was saying, how the world seemed foggy, out of focus, downright unreal, and how it feels as though it's all made up in your head, but it doesn't stop there. *You notice how that is.* That's the crazy-upon-crazy part of it." He stops only a second. "Thing is, you see how everybody else is acting, and it's not like they're in their heads the same way you are. It's like they're living *for real*—they're into what they're doing without being so mindful of everything. I just don't know if I'll ever be able to do that again, anyway, not like I used to."

"You mean being immersed in what you're doing, not being so self-conscious all the time?"

He nods, with tears in his eyes.

His troubled waters *are* running deep. I'm becoming increasingly nervous about his profound internal pondering. I want to say or do something that will stop this reality-unreality talk, but I'm not sure what could effectively do this. And his desperate need to tell stops me from throwing an obstacle in his path. He continues, wiping his eyes with his handkerchief. "It's like there's one world right there that you're dealing with in front of you, and the other one is what you *think* is going on. But both are in your head, only for a while I thought it was only the thinking-world one."

He must see the puzzlement on my face, because he attempts to clarify. "The world inside felt like the only real one, and the one outside everybody else was in, seemed unreal, except I thought I was supposed to be seeing it as the real one, you understand? I'm saying, I think that's what Darlene had been trying to tell me about herself, too."

His expressions bring to mind the way the unschooled hearing speak to the deaf, through loud repetition. He doesn't know the words, so he keeps going over and over what he can express, sometimes with broad gestures and emphatic voice, hoping that these will carry the message.

"You mean regardless of which world you're in, whether it's your immediate experience or your perception of it, these both are made-up, because they're in our heads as stories, is this what you're saying, Dad?"

He nods vigorously. "Don't you think that's so?"

I hesitate a moment before answering. "Well, Dad, everything's in our heads, as you've said so well. But, I guess, I'm trying to figure out what you mean by 'story' in regards to reality and unreality." Suddenly, I have a quick, involuntary intake of breath. My voice comes out in a shaky burst, "We're interpreting all the time with this constant flow of...." I start to say 'information' but I'm afraid this will veer our talk in a direction that's even further from what I need to know, which right now is whether he's okay or not.

I say instead, "...experiences. They are going on around us all the time, and we're constantly observing them. If that's what you mean by an 'inside story,' I couldn't agree more. After all, we only have our minds to take in and interpret what's happening—our *thinking* about that, as you've put it. But our inside story/making-up/perceiving/thinking keeps going on even when we're dreaming, so whether it's totally conscious or not, it's what our minds do, you know what I mean? We're in our heads all the time, in a sense."

"You're saying that's all we got—if your head's cut off, there's not much going on after that?" He's grinning when I look over at him, and we both laugh.

"And not much is going on with the body, either," I add. "I can't see Anne Boleyn dancing around her court without her head!"

"Don't know who she was, but I remember the 'headless horseman.' Heard about him in school. Scared the devil outta me, especially when Miss Kretsch read it to us—now there was a scary woman. She didn't have much hair, and she talked with a lisp. Her hands were all crippled, and she walked with a limp. So the headless horseman stayed in my memory good and plenty. But there you have a man who rode around on his horse without his head."

"*The Legend of Sleepy Hollow.*"

"That's the one," he says.

"But it's only a story!" we say together, pointing at each other, then laugh.

I want a drink, very badly. A small headache is starting in the back of my neck flowing toward my sinuses, settling behind my eyes. I have no idea where this man is going with all of this, but I feel as though much more, and I'll shake apart, my own EDTs overtaking me—Emotional Delirium Tremens, my own word invention.

He shakes his head as though clearing his thoughts. "You know, as nuts as this sounds, sometimes I think it would be better if we were like moles, or no, even better yet, like Helen Keller. Then our eyes and ears wouldn't get in our way. We couldn't get so caught up in all the nonsense." He laughs. "But then I'm not sure how we'd drive ourselves to the grocery store."

And I'm not sure how he thinks having fewer senses would cure him of his thoughts, but I laugh with him again.

"Well, the headless horseman was able to do it, because he was a ghost," I say. "Might do well to ask Helen Keller what she thinks about this idea of yours, Dad, since she actually was out there quite alive and thriving without her eyes and ears. Could be you're right. But since she's been dead for a while, I guess we'll have to wait until you and I pass to the other side to get our answer."

Turning serious, he says, "Point well made."

Point well made? Good Lord. He's a wonder.

I want him to go back to the thread of his talk about mother, before all these asides. But then again it would be nice to give the whole conversation a rest, even though I'd like to know more about his mental and emotional stability. Then I see he has no desire to give up the idea he's trying to clarify to me.

"Where was I?" he asks.

I pick up the thread of our talk. "I get what you're saying about living in a storytelling reality while needing what's really happening to be honest and true, but you were beginning to say something about...." I want to ask him how he used me with Mother, but I skirt around it because he's asked me to be patient with him, to allow him to tell me in his own time. But, once again, he doesn't wait for me to finish my sentence.

"I want to live in the world without...." He drifts off and waits for his thoughts to gather.

I have a knee-jerk response. "Subterfuge?"

"What's that?" he asks earnestly.

I smile because I didn't intend to use the word, certainly not the cliché. "Without deception, in this case, self-deception—without lying to yourself."

"That's right. I want to get honest about my feelings and my thinking too."

"That's a wonderful goal, Dad. Most of us don't examine our feelings enough to do that." I wince at my therapeutic condescension. "But don't you think it's important to just feel, to simply live. Maybe that's what you mean by being honest?—getting back into things, letting them flow in a natural way?"

"Okay, but I wanna stop making things up like I used to, is what it amounts to. I wanna know what's real and what's not. I wanna stop making up how things are by how I want, need, them to be. You know, trying all the time to make that happen so it's real all the time."

"You want to know what you're really feeling about what's going on instead of trying to manipulate it into something you want it to be. I get that." I sound like my therapist. Clarifying what's just been said, so that I can know for certain what he really means. Or is my desire for clarification really a way of embedding a thought, so that he'll recall it later and act on it? It's a heady game we therapists play with others! I wonder suddenly how well my therapists have done with their own self-diagnosing and personal curative solutions?

"Yeah, like I told you, I loved your mother, as much as I could understand what love was back then—" he snorts, *"back then,* sure, like I know now." He hunches his shoulders as though he's cold and needs to protect his neck, then releases his muscles and air through his mouth. Waving his hand at me, he says. "I'm hoping you know what I mean."

I smile, nodding a little. I reassured him earlier that I knew he loved Mother when my brother and I were kids, but I can't imagine how he loves, except maybe through loyalty and his attempts to get approval by his generous efforts to others—fixing their cars, rigging new electrical boxes and outlets, making bread and cinnamon rolls for the elderly or sick in the neighborhood. For me and my brothers, his love was what he called "being a father," which I interpreted as his earning a living for us, taking up the slack for mother's days of inertia, and the discipline. There was that.

But what was his love for her? A lust for what she had the courage to do that he couldn't? What did he see in her that held him so devoted for all those terrible, hard years? I know something of their courtship, but very little about the fierce yearning he had for her that compelled him to step beyond his terror of "the other" and pursue her. I realize I still view him as weak, even gutless, not perhaps where we, his immediate family, was concerned—his working hard and not running out on us—but certainly where the world out there was concerned, that he encountered, still encounters every day. Would he fight for me if we were under siege? I'm not sure. I'm not sure he'd fight for himself, but maybe that's what's changing I need to pay attention to, that he's telling me to notice.

He's saying, "Truth is I didn't really know anything about how to be with people, connect with them, understand them, let alone how to look at my feelings about them. You know, in detox we talked about what Dr. Hyatt called 'our emotional lives,' It's the first time I really stopped and thought about my feelings. Before I just *felt* and didn't think about why, hardly at all. So when I say your mother was a story to me, I mean I didn't know how to look at her other than how I needed her to be, the made-up Darlene."

"How was that?"

His reply is instantaneous, barbed, bristling, "Sick, okay?"

And just as suddenly his cutting tone is gone. "God help me, I wanted her to stay sick so she'd need me. But that isn't what I told myself. I told myself she was really hard to live with, and I stayed because she was a bad habit I couldn't break, like my brother Willard had told me she was when I married her."

"Really? A bad habit you couldn't break? There seems more to it than...."

"It was my duty to take care of her," he interrupts quickly. "You didn't just up and leave somebody back then. People would think you were a bum. But you're right, a-course. There was more than my being caught up with her. There's a lot in this, Caroline. A lot more than I want to admit, especially to my kids."

He's undeniably upset, even suddenly angry. But before I can soften the situation, he goes on.

"I woulda been alone, and, c'mon, look at me! I would never've gotten anybody like her again, as hard as she was. I wanted to keep what I had!" I want to ask him what that was, but he's not to be interrupted. "And then there was the booze-thinking, you know, me thinking I was the poor victim guy—she acted bad, and I got to feel sorry for myself, so I used that to drink and 'swallow' in my misery. It's what we called it in therapy.

"Hell, I never took charge of anything in my life. I took it, like I always took it with everybody—my family, at work, at church, you name it. But the worst was when I told myself that this was love—me wanting her to need me, me thinking I was the victim, this was love." He shakes his head. Dr. Hyatt has taught him well, perhaps too well. He's been out of follow-up therapy long enough now to be more into the flow of his life. I'm feeling, once again, that he's still stuck in the rhetoric of figuring everything out.

But am I being fair? I'm telling him to just feel when he's trying for the first time in his life to ask why he's feeling what he does. It takes time to get back into your life with tools in place, so that you don't feel and do without reflection the way you used to, the thoughtless living for which you pay the consequences in pain and loss. He's had an enormous amount of upheaval and change to handle. And for a loner like my father, what would being more in the flow of life look like? I'm not sure. Obviously he's actively involved in his garden, the house, reading. It's not like he's paralyzed. And he's attempting to demonstrate what he's learned about himself and his world now to me.

I know how it's been with me, this searching for a way past the booze and into some clarity about what's gone on and what's coming next. I dread the horrible self-consciousness of it. I close my eyes and breathe in the claustrophobic air around his voice. I dread the walk back into the self-examination of my own treatment again—the appointment that's already set the minute I'm back home, the one I can't break without the consequences I really couldn't face if I did—the courts, the judgment, the rehab, the effect on my teaching-counseling career. It's as though what he's been through and his reflections on it are a dry run for what's happening in my own life.

"Are you hearing what I'm telling you, Caroline?"

He's been talking, and I haven't heard a word. "Oh yes, Dad," I manage to get out.

"You look like you're a million miles away."

"I'm sorry. I'm listening very carefully, honestly I am. This is so true, what you're saying, I'm thinking about it in relation to myself, not just you." Truth is I haven't followed what he's been saying for a while. But he seems encouraged by what I've said, so he continues.

"And here's what I want to add to this. Okay, so I made up stories in my head like everybody else, but what I found out was that I was covering up a lot of what I didn't want to admit with these stories I dreamed up, you see?" I'm wondering how soon it will be before he asks himself how he can know a thing is true. I haven't a clue what I'd say to him—should he ask—about any of his notions of lies, truth, and cover-up.

He's on a roll. "And then I found out I wasn't only covering up the truth, I was deliberately making up *lies*. Well, hell, a-course they were lies, what else could they be? They were covering up what was really underneath I didn't want to know as the truth. That's how it works when you pinch your eyes closed and don't look at what you're afraid to.

"So in therapy, I started looking underneath my 'made-up scripts,' as Dr. Hyatt called them. We've been calling them stories. Same thing. But looking underneath is what I've been trying to do ever since."

So this is his conclusion. Truth is what's underneath. I want to ask him what happens if he doesn't find it there, or worse, if he finds out that what's underneath isn't the final truth? But I know what a cynic I've become and introducing such skepticism now could be disastrous for him.

"Okay, here's the truth. You wanna know the truth?" he exclaims, leaning forward in his chair, his eyes accusing me. "Right this minute, I want to have a drink, Caroline. *Right this very minute I want a drink,* because I don't want to tell you the truth about what I'm thinking and feeling. I don't want to see what you might do when you hear it. I don't know how I'm even doing it without a drink.

"*The truth is,* I have to tell, because it's a sickness if I don't. I won't be able to not drink if I don't say. I have to say all this to your mother as well—all of it, every stinking word of it—and the only way I can deal with that is to tell you first."

He swallows and breathes in and out loudly. His hands are trembling. His voice is shaking, but he forces the words out toward me.

"Because—because I'm afraid of you. Just wait a minute, honey. I'm going to tell you how that is, but you have to give me a minute." He takes a jerky gasp that shudders his whole frame. "I'm wading in the water now, right up to my neck. It's sink or swim."

In the silence he digs his heels into the carpet and pushes gently back and forth, gliding slowly. He seems to be studying the clock on the secretary, one of the ornate pieces of furniture Mother didn't take with her when she left. Suddenly, I realize that this desk has china on it from her trip to Europe, after she'd left him. Why did she leave it behind, here in his living room for him to see constantly? Did she plan in some overt way to hurt him, or did she, in a more subliminal way, intend to tell him—and perhaps her too—that she was never quite gone, could possibly return anytime to live here again? The house is in her name. Was she thinking she could claim the rooms as her own, even as she was out there doing what she liked?

And then a deeper understanding comes to surface. *Everything* is hers, the house, the furniture, the framed pictures on the wall, the cooking utensils—he is *renting* his life here from her. She's his landlord in a furnished home they had lived in together. He can't sell a stick of furniture or anything else in this house without her permission. Why did he allow such a thing? A horrible anger begins in me for her brazen emotional usury of him, to say nothing of the ways she's wheedled favors out of him—his checking and repairing her car, her getting vegetables from his garden, using his washer and dryer for her laundry, where did it end? It's enough to gall a saint. But hasn't this been their dynamic all along? Is this what he's alluding to when he says he has to confront her as well?

I hear his voice coming back to me, but once again, he's sliding past telling me why he's afraid of me, or he's taking another long hike toward it.

"I think your mother had her own stories going on. The one she tried to work all the others around was that she wanted us to be living in a movie. She used to go to the movies with me, on dates, you know, before we were married, had you kids and joined the church. I'd watch her face when she didn't notice, which that was pretty easy to do, really, because she'd get all lost in the story up there on the screen. What she saw in the movies became a dream, something she wanted to have, do—*be*.

"She was miserable all the time, because, after we got married, she resented how we lived. It didn't ever fit what she dreamed from the movies, and then there was the Mennonite script, about trying to live so you went to heaven and not to hell. Put those together in a sack, shake them around, and see what you come up with!"

He leans back and gliding a little faster, pursing and stretching his lips across his teeth, breathing hard through his nose. "I learned in therapy about this dreaming. We have these ideas about how our lives should go, but then these scripts or stories or dreams or whatever you wanna call them, they're so loose in our minds, we don't have a clear picture of exactly what we want or even if we do, we don't have any idea how we can get it from where you are.

"The problem starts when you go about your ordinary life, and things happen that make your life hard. Then you get upset because life doesn't fit what you've been wishing for. My movie, if you want to call it that—Dr. Hyatt calls them 'scripts,' which is what a movie's story is—well, I had mine. And I felt self-righteous about mine, oh yeah, really thought mine were better than hers, because my little movie was a house full of people who belonged together and loved each other and wanted the best for each other, with me running the show! While hers was about the house—your mother had a very high opinion of that—but hers wasn't that different from mine, really. She just knew what the house looked like, and you kids in it, and me, too, a-course."

He glides some more, faster, his hands rubbing the arms of the rocker. "Most of the films we saw, hell, money was flowing outta the faucets—you could turn it on for anything you wanted. In these movie scripts, people are all bankers, lawyers, doctors, college professors, inheritors of wealth. Money was simply *there*.

"Well, your mother and me dated right at the tail-end of the Great Depression, and we went to these movies where the people were living in mansions with incredible riches. That dog, what was his name—oh you know, in *The Thin Man*—that wire-haired terrier?" He stops rocking and looks at me, "Asta, that was his name. Asta had a better hair cut than I did!" I am laughing out loud when he says, "Think about those movies back in the thirties before we got married. Hell, the amount of money they showed us was enough to curl your hair, and I don't even have any to curl—didn't then, not even in my twenties!"

We both laugh, and I'm glad for the break. I offer, "*Like Bringing Up Baby, The Philadelphia Story, Holiday,* you mean?"

"You seem to know a lot of them yourself," he says, surprised.

I shrug and say, "Mom named Kat after Hepburn, Dad. These were all Hepburn's films, but there are a zillion others from the screwball comedy years of the thirties and forties. They don't make them like that anymore.

"All I remember is that everybody in them came from money or had high-class jobs—the men anyway. The women waited on the men and did charity work. Well, we sat and watched those stories, and hell, we wanted those things. Your mother wanted the dresses the rich women wore. I wanted the automobiles the slicked-up actor-guys drove. You tell me how you're gonna get those things on a mechanic's salary, especially starting out in life when there weren't even enough cars to work on?"

I'd heard Mother's side of this story. She'd taken a good look at herself during and after the divorce, had gone to therapy and straightened out some kinks in the defenses she'd lived by for over half a century. But she still had a good-sized wall between her and my father—dented and battered as it was—especially when it came to his side of the story about all this. And he'd told me some of his side already. He wasn't exactly repeating himself, because I didn't know how much and in what ways therapy had affected him, but I'd heard his living-with-mom's-dreams stories before. So some of what I was hearing was over-plowed territory.

Now, I mainly wanted to know why he felt afraid of me. He said it had to do with Mother and his attachment to her. I could guess at what that might be.

After all, I had my own story to tell, and had told it both in and out of therapy, to Mother and my sister, though not to him. What I needed to understand was how he'd come to feel, if not comfortable, at least courageous enough to talk to me, but still say he's afraid of me. There was no rushing to the end of his story. He was prepared to tell it in his own good time.

"So why did life treat me so dirty, I asked myself? *Life*, well, hell, my life boiled down to your mother, didn't it?" As an afterthought, he says, sheepishly, "Well and you kids too, but your mother was at the center, wasn't she? I felt I certainly didn't deserve any of the guff she was dishing out to me. And a-course, thinking like this, everything's going to turn out wrong, which it did, a-course. But I want you to understand—regardless of what she's told you—your mother was pretty much doing the same thing. She blamed me and her mother and dad, you kids—especially you, hell, you couldn't ever do anything right.

"So she had this movie about what she wanted and blamed everybody around her who couldn't make it happen. And me? Well, a-course, I blamed everybody too, only it always swung back around to her."

I take a chance and interrupt him. "Why do you think you focused on her so much as the bad guy... person in your life, Dad?"

"Huh?" he asks, as though he's suddenly hard of hearing.

He's told me in so many words, but I want him to tell me outright. This might not be fair, but he's hit me pretty hard—with the being afraid of me idea—and then taking Mother to task, in more ways than I can count, over the years.

"Why did you make Mother your scapegoat for this victimhood in yourself?" I ask him directly and catch how fast my heart is beating in my chest.

"Well, I *wanted* her," he says, almost angry at me for holding him to the thing he's told me he wants to tell me. "I wanted her to love me, and she... she couldn't. I thought at the time, she *wouldn't*, but I knew better." By the time he gets this out, he sounds utterly defeated. In a whisper he echoes, "I knew."

"That's pretty hard on yourself, don't you think?"

"No, I don't think so, because, back then, I knew and didn't admit it, Caroline." He clears his throat. "There're things we know about people, especially people we live with every day. I knew that she didn't love me, but she needed me, so she...."

"Used you?"

"I let her. That's the point. No, more than that. I *wanted* her to. If she couldn't love me, well, then I'd take her...." He doesn't finish his thought, but I do, to myself. He started to say, "pity," which is too shameful for him to admit to me. At least he has a bottom line to his self-degradation. I don't know if this discussion can go on, or, even if it is a discussion. I feel his rage directly at Mother, but at me, too, by extension. Is this the fear of me he's talking about? Did he think, back then, that it was me standing between him and Mother?

"Back when your mother and me were living this all out with you kids, and my job was constantly a worry—not about losing it, but about never having enough money...." he trails off again, then after a while says, "Hell, you can say that, that she used me. And I can say I let her. But what does that mean with her being so sick?"

He rocks, and I remain silent. "You tell me to forgive myself just as Dr. Hyatt told to do. And I'm trying to, Caroline, ever goddamned minute of the day and night." His eyes are fiercely dark—as indigo as I've ever seen them—hard as b-bs taken out of a furnace and thrown in my face. His voice is tight, but he is clear about the point he's wanting to make.

"Goddammit, Caroline, we—neither one of us knew anything about—I started to say, life. But that's only true if by life I mean anything and everything. I didn't know the first thing about how most people really lived outside our life in the Mennonite church. I heard a million times from the pulpit about how these people who weren't like us were 'worldly.' What the hell does that mean? I guess I thought they lived in sin all the time—smoked, drank, committed adultery on their wives and husbands, got money dishonestly by beating the poor guy out. They worshipped Baal—worldly idols—that's how we talked about it."

"But wasn't that what the movies were about that you saw? All those things you wanted so much?"

"Sure. That's why we weren't supposed to go to the movies. It makes you crazy for wanting those sinful things! It's why we stopped going to the movies and started going to the church more. But that's another story, isn't it? We just substituted the wanting-riches story for the going-to-church-all-the-time story. Your mother had her own fears and the idea of 'going to hell' was the glue that held all of her religious-movie-stories together. Mine was making a family like the church thought it should be, the most important part being a good father. That was my glue." He smiles and says, *"Life With Father,* only William Powell as a Mennonite!" We both laugh at the image he's created.

"Or *Father Knows Best,"* I say before I realize my implication.

He ignores the darker side of this, if he catches it.

He says, "Oh sure, I knew best all right!"

Suddenly in my thoughts I hear the bathroom door lock, his back-then voice yelling, as he's coming at me with the strop, "You gonna mind? You gonna do what I say?"

Now I hear him saying, "Robert Young, hey, I remember that one. It was on the radio in the evening once a week, and then when we got a television set, we watched it on there. Remember our first set? 1954, things were picking up a little better at my job after the Korean War ended. Cars went up in price, so people got their old ones fixed instead of buying new ones. They never stopped production like they did during World War II, but only the rich could afford those offered every year."

"What did that mean to you, Dad?"

"Well, it meant I was a good provider."

"No, I mean about you being a good father. What did that mean to you at the time?"

"That's what it meant, Caroline, being a good provider. I pretty much put most of my eggs in that basket. But it also meant making sure you kids grew up right—in the church. And that meant giving up the worldly things.

"We relied on the preachers to tell us what the right things were. Sometimes we followed what they told us, sometimes not, but to my mind, they knew better'n I did." He stops and I let the silence fill the space between us.

"What I think Dr. Hyatt was trying to get all of us in detox to see was that we're alone, nobody can save us, not the preachers, or our wives and husbands, not even Jesus Christ. He didn't say that—he wouldn't ever've said such a thing, because he told us from the outset that he didn't want to interfere with our religion—but that's what I've come to believe, anyway, working my garden and sitting out here drinking my tea. Jesus or not, you gotta help yourself. He can't get you out of it."

"You mean, Jesus can't get you outta your troubles?" I echo, just to make sure I'm understanding him correctly.

"You have to see this Jesus story for what it is, or it becomes something you hold onto, so you don't have to deal with your messes or face up to being alone and especially the fact you're gonna die." He adds thoughtfully, "And your loved ones."

Seeing the Jesus story for what it is? Did he actually say this?

When I look over at him, he's softly crying. I don't know quite what to do. I start to ask him if he's all right, when he begins again in a voice that grows steadier as he talks.

"You know, you get past the tears—anyway I have by now, most the time. I was terrified I'd cry my whole life. I know you saw that in me."

Has he's forgotten how we cried together sometimes, each to ourselves, after the punishments he gave me, his holding me against his chest, rubbing my back?

Now, he's saying, "And in therapy once I started crying, I couldn't stop. It was awful, just so awful. Dr. Hyatt asked me in our private sessions, 'Where do you think that comes from?' And I'd tell him over and over, 'I'm scared, can't ever imagine not being afraid.' That's when I learned what the DTs were. It's believing that your world is gonna come apart, and you'll never get it back together again. Humpty Dumpty Sickness." He grins to himself, but he wants me to be in this therapy circle by his side, going over Dr. Hyatt's and AA's teachings with him again. He's proud to have me here listening to his story, even if it shames him.

"Darlene's gonna disappear, I told myself, back then. You kids are gonna leave with her. One day I'll come home from work, and the house'll be empty. There'll be nobody, nothing there but me. I lived in terror all the time. I'd think, *'I'm not gonna make it, I'm not gonna survive, because nothing is gonna hold up in the end, it's all gonna be gone.'* I asked myself, *'when you take your last breath, what's gonna be in it? A whimper, a cry, a shout, a whisper, a prayer, what?'*

"All this work we do, it stands for something doesn't it? For love or hope or family or work or religion, going to heaven, is that it? My God, what's it all *for?* Something! It's gotta be for *something*, don't you think, that you're living for, I mean, doesn't it, for more than just the next thing?"

The air is crackling around us like thunder. Through the kitchen window my eyes follow the lights my father has forgotten to turn off which are illuminating the backyard patio, bordering the walk toward the vegetable garden and around the flower beds to the outdoor bench under a canopy of ivy and grapevines. I think I hear the tiniest sound out there, the crawl of every living thing in the air, the visceral leap of life from the stars to the grass, falling, falling, falling to the roots of all my father's flourishing plants blooming in a fierce profusion upward during the day toward the sun, but which are already fading and dying in the night, slowly bending back down to the earth from where they came—flowers in the fragrant air of our funeral services, covering the odor of our body's decay. To think of his, my father's, funeral in this moment is excruciating, unbearably real. The image of mine is still distant. I watch myself in the movie script I've invented in the darkness under my still pinched-closed eyes.

"What I believed, Caroline, was that religion would make everything better, because my life had some meaning, underneath all the troubles. It was the big picture story, the biggest movie of all—maybe that's why your mother believed in their stories so much. Maybe they put up on a big screen those we have in our heads already, instead of the other way around.

"Well, it's like I told you, the Bible stories are like that, aren't they? And they're sanctified by blood—it's always somebody's blood that makes the stories sacred. First and foremost, it's Jesus's blood for all of humanity—he's the big sacrifice. And then it's the blood of your family, isn't it? The big stories are always about sacrifice, life for life. It's always that, whether it's your real kin or members of a church or a nation or your buddies on the battlefield."

He's working himself up to some point, and I don't know how to help him get there. So again I wait. "It's the Jim Jones story, this man who made his family, you see that? This huge family, and then he tells all the members of his family what to do, what will be so right, so holy, they couldn't resist him, because it'll give meaning to what they were doing, meaning they thought they couldn't do on their own. You know how many members of his congregation died in the name of this family he concocted for himself? *Nine hundred and nine.*" My father has pivoted his emotions instantly, that trigger I know so well, when everything affecting him converges into one focused release. He's suddenly filled with near trance-like anger, his chest is heaving, his voice coming out in spurts.

"All in the name of family, a family with a story so right the members in it can't do anything else but what the person says." He sits trembling, his whole body shaking.

"Dad," I say, attempting to bring him out of this place he's gone to.

"What?" He's angry at my interruption. He's all but shouting.

I stare back at him in silence, not a muscle moving, trying to hold very still, keeping my gaze steady, without malice or fear.

He looks away and continues, his tone softening as he speaks. "Whatever this family is that you belong to, it has to be sanctified by some kind of bond, if not blood, *something*. The Mafia have an oath that states they 'make their bones' through killing somebody, don't they? The Mormons have a holy seal into their family. Our church had baptism. Once baptized you're a member of that holy community. With us, it was the blood of Jesus and the water of baptism that binds all the members together."

My father looks at me with tears in his eyes, his lips trembling which he attempts to hide by stretching them in a grimace over and over again and wiping his nose with the handkerchief he's pulled from his pants pocket. He's taken on an enormous burden. I think of the countless bloodbaths in the name of holy wars and to appease the gods down through world history.

"I've believed these stories all my life," he says, with such conviction, I want to walk across the room to console him, but I know that it's only because I'm sitting where I am that he can tell me what he is. "And now when I look at it, I realize even while I question the story about sin and redemption, I still believe it. But more than anything else, Caroline, I want to understand it, for me. For nobody else but me. I'm sick of hearing the preachers tell me I'm going to hell if I don't believe Jesus died on the Cross for my sins."

He rocks viciously, almost victoriously, then comes to a halt and says, "Who knows? Maybe I can't not believe. Maybe I'm predestined to believe, or maybe I'm terrified not to. I don't know anymore. I simply don't know."

He shuffles his feet, then sits still, hunching over, and after a while rights himself again, looking across the room at me with a steady gaze. "What I do know is our story is paid for by the blood of our martyred ancestors, Caroline. You ever read *Martyr's Mirror?*"

I shake my head. "I know about the book, but I've never read it."

"It's the story of thousands of Anabaptists who died in order for us to have our church family. They were drowned, beheaded, burned, and buried alive. When you know such things, you belong to something sanctified, something holy. Our Christian community goes back hundreds and hundreds of years." He looks at me, tears running down his face. "How can I abandon that, even when I now question it?" His turmoil is written on his face, as he glances at me and then stares out into space between us.

I am reminded of the scripture I memorized as a child, having quoted it many time in recitation in front of audiences, Mark 9:24, *And straightway the father of the child cried out, and said with tears, Lord, I believe; help thou mine unbelief.*

"If you feel this way, Dad, why don't you go back to church?"

"I go and try to belong. But the people there don't ask questions. They want to sit like sheep, like I used to, and listen to what the preachers tell them and believe it. I want to—to believe for *myself*, don't you understand? Not like they say I have to." He wipes his face with his handkerchief again, blows his nose. When he looks at me, eyes glistening, he says, "I want to be free to not drink the Kool-Aid and not get shot for not doing it, you see what I mean?"

I look away from the sheer gut-wrenching honesty of his words.

I've let him down when he's needed me most. I haven't been there for him during our family's severance. Have I abandoned him like Mother has left him behind, sliding in and out of his life at my own convenience? Are my visits like the leased offerings of her china on the secretary that he stares at every night during television news? His need for family is so deep. Can any of us fill it?

I'm realizing the truth-seeking searches he's learned in therapy may be taking away his linchpin, not just the unhinging of our immediate family— that's already done— but the destruction of his history, even his genealogy, the sense of kinship from his ancestral family whose traditions have defined his identity as far back as the Reformation.

"So, I can't stop believing," he says as though refuting my thoughts. "It's a little like those men on the battlefield who believe in the war because of the sacrifice their buddies have made to the cause, whether they think the war is just or not. Or like in Vietnam when soldiers revolted against their officers, while they continued to fight, not just because they knew if they didn't, they'd end up in jail, but because of the sacrifices that'd been made. You tell me how deep loyalty and fear go, Caroline, when it comes to beliefs like this.

"I'm so scared, I don't even know anymore why I believe what I do for sure. I sit here and ask myself if I'm believing only because I'm afraid not to. If that's so, that's not a very good reason for believing, is it? Is God even gonna honor that kind of belief? Do I care? If I don't, am I willing to pay the consequences if I'm wrong? You ever read *Revelation?* There's a God of Wrath. It's not all just about the God of Love. God demands obedience. There's a heaven *and* a hell. About that Mother's preachers got it right."

When he's silent for a while, I say, "I have my own fears, Dad." I skirt the issue of his Biblical God, heaven and hell and blood-sanctified community. "I've read somewhere that it's the one human emotion most like fire—it can save you, even while it can destroy you. On the one hand, our fears keep us from danger and from doing ourselves harm—you can wake up out of a deep sleep when your body and consciousness registers smoke in the air. On the other hand, our fears can eat us alive and cause us to act in ways that are destructive to ourselves and others—like when we think we smell smoke in a theater and yell 'fire' when there is none. Most psychologists believe that fear is motivated by our need for security. If you look at it like that, fear keeps us safe."

"Dr. Hyatt told me to think of my fears like a huge snowball that's become hard as rock that I keep rolling in front of me everywhere I go. It's my fortress and my weapon, but it keeps getting bigger and bigger and harder and harder the more I roll it in front of me to save myself. And even after it's so big that I can't roll it anymore, I can't give up trying to push it in front of me. I feel if I give up, the rock will roll back over me, I swear." He pulls out his handkerchief again and blows his nose, stuffing it back once more into his pocket.

"I'm afraid of you most of all because I need you, Caroline, and I don't want to." So there it is, finally out, though I haven't a clue as to what this means to him. "This feeling is just too much like I felt for your mother. But the thing that's different, it seems to me, is that I gave you up once, for her, because...." He hesitates once again.

"I was the sacrificial lamb, you're telling me?" I ask, couching my idea of coming between him and Mother in the metaphoric language of the *Book of Revelation* which my father doesn't know I've read, about the wrath of God written there toward non-believers and those without obedience.

He nods.

I've had my own knowing about all this. I was the one, more than his boys, to carry the cross for the perfect world he and Mother couldn't make together, the one sanctioned by the church, made sacred through death and blood. The boys were boys and not expected to meet the same sacrifice in the family history as their eldest daughter who was led to slaughter for their guilt and fear in the face of God. How very familiar, yet peculiar, this repeating of history is through the stories—sacred and otherwise—that shape all of our lives.

"But now, I want you to be my family—not all of it, just your part of it," my father is telling me. "That's if you can." He is shaking again, his voice wavering, but he's seeing it through, looking toward some group of angels on the far wall lending him support—probably Dr. Hyatt and his circle of friends from therapy and all those drinking buddies sitting every week with him in AA.

"But I don't trust myself," he continues. "I don't know if it's still about me being scared more than about…." He waves his hand out and brings it back to his lap, settling into a steady rocking rhythm in his chair, gathering himself.

"Love?" I ask, amazed I've asked such a thing of him. The word sits like some wild animal between us. I will it to seek warmth and comfort instead of some feral terror that, charging, could rip us apart.

He nods his head, as he sobs. I walk over to him, sink to my knees and put my arms around him, holding him as he did me so long ago after such horrible injury was done between us. I hold him awkwardly against me until his sobbing subsides. The whole time of the embrace, he holds himself stiffly against me, still unable to surrender to what he must feel could eat him alive.

When I stand, he continues to look down, so I pat him lightly on his shoulder. I don't say what I know he's waiting to hear. I see all too well what these therapists are to us—the one I feel I've become over this day and night of my visit—the stoic support we receive, while we strip our lives down in front of them. But I refuse to lie to him. I have to be ready myself, to gather the courage to know it's real, honest, true when I say it. I can ask love of him, but I can't say it yet. This realization leaves an emptiness too enormous to accept. I begin walking toward the kitchen to do something, anything, to fill the vacuum he and I have, once again, created.

"I'll make tea," I say to him. Alone in the kitchen, waiting for the kettle to boil, I listen to my father rise from his rocker and walk slowly to the bathroom. I study the reflection of myself in the kitchen window over the sink, seeing the eyes of a woman unsteady about her intention in the question she's put to her father. What a horrifying thing I've just done. How can I ask of him what I myself am not ready to give? Do I want a guarantee before I will invest my own feelings in what he's asking of me? Do I want to belong to this family of his? Not of his, not even of ours, anymore. It's the family of him. Of him.

Once the pot is between us, the filled, creamed and sugared cups by our sides, my father says, as though the thought of love has not passed between us, "These Bible stories are life and death matters, Caroline, because if I stop believing, I don't know if I can believe in another single thing anymore."

Hidden in this, I'm certain, is a suicide note. He's had his own recouping going on in the bathroom. He's left me with far too little choice in what I can reply, so I decide to go for broke.

"I believe there is love and there is fear, Dad. They're the two sides of a coin. None of us think about either one very much, except for the losing of one and the letting go of the other—you're so right about that. We just live them out, until something happens that forces us to look at them.

"Therapy can help us become aware of how we're living them out and maybe even why. But if it's good therapy, we get how knowing this is not the cure. Just because we understand how we're feeling and doing our loves and fears, doesn't mean we can readily change what we're feeling and doing." He rocks and nods. "The healing comes from the same place the sickness comes from—from inside ourselves. I think sometimes love's like a little mouse you hold in your hand. I read somewhere that rodents can die from both fear and boredom. You can scare love to death, and you can let it drift into oblivion. But I like the metaphor Dr. Hyatt gave you. I don't know any better than you do, Dad, how to stop rolling the petrified snowball in front of me. So you're not alone in this. We all have to believe in something, just as you say. And what do we have other than our inventions?" He continues to rock, now saying nothing. We undoubtedly both realize I could have answered with "love" but decided against it.

When the silence grows heavy, I add, "By the way, the word 'petrified' means literally 'to turn into stone.' As a metaphor it can mean, 'to be paralyzed with fear.' It's close in sound to the word 'terrified'...." He interrupts me and asks how I know this. I tell him I've read a lot of poetry, so I look up words all the time, just like he does now.

"The word, 'petrified' stayed with me, because I'm afraid a lot, too. When we're afraid to love, it's usually because we're afraid we're going to lose that love, maybe even ourselves in it, that's when the snowball grows so large we can hardly move it, so much so, sometimes we stop moving it altogether, and we hide behind it so we're never seen. We aren't available to others for love anymore." He rocks, listening, so I go on with my thoughts, speaking out loud as they come to me. At least, this I can give.

"Sometimes we can't help ourselves, you know, like you fell in love with Mother and wanted her so badly to love you. So just like you did, we all come out from behind the snowball long enough to connect, but then once we do, we run right back behind the fortress and fear again. And so, we hide that way as long as we can. Almost always something has to happen to make us give up the snowball pushing altogether. I don't think we ever stop being afraid, but we can lessen its influence by admitting what we're doing and openly love—show it, express it, and live with it honestly. I'm often not able to act on my own advice, but there it is, the truth as I believe it."

"You were such a beautiful child, Caroline," he says unsteadily, bringing the gliding to a stop. "You have no idea how much I loved you when you were little." His voice catches, but he struggles on. "I still do, you gotta know that. But you were such a joy as a child, the center of your mother's and my world. We couldn't imagine anything more wonderful happening to us."

"But Mother got sick," I say, trying to help him through his upset.

"No," he says firmly. "Oh no. She wasn't sick until after Theodore was born. But she was a demanding Mother from the start. They say you're hardest on your first child and maybe that's so. She wanted you to be perfect, and you were a kid with your own mind. She—we wanted your mind to be like ours. We were young, didn't know what we were doing, knew absolutely nothing about raising kids. We were lost about what to do with you. You were all the time into scuffles out in the yard. You did things we didn't think other girls did, like wanting to be with boys, especially play their games with them. Most men—anyway, back then—let women handle their daughters, because we were brought up to believe they knew them better than we ever could.

"In your mother's case, she was especially determined you be like she thought a girl should be, and you were just as determined to not fit that mold. You'll have to talk to your mother about how she sees this, well, maybe you already have, but while you were still little enough to do what we said, we laid down the law. And that was both of our doing. I don't want to go into all that, because you know most of it, but my—my part in—how I did that...." He can't go on, his voice is breaking.

He struggles desperately against sobbing again. He takes out his handkerchief, this time a clean one he must have gotten when he went to the bathroom, and whips his face with it. I think he's putting it back in his pocket, when I see he's pulled out what I think at first is his wallet and holds it out to me. My first thought is that he might be attempting to pay me for his wrongs, a horrid notion flashing through my mind—"paying me off"—but I see it's a cassette tape inside a plastic case with a label in his penned handwriting.

"I made this for you," he says, clearing his throat. I reach out for it, but my hand resists taking it, even as I do. I look at the label but can't make out what it says. "I'd appreciate it if you'd wait until you get home to play it, if you don't mind. I just don't know how I'd take it, if you didn't want what I have to say—I mean, you don't have to agree, that's not what I mean. We can work anything out, if it comes to that. Anyway, that's what I'm hoping."

He lets out an involuntary gasp, then adds, "I just don't want to make this all we do for the rest of your visit. I want the time we have together to be good, you know, the rest of what we have left." His eyes are expectant, caught between yearning and pleading.

I nod and hopefully reassure him. "Of course, Dad. Of course."

He gets up out of his recliner and gives me a wave, saying, "In a minute...." I hear the soft slap of his footsteps in his slippers as he retreats to the bathroom again. I study the tape's label. The words simply stare up at me, "For Caroline." I place it on the coffee table next to the couch and wait.

When he doesn't come back after some minutes pass, and I hear running water from the lavatory, I turn on the television, the volume up enough for him to have his privacy. I'm watching an episode of *The Golden Girls* when he finally returns, looking as though he's showered. His hair and bald head is wet, but he's still wearing the same clothing.

He says, "You wanna find a movie?"

I nod, and he picks up three VHS tapes he's placed carefully on his television stand, handing them to me, one at a time. "I didn't know what you liked for sure. The guy in the store told me ones he thought might be best."

He holds out the tapes in much the same gesture he'd used for the cassette tape he'd given me earlier. He's picked *Raiders of the Lost Ark*, *Tootsie*, and *Two Mules for Sister Sara*. "I'm hoping one of these is something you haven't seen." I hadn't seen the Harrison Ford movie, but I tell him I'd like to see *Two Mules for Sister Sara*. "I'm not surprised," he smiles. "This Shirley What's-her-name is one of your favorites, as I remember."

"And you like Clint Eastwood as I remember," I say, seeing he's pleased.

"It'll work then," he tells me.

In the bedroom my mother lived and slept in apart from my father—before she left him for good, as Dad puts it—I sit in the Mission-style rocker next to the bed and wait until I hear him snoring in his bedroom. I carefully pull out the suitcase I've pushed under the bed, open it, unzip a side sleeve to retrieve one of the pints of vodka I placed there when I packed at home. Since I couldn't take a glass with me to the room without arousing my father's suspicion, or my suspicions causing me to over-explain, I go into the bathroom, find a glass with a toothbrush in it. My mother's, I muse, setting the toothbrush aside and washing the glass thoroughly with hand soap. I wonder if she spends the night back here after watching a movie with Dad, so she doesn't have to drive back to her apartment in the dark.

After drying the glass, I pour at least three ounces of vodka in it, filling the glass with diet Coke I'd taken in the afternoon from the refrigerator and left in the room. Just before I lift the glass, the approaching appointment with my therapist, Sylvia Hoffman-Deitch, slides into mind. I grimace at my image in the mirror, then glance away. Coward. But the drink goes down fast and easy, leaving a carbonated punch through my nostrils and throat. It barely has time to settle, before I pour another shot of the same size and blend, and, after only a sip, feel the familiar relief of the slow sink into filmy reality. The headache that had begun after supper lifts and a liquid assurance I trust starts to suffuse my mind. Halfway through the second drink, I think I might actually survive the rest of the stay. In the rocker, I drift easily and steadily toward lazy vacuity while listening to my father's distant, deepening sleep.

By the time I carry the empty glass to the bathroom, I realize I've slipped into numbing inebriation. Taking off my clothes, I throw them on a nearby chair. As I turn to walk to the bathroom, I catch my reflection in a full-length mirror on the back of the door I've closed to block out the sound of the faucet. I turn my back on the naked woman I don't want to see there, with her blotched face and unfocused eyes, her body bloated and flabby under the weight of crapulence. Soaking myself a long time in the tub, I wash every inch of my body and head. Before wrapping the towel around me and falling back into the rocker, I walk to the pint on the counter by the lavatory, listen to the cool, clean flow of the vodka pouring into the glass in my hand. With the diet Coke long gone, I drink in the alcohol that I know will bring, at least temporarily, merciful oblivion.

In the mirror, an unbidden thought snakes its way into my reptilian brain, a fight against myself I know I can't win. "Baptize your faint and impure heart," the thought-demon whispers. "Let the waters rise above your head, covering your mouth and nose until you can no longer breathe, then drink deeply until the lake is dry or you drown."

In my mother's bed, I dream I am lost in some unknown house, a large backless dollhouse in disarray, the rooms not put together in any familiar order, seemingly arranged around staircases thrown at random from ground to sky, no walls supporting them. I sense I'm both outside and inside this house, as I watch myself walking up one staircase and then another, ascending continually upward in a disjointed fashion to the side and then above, the dollhouse's roof dissolving as I reach a storm-filled sky. I'm desperately trying to locate Sylvia, calling for her from the steps leading upstairs to a cloud-filled bedroom.

Opening a door, I see all the furniture in this room is old—clean but worn, old-fashioned and overused. Suddenly a violent storm approaches. I rush toward the closet to hide, only to see Sylvia lying naked on the bed. I fall into her, reaching instant orgasm, and, at that moment, she evaporates into the storm. Just as quickly, in a swirling so intense I think I'm dying, I attempt to raise myself from the bed, hearing my father calling me, but I'm paralyzed in a suffocating dread, bound to my place, unable to breath or move. I open my mouth to scream, but I awaken to the morning sunlight filling my mother's bed with golden heat and shimmering luminosity.

I race to the toilet and wrench myself dry. Sinking to the floor, I smear a soaking towel over my face and arms, giving in to the trembling and nausea. On a metal footstool I find in the bedroom, I sit in the shower, allowing the water to pummel over me full force. When I finally turn the water off, my father is knocking on the door, calling my name. For a moment I'm not sure if I'm in my mother's bedroom shower or still caught in the dream.

"Out in a minute," I call through the bathroom door I've left partly open.

"You want some breakfast?" he asks, followed by, "Soon, I mean?"

"Let me dress, and I'll be out. Toast and tea are enough for now, okay?"

He taps lightly on the door with a "You got it."

I search the medicine cabinet for a thermometer and miraculously find one. Making the bed, brushing my teeth, drying my hair and dressing are all great efforts, my body weighing tons, a stone-cold heaviness in my chest, legs and arms. The thermometer reads 101°, a reading beyond any hangover I've ever had. Before leaving the bedroom, I pour the remaining alcohol down the toilet, including the full pint in my suitcase, chasing it with some Pine-sol I find under the sink, expunging any signs of my drinking from the night before. I slip the two empty pint bottles back into the suitcase sleeve.

Never, never leave evidence behind.

Shaking my head, I open the bedroom door and step into the hall. So many exorcisms. So many demons still in attendance. Only a faint nausea remains as I walk into the kitchen and sit down at the table.

"You don't look so hot," my father says, beating me to my punch line.

"I think I might be coming down with something," I say, and he glances up, pauses, narrowing his eyes, sights on me without looking away, spatula mid-air, the smell of pancakes in the air. It's the overused line of drunkards down through the ages.

"Oh, yeah? Would explain it."

"What?" I ask, running my hand through my hair, acting casual.

"You look like you're ready for today's laundry cycle, skin's got that limp and dirty look," he says. I feel heat rising to my cheeks. Dirty look in my eyes would be more accurate. But he adds, "You taken your temperature? Your mother's thermometer is in her...."

"Found it, Dad, and I'm 101. I feel like crap."

"Ah, shit, Caroline. It's no way to fly outta here tomorrow. You think you need to change your flight? You know that's not a problem with me, right?"

"I'll see how it goes, Dad. I need to get back. I've got a.... doctor's appointment I'd like to keep. So damn hard to get another one." He's studying my face carefully, but with a smile.

"Well, it would seem to be the right time. Are you sick to your stomach?"

"Little, but this tea will help." I thank him, as he puts the cup gently down on the table in front of me, surprising me with a gentle kiss in my hair before he returns to the counter, busy with buttering my toast. The tea's a strong brew with a metallic after-taste, the bag still in the cup. It'll take the full cup before I can taste the breakfast blend past the mouthwash.

"Flu's going around the college before I left," I offer.

"I thought the school was closed down for the summer," he says, pulling out his chair and sitting down to his pancake, bacon, and eggs. The thought flashes through my mind that he might be attempting to catch me in some deception. Did he notice the guilt in my face? But he hurriedly follows with, "You have students, though, tutoring, you said." He pours syrup generously over his buttered pancake and uses his fork to section off a bite.

"Summer session just ended, but I had a class of remedial students. Composition problems. Most of them couldn't write a sentence with guns to their heads, and believe me, I've thought of it! Some of them had colds. Some teachers were sick the last day I was on campus. You know how it is, Dad. People won't stop working because they've got the sniffles. What am I saying? Professors come to work with the Spanish flu during their vacation time. It's the culture."

"Culture?"

"You know," I say, smiling, feeling better with the tea. "The whole work ethic is you don't stop the daily grind, especially with the brainy-nerds who can't beat their chests to show their manhood!"

Dad laughs heartily. "Like your pops, you mean," he says, teasing me with the nickname I used for him in my adolescence.

"Guys like you don't need to make a show of it. You work on cars. Says it all."

He likes that even more, and we laugh together. I swallow back some acid-reflux and touch my forehead. It feels hot, my hands clammy, red, swollen.

"Your cheeks are awful red, Caroline. You need to see a doctor?"

"I don't think so. How long do you have to wait after eating before taking your temperature? You know?"

"Twenty, thirty minutes, same for exercise," he says with certainty, the detox expert. "But right now, it's your shower you need to wait on. It's an hour after that. You took a shower this morning, right?"

"Uh-huh," I reply, though I don't tell him it wasn't exactly a usual shower as it was more like a polar swim. I glance at the clock. "What do you have planned for the day?"

"Taking care of you, my lady." *My lady?*

"Where did you learn such language?"

"Television, a-course." He grins. "You can educate yourself if you choose the right shows." On what shows do they say things like "my lady," I wonder, but don't ask. Could he have seen the movie, *Camelot*, as a video or on TV? I can't feature it, but who knows? The portrait of my father is up for grabs these days.

"I'll have to start watching more. Where were you when I went to grad school, Dad? You should've let me in on your secret, or better yet, tutored me! I could've saved a wad—all those loans that've killed my budget for years."

He eats swiftly, smearing his plate with the last bite of his pancake, placing the fork down with a soft clink. "Good!" He exclaims about his breakfast, smacking his lips, gulping his coffee, and rising as though in a rush to work.

He stacks his dishes, reaches for my cup, but I shake my head and hug it close to my chest as I sneeze. My two slices of toast remain on a plate untouched.

"Uh-oh," he says. Handing me his handkerchief, he tells me like a child, "Use this, please. It's clean." Nodding his head toward me, before walking to the sink, he states with authority, "You're gonna start another degree right now. I'll get the couch ready in front of the TV—coupla pillows, some orange juice, Bufferin, and a hovering homecare nurse." He taps his chest. Walking down the hall, he says, "I'll get the blankets."

When I'm tucked in on the couch, he brings a hot ceramic pot of tea, two paper squares hanging down from the lid on strings, like two small kites caught against a wall.

Two hours later, chicken noodle soup simmering on the stove, my toast carefully consumed along with local news and weather, together with *Hollywood Squares*, I begin to feel better but my temperature continued to hover a degree or two above normal despite the pills and Dad's tender loving care.

I give into his entreaties and change my flight back to New York, delaying take-off for two and a half days, just in time for my therapy appointment without re-scheduling. By suppertime, I've totally convinced myself that what I have is no longer a hangover but the full-blown flu, cold, or virus. The guilt stretches like gauze over my mood, especially the underlying truth of my own brand of detox I'm keeping from my father. What good would it do for him to know I'm paralleling his life in my obsessions and compulsions?

In the evening of the second day of my extended stay—the last night of my visit—one of those violent Oklahoma storms traps us indoors watching the weather channel. "Supercells are created," my father informs me, sounding like the meteorologists he admires so much, "when certain conditions make the atmosphere unstable. The dry, hot winds across The Great Plains collide with the warm, humid air coming up from the Gulf of Mexico forming what is known as a 'dry line.' When cooler, moist air flows into that from the Rockies, it stays in the upper atmosphere, pushing this dry line east. It's the temperature and moisture differences between the upper and lower atmospheres that cause the instability." My father holds his hands out forming the upper and lower levels of an in-the-air sandwich. He moves his upper hand back and forth in the area between the two levels he's just shaped. "This air here, the hot, dry air is like a cap over the warm, moist air causing it to get hotter. A tornado can happen when all three air layers begin to lift as they move east or northeast. When this happens the cap dissolves or blows away and a tremendous updraft causes the rotation of a tornado." He circles his sandwich with his finger, spiraling upward. "It's a complex thing where certain interactions between temperature, dry and moist air, and the right wind speed come together for a supercell to take place."

He glances at me with light in his eyes, sliding back into his rocker. "It's no accident that the National Severe Weather Laboratory and Prediction Center is located just south of Oklahoma City—it's the area most prone to be hit by tornadoes in the country, no joke. I'm sure you know by now that The Great Plains is part of what's known as Tornado Alley." He grins at me and says, "So you were raised in the alley, kid! But you may not know why—about why we're in the middle of Tornado Alley, I mean."

I shake my head.

"The conditions are perfect for tornadoes to form here, because of the winds from the west, the moist, warm air from the Gulf and the sloping down of the lands across the Plains from west to east." Surely he told me parts of this during my childhood, but it sounds especially fresh and interesting on this evening in his living room, my empty ice cream bowl left over from our afternoon snack, resting quietly on the coffee table.

"This supercell is a thunderstorm with a tremendous updraft." Gary England, head meteorologist out of Oklahoma City's Channel 9 weather news, echoes my father.

Dad walks over and turns up the volume of his television set. England guides the supercell's southwestern to northeastern movement on a local map, telling us that the storm is extremely dangerous, has already cut a half-mile destructive path east of us and is advancing from a southwesterly direction and should be within our city limits in approximately twenty minutes. Taking a sheet of paper just handed to him, England reads that the National Weather Service has just upgraded the severe thunderstorm watch to a tornado warning for cities and towns along the bank shown on his map in yellow and red.

"Little slow on the draw, Bud," my father tells the television screen. I'm not sure if he's talking about the National Weather Service or Gary England. I'm guessing the former, since he's always thought England should run for president.

I have this odd sense of déjà vu, not from the many severe thunderstorms I've witnessed while living in Oklahoma, but from my dream which feels as though it's becoming reality. I'm wondering if in some bizarre pre-ordination, my dream has become the messenger of my father's and my imminent demise.

After all the unfolding talk of retribution and contrition during this visit, will we end up through some laughable twist of fate, buried together under the detritus of our searching souls? With the sky blackening, wind rising, and sirens blaring, my father shakes his head when I ask him if we need to seek some kind of shelter.

"I'm not sure it's such a good idea to run to the cellar next door with all the flying branches and debris," he says loudly, glancing out the kitchen window and nodding toward the loblolly pine and black oak swirling madly in the wind. A good-sized branch slams onto the patio as twigs snap with hail against the back windows. Standing up, swaying a little like the trees, I look around for my shoes.

"Hold on," my father says.

"That's what I'm trying to do." I'm unsteady on my feet and lower myself slowly back to the couch, feeling a little dizzy and confused. I say directly to him, "Dad, are we in trouble?"

He looks over at me as though I've asked him to answer a deeper question about the condition of our relationship now that we've unleashed the flood under the bridge.

"With this storm?" he asks, as though once again he's reading my thoughts. It doesn't answer my question in either case.

"Well, yeah, what else?"

"We're fine, honey." He looks back toward the television and Gary England's broadcast. He walks over and lowers the volume while he touches the screen. "See this here?" He points to the long angry yellow and red bank appearing to be only a nano-inch from the dot where he and I are sitting in his living room. "You watch. Right about now, this bank is gonna split, and part of the storm's going to the north, the other to the south." And as though on command, the bank starts dividing, the bright red and yellow line breaking in two on the map. England is barely audible as he announces that all points north and south of us are under immediate alert. It takes another four or five minutes before the sirens stop shrieking and ten more before the wind subsides and the rain begins to fall steadily downward. My father watches the screen with careful attention, but he doesn't turn the volume up to hear what Gary England has to say.

"How the hell did you do that?" I ask after we're settled back into our places, with him rocking in his glider and me lying back on the couch.

"Genesis." He laughs. "I figure if Moses can part the Red Sea, I should be able to take care of a little-bitty Oklahoma storm." He adds, "Well, in Moses's case, he only held up his staff, so I guess we should really give God the credit." He grins at me, sheepishly. "Well, in both Moses's and our cases, I suppose."

"Should I go out and look for chariots and dead Egyptian soldiers in the front yard?" I grin back as I pull my blanket around me.

He thinks this is very funny, laughing as he walks across the living room and opens the front door to the narrow porch, letting the fresh, cool breeze in, stepping out and jumping back inside quickly, closing the door behind him. Before he does, I rise up enough to see a couple of large branches lying near the porch in the driveway. He brushes the rain from his trouser legs and runs his hands over his hair. "You wanna help me pull them into the garage after it lets up a little?"

"I don't think I'm strong enough to pull any branches that size right now, Dad. And it may not be so great for me to get out in the damp, wet air, you think?" I pull myself up to a sitting position. I'm picturing him attempting to drag the branches he doesn't feel he can take care of himself. "Why the heck do you want them in the garage?"

He tells me, "Well, no, not the branches. I'm talking about the chariots! Gotta be hundreds out there and every single one is inlaid with gold and jewels!"

We laugh so hard, I have to lie back down to revive myself.

"You're starting to turn into a crazy old man of Biblical proportions."

"You mean like Noah," he says, not a question. "Well, a-course. You think I don't know my weather?" And that starts us on another laughter jag.

He's smiling broadly when he leaves me to go into the kitchen to ladle out soup and homemade buttered bread for our supper.

"My old man has turned into a wit," I call after him. "I'm going to hate to go, Dad. I love being taken care of."

"Well, don't and I will," he calls back.

—

Once home, I checked in with my father by phone, pouring the alcohol from various stashes in the house down the drain and listening to messages on my answering machine. The one that stood out was the reminder from my therapist of my appointment the following afternoon. I unpacked my suitcase, did laundry, took a trip to the grocery store and returned to make soup as close as possible to the one Dad had made for me. Chicken Soup Burnout, I thought and smiled. I spent the evening watching *Magnum P.I.* and *The David Letterman Show*. A small, creeping headache creased an otherwise smooth transition home. The headache continued into the following morning and grew exponentially as my therapy appointment advanced and my alcohol intake receded.

The anxiety over therapy wasn't warranted. I'd known Sylvia Hoffman-Deitch since the late seventies when I went through my first therapy. So I was more than surprised when the police sergeant processing my DWI suggested her from a list she pulled from a folder she took from a file cabinet behind her desk. I'd called and made an appointment in the police station before I was given back my license and sent packing. There would be follow-up, the sergeant reassured me, holding out the confirmation form for my therapist to sign.

Sylvia was pleased to see I was again a client, though she wasn't overjoyed it was under the auspices of the police department. I worked initially to hide my personal embarrassment of my counter transference with her in my dream while in Oklahoma, which I kept, of course, to myself. If Sylvia caught my dismay, she didn't acknowledge it. She put me at ease quickly, and because she knew my background and history with alcohol abuse, we were able to begin the session immediately with descriptions of my visit with my father which was simply a recapping of his and my conversations and our interactions. The significant and final question she left me with was why I hadn't listened to the tape he'd given me. She didn't wait for an answer, she simply issued a mandate for me to listen to it before my next week's visit and to bring the tape with me.

After supper, but before my evening of research for my classes beginning at the college soon, I put the tape in my recorder in the study, leaned back in my desk chair, feet up on the ottoman and listened.

No more delay, I told myself. The time was now.

My father's surprisingly confident voice filled the room.

"It came to me in therapy to make a tape like this one. I tried to do it with Dr. Hyatt, but it didn't work out, because I depended on him too much, and I needed to do it myself. He gave me some ideas that helped, but I've done this on my own. It's taken me some time and a lotta tries to do it right. I've written what I'm gonna say on a piece of paper, and I practiced it until I could put it on tape for you without interruptions and just like I want it. I've made the tape for another reason as well. I want you to be able to hear what I have to say anytime you want to.

"I'm promising you now that I'm planning on being a father who is more honest than the one you've had. In detox, they taught us to take responsibility for what we've done wrong in the past by going to the person we'd wronged and apologizing and doing whatever is necessary to make things right. We will have to talk about what you think some of those things are for you. I am talking to you on this tape about things that I know I did wrong, and why I honestly think I did them. The reasons I'm giving you aren't excuses, only explanations.

"Here's the thing I want to tell you, Caroline. I wanted a family. I wanted to belong to somebody. My family never loved me or wanted me as part of them. I wanted your mother to love me. I wanted you children to believe in what we did. I wanted to be a decent father. I thought that meant I was the one who said, and you were to do what I told you to without question. And then when I was in therapy in detox, I stopped and asked myself how far I went back then—and would still go—to get these things I wanted so bad. It took your mother leaving me to get me to answer that question honestly, and when I did, it tore me to pieces. Because I knew that I would have done anything, absolutely anything, to the point of destroying everything, absolutely everything, in my life—including myself—if I could get that family and keep it safe for me.

"You've heard the saying, 'I'll get it or die trying.' That's what I did. And here's the most important part I want to say to you, Caroline. I whipped you and the boys—and there's no other word for what I did, because when I punished you, I did it in anger, a terrible rage really. I can only tell you that at those times, when I hit you, I was out of my mind for wanting what I didn't think down deep I could ever have and keep. I told myself I was helping you do the right thing, helping you stay on the straight path, to be good. But I know now what I was really doing. And this was my doing, Caroline. Your mother's doing is her doing, and although I was tied to it, joining in with her notions of right and wrong and such, this was strictly my responsibility, and I made the selfish choice.

"I think I knew it back then but didn't have the courage to admit it. It was that I wanted *to own you, to take the person you were out of you and put what I wanted you to be in its place. I wanted to be the one to have that right, because I had always been so small inside. Dr. Hyatt helped me see how this can be what you do without knowing it, like the sins of the father visiting on his children. My family took away from me who I was, so I wanted to do the same. I know now that this was a way of getting even. I've learned, being alone, facing life without anything between me and it, getting up every morning without my family, just being all by myself with my troubles, I believe above all other things, you have to be able to do that, just this one thing, or you can't add anything or anybody to it without causing yourself and others harm. And by doing it, I've learned that I am what I do. I am my actions, without excuses. It was me whipping you, not the preachers or your mother or our not being able to pay the bills, or the drink, or anything else. It was me. I'm very ashamed of that now.*

"*I would like to believe that I'd never do to you what I did to you, and the boys too, years ago, ever again. And I don't believe I would. But I'm very doubtful about saying this, because I believe, for now, at least, it's a day at a time. I think we can change, but I don't believe anymore in anybody or anything saving me. I am a Christian and believe in the Scriptures, but not in order to get out of anything.*

"*For my part, I get up in the morning and live with what is here right in front of me, now, as best as I can. That's what's saving me. No more trying to get myself or other people to do some fool thing I've got in my mind I think they should or anything somebody else thinks I should do, either. It's finding out the truth for myself deep down inside. It's me being honest with no guarantees.*

"*I needed to tell you this. Because I don't know anything else to do to make what I did to you right. If you do, I want you to tell me. I want you to know that I take responsibility for all I've said and done to you that was wrong. But I also take responsibility for what I did that was right. And I did do some things right. I was a working man who took care of my family as best as I could, and I'm proud of that. But for the wrong, I apologize. I need to tell you I'm sorry for hurting you. I'm truly, very, very sorry, Caroline.*

"*I love you.*"

It took several days after my second session with Sylvia, with our listening to the tape together, with my crying over it in front of her, and with our discussion about it, for me to make the call I needed to make to my father.

"How are you, Dad?" I ask on the phone.

"Well, I'm okay, a-course." There is some hesitation in his voice.

"Whatcha doing?"

"Well, what do you think I'd be doing at this time a-day before the news?"

"Whatcha makin'? If it's breakfast for supper, I'll be right over."

"Then you better start warming up your airplane on the runway, because I'm having pancakes, and they're only inches from the griddle."

"It's gonna take me awhile to get over there."

"I can wait. I'll just scoot the batter a few more inches from the fire."

"Flappin' the jacks, huh?"

"I saw there's a part-time job opening up at Homer's Grill in El Reno, remember that place?" he asks me, conversationally.

"I remember it well, Dad. 'Homer's Down*home* Cooking.'" I sing him the brief jingle played on a local radio station. "You should apply, you think?"

"I thought about it. It was the morning shift, and I could do that with my eyes closed, but all my paycheck would get eatin' up by the commute. It's an hour's drive from here, you know."

"I think it's more likely you'd eat up your paycheck in your own pancakes." I laugh. "You could introduce your potato pancakes to the menu. Homer would like that. Big seller, no doubt about it."

"My contribution to the world, you're thinking?"

We laugh a little, then there's silence for a bit.

"I listened to the tape, Dad."

"Yeah?" I hear him breathing in a cave.

"Thank you."

"You don't have to thank me, Caroline. You don't owe me a thing, not a single thing. Really."

"I'm grateful just the same. It means so much to me that you did this. And I do want to be your family, my part of it, like you suggested. We can talk more about this along the way, if that okay."

A wait, then, in a wavering but pleased tone, "It's more than okay." Silence. "Well then," he says finally, and I hear the small turnings of the stove's dials.

"I'm keeping you from your supper. Pancakes aren't so good cold."

"You're not keeping me from anything. The batter's not got the milk poured in it yet." I wonder if he's being generous. "It can wait. And anyway if your pancakes get cold, you just heat up the syrup." He says, "Surp."

I hear him walking with the phone to the table, the cord scraping lightly on the floor behind him, and the scooting of his chair across the hardwood floors. He has turned the flames off on the stove then.

"I'll just have my coffee while we talk here, if you don't mind."

"I've got mine right in front of me, too, though mine's decaf. So let's klatch."

"What the hell is that?"

"Gabfest over coffee, usually a buncha women sitting around having their cuppa joes while they gossip. Know any dirt?"

"Do I know dirt? I'm looking at lot of it in the garden right out the window!" He says, "win-duh." Okies always sound drunk, a singing drunk. He's laughing. He's feeling relief.

"Never mind. I do have a question for you though...."

"Shoot." He slurps his coffee. I heard him blow over the top of the cup to cool it off.

"Well, first, did I attend your father's funeral? For the life of me I can't remember. It's been driving me crazy."

"No, you asked me to give you permission not to go. You were working at that new accounting job in town, working night and day to save money to go to college. This was after you quit the diner place. I didn't see any reason to push you about going. My feeling was that when you graduated from high school, you had sent my family announcements and not one sent anything, not a card, nothing. Well, I take that back, Elizabeth did send you a card with twenty dollars. But there was no reason for you to go to Dad's funeral that I could see."

I wait a beat before asking, "Do you have any pictures of your parents together, I'm thinking before your mother didn't allow such things anymore? I mean, because of her church. I'd love to have one, even if it was a copy from an original. I have one of Gramma and Grampa Dirks that Mom gave me." I'm sorry as soon as I tell him this. I hear his gears turning, 'after the divorce.' So I rush to, "I just thought it would be nice to have one of Gramma and Grampa Jantz as well."

"I have a story to tell you about that, Caroline," he begins. Well, of course, he does. "There was this marriage picture of Mom and Dad that was up in the house until my mother joined her Mennonite church out there in the country, just outside Clearview." He tells me this as though he's talking to the far end of the garden. I see him as he was our last visit, not at the kitchen table, but outside with me, at the glass-topped table in the yard, glasses of tea between us. "It was hanging in the dining room for the longest time," he begins, and I think it's going to be another story similar to the cuckoo clock, one in which he'll say another cousin took his parents' wedding picture off the wall as well. But the story doesn't seem to be going that way as he continues.

"Then all at once, Mother had it removed and put upstairs behind one of the dressers in one of the extra bedrooms nobody used anymore. Probably became she became convicted about it during a revival or some visiting preacher's sermon about sin. Maybe it was her hope that the preachers would overlook it when they came through the house or that it wasn't a sin to have it if she didn't look at it, who knows?

"But not long after your mother and I got married, I'd seen it up there, knew it was tucked way behind the dresser, you see, where nobody was likely to see it, and I intended to get it sometime when nobody was around.

"Well, one Sunday when we went visiting, I went back up there to check it out, thinking I'd get it after everybody had left, but it was gone. I asked Mother about it later, when we were alone. I figured, here again, one of my brothers or sisters took it, but she told me in Plattdeutsch, 'It was a sin that I kept those things hidden,' she said. So when the preachers found it, they burned it along with two drawers full of jewelry and photographs kept in that dresser. They spilled it all out in the yard and set it ablaze. Where the jewelry had come from, I don't know. She wouldn't say. The photographs, well, I understand why she'd hold onto those—in a bottom drawer who would care, and they were family heirlooms. She was torn between her church and her history, you see? Maybe one of us would find them on our own, then they'd be gone out of the house, and she wouldn't be sinning.

"But her church had a new preacher, Mother told me. Somehow the deacons and preachers before this had felt that dressers were off limits, you know, with all the underwear and personal things in them, stuff that they'd probably think was forbidden to look at. Good God, think about it? Who would open dresser drawers and look at Mother's underpants? I can see them shying away from that.

"Well, anyhow, I opened the drawers, thinking I'd take some of those old pictures before something happened to them. I had seen some in there of my father when he was a boy. I was shocked beyond words to find the drawers relined with newspapers and all these old knives and forks lined up as though that was where they'd always been. The utensils were plain, not silver or with fancy designs on them or anything like that, so I guess the preachers hadn't bothered with them, leaving them behind."

Then he says in a tight voice, "I took them all. And when I reached to the back of one of the top drawers, I found one fine silver soup spoon from a set we used when I was a kid for special occasions." He had tears in his voice, and I'm not sure he'll go on. I'm sure his hand is opening and closing in a fist, squeezing the telephone cord. "I put them in my coat pockets and walked past them all, them sitting there at the family table. I passed them all, Caroline, leaving without a word. I just gathered up my family and drove home. This was the last time I visited them with us all together. We went only at my Dad's retirement, his funeral, their golden anniversary, that kinda thing."

His breathing is trembling so he clears his throat, says in a stronger voice, "So now, I have a shovel, two rusty tools, a half dozen knives, forks, and one gravy spoon from the estate. Actually I don't have the knives and forks anymore. I gave them to Kat when she came to visit last time. I saved the spoon for you." I see him waving his hand helplessly toward the closet where he's probably put it to keep for me. "I meant to give it to you when you were here and forgot. I'll pass it to you when you visit next time."

When he speaks again, he speaks with more assurance. "I just wish it could have been the clock, Caroline. Being my oldest child, you had a right to that."

—

Five days later, a rather large, and surprisingly heavy package is delivered at my door from Oklahoma. I look curiously for the return address and discover it's from my father.

The cuckoo clock? Not possible! Ah, the spoon. But in a package so large and heavy?

Wrapped in white tissue in a box tightly securing it in place is a photograph album that I remember so well from my growing-up years, on the outside cover, letters in gold, now tarnished with age. In carefully drawn-out cursive so recognizably his own, my father's small note is scotch-taped on the outside. "This I give you, Caroline, with humility and love. This is your true inheritance. Dad."

When I open the book, allowing the pages to fall at random as I thumb them along, family pictures spill out on the pages, held in place by those black corner sleeves my brothers and I licked for Momma as she fastened the photographs next to her descriptions in black ink. I hold the album against my heart for a very long time, as I sit alone and cry like a child.

Cly Boehs (pronounced Klī Bāz) was born and raised in Oklahoma. She taught art on Long Island and in upstate New York, where she has lived in the Finger Lakes area for over thirty years. She has been a member of Zee's writing circles in Ithaca, New York, and various regional writing and art groups including The Georges, T-burg Writer's Group and The 3pm Club and was a playwright, stage and costume designer and participating member of the original theater group, 3rd Floor Productions for nine years. She has exhibited her art and created ritual performances in Oklahoma, Pennsylvania, and New York. She has read her stories publically for many years, including on television and radio.

She believes that we can be saved by deep conversations, books, and art, while our imagination and wonderment are what really keep us alive.

You can follow all of Cly's writing at *Mind At Play,* **www.cbfiction.blogspot.com**. She always enjoys hearing from readers. If you'd like to drop her a note, you can do so via **clyboehs@gmail.com**.

Author's Note: For readers interested in more information concerning vinyl, shellac, and vintage 78rpm recordings collecting, I highly recommend Amanda Petrusich's *Do Not Sell At Any Price: the Wild, Obsessive Hunt for the World's Rarest 78rpm Records,* Scribner, 2014.

CPSIA information can be obtained
at www.ICGtesting.com
Printed in the USA
BVHW08s2241180918
527890BV00002B/15/P